The Marriage Epidemic

June Portnoy

DELLARTE
PRESS

Dellarte Press™
1663 Liberty Drive
Bloomington, IN 47403
www.dellartepress.com
Phone: 1-877-217-3420

First published by Dellarte Press: 4/19/2010

ISBN: 978-1-4501-0006-9 (sc)
ISBN: 978-1-4501-0008-3 (hc)
ISBN: 978-1-4501-0007-6 (e)

Printed in the United States of America
Bloomington, Indiana

This book is printed on acid-free paper.

Acknowledgement Page

Thanks to my daughters, Beth and Melissa: Your smiles light up my world. Your laughter fills my heart.

Thanks also to my parents: Your unconditional love, support and encouragement mean everything to me. I couldn't ask for better parents!

Thanks also to my wonderful, devoted friends who have been there for me during the good and bad times. You have shown me the true meaning of the word friendship: Sandee Clibanoff, Renee Weihmeir, Karen Levy, Scott Goldman, Denise Gayman, Kelly Hauffer, Christy Black, Cindi Sirota, Denise Duhn, Donna Gephart, Jeanne Epstein and Rebecca Femia.

And finally, thanks to Harlequin for establishing this new imprint that gave me this opportunity to live out my dream of becoming a published novelist.

A special thanks goes out to my *ex*-boyfriends and *former* friends (you know who you are!) who inspired me to write this novel. This one's for you.

The Marriage Epidemic: 1. An infectious desire to get married. 2. Transmitted from married and engaged women to single females. 3. Highly contagious. 4. In early stages, causes nausea and chest pains at the mere sight of engagement rings and bridal gowns. 5. In more advanced stages, causes a frantic search to find a husband, based primarily on peer pressure 6. Upon diagnosis, seek treatment immediately.

Chapter 1

Leading Causes of the Marriage Epidemic:

1. Discovering your best friend found her prince when you still don't even have a frog.
2. Being challenged to find a husband, as if you just entered a marriage competition.
3. Reaching any age over twenty-nine.
4. Receiving more bridal shower invitations than bills.

The most frustrating part of the marriage epidemic was that no matter how much you washed your hands, sprayed Lysol, and kept your windows open, it was nearly impossible to prevent catching it when you were constantly exposed to engagement announcements. I found this out firsthand when my best friend arrived at my apartment early one Monday morning with a big, shiny diamond on her ring finger...

"So what do you think, Jen?" Stacy asked, displaying her diamond in front of my nose as if I wouldn't see it if she held it a few inches away.

"It's beautiful! Congratulations." As I threw my arms around Stacy's petite waist, I felt the first of many tears. I convinced myself they were tears of joy, not wanting to admit they could be tears of self-pity. This was no time to focus on my hopeless love life. My best friend was getting married! "So when did Lance propose?"

"Last night." She straightened the collar of her perfectly pressed designer shirt, while I discovered a hole in my new pajamas. "He took me to Le Chance, you know, that French restaurant on Third and Henry Streets that I've been dying to try. He said he was taking me

1

there as an early birthday present. Anyway, you'll never guess what he did."

"No, I—"

"He ordered two glasses of wine, and when I picked up my drink, I saw the diamond sparkling in the bottom of the glass. Can you imagine? He actually drove all the way downtown yesterday morning to ask the head waiter to put the engagement ring in my wineglass to surprise me. When I took out the ring, the violinist came over to our table to play 'A Whole New World.'"

"Wow that really is romantic." It sure beat my evening of doing laundry, feeding Frisky his cat food, and watching reruns of *Sex and the City*. I watched Stacy carefully get up from the kitchen table, which took up a good eighty percent of my teeny tiny kitchen, to pour a cup of coffee and cut a slice of cake. Even first thing in the morning, she looked like her makeup had been professionally applied.

"Of course, you know I thought he would never propose, that he was one of those commitment-phobes." Stacy had to walk sideways to return to the table. "When I asked him what took him so long to ask me, he said he wanted to have a good, stable job before he took the plunge. He thinks his firm might make him a partner in a couple of years. Isn't that unbelievable?" Her clear, crisp voice resonated throughout my kitchen.

"I'm really happy for you, Stace. You deserve it." I threw my high fiber, low-fat cereal in the garbage disposal and grabbed a cherry Danish.

"Thanks. I can't believe I'm getting married. Jen, will you be my maid of honor?"

"Of course, I will." I pictured Tevye from *Fiddler on the Roof* in my kitchen singing "Sunrise, Sunset."

I couldn't remember a time when Stacy and I hadn't known each other. Our mothers still talked about strolling us together in our baby carriages when we were first born.

Since Stacy and I were four, we had talked about getting married. After watching *Cinderella* for the first time, we routinely acted out the scene where Prince Charming came to find his princess. Sometimes I played Cinderella and sometimes I was the prince. We would dance around our houses, singing "Someday My Prince Will Come."

When we got a little older, we played dress-up with my mom's old dresses. I could still remember the time she let us each try on her wedding gown. I had twirled around in it for a half-hour until Stacy insisted that she have a turn. Each time it was our turn, we stared in the mirror wearing the long, white gown, wondering what we would look like when we wore our real wedding gowns someday.

As teenagers, we constantly talked about who we thought we'd end up marrying. Would it be that cute guy who sat in the last row of biology class, or the shy one in gym? One of our favorite games was trying to figure out which actor our husband would most closely resemble. After seeing *Top Gun*, Stacy hoped for Tom Cruise, but I fantasized about John Stamos who starred in *Full House* at the time.

It was around this time that we promised each other we would never get married until we both found the right guy. What fun would it be if we weren't both doing it together? We actually stuck our fingers with pins and placed our bleeding skin together to seal our pact.

As we started college, we stopped playing the game of marriage and started living it as we watched many girls we knew from high school actually walking down the aisle. We still wanted to find our Prince Charming, like when we were four, but after many broken relationships, we realized that guys didn't come riding out of the forest, carrying glass slippers for potential wives…until Stacy met Lance several years after college graduation.

I had talked her into going out with me on a Friday night to check out a new martini bar downtown. Stacy had just broken up with someone and hadn't wanted to go, but I bribed her to come with me, offering to buy the first three rounds of drinks. As it turned out, I didn't buy more than one because within the first half-hour Lance arrived.

I spotted him first, thinking he looked like a brown-eyed John Stamos, but I never stood a chance with him. He looked right past me to Stacy, who he sat next to for the rest of the evening, and now five years later they were getting married.

As I poured myself a cup of coffee, I wondered if Stacy would remember our childhood games of marriage and dress-up when she put on her wedding gown.

A part of me wished we were still sitting at my parent's home, playing make-believe and watching *Cinderella* together. Sometimes dreaming about the unknown could be more enchanting than living out your dreams.

"Jen. Jen, did you hear me?"

Stacy's cheerful voice brought me back to the present. "Uh, sorry. What did you say?" I nicked my leg on the corner of the table before sitting down.

"I was telling you how much it meant to me that you're going to be in my wedding. Did you hear anything I said?" Stacy looked hurt.

"Um, sure I did." I placed my feet with my Pound Puppy slippers on the chair in front of me while admiring Stacy's new stilettos.

"Well, I hope so." She didn't look convinced. "I just wish…"

"Wish what?"

"Uh, nothing. It wasn't important."

Figured. I was finally listening and now she stopped talking. "Come on, Stace. What were you thinking?" I wiped the icing and cherries off my mouth, while Stacy bit into her piece of crumb cake without dropping a crumb.

"I wish…that we were planning our weddings together, like we always talked about."

And I wished I hadn't talked Stacy into telling me what she was thinking. "I don't even think a fairy godmother or genie could make that wish come true. In case you haven't noticed, I haven't had more than three dates with the same guy in over a year. Call me crazy, but I don't think any of them plan to propose in the next few hours."

"You've always been able to make me laugh." Stacy giggled. "I hope I didn't make you feel bad. I should have kept my mouth shut."

"Yeah, you should have, but I know you don't know how to do that. I think your mouth would self-destruct or your tongue would fall out if you didn't say what was on your mind."

"You know me well."

"And you me. I wish I had a diamond on my finger, too. I'd even settle for a cubic zirconia at the moment."

I was glad when Stacy laughed. I didn't want her feeling sorry for me. That was my job.

"It would have been fun planning our weddings together," I said, remembering how we had planned our bat mitzvahs, sweet sixteens and all of our graduation parties together.

Our lives had always been totally in sync. We grew up in the same neighborhood, and attended the same schools, camps, and college. We lived in the same dorm and even chose the same major, both graduating with a journalism degree. I wasn't sure who followed whose lead, but one of us always had. Until now.

"I think this is the first time we won't be planning a major event at the same time." Stacy said, adding a Sweet'N Low to her coffee.

"I was thinking the same thing, but it looks like you're going solo this time." I smiled, feeling sad. For the next few minutes all I could hear was that old Three Dog Night song playing in my head, "One is the Loneliest Number that You'll Ever Do." I shook my head, trying to shake that song out of my mind.

"So, have you set a date?" I selected another Danish, this time apple, and poured a generous portion of creamer into my coffee.

"Yeah, sometime next April. That still gives you ten months to find someone."

Since when had this become a contest? Was I supposed to tell the next guy I met that he had till April to walk me down the aisle? "I wouldn't count on that happening."

"Hey, I have a great idea," Stacy said. "Remember last month when you picked me up from work and you ended up talking to Craig for over an hour while you waited for me?"

"Craig?"

"Yeah, you know, that cute consultant who works upstairs from me." Stacy finished her breakfast and blotted her lips, which amazingly still had lipstick on them.

"Oh, yeah, Craig."

"When I came back to meet you, you were in the same exact spot as when I left you there. I'm surprised you never mentioned him after that. You two must have really hit it off."

"Not exactly..."

"You have to admit, he's really good-looking."

"Yeah, but..."

"Not to mention, he's Jewish."

"I know, but…"

"And I hear he's got a lot of money. He does well as a consultant at our firm, and his father is some kind of a big shot stockbroker on Wall Street."

"You know I don't care about stuff like that." I hated when Stacy talked about guys like they were merchandise you picked out because they had the right packaging. I didn't care about a guy's gross annual income or credentials. I just wanted to fall in love with someone who loved me back. Was that asking too much?

"So should I mention your name to Craig?"

I carried both of our plates to the sink and washed them off. "Stace, how well do you know Craig?"

"Uh, not too well. The consultants don't work that closely with the marketing department. Why?"

"Have you ever really talked to him?" I picked up Stacy's empty coffee mug and placed it in the sink.

"I'm not sure. Maybe not. But two of our marketing coordinators talk to him a lot and they say he's really nice."

"Do they actually talk or do they just listen?"

"What?"

"Stace, the guy's a jerk. Do you know what we talked about the entire time I waited for you? We talked about Craig. Craig's new condo in Society Hill, Craig's red Porsche, Craig's recent promotion that's going to make him rich, Craig's dreams and plans for the future. Craig! That's it. He didn't ask me one question about myself, and whenever I tried to say something, he interrupted me to tell me what Craig thought. I don't even think he knows my name. The reason I didn't move for over an hour was because Craig was so excited talking about his favorite subject, namely Craig, that it was impossible for me to leave."

"You're kidding!"

"Listen, Stace. I appreciate what you're trying to do, but Craig is definitely not my type. You know how I hate arrogant guys."

"I had no idea he was like that," Stacy said. "Sorry for getting carried away."

"Don't worry about it." Hopefully, I would never get desperate enough to take Stacy up on her offer.

"Well, even if Craig's not for you, that doesn't mean you won't find someone else before I get married. I'll see if I can think of someone else at work who you might like."

"That's okay. I'm sure planning your wedding is going to keep you pretty busy for now." Since when had Stacy become Yenta?

"I don't mind," she said, checking her watch. "Hey, is it really eight o'clock?" Stacy got up, practically knocking over my table. "I have a meeting in an hour for that new hair spray we're marketing and I haven't finished writing the proposal. I better go."

"I have to get ready, too."

"I wish you weren't moving so far from my office," Stacy said, picking up her black leather briefcase. "I'm going to miss stopping by in the morning to catch up."

"Not to mention the free breakfasts you get out of the deal."

"That's true." Stacy giggled as she wrapped two muffins in a napkin. When she turned to leave, her long, blond hair shined and her turquoise-blue eyes sparkled. Her snug silk navy blazer and matching mini skirt accentuated her perfect figure, reminding me of a Barbie doll I once owned.

I, on the other hand, resembled a Raggedy Ann doll with my flat chest and straw-like, disheveled, shoulder-length auburn hair. Top that off with the giant zit on the front of my nose, and it was no wonder that I hadn't received any marriage proposals.

As I drove away from my small apartment in Northeast Philly and headed to work, I breathed deeply for the first time since Stacy's ring appeared in my kitchen. I didn't even get upset when the guy in the Nissan Sentra gave me the finger for passing him, or when I got stuck behind a tractor-trailer accident on I-95 for fifteen minutes. My office was my haven, my escape, the one place where I felt confident.

I had worked hard to become a senior copywriter. When I interned at Premier Advertising while attending college, I received lots of recognition and praise from the staff. No, it wasn't my journalism background, attention to detail, or organizational skills that people noticed. It was my ability to make everybody's coffee exactly the way they liked it.

Carol liked two Sweet'N Lows and low fat milk. John preferred one tablespoon of sugar and a hint of whole milk, and Joe lived on the edge by drinking his black. Other interns cringed when they were asked to fetch coffee, but I knew I had to pay my dues, and was grateful to have an internship at a Philadelphia ad agency.

Two days before graduation, John, the president of the agency, called me into his office. I had waited for this moment for a long time. Would he admire my dedication and hard work? Perhaps he would compliment me on my ability to get along with everyone at the agency. Maybe he would thank me for helping out with so many additional projects.

When I entered his office, which overlooked Independence Mall, this tall, burly man with a powerful voice said, "You make good coffee, Jen." I was hired on the spot as an assistant copywriter.

From that point forward, I immersed myself in my job. After Jared broke up with me, claiming he "just wanted to be friends," I worked sixty-hour weeks until I helped win the Yuppy Dog Food account. When Ken came out of the closet, a month after he told me he loved me, I came up with the award-winning idea for Rolio Cookies. And last year when Sean cheated on me, I developed the entire advertising campaign for Sportin Fitness Centers, which led to my recent promotion. Thanks to my lousy love life, I had a successful career.

I smiled as I drove into the parking garage adjacent to the building where I worked. While hitting the remote twice to activate the alarm on my Jeep, I suddenly had a great idea for the Peterson Auto Dealership account.

My legs took on a life of their own, pulling me toward the high-rise building that had become my second home, my oasis in the sky. Once on the elevator, I pushed the number thirty, always amazed at how quickly this movable enclosure shuttled me to my office. Since Premier occupied the entire thirtieth floor, the elevator opened to our reception area.

"Hey, Jen. What's your hurry?" asked Rhonda, the secretary who craved information like a chocoholic craved Hershey bars.

"Just came up with an idea for the Peterson account." I raced past Rhonda, not in the mood to make chit-chat. I glanced at the many framed advertising awards displayed on the bright white walls as I walked toward my office, which was the first one by the reception area. I closed the door behind me, not sure whether I wanted silence to concentrate or needed to shut out the world for a while.

I purposely didn't bring any items from home to my office. When I was at work, I didn't want to think about my personal life. Every book on my bookshelf was either from college or a reference book supplied by Premier. I had no family pictures, other than one of my cat, Frisky, and even my coffee mug was business related, consisting of our agency's logo. The only thing in my office that gave any information about me was my framed college diploma on the wall. Other than that, I'd picked up two contemporary abstract pictures from a local art show, to add some color to the white walls and gray commercial grade carpeting.

Come to think of it, my small office was kind of sterile looking, but I liked it that way so I could focus on work without letting my mind wander. Having no outside window also helped reduce my temptation to daydream. Although impersonal, my small office provided the feeling of seclusion that I craved, especially today.

But while I could hide out from my personal life, there was no escaping all the work I needed to do. Piles of file folders, each holding important information about different accounts, buried my rectangular black and gray laminate desk. Not to mention the folders under my desk, on the floor, and those sticking out of my two metal filing cabinets, which were about to explode from paper overload.

As if that wasn't enough, the red light on my phone was blinking, indicating I had voice messages. As I sat down in my gray swivel chair, I put on my computer to discover I had email, and lots of it. Oh well, at least I had plenty to do to forget about weddings for a while.

And for the next three hours, that's what I did. I was just getting on a roll with the Peterson copy when I heard a knock on my door.

"Jen, are you coming?" asked Marisa, our production manager extraordinaire. Marisa had the uncanny ability to identify the weight and finish of any paper stock in less than a minute.

"Coming where?" I asked, without looking up from the computer.

"To Lona's surprise bridal shower," Marisa said. Her words hit me like a rubber band snapping against my wrist, bringing me back to reality. "It's starting in ten minutes."

"Is that today?" I knocked over my coffee cup, which broke my glass-framed picture of Frisky. Was the whole damn world suddenly getting married?

"Are you all right?" Marisa's big round brown eyes looked concerned as she stared at me through her rimless glasses. As usual, Marisa wore practically no make-up, but fortunately for her, she really didn't need much. After all the years I'd worked with her, I couldn't remember ever seeing her put gel or hair spray in her shiny, chin-length brown hair. She had a natural beauty that didn't require the high maintenance I needed. And her full round face with a dimple on her right cheek gave her that wholesome, girl-next-door look that would have made her the perfect spokesperson for a milk or white bread commercial.

"I'm fine," I said, grabbing paper towels from under my desk.

"Why don't you call maintenance to clean up the glass?"

I leaned forward, straining my ears to hear Marisa who mumbled so quietly that I often had to ask her to repeat herself. "That's a good idea," I said, once I was certain what she'd said. I dialed the maintenance department and left a message that I needed someone to come by my office and mop up my mess. "I forgot all about Lona's party," I said, saving the file I'd been working on.

"Hers is today, Julie's is next Tuesday, and Lynn's is in two weeks, which reminds me, you owe me thirty dollars if you want to contribute to their gifts." Marisa's voice was a mere whisper and sounded flat as she recited the upcoming parties in a monotone. Needless to say, she wasn't any closer to getting married than me.

When I first met Marisa, I couldn't understand why someone so pretty had so much trouble meeting guys, but once I got to know her I realized her low self-esteem, nervous habits, and overly eager desire to find a boyfriend turned lots of guys off.

"If people keep getting married around here, I'm going to need a part-time job to pay for all these gifts," I said, rolling my eyes while putting all my notes back into my Peterson file folder.

"We should probably set aside a wedding fund because next year Theresa and Kate are getting married," Marisa said, staring at her empty ring finger. "And from what Rhonda tells me, Bob and Ryan are planning to propose some time this year too. Before long, there's only going to be a few of us left who aren't married."

She leaned against my wall, slouching as usual. I seldom saw Marisa stand up straight. "I guess we better go," she said without any enthusiasm.

"I guess," I answered just as emotionless. I grabbed a pen and notepad before getting up and following Marisa out the door.

As we walked past endless groups of cubicles, or pods as John preferred to call them, I felt grateful that I finally had my own office. Before my recent promotion, I had been stuck in one of those cubes as well. I especially appreciated my own space, considering only about one quarter of the hundred or more employees at Premier had their own offices.

We walked to the center of Premier's office until we reached the glass-enclosed conference room. John thought the glass made it look contemporary, but personally I preferred traditional walls. I always got distracted when people walked by looking inside to see what was going on.

And that glass conference table didn't make much sense to me either, especially since we had strict instructions not to put any drink on it without a coaster and not to eat anything on it without using the ceramic plates from the kitchen. Not very practical if you asked me.

"Didn't think you were going to make it," said Tiffany, Premier's top art director. She had saved us two seats in the back of the room. "We just saw Lona pull up. Jen, can't you come to one party without a notepad?" As usual, Tiffany was dressed in black from head to toe, making her appear even taller and thinner than she really was. She broke up all the darkness by wearing chunky necklaces and dangling bracelets, along with silver abstract pins, which gave her that artsy appearance that lots of the women in the creative department had.

"I had a good idea for the Peterson campaign," I said, taking out my pen.

"You really need to let go and have some fun." Tiffany moved a strand of her dyed jet black hair away from her face. She usually wore it in a ponytail since it was so long it reached her waist, but today it hung loose, and her curls practically ended up on my lap.

"That's easy for you to say. You already finished the artwork for your account."

"Yeah, but it wasn't by bringing layouts to parties." It was easy to tell from Tiffany's hoarse, scratchy voice that she smoked a lot.

"Here she comes," Rhonda yelled. A moment later, someone turned off the lights and everyone yelled surprise as Lona walked in.

"I can't believe you did this," Lona shrieked. "I had no idea."

"Like hell she didn't," Tiffany whispered to me. "Today's her last day of work before she gets married on Sunday and Rhonda told her a month ago we were planning a party for her. When else would it be?"

"I wish it was my shower," Marisa whispered. "By the time I get married, everyone here will be retired."

"I keep telling you there's no rush." Tiffany said. "You're only thirty-one. I'm the one who should be panicking considering I'm two years older than you."

"I still don't know why you're not." Since we'd arrived, Marisa had bitten all of her nails, making me feel better about my chipped nail polish.

"What's the point? It's not like worrying about it will make it happen any sooner." Tiffany spoke with an air of confidence that you couldn't help pay attention to.

Since I'd known Tiffany, almost all the guys she'd dated had been struggling musicians who were too busy trying to get discovered to settle down. Tiffany, who got an adrenalin rush just dating a drummer or lead guitarist, accepted the fact that none of these guys were looking for a commitment and just rolled with the flow. When these relationships ended, which they always did, she simply shrugged her shoulders and went on to the next one.

"I sure wish I had your attitude," Marisa said to Tiffany, while fixating her eyes on Lona, who was now opening her presents.

"Me too," I agreed, wondering how many gift cards to Bed Bath & Beyond we'd given out during bridal showers over the past year. Not wanting to think about it, I took out my notepad to jot down some ideas for the Peterson account.

But within a minute, Tiffany noticed what I was doing. "Jen, if you don't stop scribbling on that notepad, I'm going to break your pen in half. This is supposed to be a party, remember?"

"You're right," I said, sighing. I hadn't planned to exhale so loudly. But the noise that came out of my mouth was enough to stop the laughter, banter, and chatter across the conference room.

"Is something wrong?" John asked.

How to respond? My best friend who I love like a sister is getting married and I'm a self-centered bitch because all I can do is feel sorry for myself. No, that wouldn't work. Hmm…

"John, you have to stop working Jen so hard," Tiffany said, saving me from any further embarrassment. "The poor thing's so wrapped up in the Peterson account that she's practically hyperventilating back here trying to come up with another winning ad. Just look at her! She couldn't even come to the party without her notepad."

Only Tiffany could get away with talking to John like that. Thank goodness she was my friend because I felt another loud sigh ready to explode from my throat.

"Well, for heaven's sake, Jen, have a piece of cake and forget about Peterson for a while," John said. "I'm sure you'll come up with a great idea."

"Thanks." I wondered how many people noticed my zit while listening to my sound effects.

"What's up?" Tiffany whispered. "Did you have a bad date this weekend?'

If only I had a date. "No, I worked all weekend. The only time I left my apartment was for take-out at Zin Wong."

"Then what's with your vocal chords today?"

"Stacy came by this morning to tell me she's engaged."

"Oh, so that's it. You're suffering from the marriage blues, like Marisa."

"I am not," I said a little too quickly.

"Sure, Jen." Tiffany rolled her eyes.

"Really, I'm fine. I don't need to get married to be happy." I had too much going for me to let a few diamond rings get me down. I had my health, my friends, my cat, and a great career. Who needed a date on Saturday nights?

And as far as sex went, my life-size blow-up doll gave me all the satisfaction that I needed. When Stacy gave me Mr. Wow as a gag gift for my twenty-fifth birthday, I automatically stuffed him into a drawer in my night stand, never bothering to inflate him. But after my many failed relationships, I remembered my deflated friend lying alone near my bed. A few large puffs of breath brought him to life, and before long, I discovered that Mr. Wow was even better in bed than many guys I had dated.

But when Lona's fiancé came in and stood beside her, I felt like a big piece of popcorn had become lodged in my throat. Unable to swallow, I watched Dan place his hand on Lona's shoulder as if he were touching a porcelain doll. He looked into her eyes as if he could see through them into her soul. He kissed her lips as if he wanted to savor her taste. And suddenly Mr. Wow didn't seem to be "the perfect substitute for a man," as the packaging had read.

I searched for my pen, but somebody, probably Tiffany, had taken it. I waited till Lona opened her last present and everyone finished their cake. When Tiffany turned to talk to Joe, our creative director, I headed for the door.

"Hey, Jen, wait," said Rhonda.

Spotted, and by the company blabbermouth, no less. I should have smelled her coming considering she wore enough perfume to cause an asthmatic to need her inhaler. And how could I miss that purple, red, and fuchsia flowered dress with her four-inch high heels? To say nothing about her bright red lipstick and that tacky hot pink eye shadow. I imagined she must apply more make-up in one day than I did in a month.

"What's up, Rhonda?" I said, in my most confident, poised voice.

"You have icing on the tip of your nose. Here's a tissue." She handed me a Kleenex. "You wouldn't want to walk around with that all day."

So much for the concealer that was guaranteed to cover up the very worst blemishes. I thanked her for the tissue, walked to my office, and slammed my door shut, swearing I wouldn't come out until my zit disappeared or Mr. Wow turned into a prince.

Chapter 2

How the Epidemic Spreads:

1. Too much exposure to single women who talk endlessly about the misery of being single.
2. Too much exposure to married women who talk endlessly about the thrill of getting married.
3. Too much exposure to single men who talk endlessly about every topic except marriage.

"Forget it, I'm not going!"

"Didn't you read that ad I sent you?" My mom's voice sounded particularly loud on my cordless phone today.

"How couldn't I? You sent me five copies." I stared at the ads that now covered a good portion of my bed.

"Jen, the Sizzling Summer Singles Dance is the biggest social event till the fall. It's for young Jewish single professionals between the ages of thirty to forty-five."

Why had she bothered sending me the ads if she planned to recite them over the phone? "I know what it says, and I'm not interested."

"Why not? You have something better to do tonight?"

Well, she did have a point there. Chances were, I'd end up reading or watching TV with Frisky. Still, I hated these singles events. For whatever reason, they attracted the ugly, the weird, and the pathetically-desperate-to-meet-someone-no-matter-what crowd. I convinced myself that I didn't fit into that last group. "I've never met a guy worth dating at one of these things, Mom."

"Well, there's always a first time. Why don't you give it one more shot?"

I was ready to say no until I looked at my magazine rack, stuffed with bridal magazines that Stacy had brought over that morning. "I'll think about it, okay?"

"That's all I ask. You can tell me all about it tomorrow."

Hey, wait! I hadn't said I was going. Before I put down the cordless, the phone rang.

"What are you doing tonight?" Marisa asked.

"My mom's convinced that tonight's dance at the Jewish rec center is going to change my life."

"Really? Can I come, too?" Of course, I knew Marisa wasn't interested in the dance so she'd meet a Jewish guy. She'd probably go to a Jews for Jesus singles dance too. Unlike me, Marisa was Jewish in name only. Goldman, her last name, was about the most religious part about her. But Marisa never turned down a chance to meet guys.

"I haven't decided whether I'm going yet. These dances are like geek conventions." I threw a blanket over my magazine rack, covering the smiling brides on Stacy's magazines.

"Oh, come on. They can't be that bad. Besides, it's a night out."

"Why don't we hit a club downtown instead? That's where all the cool guys hang out. These singles nights draw the leftover rejects."

"And the clubs we've been going to lately draw all the jerks." Her voice was so muffled she sounded like she was talking into a tissue.

I held the phone close to my ear so I could hear her better. I wished Marisa had a monitor on her mouth so I could turn up her volume. "We could always rent a movie instead," I suggested, wondering if we could find a good one without any love scenes.

"There's nothing left for me to rent. I've already seen every new released film at Blockbuster."

Come to think of it, so had I. "I'll pick you up at seven."

When I arrived at Marisa's condo four hours later, she practically jumped into my car before I pulled into her driveway. "Do I look okay?" she asked in her hushed voice. "I wasn't sure whether to wear this dress or a pantsuit. And does my hair look all right with the hair band, or should I take it out?"

The big difference between Marisa and me was that although neither of us had much confidence meeting guys, I made a point of trying to hide my insecurities, while Marisa was quite candid about how she felt.

"I wouldn't change a thing," I said, backing up into the street and turning left at the end of her block. "You look pretty." Marisa wore a swing dress in a red, orange and brown retro floral print.

"Are you sure it's okay?" She looked nervous.

"I'm sure. Relax!" Unlike Marisa, I hadn't bothered getting too dressed up. I'd thrown on a pair of white capris with a pink and white T-shirt.

Marisa leaned back in her seat and started biting her nails. I was surprised she had any left after the bridal shower last week.

I spent the next ten minutes listening to Marisa chomp on her nails and then crack her knuckles until I couldn't stand it anymore. I finally turned on the radio to drown out her sound effects. Fortunately, her condo wasn't far from the rec center in Elkins Park. As we pulled into the parking lot, I watched Marisa bite off her last nail.

"Maybe I should look in the bathroom mirror before we go inside to the dance," she suggested.

"Marisa, you've already checked yourself out ten times in your cosmetic mirror."

It took me five more minutes to convince Marisa that she truly looked nice before we joined the crowd of singles entering the building.

The rec center's large room was decorated with surf boards, beach umbrellas, and beach balls. We sat down at a small bar and ordered two Coors Light. Well, at least it was low-calorie beer, I reasoned, wondering if I'd ever lose those extra ten to fifteen pounds.

"This place doesn't look so bad." Marisa's eyes brightened. "Some of these guys are kind of cute."

"They may look okay, but wait till they start talking."

The first time I'd gone to a singles dance, a guy followed me around the entire evening, offering to buy me drinks. He even bought me a rose. Too bad he was completely bald and looked older than my dad. Other than that, he was perfect!

The second time, I'd actually struck up a conversation with someone in my generation. He seemed nice until I realized that he wouldn't make eye contact with me. He looked at his shoes, the floor, the DJ, anything to avoid looking at me, which did wonders for my self-esteem.

After a few minutes, he began shifting from one foot to another. It wasn't until he picked up his drink, a ginger ale, that I noticed his hands shaking. He apologized for being so nervous, explaining that he suffered from social anxiety. His psychiatrist had just put him on Paxil, and thought he would be fine by now. This was way more information than I needed or wanted to know.

As he told me about his condition, I noticed beads of sweat dripping from his forehead. I was about to excuse myself when he ran out of the synagogue without uttering a good-bye. The sad truth was that he was one of the more desirable guys I had met at these functions.

Remembering my last two encounters at singles events, I wished I had marked every one of those ads from my mom "return to sender." I was just about to suggest walking across the street to the bar we had passed on our way in when Marisa nudged my arm with her elbow, a little too hard.

"What's wrong?" I asked, rubbing my arm.

"Check out that guy," Marisa said, as if she had spotted an endangered species.

"He's cute." Real cute. I couldn't remember ever seeing someone so attractive at this kind of dance before. Could my mom have been right this time?

"Here he comes," Marisa said. The way she spoke, I thought she was going to jump up and down and yell, "Goodie, goodie."

"Don't look so eager." Tiffany and I usually took turns restraining Marisa when guys approached her.

"Would you like to dance?" the Matt Damon look-alike asked Marisa.

Whew! What was that smell? I sniffed around until my nose got a whiff of Matt's double.

"No, thanks," Marisa answered, apparently aware of the stench. Then again, how could you miss it?

"What a waste," Marisa said, obviously disappointed.

"Apparently, he doesn't believe in routine showers or deodorant." I tried not to inhale. Even after the guy walked away, his odor lived on.

"Maybe he just came from the gym and didn't have time to shower."

"Nice try, but I don't think so." If Jack the Ripper was standing there, Marisa would probably find some redeeming quality in him, too.

When I looked up from taking a large sip of my beer, Marisa was already talking to another guy who had sat down next to her. Funny, I hadn't seen him walk over. Marisa was really on a roll tonight, and this guy didn't smell like a homeless person. He wasn't as attractive as the smelly guy, but he wasn't bad looking either.

"Jen, will you watch my purse? I'm going to dance."

"Sure." Had Marisa actually met a normal guy? But as they got up from their stools at the same time, I realized right away what this guy's flaw was, and by Marisa's expression, so did she. The guy, who couldn't have been taller than five foot two, barely came up to Marisa's shoulders, and worse yet, his eyes were parallel to her chest. Slow dancing with him was going to be mighty interesting. Marisa gave me a pleading look as he escorted her to the dance floor.

I ordered another beer. When Marisa didn't return right away, I ordered another one. I felt pathetic sitting alone at the bar so I became fascinated with the brochure I had picked up on my way in. It listed all the upcoming events for the Women's Senior Club. Well, at least I felt less desperate reading something instead of staring longingly at any semi-attractive male who walked by.

"Can I buy you a drink?" a guy with a nasal voice said. Ugh! This one made Quasimodo look attractive. He didn't seem surprised when I turned him down.

Now back to my reading. That casino bus trip looked like fun. In another thirty years, I'd definitely consider it.

"You look a little young to be a senior." I was afraid to look up, but when I did, I saw the darkest blue eyes I had ever seen. This guy was tall, dark, and didn't smell. What more could I ask for?

"Uh, I picked up this information for my grandmother." Figured, I couldn't be reading something trendy like *Vogue*.

"Your grandmother is a lucky lady." The attractive stranger apparently believed my lie. "So can I buy you a drink?"

I ordered a pina colada, figuring it sounded more feminine than a beer. So much for my diet. After doing three watermelon shots, I felt particularly giddy, but it wasn't just from the alcohol. I really liked this guy. Go figure.

I spent the next two hours talking to the good-looking Jewish single, whose name I soon learned was Brandon. We talked about everything ranging from our favorite movies and television shows to our interests and hobbies. It turned out that we both loved classic films and old sitcoms. We agreed that when it came to music, we were stuck in the '80s, still listening to groups like Chicago and Hall & Oates. Since we were both animal lovers, he talked about his dog, Hercules, and I told him about Frisky. He was even a writer like me, except he wrote at a newspaper. This guy had to be my soul mate. I vowed to send my mom a personal thank you card for talking me into coming tonight.

I lost track of Marisa, except when I saw a guy about two hundred pounds buy her a drink. At around ten o'clock, Marisa returned, looking tired. "Will you be ready to leave soon?" she whispered.

I excused myself from Brandon for a minute. "Any luck?"

"No, same as always." She let her glasses fall down her nose without bothering to push them back up.

"I wouldn't feel bad. You didn't exactly have much to choose from. They could have used this place in one of those *Revenge of the Nerds* movies."

"I guess." She looked depressed. "At least the guy you met wouldn't be cast in that movie."

"Yeah, for once I got lucky. Can you give me a minute to say good-bye?"

"Sure, I'll meet you at the front door."

I turned my attention back to Brandon. "My friend's ready to leave, but it was nice meeting you."

"Same here. Take care."

Take care? Take care? Hadn't he forgotten something, like my phone number? Maybe he thought I was walking Marisa to her car, and then returning to the bar.

"My friend and I came together so I have to leave, too."

"All right then, nice talking to you."

Nice talking to you? This was the time when he was supposed to ask the bartender for a pen and napkin so I could write down my number.

"So, uh, thanks for the drinks." I was running out of ways to say good-bye. Maybe I should have tried a different language.

"You're welcome." He smiled at me before turning toward the bartender to order another drink.

I couldn't figure it out. We had so much in common. We made each other laugh. We hadn't even had one of those awkward moments when we ran out of things to talk about.

As I walked past several couples making out on lounge chairs, a guy with a nervous twitch and stutter came over to me. "Would you? Would you? Would you?" I guessed that he was trying to ask me if I wanted to dance since he was pointing to the dance floor, but I ignored him.

Why the hell hadn't Brandon asked for my number after spending the entire night with me? Had I said or done something wrong? Before this creep attempted to utter "would you" for the sixth time, I marched back to the bar where Brandon still sat alone.

"Listen," I said, realizing I was slurring my words, most likely from those last two shots. "Was it my imagination or did we hit it off?" Had I really said that? I couldn't believe those words had left my mouth, but what the hell? I had nothing to lose. Brandon obviously wasn't interested, and for once in my life I wanted an explanation without spending the next week trying to figure out why he didn't like me enough to get my number.

"We did get along really well, but…"

"Then why didn't you ask for my phone number?" I hated sounding so pathetic.

"Jen, you're a nice girl and you're a lot of fun to be with, but I'm married."

"You're what? How can you be married? You're not even wearing a wedding band!"

"I don't wear one."

"How convenient! In case, you didn't realize, this is a singles dance! Single, as in not married!" I knew I was screaming, but now I was furious. How could he have forgotten to tell me that small detail about his wife at home? Weren't there any rules about letting married guys into singles dances?

"I'm sorry. I didn't mean to lead you on, but I never said I was single."

"You never said you were married either."

21

"All right. You've got me there, but if you had asked, I would have told you. Besides, I had a good time talking to you while I waited for my brother. The only reason I came here tonight is that my brother wanted to meet someone and he had nobody to go with, so I told him I'd tag along to keep him company."

"So I was just someone to pass the time with until your brother hooked up."

"I wouldn't have put it exactly like that."

"Even though it's true." Of all the guys in the entire room, I had to meet the one who was married. This was not the Sizzling Summer Singles dance my mom had raved about, although I was sizzling with rage.

"Hey, if it makes you feel better, I would have asked you out over an hour ago if I weren't married."

It didn't, but at least I knew the truth. Unfortunately, the truth hurt, and now I wanted to hurt him. I hated him for getting my hopes up, for pretending to be something he wasn't, and for making me like him too much in such a short time.

"I'm really sorry, Jen. Is there anyway I can make this up to you?"

Yeah, get divorced! "No, forget about it." I wished I could.

"Can I buy you another drink?"

He'd have to buy me a few cases to make up for what he had done. "No, that's okay." There was no way to make a graceful exit. I couldn't look at Brandon as I turned around to leave, and to make matters worse, I bumped into that twitching stutterer who had hit on me by the lounge chairs.

"Hey, Jen, this is Eric, my brother," Brandon said, placing his arm around the twitcher. "He's not married."

Gee, what a surprise.

Eric sounded like he was panting as he said, "He he he…" Before he could complete the word, which I assumed was hello, I said good-bye, and left the rec center swearing never to attend another singles event again.

I tried to put Brandon and his stuttering brother out of my mind as I watched my mother lugging stacks of flat boxes into my apartment the next morning.

22

"These should help you get ready for your move," my mother said, wiping some sweat from her brow. "So how'd it go last night?"

"Not too well." I helped her drag the rest of the boxes into my small living room, which also doubled as my family room, dining room, and occasionally my exercise room.

"Oh, too bad." My mom, a size four, wore tight denim capris, a low-cut, short pink shirt that exposed her cleavage as well as her belly button, and open-toe sandals that showed off her pedicured red toenails. I was glad my mom was so physically fit, but sometimes— okay, lots of times—I wished she didn't flaunt her body so much. It was one thing to be thin, and another thing to walk around with your nipples showing through your shirt, especially at her age.

When my mom and I went out, people often thought she was my older sister, and despite my mom's protests, I usually set them straight. I had to admit our faces had similar features and our eyes looked practically identical. Our hair color had once been the same, too, until my mother had dyed hers blond. But unfortunately, from the neck down my sister had inherited the rest. I got stuck with the flat chest and large hips.

"I thought for sure you'd find someone at that dance." She looked genuinely disappointed.

"Well, I didn't." There was no point mentioning Brandon. My mom would have a good chuckle if I told her I met a married man at a singles dance.

After putting down the last box, my mom reached into her purse and handed me a stack of ads, reading each one to me as she pulled them out. "Young Single Professional Night at Har Zion Synagogue, End of Summer Single Blast at the Hilton Hotel, Fall Frolic for Jewish Singles at the JYC. None of these are till the end of August, but I thought you might want to see what was coming up."

"Well, I don't. The guys there are all losers, and I feel like one, too, when I'm there." I handed her back her ads without glancing at them. "Do you want some coffee?" I walked into my kitchen to start my coffee maker. I was ready to change the subject.

"No, thanks, I just came from Starbucks." My mom followed me to the kitchen, holding up the ads, as if I would suddenly change my mind and grab them from her. "Jen, don't you want to find a nice guy to settle down with?"

No, I prefer to spend the rest of my life alone and miserable. What kind of question was that? "Of course I do, but these singles events aren't the place to find someone."

"Then where is the place?"

Now, there was the million-dollar question. "I don't know, Mom." If only I had real amaretto to put in my coffee instead of the imitation stuff in my International Delight creamer.

"You know you're not going to be in your twenties much longer." Good old mom, always stating the obvious.

"Believe me, I know!"

"Well, you don't have to scream. I'm worried about you. It gets a lot harder to meet men as you get older. Maybe you should try a little harder to meet someone."

"Why should I have to try harder to meet him? Why can't he try harder to meet me?" And why should anyone have to try hard to find love? Didn't it just happen?

"I remember how determined I was to get married when I turned nineteen," she said. "I went to every singles dance and night club I could find until I met your father. I was so excited when I realized that I'd finally met the guy I'd end up marrying."

From her description, you'd think she and my dad lived happily ever after. Unfortunately, I knew the truth.

It was no secret that my parents had a terrible marriage, if you could even call it a marriage. Every night when my sister and I were young, our parents put on a good show of walking together to the master bedroom, but we were on to them. Around eleven o'clock we would hear our father walk down the hallway into the guest room where he slept. Then, around five o'clock in the morning, we once again heard his footsteps, and sometimes his blanket dragging behind him, as he returned to the room where our mother slept.

Even if we hadn't caught on to their sleeping arrangement, we could tell from the way my mom looked at our dad that she felt nothing for him. She didn't look at him with hatred or anger. She didn't really look at him at all, and if she did for a brief moment, it was like she was looking at a distant cousin or an acquaintance she occasionally bumped into at the supermarket.

I'd never forget that time I left my algebra notes home the day of my midterm. I had to walk ten blocks back home to get them before the exam started. When I walked into the foyer, I heard my parent's voices coming from the kitchen. I could tell they were having a serious conversation so I quietly slipped upstairs, unnoticed.

When I came back down, I heard my mom crying. "Why do you stay with me after all this time?" she asked. "We haven't had sex in years, and we barely talk. We're nothing more than roommates."

"Because I still love you," my father answered. I looked through the railing of the steps to see my father staring into my mother's eyes like a wide-eyed puppy dog. He reached for her hand, but my mother pulled it away before he could touch it.

"I'm sorry," she said, walking toward the kitchen.

I thought I heard my father say, "I'm sorry, too," but I wasn't sure. I slithered down the steps and out the door, wishing I had never taken algebra.

⌒

"...with the hours you work, it's not surprising you don't have time to find someone. You really need to get out more, Jen."

Apparently my mom hadn't noticed that our dialogue had become a monologue. Just how long had she been talking since I tuned her out?

Meanwhile, she had meandered into the living room, frowning, as always, when she looked at my furniture. I admitted it looked a little like an IKEA showroom, and there wasn't much in my home that hadn't come with assembly instructions, but I'd bought everything when I first moved in and at the time I was earning practically nothing. Since then, I'd grown attached to my simulated wood coffee table and entertainment center. Not to mention my love seat and reclining chair purchased on sale at JCPenney. My mother, on the other hand, wouldn't consider buying furniture that didn't have a designer's name somewhere on its tag.

"You know I just want you to be happy," my mom said, staring at a lamp I'd fallen in love with at a yard sale several years ago.

"I know, Mom, but I am happy." Most of the time. All right, some of the time.

She shrugged as if she didn't believe me, and then shook her head in disgust as she picked up a ceramic vase that I'd bought at a flea market. "So do you need any help packing?"

I was afraid if I accepted, half of my stuff would end up packed in the trash.

"Thanks, but I'd rather do it myself. That way, I'll know where everything is when I unpack." And I wouldn't have to watch her scrutinize every piece of furniture I owned.

"Then I'm off to meet Barb. We have big plans today, lunch at The Trophy Inn, then shopping at the Cherry Hill Mall, drinks and dinner at Polo Bay, and then bingo at Beth El."

No mention of my dad, but that was a given. Knowing him, he'd probably sit home alone in his big leather recliner, reading the newspaper, while eating some frozen dinner.

"Tell Barb I said hi." Barb and my mom had been friends since high school, and had become inseparable since her husband died two years ago.

"And you tell Stacy to come by with that ring. According to her mother, the diamond's huge."

Apparently, the size of your diamond was all that mattered around here anymore.

I packed all afternoon until I couldn't see my bed or dresser behind the boxes. I would never have found Frisky if I hadn't heard him scratching one of the boxes. How was I going to live here for the next three weeks surrounded by cardboard?

It wasn't until I wanted to watch TV that I realized I had packed the remote. I had to unpack three boxes to find it. Sitting alone on my love seat, I began one of my favorite pastimes, channel surfing. *Sleepless in Seattle* was on HBO. Click. *When Harry Met Sally* was on Showtime. Double click. *Pretty Woman* was on Cinemax. Click click click. Where were all the good psychological thrillers when you wanted them? ABC was showing *Father of the Bride* for the fourth time this month.

Giving up, I settled on *Bridges of Madison County*. Within the first half hour, tears poured down my face, dripping on to my lap. Clint Eastwood and Meryl Streep had so much chemistry between them. How could she ever consider being without him?

When the phone rang, I grabbed a tissue box before answering it. Since the caller ID was marked private, I had no idea who it was until I heard my sister's high-pitched, bubbly voice, which matched her adorable figure and cute-as-a-button face. The only word to describe Kathy was perky. She had perk dripping from her face all the way down her body. When I looked up the word "perky" in the dictionary, I expected to see a photo of my sister.

"I know you're busy packing, so I won't keep you long, but Jeff just asked me if you'd want to go out with one of his friends from work. So what do you think?"

As much as I loved my brother-in-law, I did have a problem with Jeff's matchmaking skills. He had never fixed me up with anyone who I wanted to see again. Not to mention, I hated blind dates almost as much as I hated singles events, but as I looked up at my TV to see Clint making love to Meryl on the kitchen floor, I heard my voice accept, before my mind had a chance to decline.

"That's so great!" my sister shrieked into the phone so loud I had to hold it away from my ear. "I know you and Ben are going to hit it off."

And I knew I had to stop watching romance movies. "So what's this guy like?" I turned on CNN, trying to get Clint's expression out of my mind.

"Uh, I don't really know."

A CNN commentator described a terrible earthquake in the Middle East. Now this is what I should have been watching when Kathy called. From now on I would watch nothing but news programs and The Weather Channel. "Have you even met this guy, Kathy?"

"Well, not exactly, but Jeff says he's a great guy."

"Why is he so great?" I tapped my fingers on a box, wanting more details.

"Jen, the guy's a Jewish dentist. What more do you need to know?"

So much for chemistry and camaraderie. So much for mutual interests and hobbies. "It would be nice to know something about him before we met."

"Isn't that the reason you're going out with him? To get to know each other?"

Oh brother. I gave up. There was no getting through to her. She just didn't get it. "Maybe I should take a rain check."

"You can't be serious." The high-pitched tone of my sister's voice was enough to crack my mirror. "Why on earth would you do that? You haven't met someone, have you?"

"Well, no…"

"Is there someone you're interested in?"

"No, but…"

"Someone you think is interested in you?"

"No…"

"Then what's the problem? Why won't you at least meet him? It's not like he's a total stranger you met on-line. He's a highly respected dentist at a large teaching hospital, and he's Jeff's friend. What do you have to lose?"

Well, when she put it like that, I guessed not much. It's not like I was doing so well trying to find someone on my own. "Okay, you talked me into it."

"Great, sweetie, I can't wait to hear how it goes."

I hated when she called me sweetie as if I were a decade younger than her instead of just four years. And I hated the way she talked to me as if my purpose in life should be finding the *right* guy. And I particularly hated the way she always managed to persuade me into going on a blind date, no matter how bad the previous one had gone.

I shuddered, thinking about the last few blind dates she had talked me into. This one better be different!

Chapter 3

Early Symptoms of the Marriage Epidemic:

1. Allowing your family members to play matchmaker after you'd sworn off blind dates forever.
2. Convincing yourself that a blind date could actually lead to a marriage proposal.

"Marisa and I were thinking of checking out a new dance club on Chestnut Street tonight," Tiffany said, placing samples of her art work on the glass conference table. "I hear there's a great band playing." Tiffany gave her trademark loud hacking cough, another result of her chain smoking. "Want to come?"

"I'd love to, but I, uh…"

"What did you say?" Tiffany tapped her long black fingernails, each with a rhinestone glued in the middle, on the table.

"I sort of have a blind date," I mumbled into my hand, realizing I sounded a lot like Marisa.

"What! I thought you swore off blind dates after that podiatrist Kathy set you up with wouldn't let you walk into his house until you took off your shoes and socks."

I hated eating my words, and admitting that I was going on a blind date was like eating the entire alphabet. "Maybe I was too critical," I said, trying to redeem myself. "He did have nice carpeting."

"Didn't he try to file your toenail?"

"He said I had a hangnail."

"Jen!"

"All right, so that guy was weird, but that doesn't mean this one is, too. Besides, this guy's a dentist. The worst thing that could happen is that he'll floss my teeth after dinner. Maybe if he doesn't like me, he'll give me a toothbrush as a parting gift."

Tiffany smiled while rolling her eyes as Marisa sat down across the conference table from us. "Did I hear you say you had a blind date?" Marisa asked. "Who is he and does he have any friends?"

"Down, girl," Tiffany teased her. "Why don't you let Jen meet him first?"

"Who's the guy, Jen?" Marisa asked again, placing a large stack of paper samples on the table.

"His name's Ben Shafer and he just finished dental school. My sister said he's really cute, but she said the same thing about that guy she fixed me up with last year who had a black tooth and warts all over his forehead."

"As long as the guy is Jewish with a large bank account your sister would think he looks like Ben Affleck," Tiffany said.

"That's true," I admitted. Even though Kathy swore she went into nursing because she wanted to help people, she obviously liked the fringe benefits of meeting doctors. "But since Ben Affleck was busy tonight, I thought I'd give Ben Shafer a try."

"If you like him, find out if he has a brother who's single," said Marisa.

"Maybe if you weren't so anxious to meet someone, you would," said Tiffany. "You know how guys are more attracted to girls who don't seem interested in hooking up. And if you have a boyfriend, they really want you."

"I hate playing games," Marisa said. "If I like someone, why can't I show it?"

"That kind of reasoning is exactly why you're hanging out with me tonight," said Tiffany.

I felt bad for Marisa. Even though I had been dumped by my last three boyfriends, at least I had had relationships. Marisa rarely made it past the second date.

"What's up with Vince," I asked Tiffany. "Haven't you been seeing him for the past few Friday nights?" If I remembered correctly, Vince was the one with the body piercing and tattoos.

"Oh, we broke up yesterday," she said nonchalantly.

"What happened?"

"Nothing really. The sex was great, but when it came down to it, we didn't have much in common. Besides, he and his band are going to be touring the West Coast for the next six months. By the time he gets back I'm sure he won't remember who I am."

She closed her portfolio as if closing another chapter in her life, and I could tell by looking at her that she wasn't experiencing any feelings of loss. She handled most of her break-ups pretty much the same way.

"So you're one of us again," I said. I opened my bulging file folder to find the proposal for our new account.

"If you mean back to the meat market, it looks that way," Tiffany said, "but it's not so bad."

"Oh, yes it is." Marisa slumped lower in her seat.

We all stopped talking as Ilene Meeney walked in. Her last name suited her well. Meany, as we all referred to her, was notorious for making copywriters cry and artists storm out of the office, threatening to shove Meany's head through the wall. Whenever I worked with Meany, I knew I would have to make at least three or four revisions before she showed my work to the client, and then she would get mad at me for going over budget.

"How are you ladies today?" she asked, wearing the same business suit she wore to all client meetings, while carrying her old, beat-up briefcase. As usual, Meany had lots of gray showing beneath her short, dark brown hair. For someone who made so much money, she sure didn't spend it on her wardrobe or her hair.

Meany gave us one of her classic wide smiles as she sat next to Marisa. I swore she had a button on her hand that she hit to automatically paste that grin on her face. It was like a special effect that you knew couldn't be real, but gave the illusion of sincere joy. I imagined the button was short-acting because no sooner had it appeared than it deactivated to her normal scowl.

"I hope you've all read the proposal for Ho Wong's fortune cookies." She passed out additional information about the account. "We'll be competing against three other agencies so let's give Mr. Wong our best work."

"As opposed to our normal bad work," Tiffany whispered to me.

For the next few minutes we watched Meany scribbling away with a black felt-tip marker on the large easel she always used. I truly believed that she purposely pressed down hard on the paper to make that annoying screeching sound. Meany used a pointer to identify each goal as she read it out loud.

"Today's Goals are: One, to develop strategies and tactics to position Wong fortune cookies as a unique product line; Two, to create a campaign that establishes national recognition of the Wong fortune cookie product line; and Three, to develop collateral materials, along with a trade booth, for the American Society of Grocers Convention."

Meany, who was probably somewhere in her fifties, had been an English teacher before she became an account executive. She didn't know how to have a conversation without a piece of chalk or a marker in her hand. She seemed to get great pleasure out of making a loud thud each time she hit the easel with her pointer.

"So, are we all clear?" Meany asked as if questioning whether a classroom of first-graders could complete their homework assignment.

"Yes, ma'am." Tiffany saluted Meany, who seemed to like the gesture.

"Thank you, dear." Meany activated that smile effect for five whole seconds.

As I looked at the materials Meany had passed out, a small, dark-complected man walked in and hugged Meany. Despite our feelings about her, clients, for some reason, loved her.

When Mr. Wong approached her, she activitated her smile effect for an entire minute. "We're looking forward to putting together a campaign that you'll be happy with," said Meany. "I want to introduce you to our best team at Premier."

Funny, how we had suddenly become Premier's best team when five minutes earlier we were so incompetent that Meany had to read her goals to us so we would understand them.

We each took turns discussing Premier's capabilities, and each of our roles, and then Meany suggested that Mr. Wong describe the type of advertising campaign he expected from us. I understood about one out of every twenty-five words that he said. It was like listening to the parents on Charlie Brown. He sounded like, "Wak wak wak wak wak wak." Good thing I had the proposal in front of me or I would have had no idea what he was talking about.

Meany suggested that we each sample one of the cookies to get a better idea about what we were promoting. Mr. Wong immediately pulled out a bag from his briefcase filled with the most attractive fortune cookies I'd ever seen. Unlike the typical tannish ones you found in most Chinese restaurants, these were colorful and looked a lot more appetizing.

According to the proposal, the cookies came in chocolate, vanilla, strawberry and rocky road. I grabbed the rocky road one, assuming Weight Watchers had no record of the number of calories in Wong's cookies. Tiffany bit into a chocolate one, Marisa took a vanilla cookie, and Meany opted for strawberry.

Thrilled to have a legitimate excuse to eat chocolate, I took a large bite, ready to experience the marvelous, sweet sensation of chocolate and marshmallow. And then I tasted it. Unfortunately, it was before I swallowed. If I had bothered to smell this small, flat, sweetened dough, I would have realized that it smelled like something Frisky had dug up in the backyard. But worse yet, it tasted like vomit! Chewing it brought back vivid memories of the stomach flu I had had last winter.

Unable to swallow, I looked at Meany, who must have hit that automatic smile switch pretty hard because her smile was frozen as she swallowed her cookie. Marisa excused herself to go to the bathroom, where I imagined she planned to unload Mr. Wong's precious multimillion-dollar Chinese treat. Tiffany stared at Mr. Wong, as if he were an alien who had delivered a space creature she was being forced to ingest.

"What's in this?" Tiffany said at last.

We were probably better off not understanding the ingredients that Mr. Wong rattled off, but he seemed pleased that she was interested enough to inquire. Meanwhile, back at the ranch, I still had a mouthful of this vile, foul substance, and nowhere to spit it. I watched Tiffany drop something on the floor and bend down under the table to retrieve it, while disappearing a bit too long to find it. She looked much happier when she returned to the table with an empty mouth.

This left me holding the cookie dough. Should I hold my breath and swallow? And if I did, did I risk throwing up Mr. Wong's fortune cookie all over his lap.

When Marisa returned with a large bottle of ginger ale, I followed her lead, excusing myself. I ran to the bathroom, practically running over Rhonda, who was spraying her wavy, long blond hair with hair spray that smelled like strawberries. That, combined with Rhonda's flowery scented perfume, put me over the edge.

"What's the hurry, Jen?"

Knowing better than to tell her I was going to throw up part of our new client's product line, I ignored her question, ran to the first toilet I saw, and spit out the cookie. I continued to spit, even after the cookie was sinking in the water, making sure every crumb was out of my mouth. Satisfied that all of it was gone, I flushed the toilet, watching the little tan pieces spin around until they disappeared.

"What's going on in there?" Rhonda startled me from the other side of the stall. "First Marisa ran out of the conference room toward the bathroom, and now you. What's Mr. Wong going to think when everyone keeps leaving the room?"

Right now, the last thing I cared about was Mr. Wong's feelings. "Maybe he'll think we drank too much coffee this morning." I pushed past her toward my office. I grabbed a stack of folders and returned to the conference room, explaining that I wanted to show Mr. Wong some additional campaigns we had developed for dessert manufacturers. Of course, those desserts had been edible.

Meany hit her smile effect and even threw in a wink for good measure. How the hell was I going to promote these cookies when I wouldn't feed them to the homeless people outside our building?

Mr. Wong said something to me that I didn't understand until he pointed at a small piece of paper where half of my rocky road cookie still sat. Guessing he wanted me to read the fortune inside the foul piece of cookie dough, I picked it up and read, "Beware of meeting new people today." Not the fortune I wanted to get eight hours before my blind date.

I spent the rest of the day popping Tums while wondering whether I should cancel with Jeff's friend. Telling Ben I was feeling sick wouldn't be a complete lie, considering my stomach had been making lots of strange noises ever since sampling Mr. Wong's cookies.

But then again, what if this guy turned out to be great, and I blew my chance of finding my soul mate by never bothering to meet him? As usual, I was too indecisive and by the time five o'clock rolled around I knew it was too late to change my mind.

Before leaving work to get ready, I checked my email. Three messages from Meany, two from Marisa, and one from my mom. After reading the first five, I reluctantly read my mom's:

Jen, Barb and I are on our way to the casinos, but I wanted to wish you good luck tonight with Ben. Kathy tells me that he has a lot of potential. I hope you didn't work too many late nights this week. I'd hate for you to look tired for your big night out. If things don't work out, I'm including this link to a new singles website that I read about in The Jewish Gazette. Call me first thing tomorrow morning to give me a report, Love Mom. PS: Here's that website: phillysingles.com/jewishgaz.

I knew when my mother talked about a guy having potential, she meant marriage potential. Too bad Mr. Wong's fortune cookie had already predicted an unpleasant encounter. I shut down my computer, grabbed a stack of projects I planned to work on over the weekend, including the dreaded fortune cookie account, and closed my door.

When I walked past Rhonda's desk, she was chatting away with Meany while chomping on one of Mr. Wong's jumbo fortune cookies from his premium cookie product line. Barf! What Rhonda wouldn't do to get noticed.

I left my sanctuary, unaware that it had started raining. Just great. Now my hair would look like a French poodle's fur. My curly hair was particularly uncooperative in hot, humid, rainy weather. The big clock on the side of my parking garage indicated that it was ninety degrees, which was unusually hot for June. Just my luck, the summer's first heat wave had to begin today.

Once in my car, I blasted my air conditioning and turned up the volume of the radio to block out the persistent beeping and cursing of all the drivers leaving the city. Getting out of center city on a Friday night required patience that I didn't have this evening.

When I got home almost an hour later, I checked my mail while waiting for the elevator. Stacy had sent me two more bridal magazines. This morning she had brought over a box of color swatches for possible bridal party gowns. When I opened my door, I slid on the photos of bridal bouquets she had given me yesterday. I was starting to feel like Stacy's private wedding consultant, which was rather ironic since I obviously had no experience in this field.

While deciding what to wear, I checked my answering machine. Stacy had called.

"Hi, Jen. Are you free on Sunday to shop for bridal gowns? Someone I work with said it could take six or more months to order the dresses so I thought we better start looking. Let me know. Oh, and good luck tonight. 'Bye."

Why did everyone wish you good luck when you went on a blind date, as if you were about to have root canal or get your tonsils out? And why did my mom have to leave that message about being tired? Up until now, I hadn't noticed those dark circles under my eyes.

I used my straight iron for twenty minutes on every strand of hair and squirted enough hair spray to break the ozone layer. Unfortunately, I still looked like a long-haired Annie. My luck, Ben would look like Daddy Warbucks.

While trying on outfits, I decided that whoever decided the newest clothing trend should be snug and short had obviously never had a weight problem. Someday I would wear a shirt that showed off my fit stomach, like the teenagers I saw at the mall last week, or like my mom. But for tonight, I selected a pair of blue and white capris with a matching, but not snug, blue shirt.

When I heard the knock on my door, my heart seemed to lurch into my throat. Here I go again, I thought, walking toward that ominous figure on the other side. Please let him be normal. Please let him be somewhat attractive. Please let him be easy to talk to. I would have preferred talking to him before we met, but he had been away at some dentist convention so Jeff had set the whole thing up himself.

Holding my breath, I opened the door to see a gorgeous man smiling at me. Surely, this guy must be a UPS driver delivering a package. Or maybe his car had broken down and he knocked on my door to use the phone. No, I bet he confused my address with the model who lived upstairs. Our numbers were so close that we were always getting each other's mail. My date, a big, bald Oompa Loompa, was probably upstairs knocking on her door.

"Are you Jen?" the Ken doll look-alike asked me.

Oh my God! This was no UPS driver. This beautiful man with golden blond hair, piecing blue eyes, and muscular arms was going to take me out on a date. I silently thanked Jeff before inviting Ben in.

"Jeff didn't tell me you lived in a warehouse." He laughed easily as he looked at the stacks of boxes burying my apartment.

In its present condition, my living room would never make the front cover of *Good Housekeeping*, not that it would have before I packed either. "Sorry about the mess, but I'm moving in two weeks."

"Where to?" He had a nice smile, and he dressed like he just stepped out of *GQ*, in a royal blue Ralph Lauren shirt and black pleated pants.

"The Royalty Apartments across from the Art Museum."

He raised an eyebrow, and I was glad I had splurged for the luxury apartment. After living in this one-bedroom square box for so many years, I had decided to treat myself to a nicer place in a better neighborhood. After all, what else did I have to spend my money on except, of course, Stacy's wedding?

"That's a nice area. I have a few friends who live around there."

Which was precisely why I was moving there. The Royalty Apartments were known for their young, single professional residents, as opposed to the semi-retired neighbors I currently had. Other than the model upstairs, most of the people living here were my grandparents' age.

"Where do you live?" I barely got the words out before sneezing five times. My allergy attacks always seemed to pop up at the worst possible times.

"I have a condo in Manyunk." Manyunk was a trendy spot for young singles. Its main street had cutting edge design and gift shops, along with lots of cozy, posh restaurants. I could picture Ben coming home from work and stopping by one of its art galleries or antique shops.

"So do you like Mexican food? Because if you do, I know a great Mexican restaurant in center city," Ben suggested.

"I love Mexican food." Stacy insisted that Mexican food was too spicy. Tiffany and Marisa just plain hated it so I never had anyone to go with, and unlike Chinese restaurants, Mexican restaurants didn't usually offer a take-out option.

"Great. Let's go."

I grabbed five tissues before closing my front door and following Ben to his black Lexus, where I sank into its smooth leather passenger seat.

We made the typical first/blind date conversation. We talked about our jobs, our families, music, the weather. I tried not to stare at him, but I had never gone out with someone this attractive before.

Too bad he'd never ask me out again. Guys who looked like him were used to dating girls who looked like Stacy. I was sure he would have been happier if he had mistakenly knocked on the model's door upstairs.

But as we continued to talk, I felt more relaxed. My sporadic sneezes didn't seem to affect our conversation, which evolved from our favorite night clubs to emotional issues like how frustrated Ben was with insurance companies who threatened his new practice, and how difficult it was for me to advance my career in such a cutthroat profession. After a while, I got so caught up in our conversation that I became less intimidated by his good looks.

When we pulled up at La Casa, Ben was still smiling at me. Imagine that! We had only had a few minutes of uncomfortable silence, which wasn't bad for a first meeting. Ben took my hand as we walked inside.

"This is a really nice place," I said, following our waiter to a small table in the corner. "I don't remember hearing about it. Did it just open?" Unlike those chain Mexican restaurants decorated with bright primary colors that accommodated busloads of people, this was a small, quaint café with no more than about twenty-five tables.

"Not really. It opened two years ago, but for some reason a lot of people don't know about it. It's more of a local attraction. I used to come here all the time with my ex-fiancée because she lives right around the corner."

As if someone has just blown a bugle into my ear, my heart raced, my body shook and my head popped up from behind my menu. "Your what?" I was going to kill Jeff!

"Didn't Jeff tell you I just broke my engagement?"

"No, he didn't mention that." An ex-girlfriend was bad enough, but an ex-fiancée was worse than having genital warts. At least they went away!

"Well, it doesn't matter anyway. Patty is history and I'm ready to move forward."

All right. Don't be too hasty, I silently told myself. You're sitting opposite a great-looking guy who you've been getting along well with.

Besides, he sounds like he's accepted his break-up. Maybe Patty was a real bitch. Maybe she cheated on him. Maybe…

"Of course, Patty and I were high school sweethearts so it's hard to get over that kind of relationship quickly."

Especially when you take your date to the restaurant you used to take her to, which coincidentally is close to where she lives. "How long has it been since you broke up?"

"Two months. Next Saturday would have been our wedding." His voice trailed off as he looked out the window, probably for Patty.

"This must be a hard time for you." I wasn't prepared to counsel my date on broken relationships.

"I'm trying not to live in the past. I never thought I would be able to live without Patty, but I'm doing fine."

Then why are you still talking about her? "I'm sure you're so busy at your new practice that you don't have much time to think about her," I said hopefully.

"I suppose, but Patty was also my dental hygienist so her ghost is still with me everyday."

Wonderful. "Listen, if going out with me is too hard for you, we could do it some other time." I was ready to grab a few tortilla chips and call it a night.

"I'm sorry. I shouldn't be talking about her. Please, stay. I promise not to bring up her name again. I'm having a nice time with you, and I'm not going to let Patty ruin this evening."

I wasn't sure if he was trying to convince me or him, but the food smelled great and I hadn't eaten since tasting Mr. Wong's fortune cookie. I had finally regained my appetite.

"All right," I said.

"Great, let's start over." Ben folded his hands together on the table, giving me his undivided attention. "So what do you normally do during the weekend?"

For the next fifteen minutes, we talked about our favorite hot spots in the area. We were so engrossed in our conversation that we didn't see the waiter at our table. "Should I come back?" he asked.

"No, I think we're ready. Ladies first." He smiled at me while putting down his menu.

I didn't need a menu to know what I wanted. On those rare occasions when I went out for Mexican food, I always ordered some kind of combination fajita dinner. "I'll have the chicken and beef fajita special."

"Why not try the chicken chimichanga dinner," suggested Ben. "I always order that one."

"Maybe I can try some of yours, but I think I'll still have the fajitas."

"But the chimichangas here have been written up in local magazines. Just give them a try."

What was with this guy and the chimichangas. I really wanted the fajitas.

"Should I come back?" asked the waiter, who was rolling his eyes.

"You really have to order them, Jen. You'll be sorry if you don't," Ben said.

I didn't want to spend the night arguing over chimichangas. It would be hard explaining to Kathy that my blind date was a disaster because I insisted on eating fajitas. "Okay, you win, I'll order them, but they better be good."

"You won't regret it." Ben smiled like a football player who had just scored a touchdown. I was glad I could make him so happy. He was just trying to be nice.

"Would you like a drink?" the waiter asked after Ben had ordered.

"I'll have a strawberry margarita," I answered, already anticipating its cool, thick, sweet taste.

"Can I make a suggestion?" Ben asked.

"Sure." I had a sinking feeling that it meant changing my order.

"Why not try the Midori melon margarita? You can get a strawberry margarita anywhere, but this margarita is a house special."

I hated melons, but the waiter looked impatient, and I didn't want to go another round with Ben about why I preferred the strawberry margarita. "Okay, I'll give it a try."

"Great. We'll have two, please."

We were once again engrossed in our conversation when dinner came, and when I tasted it, I was glad I had changed my order. The chimichangas were great, and surprisingly, I liked the margarita, too. I shouldn't have argued with Ben about my entrée. All this dieting was obviously making me irritable.

When it came time for dessert, I let Ben order for both of us. He ordered two fried Mexican ice creams, which we both agreed was the perfect dessert.

"So would you like to take a drive to my place?" Ben asked, while giving the waiter his credit card. "It's only about fifteen minutes from here."

I wished I could remember which underwear I had worn. Were my panties the pretty black lace ones, or the old ones with the small hole in the center? I had gotten dressed so quickly, I didn't bother to take inventory of my lingerie, assuming my date would be over before dessert. Maybe Ben would dim the lights so he wouldn't notice. Then again, maybe we would just watch TV.

I was impressed when we got to Ben's apartment. Unlike many guys I'd dated who had clothes lying all over the place, newspapers and magazines thrown on the sofa, and the bare essentials for furniture, Ben's place was immaculate and fully furnished.

"Would you like a drink?" he asked.

"Okay." I was getting nervous, waiting for him on his sofa. How many times had he made love to Patty here? How would I compare to her?

"Here's your drink." Ben sat down next to me, close enough for our legs to touch. And then he kissed me, at first softly, and then deeper and passionately. After a short time, I felt his tongue inch inside my mouth. It had been so long since I had been with anyone that when I felt his hands search for my bra strap, I was ready to give myself to him.

Hey, what was I doing? If I had sex with him on the first date, he might never call again. But as his hand caressed my inner thigh, I decided I didn't care. To hell with a second date! When would I have the chance to have sex with a guy who looked like this again?

His hands slipped into my panties as I lowered my hand inside his pants. He moaned and I groaned. I knew it wouldn't take much more for me to come. My panties were already soaked.

"Aah! Ooh!" he shouted as I felt his hardness with my hands. I couldn't believe I was making this gorgeous guy make these sounds. "Oooohhh, don't stop. Now, now. I want you, *PATTY!*"

Patty? He might as well have slapped me on the face or poured boiling water over my head. I got up so quickly that I knocked him off the sofa.

"Jen, I'm so sorry. I didn't mean to say her name."

I searched under the cushion for my bra and shirt, suddenly aware that the only thing I still wore from the waist up was my Star of David charm. "You're obviously not ready to move forward like you said you were."

"I am ready," he said, unable to zip his pants. I was glad that he was still big and hard. Let him take a nice cold shower. I wasn't about to help him out with this problem.

"I'm leaving."

"Don't go. I really like you. I must have called out her name because you tasted so much like her when I kissed you."

"Huh?"

"Patty always ordered the chimichanga and Midori melon margarita at that restaurant. I smelled her on your breath when we were close."

"What did you expect me to taste like after you insisted I order those goddamn chimichangas and that margarita? I would have been perfectly happy with the fajitas, but no, I had to have the chimichangas!" I was ready to strangle Ben with my bra as I fastened it behind me.

"There are hundreds of restaurants in Philadelphia, but you had to take me to the one you took your ex-fiancée to!" I continued shouting. "Taking me there was like foreplay to you! You got me smelling and tasting like Patty so you could have some sick fantasy that she was with you! I don't even like melon!" I pulled up my pants and slammed the door behind me.

Reaching inside my purse for my cell phone to call a taxi, I gained a new respect for Mr. Wong. His cookies might taste like vomit, but his fortunes were one hundred percent accurate.

Chapter 4

Most Marriage Epidemic Sufferers Experience the Following Emotions:

1. **Frustration**: You don't understand why so many women are strutting around with diamonds on their fingers when the only stone shining on your finger is the ruby on your school ring.

2. **Anger**: You become irritable and mad anytime someone mentions the "M Word" (marriage) and the "W Word" (wedding).

3. **Defensiveness**: You feel a need to explain why you're still single, as if you have a rare disease.

4. **Acceptance**: You surrender! You hate being alone and staying home Saturday nights. You can't fight the symptoms from the epidemic anymore. You're ready to settle down.

"Why don't you treat yourself to something nice?" said Stacy, as we rode in her bright yellow Volkswagen Beetle toward The Pampered Bride Salon on the Main Line. "I know! We can stop at Bloomie's on our way home and pick up those diamond earrings you've been looking at for the past six months. After that chimichanga fiasco with Ben, you deserve them."

Just hearing the word "chimichanga" made my stomach churn. While riding home from Ben's ex-fiancée-infested condo on Friday night, I had sworn off Mexican food and blind dates forever. "I'm really not in the mood to shop for earrings. Let's just look for gowns, like we planned." I wasn't in the mood to do that either, but I didn't want to let Stacy down.

Stacy squeezed my hand and smiled. "If you change your mind, let me know. Is there anything else you've been wanting besides the earrings?"

"Yeah, he's about five foot, ten inches, attractive, funny, smart, and ready for a relationship. Do they have any of those at Bloomie's?"

"I'm afraid not," Stacy laughed.

"Well, when they start carrying that type of merchandise, let me know. Until then, let's just shop for you today."

"I understand. I'll drop the subject."

"Thanks." The bright sunlight reflected off of Stacy's diamond, making it twinkle like a star. Somehow the sun didn't have the same effect on my college school ring.

We drove in silence for the next few minutes as we entered the Main Line. I was always amazed that people lived in these huge, aristocratic-looking homes surrounding this community. I couldn't imagine what these people did for a living to afford such glamorous homes. Apparently, they weren't writers at advertising agencies.

"By the way, Lori's meeting us at The Pampered Bride," Stacy said.

"Oh, great. I haven't seen her since she left for Italy." Lori would be fun to shop with. She always had some outrageous story to tell about a guy she had met or an exotic vacation spot she had visited.

"Neither have I. I can't believe she's been gone almost a year. I was beginning to wonder if she was coming back until she called me last night. She got back last week and she seemed excited about being in the wedding party."

"I hope she sticks around long enough to get fitted."

"I'm a little worried about that, too." Stacy parked her car at a meter.

I was glad Stacy wanted to look for gowns in Narberth. I liked its quaint, small-town feeling. Plus, you could walk through the entire shopping district without ever needing a car. "Does Lori have a job?" I walked beside Stacy as we passed a small church.

"No, her boss at McGraw's Pub was supposed to keep her job open for her until she got back, but when she stayed in Europe so long without getting in touch with anyone at work, they hired someone else."

"That's typical. It's amazing she still keeps in touch with us. Remember all the friends she dropped after college?" In her usual cool fashion, Lori had simply shrugged off her discarded friends by saying they no longer fit into her new lifestyle.

Stacy and I had always thought the real reason she stopped speaking to them was because those friends couldn't understand why she wanted to work at a bar after receiving her degree. Obviously those people didn't know her very well or they would have realized that Lori wasn't the type to get dressed up in a business suit every morning and work at a nine-to-five job. Since her degree was in recreation, you could rationalize that her job was related to her degree. After all, drinking was a recreational activity!

"Well, I'm glad we're all still friends," Stacy said. "We've certainly known her for a long time, not to mention living with her those two years in college." Stacy walked with her head up high and her shoulders back as we approached the bridal salon.

"Those were fun times." I missed college. Even though I rarely had boyfriends then either, it was more acceptable back then. "Is Lori dating anyone?" I asked.

"She's always dating someone."

I smiled, thinking about all the guys she had brought into our apartment. At first, I'd felt uncomfortable seeing naked men who I'd never met parade past the kitchen, but after a while, I got used to it. "So she's still playing the field?" I said, always fascinated with Lori's social life.

"I forgot to ask her," Stacy said, "but I'm sure she'll give us all the details when we see her."

I felt better, knowing Lori was back in town. Now that Stacy was engaged, she rarely went clubbing anymore. She was so busy on weekends meeting with florists, DJs, and calligraphers that she barely had time to meet me for a cup of coffee at night. I understood that she was busy, but I missed hanging out with her. Not to mention, I now had one less friend to go out with on weekends.

Lori, on the other hand, was always willing to go out, as long as it involved alcohol and men. She hated sitting home watching videos, but after the effect that the *Bridges of Madison County* had had on me, the only movies I watched now were horror flicks and murder mysteries, and even they made me cry when a romance developed between the killer and one of the lead characters.

After all these years of wondering why Lori preferred short flings to relationships, I finally understood. If you didn't get involved, you couldn't get hurt. No more waiting for the phone to ring after the first date. No more wondering why the love of your life doesn't want to see you again. Maybe I should be more like Lori and stop searching for a meaningful relationship. Would it really kill me to have some one-night stands? I had almost taken the plunge with Ben, so maybe that's where my life was headed. Maybe casual, meaningless sex was the answer.

For the first time since Friday night, I felt more focused as Stacy and I walked into The Pampered Bride.

Despite my new lease on life, as soon as I took one step into The Pampered Bride, my eyes filled with tears. We were surrounded by beautiful, long white gowns ranging from traditional and simple to chic and gaudy. But regardless of the style, they were all symbolic of a new beginning, a future filled with love, romance, and commitment. The only new beginning I had to look forward to was moving to a larger apartment with more empty rooms.

In the middle of the high racks of dresses, a woman with sculptured nails, a diamond necklace that glittered along with her enormous diamond ring, and a dress that looked like something I had seen in *Vogue*, stood at an espresso bar, in front of a long list of exotic-sounding coffee flavors. "Can I help you?" she asked in a husky Kathleen Turner voice.

Stacy started to answer when we heard a familiar voice coming from behind a rack of strapless bridal gowns. "Hey, you guys. I'm over here!"

Forgetting about the saleswoman, we raced toward the voice, which is when I saw Lori's face on top of someone else's body. Lori, who had always been well endowed, now had breasts the size of Pamela Anderson's.

If this had been anyone else, Stacy and I would have hugged her, especially after not seeing her for so long. But since we knew Lori wasn't the touchy-feely type, we simply smiled at her, unable to take our eyes off her chest.

"Do you like them?" she asked, as if asking our opinion about a new pair of shoes. But these were no shoes, and I wasn't sure how to respond. I couldn't exactly say no because obviously Lori was past the point of no return, but I wasn't sure I could say yes either.

"Can I help you ladies?" The Kathleen Turner sound-alike had emerged from the coffee bar.

"We're just looking right now," Stacy answered, staring at Lori's cleavage. The woman pointed her nose up as she walked away, obviously not too pleased that the only things we were looking at were Lori's breasts.

"Well?" Lori asked again. "What do you think?"

"I take it those aren't socks in there," was the only answer I could come up with.

Lori laughed. "Oh, Jen. I missed your sense of humor. These better not be socks, considering how much money I paid for these babies."

Lori was always full of surprises, but this one really caught me off guard. Not to mention, if any of the three of us needed breast implants it was me. I wondered what bra size Lori was now, and if they even made bras that large without special ordering them.

"What made you decide to get that done?" Stacy asked, talking to Lori's left breast.

"One day when I was surfing the web, I saw an ad from a plastic surgeon in Italy who talked about the benefits of getting breast implants. According to him, there's a direct correlation between your breast size and your self-esteem. You've heard the expression, 'when in Rome, do as the Romans do,' so I did."

I didn't want to burst Lori's bubble by telling her the Italian surgeon was probably referring to people like me, who resembled a male from the side. And if breast size determined your self-esteem, maybe that explained a lot about my personality. Maybe I was doomed to a life of insecurity simply because I had a small chest.

"Now if you guys will take your eyes off my boobs for a minute, you might notice something else new about me," Lori said.

I was ashamed at my reaction, but what did she expect us to look at when she walked in wearing two giant cantaloupes under her shirt? And what else could possibly top the implants?

When I tore my eyes off of Lori's breasts, I noticed how unusually pretty she looked. She was always attractive with her Angelina Jolie look-alike facial structure and her Eva Longoria straight dark hair. And she certainly didn't have to worry about losing any weight while she was away. For a while Stacy and I had been concerned that Lori might be anorectic. But today, she looked especially beautiful and I couldn't figure out why. Had she done her hair differently? Maybe new makeup?

"I had my eyes done, too," Lori said, seeming to burst with excitement. "I was going to try Botox, but while I was at it, I decided to go all the way."

Looking closer, I saw how youthful her eyes now appeared. Not that they were old-looking before, but Lori's obsession with being tan all year round had resulted in some wrinkles around her eyes that were now gone. Her eyes, which were a grayish blue, seemed to look more blue than gray now.

I stood back, trying to take in Lori's new appearance. Besides the surgery, there was still something different about her. Maybe it was the way she smiled and laughed more. Lori wasn't the most expressive or emotional person. She was usually on the serious side until she had a few drinks in her.

And there seemed to be a softness about her today. Even though I liked Lori, she wasn't one of the easiest people to get along with. There was a toughness about her that made getting too close to her difficult, but today she seemed more relaxed. Even her voice, which could be harsh and abrupt, sounded gentler.

"Wow," Stacy said. "You've been busy this year. You look great." Stacy was now talking to Lori's right breast.

"I feel great," Lori said. "I had gotten to the point that I hated looking in the mirror because all I saw were those awful lines around my eyes, reminding me that I was getting older. I hated those constant reminders so I decided to do something about it."

"Was it painful?" I asked.

"Like getting socked in the eyes with a football, but it was worth it. Now I don't feel so bad about being thirty."

Just hearing Lori say that number gave me a lump in my throat. I had one more week of being twenty-nine, and the leap from my age to thirty seemed as great as jumping over the Grand Canyon. Looking at one of the many mirrors at The Pampered Bride, I once again saw those gray hairs peeking through my head. The florescent lights magnified a few creases around my eyes that I thought I had concealed with makeup. Hell, maybe I should jump on a plane to Italy and get socked in the eyes, too.

"Are you sure you don't need help?" the same saleswoman asked once again.

"Not right now. Thanks," Stacy said in her sweetest voice. This time the saleswoman sighed loudly before approaching another customer.

"I have one more surprise," Lori said, "and this is a biggie."

I still hadn't recovered from the other two. If she got her tush tucked, too, I refused to look.

"Well?" Stacy said. "Don't keep us in suspense. What is it?"

"I'm getting married," Lori said.

"You're what?" I said, perhaps a little too loud because the saleswoman shot me a dirty look from across the room. I couldn't believe what I was hearing. Lori, queen of casual dating for fun, was settling down forever? I would have rather looked at her tush.

"Oh my God!" Stacy impulsively reached over to hug Lori, who stiffened a little at the gesture, but managed to hug her back. Stacy was careful to hug her from the side, apparently not wanting to mess with the plastic surgeon's work. "Congratulations. Who's the guy?"

"His name is Tony Riccio, and we met in Italy, which, by the way, is why I was gone so long."

"Don't tell me you're moving to Italy," Stacy said.

"No way. I loved Italy, but I wouldn't want to live there. Besides, Tony is from South Jersey. He was visiting Italy to expand his franchise."

"He has his own franchise?" Stacy raised her eyebrow.

"Yeah, it's a coffeehouse, like Starbucks, except they serve over fifty flavors of coffee and tea. His grandfather started the business, and Tony and his father have been opening new shops every month for the past few years. They have over twenty-five stores all over the country. The one in Italy is the first one outside the U.S."

"What's it called?" Stacy still glanced occasionally at Lori's left breast.

"The Jumpin' Java."

"Didn't they just open one up on Market Street?" Stacy asked.

"They did, and it's doing really well."

Not only was she getting married, but she was marrying an entrepreneur who owned his own business! This was quite a switch from the construction workers and truck drivers she usually dated. Who would have thought she'd end up with a white collar professional?

"If you're getting married, why don't you have an engagement ring?" I asked. "Or is this just another passing fling?" I immediately wished I could retract my question.

Lori and Stacy looked at me with their mouths open, apparently startled by my remark. I realized it wasn't the appropriate thing to say and I felt bad about it as soon as I said it, but I was getting tired of hearing engagement announcements, and the words had slipped out faster than I could catch them.

I couldn't believe that Lori, of all people, was settling down. Could this be the real reason she seemed so different? While lost in my thoughts, Lori and Stacy continued staring at me, still looking surprised at my harsh question. This was the kind of thing that the old Lori would have asked and gotten away with before. Regardless of that, I knew it was rude and I had to redeem myself.

"I'm sorry," I said, while cracking my knuckles. "I'm just surprised at how fast this all happened."

"I understand." Lori's heated expression seemed to cool down a little, but she turned her attention to Stacy. "After the surgery, I was laid up for a while. But once the bandages came off and the swelling came down, I felt great. I was tired of staying in my hotel room, so I went out as often as possible, meeting new guys every night."

I wondered if those guys ever got past her breasts to see her youthful eyes.

"Anyway, I was just playing the field. Italian guys love American women so I was making the rounds until I met Tony. I went into The Jumpin' Java, needing a large cup of coffee for a terrible hangover I had from the night before and we began talking.

The next thing I knew it was three hours later and we were sitting at a corner table, unable to leave each other. We headed over to a nearby restaurant and spent the rest of the night talking over dinner and drinks." Her eyes beamed as she spoke.

"I knew right away that he was different than anyone I had ever dated because he took the time to get to know me. Me, not the party animal who everyone wanted to get into bed, but the person inside. He's the first guy who really cares about my opinions and feelings."

I wasn't sure if I saw a tear forming in Lori's eye, but I definitely heard her voice crack when she talked about him. After all these years, it was the most emotional I had ever seen Lori. She must really love this guy, and that was the biggest surprise of the day, even more than Lori's explosive bosom and her fountain of youth eyes. Lori was in love. It was the end of an era.

"The thing that really amazed me," Lori continued, "was that after all the work I had had done on my body and face, Tony didn't even kiss me till the third date. We didn't have sex for two months and that's when I knew I loved him. After having sex for fifteen years, it was the first time I ever made love."

"Aah," Stacy said, apparently eating up every word she said.

I, on the other hand, felt like I was looking and listening to a Lori imposter.

Where was that flirtatious party girl who expressed herself with sarcasm and curse words? What happened to that person with the stoic expression who needed a shot of tequila in order to crack a smile? Apparently, love really did work in mysterious ways.

Stacy was still smiling at Lori, but I wanted to cry. It was such a beautiful description of what I was looking for and how I wanted to feel. And of all people, I never expected to hear it from Lori. Unlike Lori, I had always waited to have sex until I was in a relationship that I knew would continue after the next morning. I was the good girl who was against sleeping around for the sake of it. And where had it gotten me? So much for my high morals.

"To answer your question, Jen." Lori barely met my eyes. "Tony and I are looking for rings this weekend. He hadn't planned to propose so quickly, but on our last night in Italy he took me to the Trevi Fountain. We each threw in two pennies over our shoulders, and then he kissed me. I remember hearing Italian music playing from one of the nearby cafes, and the next thing I knew Tony looked into my eyes, told me he loved me, and asked me to marry him. I didn't have to think about it for a second. Even though we had known each other for less than six months, I knew it was right."

"It sounds like something that would happen in a movie," Stacy said. "I'm so happy for you."

Of course, I was happy for her, too. How could I not be, seeing her face all lit up like a Christmas tree? Despite my excitement for her, I felt defeated. Where were all these great guys coming from and why couldn't I have one? Just one!

When the saleswoman reappeared, she was tapping her left foot on the marble floor. "Are any of you planning a wedding?" she asked, as if we had come to her posh salon solely to chat by the tiaras.

"As a matter of fact"—Stacy smiled at Lori—"she and I are both planning weddings. But if you're too busy to wait, we could go somewhere else."

The saleswoman's scowl turned into a large smile, showing all of her teeth and even her gums. "Oh, we're never to busy to help a customer. In fact, would you like a cup of cappuccino until you're ready to shop?"

"That would be just great," Stacy said to the saleswoman. Turning toward Lori, she asked, "So are you ready to look for gowns or is it too soon?"

"Are you kidding? Since Tony proposed, all I could think about was trying one of these babies on. Let's do it."

Stacy and Lori walked to the front of the store, where all the bridal gowns were hanging, and I walked alone to the back of the store to look for a maid of honor gown. Being a writer, I hated clichés, but I couldn't help mumbling "always a bridesmaid, never a bride" over and over again as I grabbed three teal dresses off the rack. Once in the dressing room, I threw my shoes into the corner and shoved my clothes into a ball.

The first gown revealed more than I wanted any stranger to see. The second gown, just the opposite, looked like something a nun would wear if she wore teal, and the third one was one of those snug-fitting gowns that made everything that wasn't firm on your body, bulge out. Unfortunately, there was a lot bulging through the material. Not the look I was going for.

I was hot, thirsty, and tired, and longed to seek refuge at my computer at home. I picked up my clothes and put them back on before returning the gowns to their respective racks. I was more than ready to leave, but when I walked to the front of the store, Lori and Stacy were leisurely sipping champagne, compliments of the house. The saleswoman, who had suddenly become their best friend, was holding a tray of gourmet pastries in front of them. Lori and Stacy each took one. As I walked over, the saleswoman carried the goodies away, not even offering me a glass of water.

"How's it going?" I asked.

"Great," Stacy said. "Wait till you see the dresses we picked out to try on."

"Stace, what do you think of this one?" Lori held up a strapless blush-colored bridal gown covered with sequins.

"I think it's very you," Stacy answered diplomatically. "Do you like this one, Lori?" She held up a more traditional white dress with a long train.

"Yeah, they're showing a lot of that style in Europe." Lori bit into what looked like a chocolate éclair while my stomach growled.

Was anyone going to ask my opinion, or had I suddenly become the invisible woman?

"Have you picked your florist yet?" Lori asked Stacy.

"No, but I have an appointment with two this week." Stacy finished her champagne, while I longed for any kind of alcoholic beverage. "I'll let you know if I like them," she offered. "Do you think you'll have a DJ or a band?"

"Tony's friends play in a band, and they offered to play at our wedding. If you want, I have a CD of their music I can lend you."

"Thanks. Do you know any good photographers or videographers?"

And so the conversation continued…without me. I understood that they were both excited about planning their weddings, but that didn't make me feel any better about being left out. It was like they had just formed some elite club that single people couldn't join.

There was nothing I could contribute to their discussion. Ask me about the newest club in Philly, and I'd rattle out the top fifty. Ask me about the trendiest restaurant in the area, and I could provide a list of the best in each county. But ask me which caterer had the tastiest pigs in a blanket, and I was lost for words.

"Jen, it's probably going to take a while to try on these gowns," Stacy said, startling me by acknowledging my presence. "Any luck finding a gown?"

"Not unless you want me to look like a religious figure or a beached whale."

"Huh?"

"Never mind. No luck yet."

"Well, maybe you can try on some more gowns while Lori and I try these on. We can meet back here in an hour." Stacy followed Lori into the dressing room while the saleswoman refilled their champagne glasses. Once again, I had been segregated to the back of the store.

There was no champagne or pastries back there. Not even a salesperson. Even the water cooler by the fitting room was empty. Another woman entered the shop and was directed to the back. She was quite large, which ironically made me feel skinny and petite by comparison. The hefty woman nodded to me as she walked to the rack filled with peach gowns next to the one I was looking through.

"When's the wedding?" she asked me.

I was so glad to be able to answer a question that I responded immediately. "Next April. When's yours?"

"In February, and mine's in March. For the next year, I have weddings almost every month. Thank goodness, I'm getting married, too," she continued, unphased that I no longer responded. "My friend from work just turned twenty-five and every guy she meets is either married or already has a girlfriend. She tells me all the time that it gets much harder to meet someone as you get older. I'm glad I don't have to worry about that," she said, as if describing a terminal illness.

Her friend was only twenty-five and having trouble meeting someone? And this woman, who could have easily weighed close to two hundred pounds, was getting married when I still didn't have a boyfriend! My moment of bonding was over. No longer interested in talking to anyone at The Pampered Bride, I grabbed five gowns and slammed the fitting room door behind me. I wondered if anyone would look for me if I didn't return to the front of the store. Would they even notice?

About forty-five minutes later, I caught up with Stacy and Lori. Stacy was sure she had found the perfect dress, but wanted to show it to her mom before buying it. Lori was still undecided. Amazingly, I had found a pretty gown with a princess waist and a big bow on the back that almost made me look thin.

Stacy approved of my selection, and I bought it for a mere four hundred dollars. The saleswoman, apparently pleased that I bought something, offered me a cold glass of water.

"Do you have anymore pastries," I asked, tired of being treated like a second-class citizen because I was *only* buying a maid of honor gown. I knew it was called The Pampered Bride, but couldn't anyone pamper me a little, too? Just because I wasn't getting married didn't mean I didn't get hungry.

"I'm sorry. We had so many brides come in today that they're all gone. Wait a second. Let me see if I have anything in the back."

"I thought you were on a diet," Stacy whispered to me.

Damn, for a split second, I was so busy standing on principle that I forgot. The saleswoman returned with that toothy, gummy smile. "Here," she offered me. "How about a Twinkie?"

Eyeing the empty gourmet pastry tray and the empty champagne glasses stacked on a table by a bridal display, I stuffed the Twinkie into my purse and followed Stacy and Lori out the door, relieved to be on the other side of bridal hell.

"I told Lori we'd drive her home since Tony dropped her off," Stacy said as we returned to her car.

Great, now I would become invisible for another half-hour. "Great," I said, taking a large bite of my Twinkie.

As Stacy turned on the ignition, my cell phone rang. "Hi, sweetie. Are you still with Stacy?" My mom's voice echoed from my phone. The one thing I hated about cell phones was that anyone sitting close to you could hear your conversations, especially if they had a voice as loud as my mother.

"Yeah, we just finished."

"Oh, good. I was hoping you could bring Stacy over. I still haven't seen her ring, and I have a present for her."

"Tell her yes," Stacy said, without me having to relay the conversation.

"We'll be there in about forty minutes. Lori's here, too."

"Well, ask her to come by, too. I haven't seen her for ages."

Lori smiled at me as I turned off my phone.

Without saying anything, Stacy got on the Schuylkill Expressway, instead of the Roosevelt Boulevard extension, like she would have taken to drive me back to my apartment, and headed toward my parent's house in Pleasantown.

For the next fifteen minutes, Lori and Stacy talked about how hard it was to decide who to invite to their weddings.

"Do you believe my mom wants me to invite all my second cousins," said Lori. "That would add almost thirty people to the guest list. I haven't had the heart to tell her yet that Tony and I want a small wedding where we can talk to all of our guests."

"My mom would kill me if I told her that," Stacy said. "She waited her whole life to throw me a wedding, and considering I'm an only child, this is her big moment. I won't get away with less than two hundred people."

Were they being self-absorbed or was I feeling sorry for myself? I still wasn't sure, but I felt like I had faded behind a cloud as these two rays of sunshine rose high above me.

As we approached my childhood home, I felt even more depressed. Pleasantown was far from pleasant these days. Graffiti covered storefronts. Homes that had once belonged to my friends' parents were now rental properties. When I had lived here, the worst crime in the area had been jaywalking. Now the newspapers were filled with stories about robberies or murders taking place almost everyday.

Despite the changes, my parents refused to move. They hated change and refused to admit anything was different.

Stacy pulled in behind my dad's car on Richman Street. "Your mom's so sweet to get me a present," Stacy said.

Was someone talking to me? It had been so long that I wasn't sure they realized I was still there. As we walked up the thirteen steps that led to my parent's front door, I searched for my keys, finally locating them behind the half-eaten Twinkie. I opened the door, hoping my mom wouldn't swoon too much over Stacy's ring.

"Surprise," people screamed. Was it Stacy's engagement party? But no, I would have known about that. Maybe Kathy was pregnant. But that couldn't be because she was already inside, waving at me.

As someone turned on the lights, I saw Marissa, Tiffany, and at least ten other people from Premier. The room was filled with relatives I hadn't seen since my sister got married four years ago, and next to my mom stood Barb. In the very back of the living room, I saw my father smiling at me. And then I saw the "Over the Hill" balloons, banners, streamers, and tablecloth. The number thirty appeared everywhere I looked.

"Are you surprised?" Stacy asked, giving me a big hug.

"Uh, yeah." I seemed to have forgotten how to talk. I cleared my throat a few times, hoping to find my voice. "Stace, did you plan this?"

"It was your mom's idea, but she asked me to find a way to bring you here. I was hoping you'd agree to go shopping for those earrings after we were done, but when you didn't, Lori and I had to stall for an hour so we wouldn't get you here too early."

I couldn't believe it. The whole time I was feeling sorry for myself, Stacy and Lori were planning to take me to my surprise party. Now I really felt like a spoiled brat. Everyone took turns hugging and congratulating me, and I felt special and loved to have so many friends and family members celebrating my birthday with me.

As I walked over to my parent's dining room table to get a drink, an "Over the Hill" banner with the number thirty fell from the ceiling and hit me over the head. It hit me like a ton of bricks, even though it was only paper. Somehow holding the sign with the numbers made this moment feel more real. I was turning thirty, without any prospect of finding a husband, a soul mate, a partner for life. Everyone, even Lori, was getting married. I didn't want to spend the rest of my life alone. I began to sweat and my heart raced so fast I thought I was having a heart attack.

According to the girl at The Pampered Bride, I was truly over the hill, and too old to meet someone. According to Lori, the only way to feel young now was to hire a plastic surgeon.

"Jen, what happened with Ben?" Kathy asked, putting her arm around me. "He wouldn't give Jeff any details, but he kept mumbling something about Mexican food."

"I'll fill you in later," I said, having trouble catching my breath.

"Sweetie, here's a little something I want you to have," my mom said. "The big present is stacked with the other gifts."

Even though my hands were shaking, I managed to tear off the wrapping paper to see a book called *Thirty-Something Singles*.

"I hear it's on the *New York Times* best-seller list." My mother looked proud at her selection.

"Just perfect, Mom." My mother seemed oblivious to my sarcasm.

"Jen, where's Stacy and Lori," asked my grandmother. "I haven't had a chance to congratulate them yet."

"Don't know, Nan."

"So now that you're thirty, are you thinking about settling down?" asked my Aunt Fannie.

"Why should I settle down? Maybe I like being single!" I screamed at my poor eighty-year-old aunt.

"Uh-huh." My aunt Fannie nodded and smiled at me like she was trying to appease a mental patient. "Whatever you say, sweetheart." It was easy to tell from her expression that she didn't believe me anymore than I did.

"Perhaps she already has a fella," Aunt Betty said, apparently forgetting I was still standing there.

"No, Sylvia says she can't find anyone," Aunt Fannie said, as if I couldn't hear her relay my mother's comments.

"Jen, I have to leave early, but I got a few things you might need," laughed my uncle Lenny, holding something behind his back. My uncle, the family jokester, laughed hysterically as he handed me a cane, hearing aid, and bed pan. "Thought these might come in handy now that you're becoming an old lady." I heard him chuckling all the way through the living room, out the front door.

I felt dizzy as I pushed my way past more people and found myself sitting in my childhood bedroom on the bed I had slept on till I started college. I sat clutching my knees to my chest, rocking back and forth. I wished my mom was getting ready to tuck me into bed. I wanted my dad to come by and read me a story. For a split second I felt safe and secure.

But as I looked around my old room, I saw my old closet filled with workout clothes. My mother's exercise bike now occupied the spot where my desk once stood, and a treadmill had replaced my chest of drawers. I felt sad, picturing how these four walls had once surrounded my stuffed animals, dolls, and later my posters of New Kids on the Block.

"Jen, it's time to cut the cake," I heard my mom call. "Has anyone seen Jen?"

Before cutting my thirtieth birthday cake, I took one last look at my former bedroom, now my mother's exercise room, and closed the door behind me.

Chapter 5

Age-Related Risk Factors:

1. Once you turn thirty, your chance of contracting the marriage epidemic increases as your single friends decrease.

2. You become more susceptible as your friends become pregnant, and are most likely to catch it as you approach the end of your child-bearing years (usually between thirty-five and forty).

3. Possible Remedy: Avoid engaged and married females until you reach menopause.

I watched the hairdresser through the mirror as he placed what seemed like the hundredth piece of foil on my hair. He had already been at it for at least thirty minutes and I couldn't believe how much work was involved to get that natural, youthful look.

My mom had talked me into going to her hair salon. Supposedly her hair stylist was a master at hair coloring, but after meeting Thomas, I had some serious doubts. I didn't mind having a man do my hair, although Thomas was about as manly as a pre-adolescent boy. I was more concerned that Thomas was almost completely bald. It was like going to an orthodontist who had crooked teeth or seeing a dermatologist who suffered from acne. How could you trust these professionals when they obviously couldn't manage their own problems?

At last, Thomas put the stack of foil on the counter in front of us and lowered my seat. "Okay, darling, you can go sit under that last hair dryer on the end until the timer goes off." He spoke in a high-pitched, sing-song voice that made my voice sound deep.

"You're sure it's not going to be too blond?" I felt each rolled piece of foil bounce as I walked toward the row of hair dryers.

"Don't worry. Thomas is going to make your hair look beautiful."

"You know I just want blond highlights, nothing extreme."

"Of course, sweetheart, we already decided on strawberry blond highlights, right?"

"And it won't end up darker than my natural hair color, right?" Marisa had gone to one of those cheap hair salons where students work on your hair and had come back with black hair when she had wanted her hair two shades *lighter.*

I think Thomas would have been happy if I had gone there, too. "Just relax, Jen. Do you always have so much trouble making changes with your appearance?" Without waiting for an answer, he put a huge circular dryer over my head that made me look like a space alien.

For the next twenty minutes, while the fumes from the bleach made my eyes tear, I thought about Thomas's question. Did I usually have this much trouble making changes? I had worn that eighties feathered hair style well into the late nineties, and I had refused to believe that blue eye shadow was no longer in style until every cosmetic company discontinued it. Maybe I needed to make more changes in my appearance, and in my life. Letting go was never one of my strong points, which is why I had stayed in my shell of an apartment so long, refusing to get rid of my old furniture.

Wiping a tear from my burning eyes, I prayed my new look would make me look younger. At least I wouldn't be gray anymore. Over the past few months, I had tweezed so many silver hairs from my head I was amazed I wasn't as bald as Thomas.

The timer startled me, and within a few seconds Thomas was back analyzing each strand of hair.

"What's wrong?" I jumped up, forgetting about the space helmet covering my head.

Thomas looked concerned as we both heard the loud clang of my head collide with the hair dryer. "Are you all right, Jen?"

"Fine, but what's wrong with my hair?"

"Nothing is wrong!" Mild-mannered Thomas looked like he wanted to hurt me. "I always check everyone's hair to see if they need more time under the dryer. You can get washed now."

I inhaled a breath of fresh air as I sat down by the sink. I wondered if the cold water against my hot, bleached hair would make my hair sizzle and fall out, but fortunately there was no chemical reaction. "Thomas did a nice job," the hair washer said.

Of course, she probably told every customer that. Maybe it was part of her training. She had to say something, and she couldn't exactly say, *That's the worst job Thomas ever did in his entire life.*

My heart pounded before looking in the mirror, but when I did, I felt relieved. No, not just relieved, ecstatic! Thomas had done exactly what I instructed him to do. The blond streaks were dark enough to cover all the gray hair, but light enough so you almost weren't sure if I had had my hair dyed or had sat in the sun for a long time. It was perfect! Maybe this was how Lori had felt when she saw her new boobs for the first time.

As Thomas dried my hair, the blond streaks became more pronounced, making me feel almost glamorous. It was the perfect gift from me to me, and was just the lift I needed twelve hours before I turned thirty.

But when I woke up alone the next morning, I forgot about my hair. If only I could have begun my birthday with a nice, warm male body wrapped around mine instead of Frisky curled up by my feet. I tripped over the stacks of boxes between my bed and my bathroom and stumbled to the mirror to pull back the creases around my eyes. There was no fighting it; I was getting older. I grabbed my terry cloth robe from the bathroom and pushed aside several piles of boxes, trying to make my way to the living room.

I had taken the day off from work to finish packing, but now that I was home I wished I was at work where I wouldn't have time to obsess about my age. As I started packing a stack of women's magazines, an article about botox treatments in *Cosmopolitan* caught my eye. I sat down on my couch, ready to read it when Stacy let herself in. "Happy birthday, for real this time, and I love your hair," she said.

"Thanks." I was glad I had gone through with it. For only one hundred and fifty-five dollars, I was rid of my gray hair for at least a few months.

"So are you ready for the big move tomorrow?" Stacy sat down next to me, placing a large nondescript brown bag beside her.

"I hope so. The moving truck will be here first thing in the morning." I had strategically planned the move around my birthday as another distraction from my age.

"I can't believe how many boxes you have to move. Are you sure you don't need any help?"

You could take your three boxes filled with bridal magazines and swatches home. "No, I'll be fine. Thanks." But as I looked around at all my stuff that still needed to be packed, I wasn't so sure.

For the past few weeks, every time I should have been packing I'd found something more important to do, like tweezing my eyebrows, sending a text message, or watching a new reality show. Now that I was down to the wire, I had a feeling I'd be up all night if I wanted all my things to end up at my new apartment.

Stacy picked up a bridal magazine I'd neglected to pack and started flipping through the pages. "Lance said he'd move anything breakable that you don't trust the moving people to move."

I never understood why people spent a fortune on moving companies, and then ended up moving most of their stuff anyway because they didn't trust the company they hired. "No. That's okay, but tell him thanks." I wished I had a Lance to come by for moral support. The only male in my apartment, Mr. Wow, was already securely packed in one of my boxes.

"Well, let me know if you change your mind. Oh, I almost forgot, I brought you a housewarming present." Stacy held on to the magazine as she bent down to get it.

"You didn't have to do that, especially after you bought me those earrings for my birthday."

"It's just a little something." Stacy pulled out a huge bottle of champagne from the brown bag she brought. "Congratulations!" We automatically reached over to hug each other as we'd done for so many happy occasions over the years.

"Thanks, Stace. That was really nice." If only I had someone to drink the champagne with on my first night at my new place.

⁓

Even though I was supposed to be home packing, I stopped by the office to give Tiffany the copy for Mr. Wong's campaign. Okay, so maybe I was looking for an excuse to get out for a while.

"So how's it feel to be thirty?" Rhonda asked, as if I had just acquired some debilitating ailment.

It feels like shit, I wanted to scream for the entire office to hear. *It feels like a loud reminder that time is running out to find the right guy before it's too late. It feels like I'm about to lose my youthful appearance. And it feels like I might be headed for a nervous breakdown.* "It feels great," I answered instead. "You know what they say about looking as young as you feel." I didn't tell her I felt about eighty today, minus the new hair color.

"You do look nice. Your hair looks great!"

A compliment from Rhonda? Now I was worried. She must want something. But what?

I was still trying to figure it out while I walked past my office to the opposite side of the thirtieth floor where Tiffany's office was located along the art department's long hallway. Marisa sat in front of Tiffany's desk with her head down. She pushed her glasses up with one finger to wipe a tear away from her eyes.

"Has Meany been making changes to the paper stock again?" I tried to lighten the mood, but Marisa continued to cry into her tissue without bothering to take her glasses off.

"Marisa's been waiting for over a week for that guy she met to call her," Tiffany said. "I told her it was time to move on and forget about him." Tiffany, whose voice sounded particularly raspy today, had a mild coughing attack until she took a sip of her Sprite.

"But I really liked this one," Marisa said. "Tif, you saw how well we hit it off."

"Is this the guy you met the night I was on my blind date?" I asked.

"That's the one," Tiffany said.

"Jen, do you think he might still call?" Marisa blew her nose before looking up at me, as if I held the magic answer. If it was possible, she spoke quieter today than normal.

I hated to burst Marisa's bubble, but the unwritten bylaws of dating generally required that the guy call within the first week of the initial meeting, and within the first several days if he was really interested. "I don't know. What did...uh? What was his name again?"

"Zack." Marisa got this weird dreamy expression as she said his name.

"Right. So what did Zack say when he took your number?"

"He said he'd like to take me to the grand opening of a restaurant that his friend is holding, and that he'd give me a call." She finally took off her glasses to dry them with a tissue.

"When's the opening?" I hated seeing Marisa so upset, but almost every time she met someone, Tiffany and I spent hours the next week analyzing why he didn't call her.

"He didn't say, but don't you think it's a good sign that he asked me to a specific place? He didn't just say that he'd be in touch sometime. We actually have a real date."

"That would be true if you had an actual date, time, and location of the grand opening," Tiffany said. "But considering Zack hasn't filled you in on the details, I wouldn't count on going."

"Do you know the name of the restaurant?" I wanted to give Marisa a glimmer of hope, if possible.

"No." Marisa put her head down again and began twirling her hair around her finger, a habit she usually reserved for guys who didn't call.

Tiffany gave me one of those "here we go again" expressions as she placed a pack of cigarettes on her desk. This was usually her subtle way of telling us we'd soon have to leave so she could go outside to smoke.

"Well, you never know," I said. "He could still call."

"That's what you said the last three times." Marisa tugged on her hair so hard I was afraid she'd soon be holding a strand in her hand.

I had to admit, she seemed more upset than usual about this guy. "What made Zack so special?"

"I don't know." Marisa seemed to be trying to figure it out herself. "There was something about him…He was different."

"Apparently, he was just like every other asshole guy in America who takes your phone number and doesn't call," Tiffany said. "That's why I don't get bogged down worrying whether a guy will call or ask me out again. It's just not worth it."

But by Marisa's expression, I could tell it was worth it to her. I handed her another tissue, wishing I could do more.

"So what brings you here on your day off?" Tiffany asked, obviously looking for an excuse to change the subject. "Or did you come in to show off your new blond hair, which, by the way, looks great. That idiot blind date of yours doesn't know what he's missing."

"I'm sure he'll survive." I was tired of talking about men. "I dropped by to give you the rough draft and tag line for the Wong account." I pulled the copy out of my briefcase.

"Mr. Wong predicts that his fortune cookies are different than anything you've ever tasted." Tiffany read from my draft. "Well, the tag line is accurate, but what do you want me to use as visuals? A woman heaving her guts out?"

Marisa smiled for the first time since I walked in.

"Maybe Marisa can order puke yellow paper stock to use for the brochure," Tiffany continued.

At last, Marisa laughed. "I'm sure going to miss you if you get that job," Marisa said.

"Job, what job?" I asked, turning my attention to Tiffany.

"Oh, it's no big deal," Tiffany said. "I went on an interview for a creative director's job at JBM&P Advertising."

"You're kidding! Why didn't you tell me?"

"How could I? Since your blind date, you've been locked up in your office, writing about foul-tasting cookies."

"I'm sorry. I didn't mean to become a recluse. So how did it go?" I pulled up a chair by Tiffany's desk and sat down.

"Put it this way. My chances of being recruited into a circus are probably better than getting a job offer from this place. They're looking for someone with lots of web design experience and obviously I don't have that."

"I always thought you'd make a great tightrope walker," I said. Tiffany rolled her eyes, trying to swallow her smile.

"Besides, you never know," I continued. "With all your experience, maybe they won't care about that." I couldn't imagine working at Premier without Marisa and Tiffany. We had all begun working here within six months of each other, and we immediately stuck to each other like glue. But, of course, I knew eventually we would all move on. In this field, it was unheard of to stay at the same job for very long. The three of us had nearly set a record for being at the same agency for over eight years.

"I don't know why you're so anxious to find something else," Marisa said, looking depressed. "I thought you were happy here."

"I am happy, and it's been a great gig for a while, but I'm ready for something different, where there's room to advance." Tiffany glanced at those cigarettes on her desk.

"Marisa, you didn't think we'd all work here forever, did you?" I asked.

"I guess not," she said, but from the sound of her voice, I wasn't sure.

"You're not looking, too, are you, Jen?" Marisa sounded frantic.

"No, not yet. I'll probably be here for at least another year or two now that I got that promotion. Not to mention, in this economy finding a new job isn't going to be easy."

"Are you still thinking about a management position?" Tiffany asked. She and I had spent many hours talking about our careers over vodka and tonics.

"Yeah. I'd love to find a job where I oversaw the writers for a change." As much as I loved my job, I had to report to so many people that by the time I was done writing, the copy barely resembled what I originally wrote.

Tiffany and I had talked about opening our own agency someday, but if that ever happened, it wouldn't be for a long time. You needed lots of money to start your own business, and neither of us had an excess of that floating around.

"Don't you still want to write?" Marisa asked.

"That's the problem. I want a job where I can manage a writing staff and still write. I wouldn't be happy if I had to give up writing, no matter how much money I made as a manager."

"I bet John would let you do both," Marisa said, looking hopeful.

"Get real," Tiffany said. "John won't consider hiring a manager or director without twenty years of experience, especially Madison Avenue experience. Let's face it. We've all hit a brick wall. There's nowhere for us to go here, but out."

"Do you think you'd look for another job in production?" I asked Marisa. Marisa rarely joined in when Tiffany and I talked about our careers, so I wasn't sure what she wanted to do when she left Premier.

"I just want to get married," Marisa said.

"You've been watching too many reruns of *Ozzie and Harriet* on TVLand," Tiffany said, rolling her eyes.

"Getting married doesn't mean you have to give up your career," I said. "I would never give up a job I loved for a guy."

"It's different for the two of you," Marisa said. "You both have cool, creative jobs. Believe me, there's nothing creative about watching thousands of sheets of paper roll through machinery during a print run."

I felt bad for Marisa because she wasn't doing anything that came close to what she'd aspired to do. Marisa had been an art history major in college and had hoped to work in a museum as a curator some day. Because of budget cuts, most museums had job freezes when Marisa had graduated. A temp agency had sent her here for a part-time production assistant job, and she never left.

Marisa's mother died right before she came to work at Premier and since she was never close to her father, Tiffany and I had become like her surrogate family. Tiffany and I always thought the reason she stayed so long was because leaving us would be like losing another two family members.

"Have you thought about applying at a museum again?" I suggested. "It doesn't hurt to send in your resume." I didn't want to push her to leave a place where she felt so comfortable, but I hated thinking of someone as intelligent and talented as Marisa wasting her time at a job she didn't like.

"I really just want to get married and have children," she said. "That's all I've ever wanted to do. A good family life is important." Her eyes filled with tears again and I could tell she was probably thinking of her mother, who'd been sick during most of her childhood. "I thought you wanted to get married and have a family, too, Jen."

"You know I do, but I still couldn't imagine quitting my job so I could stay home and raise a family."

I wanted to talk to Marisa some more about the real reason she didn't attempt to find a job she liked better, but as usual, Rhonda interrupted my thoughts with her whiny voice coming through Tiffany's intercom. "Is Jen still in your office?" she asked.

"I'm here," I screamed back, always amazed how Rhonda kept tabs on every employee at Premier.

"Someone named Lori's on the phone for you. It sounds like a personal call."

Tiffany stuck her tongue out toward the intercom. Rhonda was back to her old self.

"I'll take it in my office." Why did I let Rhonda make me feel guilty about receiving a personal call on my day off? And why couldn't a big agency like Premier hire a receptionist who was satisfied answering phones without becoming the office's Agatha Christie, tracking down clues to learn about everyone's personal lives?

I looked back at Marisa, who seemed relieved that Rhonda had changed the subject, and Tiffany looked equally pleased to grab her cigarettes and head for the front door.

Since Tiffany's office was so far from mine, it took me a good few minutes to return to my office. Once inside, I felt a feeling of calm engulf me as I flicked on the light and turned on my computer. Finally, I hit the flashing light on my phone. "Hi, Lori. What's up?"

"I would wish you a happy thirtieth, but if you're feeling like I did on my birthday, you're probably sick of hearing it."

"I am, but thanks anyway."

"The real reason I'm calling is that Tony and I set a date for our wedding, and I'd like you to be one of my bridesmaids."

"Thanks for thinking of me." I clenched my teeth together so tightly that I was sure they would break. If she bought her gowns at The Pampered Bride, I was holding out for at least one gourmet dessert and one glass of mineral water before I tried on a single dress. My days of drinking from water coolers in the back of bridal stores were over. "So when's the wedding," I asked in my most cheerful voice.

"September 2."

"September 2? What's the rush? It's not like you're pregnant... Lori?...Lori? Are you there?"

"Actually, I am pregnant."

"You're what?" Lori having a baby seemed as unbelievable as me fitting into a size two. There were a lot of adjectives I could use to describe Lori, but maternal wasn't one of them.

"Believe me, I'm as surprised as you are," Lori said. "I just found out two days ago. Thank goodness, we were planning on getting married anyway."

Were congratulations in order? What was the appropriate response when your engaged friend announced her pregnancy? "Well, that's great," I finally said, still unsure what the proper etiquette was.

I felt ashamed of myself, but my first thought was how on earth Lori would breast-feed a baby with her new, well-endowed chest. With breasts her size, she might need Tony to hold the baby in another room in order for the little fella to reach the milk. "So when's your due date?"

"Mid February."

Wishing I had been better at math, I did some quick calculations, determining Lori had conceived two months ago. Hadn't she said that Tony just proposed?

"Of course now my parents think the only reason I'm getting married is because I'm pregnant," Lori said, as if reading my mind. "But I don't care what they think. I know the real reason we're getting married."

I wanted to ask her what it was, but then I remembered how in love Lori seemed to be, and I imagined a baby wouldn't affect their relationship if they were meant to be together.

"Anyway, now that I've gotten over the shock, I'm really excited," Lori said, and she actually sounded it. She once again spoke in that new softer voice that I was still trying to get used to. "I'm also relieved in a way because I just read in *Today's Modern Woman* that after you turn thirty-five your chances of getting pregnant go down, so at least that's one less thing I have to worry about now."

And one more thing I needed to worry about. Just great. I stroked my Star of David charm that had belonged to my grandmother before she died. "So how does Tony feel about the baby?"

"Well, it wouldn't have been his first choice, but we can deal with it."

Not the typical reaction a mother-to-be generally had, but then again, this was Lori. "I'm sure everything will work out fine."

"Thanks. I'll call you soon about buying dresses. We'll have to find something off the racks since we won't have time to order them. Promise you won't tell Stacy until I talk to her. I want to tell her myself, but I haven't been able to reach her."

"My lips are sealed." I hung up, wondering what it would be like to be pregnant, and worried that I'd never get the chance to experience it. I was getting older, and that goddamn biological clock was ticking so loud today it sounded more like a time bomb.

My mother's email only made the ticking get louder. *Hi, sweetie, Happy Birthday! I've attached an article from today's issue of the Philly Herald. One of the columnists from the society page did a survey of single women over thirty trying to find the right guy and the results aren't very encouraging. Do Lance or Tony know anyone who wants to meet someone? Please don't be mad at me for caring. I don't want to see you end up alone, like Aunt Sophie. Barb and I are on our way out for drinks. I'll call you tomorrow. Love, Mom.*

I deleted the email without reading the article. I hated when she compared me to Aunt Sophie, who weighed several hundred pounds and had rolls of flab hanging from her arms. Perhaps these were the reasons Aunt Sophie never got married!

I skimmed over a few work-related emails until Kathy's message got my attention. *Jen, have you visited Mom and Dad lately? Things have gotten out of hand. Call me. Kathy.*

Not wanting to deal with any problems on this day of all days, I reluctantly called my sister at work and had her paged at the hospital. It was unusual for my bubbly, cheerful, cutsie, happy-go-lucky sister to express concern about anything, but when she came to the phone I heard distress in her voice. "What's wrong?" I asked Kathy.

"Jen, when was the last time you visited Mom and Dad?"

So much for small talk. "I saw them at my party last weekend, remember?"

"I mean have you spent any time with them alone recently?" She dragged out the word alone.

I felt horrible admitting that I hadn't. My mom made it impossible not to see her regularly, but my dad usually faded into the background. Sometimes even when he was in the room, I forgot he was there. "I guess it's been a while."

"Well, I stopped by yesterday to show them the blueprints for our new house. When I came in, Mom was screaming at Dad for losing the remote control."

"That's nothing new." I opened and deleted a few emails while still listening.

"No, Jen, this was worse than usual. She exploded when Dad accidentally spilled a small drop of coffee on the counter and she went ballistic when he put the sugar on the wrong shelf."

71

"What did Dad say?" I rubbed my forehead, feeling a bad headache coming on.

"As usual, he sat there and took it." My perky sister had become perkless, which made me realize how bad things must be.

"What do you think caused Mom's explosion this time?"

"You know my theory." I could picture my sister scrunching up her nose with a look of disgust.

"I know what you think, but I still don't believe that Dad had an affair," I said, trying to remain calm. "He wouldn't do that."

"They say it's the quiet ones you have to watch out for!" The only time I ever heard Kathy sound angry was when we discussed this subject, and right now she sounded livid.

"But this is Dad!" I insisted. "He's the most mild-mannered, sweet, polite guy I've ever met." I would marry him if he wasn't my dad!

"Well, what else would cause Mom to attack him all the time, and make Dad stick around to take it? He probably feels so guilty about what he did that he feels like he deserves it."

"I think you've been watching too much Dr. Phil." I didn't want to think about my parent's marital problems. It made my fantasy of finding my prince and living happily ever after go down the toilet.

"Jen, this is serious." She sounded like she was gritting her teeth.

"So if Dad did cheat on Mom, why would she stay with him all these years?" I said, ready for this conversation to end.

"She was probably too scared to leave him. I bet he had an affair when we were kids and Mom felt trapped into staying with him. It's not like Mom could go out and get a job. Can you imagine Mom working a cash register while making sure her nails didn't break?"

"If it happened that long ago, why is Mom so mad now?" And why was I here listening to this when I should have been home packing? I pounded my fist on my desk, mad at myself for being there to get Kathy's email.

"That's what I can't figure out. Any chance you can stop by their house after you get settled at your new place and see what's up?" The unusual pleading in her voice made me give in.

"I suppose," I said, wishing I had normal parents who were leaving for their summer home down the shore.

I could almost hear Kathy's sigh of relief as we hung up. And why shouldn't she feel relieved? Now that she had passed the torch to me, she could stop worrying about my parents for a while. I decided to leave before I got anymore personal phone calls or emails that I didn't want to receive.

Shutting down my computer, I popped two extra-strength Tylenols into my mouth. Nothing like a stressful conversation about your parent's relationship problems to help celebrate the birthday you've been dreading for the past year.

Chapter 6

How to Prevent Additional Symptoms from Occurring:

1. Find a new apartment building filled with eligible singles, and hope you don't end up living next door to a married couple with kids.
2. Find a new boyfriend and hope he has more to offer you than a clean pool and free coffee refills.

After almost three weeks of hot, dry, humid weather and a draught emergency posted throughout Philadelphia, the skies opened up with a torrential downpour the day I moved. Meteorologists predicted two inches of rain for the day. Farmers celebrated the weather, as I cursed Mother Nature for pouring buckets of water over everything I owned.

Even though the movers tried to protect my stuff, my couch ended up with a big water stain and most of my boxes were soaked when they arrived at my apartment. One of the movers slipped on the mud, breaking a lamp that my grandmother had given me. By the time I walked into my new home, all of my belongings smelled like mildew. I hoped this wasn't a bad omen.

As I walked in the front door and stood in my new living room, I wanted to check out every inch of my new bachelorette pad. It had been over two months since I'd last seen it. But just as I was about to check out the built-in wall unit, I felt myself shiver from the sopping wet clothes I still wore. Damn! I'd have to change into something dry before I went exploring.

I walked down the hall to where I remembered the bedroom was. I was glad the movers had at least made a wide path between the piles of boxes for me to walk through. Still, I felt blinded by the sight of tan cardboard everywhere I looked. It was going to take a mighty long time before I unpacked all this stuff.

The boxes in my bedroom were piled up to my bed. How the hell was I going to find my clothes in this mess? Unfortunately, I'd been in such a rush to pack that I hadn't had time to label the boxes. I barely had time to tape each box closed. Needless to say, every box now looked identical except for its size and water stains.

Since all the boxes looked the same, I randomly chose two, hoping I'd get lucky. As usual, I didn't. One box contained tampons, sanitary napkins and toilet paper, and the other one held Mr. Wow and two vibrators. Figured! God forbid the first box I opened would contain my silk flower arrangements or the set of fine china I had foolishly bought to impress Ken before I found out he was gay. No, I had to be surrounded with feminine hygiene items and sex toys.

Finally, I found an old sweatshirt in the fifteenth box I opened. I put it on, despite the hot temperature outside.

As I looked around my new bedroom, it suddenly hit me. This place was mine! I wanted to jump into someone's arms to celebrate this moment, but the only male nearby, as usual, was Frisky. Not the special person I was looking for, but since I had no other alternative, I bent down and gave Frisky a big hug. He purred and licked my hand. Now why couldn't I have that effect on guys?

It would have been nice giving a tour to a tall, dark, and handsome boyfriend, but instead my small furry and cute cat followed me into the living room as I began to survey my new place. I loved the light ash hardwood floors that covered most of the apartment. It was a nice change from the old gray rugs in my former apartment, which Frisky had used on occasion as a litter pan. I'd have to make sure he stayed away from the sisal carpet in the living room. The motorized wooden blinds that covered the length of my balcony's sliding glass doors were enough to make me lazy. With the flick of a switch, I could open the blinds without ever having to get up from the couch Talk about luxury!

I looked up at the ceiling, admiring all the recessed lights. It really brightened the room and gave it a feeling of warmth. And the camel-painted walls throughout the apartment were neutral enough to go with all my furniture even if it had come from IKEA!

I followed the hardwood floor to my dining room. My first dining room ever! Too bad I had nobody to dine with. Then again, I had no dining room set to eat on, so it worked out okay. The room looked bare with just one pendant ceiling light above the rectangular sisal carpet. I'd have to do something about that.

I walked from the dining room into the kitchen, my favorite room in the apartment. Just knowing I could fit more than two people comfortably in here was exciting. I stroked the natural cherry cabinets and the black granite counter tops. All the stainless steel appliances looked so shiny and clean they *almost* made me want to take up cooking. But I imagined the microwave would still get the most use. I purposely left the kitchen from its second entranceway, which led back to the living room. Imagine two entrances to get into the kitchen when I barely had one before!

Apparently all this excitement was too much for my small male companion because when I returned to the living room, I discovered Frisky sound asleep in a box of underwear he had unpacked to make room for himself. With the exception of one bra draped over Frisky's tail, I now had a pile of lingerie in the middle of the room.

Deciding it was time for a bathroom break, I retraced my steps down the hallway and through my bedroom to my beautiful new bathroom with its terra cotta floor and tiles. I felt like a movie star peeing next to my jumbo-sized Jacuzzi with its four adjustable jets. Was it too much to hope for that I'd find someone to share this whirlpool tub with? I flushed the toilet and decided that maybe it was.

While washing my hands in my pedestal sink with its marble surrounds, I realized I needed some new towels to fit in with this bathroom. Perhaps something with a hint of brown to go with the earth tone color wallpaper?

When I reentered my bedroom, I opened my tan silk drapes and used yet another remote control to open the pleated shades beneath them. The white plush carpeting in this room was the only thing about this apartment that concerned me. I usually applied my makeup at my vanity in my bedroom, but my cosmetics were known to stain even the darkest rugs. It would have been better if the hardwood floor extended into this room also, but the carpeting did make it feel cozy.

I closed my eyes, imagining what it would be like to walk into this room with my significant other after making love in the Jacuzzi. We would come out draped in towels, enjoying the sensation of the soft, cushioned fabric beneath our feet. Then we would jump into my bed, which in my daydream was a king-sized water bed (instead of my actual lumpy twin mattress) and make love to celebrate my new apartment.

This fantasy came to a screeching halt when I looked over to see Mr. Wow deflated in his box with a big smile on his face. It was almost like he knew what I was thinking, and found the notion of a guy in my tub to be as likely as him coming to life.

Feeling frustrated, I decided it was time for some fresh air. I left Mr. Wow in my bedroom and headed for my balcony, which overlooked Kelly Drive and the Art Museum. As I reached over to open the balcony door, I felt Frisky nuzzling my legs. I laughed out loud when I saw my favorite male companion looking up at me with my bra on his head. Unfortunately, this was the closest I'd get tonight to having a male touching my undergarments.

I pulled the bra off of Frisky as we both stepped outside. Even through the fog and mist, I saw young couples holding hands while walking along the Schuylkill River. I wanted to be one of those couples! Looking down at Frisky licking his butt, I had the sinking feeling that instead of holding someone's hand, I would be holding someone's leash.

Okay, no more negative thoughts. This apartment was awesome, and I deserved to be happy. This was a real step up for me, and I worked hard to afford it. I was reminded of that old sitcom, *The Jeffersons,* where the couple moved from Queens to Manhattan.

I carried Frisky inside, singing *The Jeffersons* theme song at the top of my lungs, "I'm moving on up, to the east side, to a deluxe apartment in the sky." I sang and danced around the living room swinging Frisky back and forth until I heard a knock at my door. Frisky seemed disappointed when I put him down.

When I opened the door an attractive guy with beautiful hazel eyes and short dirty blond hair stood outside without smiling. Oh God, he probably heard me singing. He must have thought I was a total spaz.

"Um, hi," I said, wishing this wasn't the first impression any of my neighbors had of me. I imagined everyone talking about the new crazy girl in apartment 211 who belted out theme songs from old television shows.

"I don't mean to be rude, but would you mind keeping your voice down? Your singing woke up my baby and my three-year-old daughter."

Until now, I hadn't noticed the loud cries coming from next door as a female voice tried to console them. "Oh, uh, sorry."

How was it possible that he had a family? This place was supposed to be swarming with young, single professionals in heat. Just my luck, I had to live next door to a married couple with kids. It was the story of my life. "I promise to keep it down."

He thanked me before I silently closed the door. I didn't hum one verse as I unpacked a few boxes. I was so quiet that Frisky fell asleep on a shelf in my walk-in closet.

As I unpacked some bathroom items, I felt disgusted with myself. How could I have lived with such worn out and shabby towels for so long? And look at that shower curtain liner. It had a black stain along the bottom. I couldn't even stand my soap dispenser anymore. The soap was so caked up along the sides that I had given up removing it a long time ago.

Had I ever replaced any of my original household items? Why had I been complacent to live with my torn bath mat, faded comforter, and burnt oven mitts?

Well, not anymore. It was time for a change. I felt like Wilma Flintstone and Betty Rubble as I grabbed my credit cards. I was about to yell, "Charge!" like they always did, but then remembered the crabby kids next door. I restrained myself and quietly headed for the mall.

After three hours at Bed Bath & Beyond, and one hour at Super Fresh buying groceries for my empty refrigerator, I returned home anxious to unpack all my new findings.

I lugged the first two of ten bags from my car, unaware how slippery the parking lot still was from all the rain, which had finally stopped. Within two feet from my car, I slid into a huge puddle.

Meanwhile my bananas fell to the left, while my tuna fish cans landed a few feet away on my right side. In between, a stack of frozen foods, consisting of Lean Cuisines and Weight Watcher Smart Ones, floated along the rain water like boats coasting along a river. Behind me, soap dishes, a toothbrush holder, a tub mat, a dustpan, trash cans, and a sink rack blew threw the courtyard from the harsh winds.

My shoes were soaked and my windblown hair must have looked like Kramer from *Seinfeld*, but I had to salvage as much as I could. I ran toward my apartment complex chasing a mop and bucket, and had just caught my toilet bowl brush sliding along the pavement when I stared directly into a pair of worn out looking sneakers.

"Well, either you're coming from a Rubbermaid convention, or you just moved in," a deep male voice said. I looked up to see a great looking guy, probably about my age, grinning at me. Was he smiling or laughing at me? I wasn't sure as I tried to push down my matted, tangled hair.

I stood up to face the mysterious stranger holding my newly purchased mop. He had bright green eyes and dark brown hair that he wore long on top, but short on the back and sides. It was easy to tell that this guy worked out a lot because his white tank top and denim shorts showed off his muscular arms and legs.

"So which is it?" he asked again. "Did you just rob the housewares department at Wal-Mart, or are you new to the Royalty Apartments?"

"You were right the second time. I moved in today." I tried to wipe some mud off my shirt.

"I knew it," he said. "The Bed Bath & Beyond bag gave it away. By the way, I rescued one of your dustpans rolling into the parking lot." He handed me the dirty new dustpan. "Can I help you clean up?"

"Yeah, if you don't mind." Oh, please let him live on the same floor as me. That would more than make up for those screaming bratty kids next door.

"So what's your name?" he asked, as we picked up my purchases. "Or should I call you Rubbermaid girl?"

"I'm Jen."

"I'm Chris. Didn't anyone ever tell you that brooms don't float in the mud?" He handed me my muddy broom.

"I guess I missed that class in home ec."

"That's okay. I think I remember enough to help you out." And he did. For the next ten minutes, Chris and I ran after my food, juice, and cleaning supplies. He even challenged me to a race to retrieve my toothbrush holder rolling down the parking lot. Then he re-bagged whatever items we had saved and carried them through the parking lot to the front step of my apartment complex.

"Thanks for all your help." I looked up at Chris, who was probably no more than five feet, nine inches tall, not real tall for a guy, but the perfect height for me.

"No problem. Oh, there is one more thing I can help you with." He took out a crumbled but clean tissue from his pocket and wiped a huge wad of mud off my nose.

How mortifying!

He obviously sensed my embarrassment because he took my hand as if to console me. "Don't worry about it. I think you're still pretty cute even with mud on your nose."

This guy was either a smooth talker or needed glasses, but whichever it was, I couldn't help feeling flattered, especially since I hadn't received a compliment from a guy in a long time. And he had the warmest, softest hands I'd ever felt on a guy. My hands weren't that soft.

"Thanks, but walking around with mud on my nose is not exactly the first impression I like to make."

"I'd say you made a very good first impression." He grinned widely and winked at me, which made my heart lurch more than I wanted to admit. But there was something very passionate about the way he looked and spoke to me, as if he didn't see anything else when I talked. His expression was so intense it almost scared me. For a few moments we just stood, still holding hands by my front step, staring into each other's eyes, and I was beginning to feel hot all over just being so close to him. It was almost like we had formed a cocoon that nobody else could enter.

This was crazy. How could I feel so much chemistry toward someone I didn't even know? Yet my heart was doing some major fluttering.

Finally, I thought I better break the spell before I had to run upstairs to inflate Mr. Wow. "So which apartment do you live in?" It seemed like a lame question after all the sensations I felt, but it was the first thing that popped out of my mouth.

I pictured us running into each other in the laundry room where we'd hang out for a while and talk. I pictured us lounging at the apartment's swimming pool during the summer, sharing wine coolers and chips. I pictured him dropping by after a long day at work to invite me for a drink in the lounge downstairs.

"Oh, I don't live here. I'm the pool cleaner. My apartment's a good fifteen minutes away."

Okay, I certainly did not picture that. It was like someone had just hit the pause button on my daydream. I had always prided myself in being open-minded about a person's profession, but a pool cleaner? My mother would be so proud.

"Of course, this is just a part-time job. I don't get too many job offers during the fall and winter." Chris smiled widely, showing off his perfectly straight white teeth. He could have been a model for a toothpaste commercial.

His smile made my heart leap. Come to think of it, everything this guy did seemed to create some kind of sensual sensation in my body. I returned his smile, relieved he didn't clean pools full-time. "So what do you do when you're not cleaning pools?" Maybe a graduate student working his way through school?

"Starting Monday, I'll be the new assistant manager of Big Al's Mini Mart. It's the one by Big Al's Gas Station on Tustin Avenue. The pay's not great, but I hear the free coffee refills make up for that." Chris laughed at his joke, but I had some trouble joining him.

I couldn't imagine my family and friends being anymore impressed about me dating someone who worked at a mini mart than someone who cleaned pools for a living. Then again, what were the chances that he was going to ask me out anyway? Just because I was sitting here lusting all over him, didn't mean he felt the same way. Judging by my track record, he'd be telling me about his live-in girlfriend any minute now.

"Where do you work?" Chris asked, motioning for us to sit down on the step.

I followed his lead, feeling disappointed when he let go of my hand, which suddenly felt cold and empty.

"No, let me guess," Chris continued. "You're a scientist doing experiments on how long buckets and mops will float in muddy puddles."

"Not exactly," I laughed. "I'm a writer at an advertising agency."

"Now I'm impressed, although a scientist would have been cool, too. Do you write for TV or print?"

"Just print right now, but I'd love to get into TV someday."

He nodded, looking genuinely interested. "So have I seen any of your ads?"

"Maybe. I wrote the Sportin Fitness Center ads. You might have seen them in some national magazines."

"No kidding? You wrote those?" His eyes lit up as if I just told him I had won the Pulitzer Prize.

"You *have* seen them?" I wasn't sure if he was trying to be nice or if he was being sincere.

"Of course I did. I work out there. Did you write the brochures and billboards, too?" He seemed genuinely impressed, and I was touched by his interest, especially since nobody else ever asked so many questions about my job. The only questions my mom asked related to whether I worked with any cute, eligible account executives. And since Stacy got engaged, she was most interested in whether I could get out of work early so I could go wedding shopping with her.

"I wrote all the collateral materials for that campaign," I said proudly.

"I'll have to take a closer look at them when I'm there later." He smiled easily. In the short time I'd been with him, it seemed like he wore that smile most of the time.

"Do you work closely with the artists when you write, or do they design the artwork after you're done writing?"

Now I was impressed. Most people stopped asking questions after I told them about the Sportin Fitness ads. But Chris sat back, leaned against his hands, and looked eagerly into my eyes for more answers.

I spent the next twenty minutes explaining to him how advertising campaigns were created and what my role was in developing them. I thought he'd get bored, but he continued asking more questions, probing me with his eyes and smile for more information. After a while I wasn't sure what I was saying anymore. I felt hypnotized looking into his eyes and tingly all over being so close to him. Was this guy for real, or was I having some kind of a weird dream where I felt like I was awake?

"It sounds like a great job." Chris sat up and leaned toward me.

"It is." I felt my body quiver as he moved closer to me. "Sometimes the long hours can get to me, but overall it's worth it."

"Well, no job is perfect, but if you like what you do, you have to take the good with the bad." He had an exceptionally sexy voice.

I wondered if anyone ever had an orgasm just listening to someone talk.

"So what do you do when you're not at work?" He looked so deeply into my eyes, I felt like he was looking right through them into my soul. It was hard to remember what I did in my spare time when he looked at me like that, but he was anxiously waiting for a response. But what could I tell him that would make me sound intriguing, or at the very least, interesting? That I spent most of my time in video stores and Chinese restaurants? Not exactly the glamour girl image I wanted to portray.

"I like going to nice restaurants." And I did. Just nobody had taken me to one recently. "And I like going to the movies." Boy, did I sound boring.

"In that case, would you like to go out to dinner with me sometime?"

Yes, yes, and yes! "Yeah, that would be nice."

"Great. I don't know if you'd consider Friday's to be a nice restaurant, but unfortunately, that's all I can afford right now. I hope that's okay."

"Yeah, of course." Damn, why did I have to throw in the word *nice*? Now I sounded pretentious. "Friday's sounds great."

"How about next Saturday night?"

Considering I had no plans for at least the next twelve or thirteen Saturday nights coming up, I imagined I could make it. "I think I'm free."

"Great. Do you have a pen and paper so we can exchange numbers?"

I searched through my pocketbook, aware of his eyes traveling down my body. I certainly hoped he was a small breast kind of guy. But when I finally looked up, having found a pen and notepad, Chris had a wide grin on his face. Apparently, small breasts were okay with him.

After writing down our phone numbers, we each got up, still unable to unlock our eyes. "By the way, Jen, would you mind driving? I hope that's not a problem, but I don't have a car."

"No, that's okay." I hated myself for being disappointed, but I had never driven on a first date. In fact, I couldn't remember ever driving any of my boyfriends around. Did that make me a snob, or did I just have higher expectations of the guys I dated? As I pondered that thought, I looked at Chris, once again feeling his electric current that went right through me, and I no longer cared whether we had to take the subway to get to Friday's. "So where do you live?"

"Oh, I guess it would help if you knew that." He laughed. "I'll write down my address." The skin on his finger rubbed against my hand, making me want to pull him back down on the step to make love to him right there and then. Needless to say, I controlled myself.

"Here you go." He returned the paper to me, once again rubbing against my flesh and I thought I was in heaven—until I saw the address.

"You live on Fifth and Franklin?" *One of the worst neighborhoods in Philadelphia!*

"Yeah, do you know how to get there or do you need directions?"

I knew exactly how to get there because I had once gotten lost around there on my way home from a frat party at Penn, and I'd sworn if I got home alive I'd never drive through that neighborhood again. "No, that's okay. I know the area."

What was I doing? Despite my desire to have sex with this guy on the spot, I didn't even know his last name. What if he was some kind of a psychopath? What if he attacked me in the car?

But when I looked up at Chris, staring into my eyes like the world had just stopped, I knew my heart would stop, too, if I didn't see him again. And as I looked deep into his eyes, I felt confident that I could trust him. "What time should I pick you up?"

I finally had something to look forward to on a Saturday night.

Chapter 7

Incubation Period of The Marriage Epidemic
Ranges From One Day to Several Years
Depending On:

1. The number and frequency of annoying engaged friends who question your desire to find the right guy.
2. The number of guys you must date before finding someone who remotely qualifies as a potential husband.

"He does what?" Even over the phone, I could picture Stacy's horrified expression.

"You heard me. He's an assistant manager at Big Al's Mini Mart." I left out the part about him cleaning pools.

"Is he one of those gas station attendants with dirt under his nails?" Sitting at my desk in the corner of my bedroom, I scribbled lines on a piece of paper until I made a hole through the middle of the page.

"No, Stace. He doesn't work at the gas station. He works at the convenience store attached to the station."

"Oh. That doesn't sound much better than pumping gas."

"Stace, will you *please* be happy for me. It's the first time I met someone in a long time who I hit it off with. I don't care what he does for a living." Okay, maybe I cared a little bit, but I was too excited about seeing Chris again to let it get in the way.

And just because he didn't have a great job now didn't mean he would never find one. For all I knew, maybe he was working all these odd jobs to save up for college.

"I am happy for you, but I can't see you dating someone who works at a gas station."

Apparently, Stacy had totally missed what I had said.

"I always pictured you with a doctor or lawyer," Stacy continued.

"Like Lance." I filled in the last two words for her.

"Well, somebody more along those lines."

"Lori never dated doctors and I don't remember you giving her a hard time about it." I started scribbling on a new piece of paper, this time with a black marker.

"Yeah, but that was Lori. She didn't go for that type of guy until Tony. Besides, I don't feel the same way about her as I do about you. You have so much to offer, Jen. Why settle for less?"

I stopped scribbling long enough to consider what she said. It was nice that she thought so highly of me, but wasn't I entitled to make my own decisions? And who asked for her opinion anyway? "Stace, we haven't even gone out once. I'd hardly say we were dating." The way my luck had been going with guys recently, chances were I'd never make it past the second date.

"Listen, Jen, forget what I said. If you're happy, then I'm happy for you. And like you said, it's only a date."

"Exactly." I didn't tell Stacy that I was hoping there would be more. Since I met Chris I couldn't stop thinking about the way my body had trembled for thirty minutes after he left. He definitely had some kind of hold over me.

"So, how are your wedding plans going?" I tried to wipe the ink from the black marker off my hand. It better not be permanent.

"Wonderful! We picked out a wonderful band and got the most wonderful florist. Wait till you meet the wonderful photographer we chose!"

I lost count of how many *wonderfuls* Stacy said. Funny, I didn't remember Stacy ever describing anything as wonderful before.

"I'm glad everything's going so wonderfully well. Anyway, I've got to run. I'm stopping over my parent's house, and I'm already late."

In her usual Stacy fashion, she had spoken her mind, but this time I found her comments especially irritating. Just because she struck gold with Lance didn't mean I couldn't strike oil with Chris, even if it was just peanut oil.

As glad as I was to be off the phone with Stacy, I was just as depressed at the thought of talking to my parents. What on earth was I supposed to say to them? So, Dad, have you been having a midlife crisis lately? Or, so, Mom, any need for birth control these days? This wasn't the type of conversation you wanted to have with your parents.

Stalling for time, I signed in to my work email and found one message from Marisa.

Jen, he still hasn't called. What should I do? Marisa.

I saved her message until I could think of a good answer. I was about to put on my Star of David necklace when I heard a knock on the door. Maybe it was Chris. I wasn't sure which days he cleaned the pool. I flung open the door to see the attractive man from next door holding a fidgety baby. Next to him was a woman, probably in her early thirties, and a girl around four picking her nose.

The whole family was here! Had I hit the keys too loudly on my keyboard and woken them all up? Maybe they were annoyed at the long shower I took. Just how thin were these luxury apartment walls anyway?

"Hi, hope we're not interrupting you," the man said, trying to hold on to his squirming child.

"No, not at all. Do you want to come in?" Why had I said that? I didn't want that bratty kid running around, knocking over all my breakable things. My apartment wasn't exactly child-proofed.

"No thanks," he said. The stubble on his face gave him a rugged look. "We stopped by to apologize for the other day. I shouldn't have complained about your singing."

Once again, I felt my cheeks grow warm. "Don't worry about it."

"It's just that Josh is a terrible sleeper, and the slightest noise will wake him, which naturally disturbs Jessica." He looked down at his daughter, indicating that she was Jessica.

Oh good grief. Why couldn't I have moved next door to that guy down the hall who blasted his radio every night around ten? I'd rather listen to music than a screaming child.

"We also came by to introduce ourselves. I'm Randy and this is my wife, Lisa." Lisa looked like she just rolled of the bed. Had she even brushed her mousy frizzy brown hair today? Judging from its split ends, it looked like it had been a while since she'd had a good haircut.

"I'm Jen." I sniffed a few times, feeling my allergies flaring up.

"Do you have any children?" the little girl asked me. She had the cutest dimples and I was impressed by how well she spoke for her age.

"I'm afraid not." She had the most adorable chubby face with brown curly hair that flowed down past her shoulders.

"Why?" she asked, staring up at me like I had let her down.

"Because I'm not married." Not that that mattered these days, but I wasn't about to corrupt this innocent child.

"Why?" Okay, this darling child with the big brown eyes was looking less cute with each subsequent question.

"Jess, you're being nosy again," Lisa said, chuckling at her daughter, apparently amused by her questions. I, on the other hand, felt like I was talking to my mother.

"She's very precocious," Lisa said proudly.

"Apparently so." I was ready to bid this family adieu, but nobody seemed to be moving away from my front door.

"So do you have a roommate or do you live alone?" Lisa asked, rubbing a stain that looked like chocolate milk on her beige T-shirt.

"I live alone." Why did I feel pathetic admitting that? After all, this apartment complex was apparently swarming with single people who lived on their own. Still, seeing this happy foursome made me feel lonely.

Lisa nodded while slipping her arm through Randy's as if to claim him. "Well, you'll probably love living here. We're surrounded with young single people looking to meet someone." The tone of her voice made it obvious that she wasn't too pleased with the married to single ratio.

"Have you lived here long?" I asked. *And more importantly, any plans for moving in the near future?*

"I guess it's been about two years, hasn't it Randy." Lisa's black pants had white lint all over them as if a tissue had exploded in the washing machine.

"That sounds about right. I'm waiting to pay off all my student loans before we buy a house. For now, this place is ideal considering I'm within walking distance from work."

Randy looked directly into my eyes while he spoke as if he wanted me to understand why they had chosen to live here. He sure was cute even in his blue and white jogging suit. Lisa had done pretty well for herself considering personal hygiene didn't seem like one of her top priorities.

"Mommy, I'm bored," complained Jessica, tugging at her mother's sleeve. "I want to go home and watch *Blue's Clues*.

"Just a minute, sweetie. Mommy and Daddy are still talking."

"I don't care. I want to go home right now!" She stomped her foot to make her point.

"Jessica, you'll have to wait till we're done talking," Randy said, looking at me apologetically.

"Don't be too hard on her Randy," Lisa responded. "She has been cooped up in the apartment all day."

"Yeah, I want to go to McDonald's," Jessica wailed.

"Okay, darling," Lisa agreed. "We'll go as soon as we say good-bye."

"Good-bye," Jessica immediately said, pulling on Lisa's arm.

Well, it was obvious who was in charge in this household. "Good-bye, Jessica. It was nice meeting you," I lied.

"You'll have to come over for dinner some Saturday night so we can get to know each other better," Lisa said.

"Yeah, and I can show you all my Barbie dolls and my princess castle," Jessica chimed in. "I'll even teach you how to play Candy Land."

Well, that certainly sounded like the way I wanted to spend a Saturday night. Thank goodness, I actually had a legitimate excuse for this weekend, but what about the next? While praying that nobody would invite me for a specific date, I heard a loud belch and the next thing I knew a flood of white liquid poured out of Josh's mouth onto my new leather sandals.

"I'm so sorry," Lisa said. "Tell Jen you're sorry, Joshy."

I wasn't surprised when their infant didn't offer an apology. "That's okay. I'm sure it will come out." Wondering whether I had breast milk or formula on my feet, I closed the door, vowing to avoid contact with my next-door neighbors as long as possible.

~

I wasn't sure which was worse, having baby spit up on my shoes, or talking to my parents about their marital problems, and I had to endure both the same day. When I walked into my parent's kitchen, I found my mom sitting at the table, reading *Glamour*.

"Jen, you scared me. I didn't hear you come in. Is something wrong?"

My mom looked worried, probably because I rarely stopped by unexpectedly. She usually had to use guilt tactics to get me to visit. "Sorry. I should have knocked."

"Don't be ridiculous. This is still your home."

It had once felt like a home. I remembered family vacations to the beach when I was young. My mom would bury my dad in the sand and we would all laugh, happy to be together. I always looked forward to dinnertime when I could tell my dad about my day. My parents would sit together for at least an hour after Kathy and I left the table.

As I got older, my parents stopped laughing. My mom got louder and my dad got quieter. According to Kathy, there had always been tension between them, but I didn't notice it until I was about ten. Maybe I hadn't wanted to. Since Kathy was older than me she remembered more than I could.

"So what brings you here today? You're not sick, are you?" My mom, wearing a halter top and flared stretch jeans, walked over to the refrigerator.

"Don't worry. I'm fine. I stopped by a friend's house from work and she only lives a few blocks away so I thought I'd come by." This was a lie, but it was the only thing I could think of.

"That was nice. Do you want something to eat?" She opened the fridge.

I shook my head while my mom took out a vegetable tray and carried it across the kitchen to where I sat at the table. Staring at enough carrot sticks, broccoli, zucchini and celery to feed the entire neighborhood, I felt like I had stepped into the produce section at the grocery store.

"Where's Dad?"

"Who cares?"

"Mom, why did you say that?"

"Would you like some Romaine lettuce?" As usual, my mom didn't wait for my answer as she served me a large portion of vegetables in her new Lenox bowl.

I reluctantly ate a small carrot. "Mom, are you and Dad doing all right?"

"As well as ever." My mom bit into a piece of celery.

90

Not the reassuring answer I was hoping for.

I heard the door creak as my dad walked in. "Hey, princess," my dad said, as he sat down beside me. I felt sad seeing him look so old and haggard, remembering how attractive he had once been.

His hair, which used to be thick and dark brown, was now gray and thinning. His stomach, which had been flat and firm, had become big and flabby. And his face, which had been completely smooth, was now buried in more wrinkles than most men his age. His blue eyes looked tired, like they needed a long overdue vacation, and his lips looked equally listless having become permanently turned down at the corners for so long.

But I still recognized the heart of gold beneath all the wrinkles, creases, and bulging stomach, and wished I could make it start beating a little faster again. My dad had slowed down so much the past ten years or so it was almost like he moved in slow motion.

My mother interrupted my thoughts as she crunched so loudly on her celery stick, I thought for sure she'd break a tooth.

I turned my attention to my dad. "How are you, Dad?"

I loved the way his face lit up whenever he saw me. Seeing myself through his eyes was the only time I felt special and it was also the only time he seemed happy these days. And now looking at his gentle eyes and his loving smile filled with adoration, I couldn't imagine him ever cheating on my mom.

"Harris, I found your socks rolled up in a ball again under the bed." My mother went into attack mode before my dad had a chance to speak to me. "Won't you ever remember to put them in the laundry?" My mother didn't look up as she cut a zucchini stick.

"Sorry, Sylvia." My dad looked down at the floor like a child being reprimanded by his mother.

"And you forgot to take out the trash yesterday. Now we have to wait an entire week for the next pickup. The neighbors are going to think we're pigs."

"I'll make sure to remember next week." He continued staring at the tiled floor.

"Harris, have you looked in the mirror recently? Your hair's a complete mess." My mother crunched louder while my dad looked like he had developed another crease around his eyes.

"I'll make an appointment to get it cut tomorrow." He slumped in his seat as if he had no energy to sit up straight, let alone argue with my mother.

"How about today?" She managed to scream at him while continuing to chew her healthy snack.

"I'll take care of it." But he didn't sound very convincing, just sad.

I felt like I was watching a boxing match where my dad let my mom get every punch. "I think Dad's hair looks nice." Well, someone had to stand up for him.

"Sure, if you like that disheveled look."

Okay, this wasn't going well. Someone really needed to put a muzzle around my mother's mouth. I had to do something to get them in a neutral place where they could be civil to each other, but where? And then my eyes glanced over to my dad's Phillies shirt. "Dad, you still get season tickets to the Phillies' games, don't you?"

"Sure do. I happen to have an extra ticket for tonight's game. Would you like to go with me, princess?" He sat up straighter and finally removed his eyes from the floor.

"Uh, I kind of have plans with the girls. Sorry, Dad." It was way too early to tell my parents about Chris. "Why don't you take Mom instead?"

I thought my parents were gazing into each other's eyes until I realized that my mom was staring at the clock on the wall, while my dad was preoccupied with an ant crawling up the cabinet. "Barb and I got tickets to see *Cats* at the Galaxy Theater tonight," my mother answered, scrutinizing a hangnail.

"What about next week's game? Aren't they playing a home game on Sunday?"

"Yeah, but…"

"And Mom, didn't you always tell me how you and Dad loved going to baseball games when you first met? In fact, wasn't your first date at a Phillies game?"

"That was a long time ago, Jen."

"So what?"

"Yeah, so what, Sylvia?" My dad stopped looking at the ant and his eyes looked slightly hopeful.

"I guess I could meet Barb for drinks after the game," my mother said.

Okay, so this wasn't the loving response I was looking for, but at least it was a start. I listened as my parents hesitantly made plans to see the game the following week. While my mom looked less than pleased about her upcoming date with her husband, my dad looked rather enthusiastic at the prospect. His eyes seemed to wake up and his lips even moved into a smile.

Kathy would be upset that I hadn't found out what was going on between them, but I didn't feel like prying into their personal life. Unlike Kathy, I wasn't here to place blame on either of them. I just wanted them to be happy.

Even though the block of ice between them still needed a lot of chipping before it cracked, I hoped that I had at least helped melt it a little. Thank goodness that was over! Now that I had played Cupid for my parents, I hoped that as a reward, Cupid would be waiting for me when I picked up Chris for our first date.

At it turned out, Cupid was nowhere in sight when I picked up Chris, but half the Philadelphia police force was. As I approached his neighborhood, his street was blocked off for a drug bust in a housing project across the street from his run-down apartment complex. I nearly turned around and cancelled our date, but my need to see him again motivated me to walk past all the police and anxious spectators till I reached him. As soon as I saw him waiting for me outside on the curb, I was glad I hadn't changed my mind.

And now sixty minutes later, seated safely in a booth at Friday's with our dinners and drinks, I felt mesmerized by his smile, which I hadn't been able to get out of my mind since we met. His eyes seemed to twinkle as he spoke.

"Have I mentioned how pretty you look tonight?" Chris once again looked at me as if nobody else in the room existed.

I couldn't believe this gorgeous guy was calling *me* pretty. Instead of thanking him, I merely blushed and took a sip of my Cosmo.

"Not good at taking compliments, huh? I'll have to work on that. By the way, I realized this morning that I don't even know your last name. Or do you just go by your first name, like Cher and Madonna?" Chris gave me that movie star smile that made my heart beat fast.

"I'm afraid that Jen isn't nearly as exciting a first name as Madonna. My last name's Greenberg. What's yours?"

"It's O'Reilly. So we have a Jew and an Irishman. It sounds like the beginning of a joke." Chris chuckled and I couldn't help joining him, but somehow I doubted my mom would be laughing.

She had been brought up with a strict Jewish upbringing and couldn't contemplate Kathy or me marrying anyone who wasn't Jewish. Well, at least Kathy hadn't disappointed her.

Chris certainly wasn't the first guy I'd dated who wasn't Jewish, and if I ended up with someone who didn't share my religion, it wouldn't be the worst thing in the world. But it certainly would complicate things. I suddenly had a vivid picture of my dad's mother cooking matzo ball soup and I automatically reached for my Star of David charm. Oh, shoot! I'd forgotten to put it on after that baby next door spit up on my shoe.

Well, maybe that was for the best tonight. I wondered if Chris was religious. Would he mind that I wasn't Catholic? But I was truly jumping the gun here. We hadn't even made it past our first date. Maybe it was time to switch to a less controversial subject. "So did you go to high school around here?"

"I went to South Jersey High. I lived in New Jersey till I was seventeen," Chris said, taking a large bite out of his cheeseburger.

"I know a few people who went there. What year did you graduate?" I used my fork to play with my Cobb salad.

"I never graduated. School wasn't for me." He took a sip of beer from its bottle.

Instead of playing with my salad, I ripped the lettuce leaves into small pieces. Of course, education wasn't everything, but it sure helped you get ahead in life. I couldn't imagine not graduating from high school. Come to think of it, I never knew anyone who hadn't. All of my friends had graduated from college, and some had gone on to graduate school. "Do you regret never graduating?"

"Not at all. I've managed to find some great jobs without a high school diploma." The music and noise from the bar made it hard to hear Chris, but I picked up enough to get the gist of the conversation.

Okay, the list of Chris's negative traits seemed to be growing. I couldn't get involved with a high school dropout with no ambition who lived in the slums. Could I? This was without a doubt one of the craziest things I'd ever done. In the past, I would have dropped him as soon as I saw where he lived, but something about this guy kept me wanting more.

"You look concerned. Does it bother you that I dropped out of school?" He took one last sip of beer until the bottle was empty.

"Well, uh, I do think that graduating from high school is important, especially if you want a good career."

"I think education is a great thing, too, but I also think people can sometimes learn more from firsthand experiences than from sitting in a stuffy classroom where some instructor rattles on about meaningless facts. I'd rather experience life than read about it in a textbook."

"I guess." I was trying to remain open-minded, especially since he had taken my hand from across the table, creating an overwhelming rush of heat throughout my body.

"You don't sound convinced." He stroked my hand with his silky soft skin, causing me to shiver with excitement. "I know dropping out of school sounds crazy, and I really tried to hang in there, but I was too anxious to get out into the world and start living my life. Besides, I've learned a lot from every job I've had." Chris held up his empty beer bottle to the waitress, indicating he wanted another one.

"So where have you worked?" I picked a few pieces of cheese out of my salad with my fork.

"See, that's the point." His eyes twinkled like beautiful bright stars. "I've had so many different types of jobs that they probably covered every subject at school that I missed. While you were reading school books about the Civil War, I was working as a tour guide at Gettysburg visiting the actual sites where history was made."

I nodded, really wanting to understand how anyone could rationalize dropping out of school.

"Instead of reading about the pH level of water in science class, I learned about it by working at the Baltimore Aquarium," Chris continued. "Not to mention, if I hadn't worked as a security guard at the Art Museum, I would never have been able to describe post-modernist art from looking at it on slides in school. And I bet I'll learn more about merchandising and management at Big Al's Mini Mart than I would have remembered from reading textbooks in marketing class."

"I guess when you put it like that, graduating from high school doesn't seem as important." Had I really said that? Maybe it was because I'd never guess from talking to him that he dropped out. He spoke better than some of the people I knew who had received master's degrees. Or maybe it was because when he spoke everything he said seemed to make sense.

Chris squeezed my hand, as if to thank me for understanding. "By the way," Chris said, still smiling, always smiling, "I read all your brochures at the Sportin Fitness Center this week, and I was really impressed. I especially liked the one that compared Sportin Fitness to other fitness franchises. You did a great job showing all the advantages of going there instead of joining the others. If I weren't already a member, I think I'd sign up."

Wow! I was amazed that he had gone to the trouble of reading the brochures. This gesture definitely got added to his list of positive traits. Going out with Chris was becoming like a seesaw ride. First he was on the bottom, when he talked about dropping out of school, and then he was back on top, when he described how he went out of his way to find something I'd written. "Thanks for bothering to read them." I put my fork down and pushed my plate away, having had enough of my salad.

"I wanted to. I'm really interested in your job. I walked by the billboard you wrote to check that out, too. There's one a couple blocks from my apartment. Those graphics were awesome, and the message you wrote was powerful. 'Live healthier, live longer, start living today at Sportin Fitness Center.' The copy worked really well with the artwork."

It was weird hearing anyone quote my copy. Weird, but nice.

"So now what should we do?" Chris finished his burger and ate one last French fry before placing his napkin over his plate. "I know. Why don't we go dancing at Tailgaters and then spend the rest of the night hitting the slot machines in Atlantic City."

I wasn't used to so much excitement in one night. In fact, I wasn't used to much excitement at all. "Don't you ever get tired?"

"Never. Is there something else you had in mind? I'm up for anything."

That was obvious. "I'm not really sure." Why couldn't I think of any cool place to go to? Probably because most of my dates thought movie theaters were the most thrilling activity in the area.

"If I were you I'd check out the Hot Spot downtown," suggested our waitress, who came by to give us the check. I hadn't even noticed her until she spoke. She looked a little like Kelly Ripa and wore a skirt under her Friday's shirt that barely covered her hips. "I hear they have a great jazz band playing tonight." She smiled at Chris, completely ignoring eye contact with me.

"Thanks for the idea," Chris said, without glancing in her direction.

"No problem," said our buxom waitress. "If you have any other questions, just give me a holler. I'm Ginger."

Figured she couldn't have a name like Hilda or Gertrude.

Ginger moved so close to Chris that I thought she was going to sit on his lap. "You can pay me when you're ready." Ginger still hadn't acknowledged my presence as she spoke only to Chris.

"Thanks, Ginger. So, Jen, what do you think? Would you be interested in some jazz music after we leave?"

It sounded great and I was afraid if I said no, Ginger would gladly take my place.

"That's fine with me." I watched Ginger slowly walk away without taking her eyes off of Chris. He's mine, I wanted to scream to her and every other attractive female in the restaurant who was checking Chris out.

"Great." Chris got uncharacteristically quiet as he opened his wallet.

"Is something wrong?" I wasn't used to seeing him without that big smile on his face.

"I feel terrible about this, Jen, but it looks like I'm a little low in cash. Would you mind paying for yourself tonight? I promise I'll make it up to you."

I was getting that uneasy feeling again as that seesaw came tumbling down. What kind of guy took a girl out for dinner without checking to make sure he had enough money to cover the check? Or was I was being too hard on him? After all, we all made mistakes and he did sound like he felt bad about it. "No problem. I have enough money."

"You're the best." He flashed me that smile that could have warmed an entire room of Eskimos.

While I took out my wallet, Chris got up to take out a package of Marlboros. I hated the smell of cigarettes, and made it a point not to date guys who smoked. So why was I making all these exceptions for Chris?

"Don't worry. I won't light up until we get outside." Chris bent down and kissed me gently on the lips, and I felt like Bobby Brady on the *Brady Bunch* when he got his first kiss. Like Bobby, I really did see fireworks! Large, colorful ones that lit up the entire restaurant.

Okay, so maybe this was the reason why I was letting him off the hook for all the things I typically wouldn't put up with. But besides the intense physical attraction I felt toward Chris, he showed more of an interest in me than most people I'd known for years.

We walked outside into the moonlit, warm summer evening, and I muffled a cough while Chris smoked. As I watched him puffing away, I imagined what my mother would say if I told her I went out with an Irish Catholic high school dropout who worked at Big Al's Mini Mart. He certainly wasn't the Jewish doctor she was hoping I'd meet.

Chapter 8

How the Marriage Epidemic Distorts Your Thinking:

1. You no longer care if you marry a high school dropout even though you always thought you'd end up with a college graduate.

2. You no longer care if your husband has no ambition or goals. After all, how important is security anyway?

3. And who needs a house in the suburbs when you can live a perfectly happy life in the ghetto?

"You haven't said anything about Clarke for a while," Stacy said. "Are you still seeing him?"

"Yeah, occasionally. And his name's Chris." I held the phone under my chin as I searched for the copy I had written for Sterling Pharmaceutical's foot fungus account. I thought I had put it in my desk drawer when I got to work this morning.

"Come on, Jen. What gives? Why are you keeping him such a secret?"

"Maybe because I had to practically resuscitate you after I told you what he did for a living."

"Oh, I hope you're not mad about that. I didn't mean to come off so strong about him pumping gas."

"He doesn't pump gas! I told you, he works at the convenience store inside." No matter how many times I told her what he did, she would always think of him as a gas station attendant. "Not that there's anything wrong with that," I could hear Jerry Seinfeld say.

Even though I had only been dating Chris for less than two months, it felt a lot longer. Maybe that was because in such a short time, he had encouraged me to experience so many activities that I normally would never consider trying. On our second date, he had talked me into riding a wave runner with him in Ocean City. This was a major accomplishment for me, considering I typically avoided water that went above my knees, due to my fear of drowning. By the end of the day, I was driving the wave runner, while Chris hung on to my waist.

The following week we had gone hiking up a huge hill that I was sure I'd never be able to climb. Since I wasn't exactly the outdoor, athletic type, I had suggested staying at the bottom of the hill with a good book while Chris hiked up alone, but once again he'd insisted that I at least try. And once again, I had done it, thanks to Chris's rendition of "The Little Engine that Could," all the way up the hill. As he chanted, "I think I can, I think I can," I realized I could.

And just last week, he had taken me to Great Adventure where we'd ridden the Nitro. This colossal mega roller coaster wove us through seven steep drops and horizontal loops at hyper speeds of close to eighty miles per hour. I had felt nauseous just looking at it, but Chris didn't let that stop us. As I told him all the reasons why I wouldn't go, he told me all the reasons why I needed to take risks and try new experiences. Realizing I rarely did, I clutched his hand, closed my eyes, and braced myself for the worst ride in my life until we blasted off up to two hundred and thirty feet. Soaring through the sky at such a high speed gave me an adrenaline rush that made me feel like I could move mountains or part the Red Sea.

Just the idea that I was letting Chris talk me into all these new experiences still amazed me. Hell, just a few months ago I got mad at Ben for talking me into changing my order at that damn Mexican restaurant. And now here I was hiking up hills.

I still wasn't sure what it was about Chris that made me give into his requests every time. But I think it had something to do with the way he looked at me with such assurance whenever he suggested we tried something new. No matter how much I resisted, his complete confidence in me was contagious, making me believe I could do anything I put my mind to. And I did.

For my entire life, I had been so cautious, always looking for the safe alternatives. Chris brought out a free-spirited side of me that I never knew I had, but was grateful I had discovered. For the first time, I felt like I was living life to the fullest and I had Chris to thank for that.

"So is it serious?" Stacy asked, as I took out every folder in my desk and leafed through them hoping to find the missing copy that I had stayed up all night writing.

"We're keeping it casual for now." I didn't mention that I spent every moment that I wasn't working, thinking about him, and that when I wasn't with him, all I wanted to do was see him.

The other reason I didn't want to say too much was that I still had mixed feelings about Chris. There were so many things that I liked about Chris, but there were equally as many things that I didn't like. Unlike Stacy, I didn't care that Chris wasn't a white-collar professional who made six figures. I didn't look at guys as status symbols, like obtaining a new car or piece of jewelry.

What bothered me most about Chris was that he wandered aimlessly from job to job, without any long-term goals and plans for his future. And even if he didn't go to college, I would have preferred that he had graduated from high school. But did these things really matter, or was I being as superficial as Stacy?

If I had been twenty, I was sure I would have felt different. I could have dated him for a while, and if things didn't work out, I would still have time to find someone else. But I wasn't twenty anymore, and every relationship seemed so much more critical now. I didn't have years to waste on the wrong guy. The pressure was on!

Unfortunately, my heart was starting to take control of my mind. Even though I was beyond ready to sleep with him, I was afraid of getting too close to Chris until I was sure I wanted a long-term relationship. I knew once we slept together, I'd never be able to let go. Apparently that cautious side of me still existed.

"Well, even if it's not serious, why don't you invite him to my engagement party next week," Stacy suggested. "Even if he doesn't have anything in common with the other guys, I'm sure they'll find something to talk about."

Interpretation: You can bring him, but he sure as hell won't fit in with anyone there. "Thanks, but I'll come alone."

"If you change your mind, let me know."

"I will." *Not!* "So anything new this week with your wedding plans?"

"Oh, Jen, I found the most wonderful caterer. Wait till you taste the wonderful hors d'oeuvres we picked for the reception."

Ms. Wonderful was back. "I can't wait." It was hard to believe that everything was going so wonderfully. Or was I just jealous? Maybe her wedding plans were going unusually smooth. Everything else in Stacy's life always had. Maybe I was in a bitchy mood because I couldn't find that damn foot fungus copy that I needed right away.

"Speaking of weddings, I have some big news about Lori's wedding," Stacy said.

"What is it?"

"The wedding's off!"

"What happened?" I was so surprised, I stopped looking for the missing fungus campaign.

"She's been so sick from the pregnancy that she doesn't have the energy to plan a wedding. She's afraid that once she gets better, she'll be too big to fit into a gown."

"I guess liposuction is out of the question."

Stacy laughed. It felt good to be back on common ground.

"So are they going to wait to get married till after she has the baby?"

"No, they're getting married at City Hall in a few weeks."

"But she won't get to walk down the aisle." I took a sip of my cold coffee that I'd bought over an hour ago.

"That's what I said, but she doesn't care. As long as she marries Tony, nothing else matters, not even canceling her wedding. She'd rather spend the money on a nursery than pay for a wedding. Since she heard the baby's heartbeat, Babies R Us has become her second home. She bought one of those fetal heart monitors so she could hear the baby's heartbeat. When I visited her last week, she spent most of the time patting her belly or talking to her stomach."

"Lori did that? I can't believe this is the same person who once set a record for sleeping with the most fraternity brothers in one semester."

"Neither can I. Tony's had some effect on her. Wait till you meet him. He's such a great guy."

I imagined the fact that he was a successful businessman didn't hurt either. "Listen, Stace, I've got to go. I have a meeting soon."

"Ok. Tell Curt I'm looking forward to meeting him sometime soon."

Before I could remind Stacy that his name was Chris, she hung up.

I crawled under my desk to look for the lost copy. "Jen, is that you under there?" I looked up to see Tiffany and Marisa looking down at me, literally.

"I can't find the copy for the Sterling account. Quick, Marisa, look in my desk drawers. Tif, will you look in my bottom cabinet drawer, and I'll run out to my car to see if I left it there."

"What does it look like?" Tiffany asked.

Her breath smelled like she'd been smoking, which made me think about Chris. Hell, everything made me think about him lately. "It's in a dark blue envelope."

"Looking for this?" Rhonda walked in holding the folder. Her bright orange and magenta pant suit was blinding.

"Where was it?" I asked. For once I was happy to see Rhonda.

"I found it next to the bathroom sink. Good thing I found it! If it weren't for me, this could have been lost forever." My gratitude toward Rhonda vanished as I envisioned stuffing her head in the toilet.

After she left, Tiffany closed the door. "So things with you and Chris must be getting serious," Tiffany said.

"Why do you say that?" I wiped off the folder, which had apparently gotten wet from the sink.

"Come on, Jen. You're always two weeks early with your copy, but since you met Chris I barely see your tag lines before the kick-off meetings."

"I guess I've been a little preoccupied lately, but you have to admit, I've still never missed a deadline."

"You've got me there," Tiffany said. "So, what's with Chris?" She moved a pile of folders away from the foot of my desk and pulled over a chair.

"Yeah," Marisa said. Her eyes looked red and puffy, like she'd been crying a lot.

"Is he the one?"

The older I got, the sooner people asked that question. "I don't know." I tried to straighten up my desk, which seemed to be eaten up by file folders. "He's not exactly the type of guy I ever imagined marrying."

"So who says you have to marry him," Tiffany said. "Do you like being with him?"

"Yeah, but…"

"But nothing. Why get so hung up on marriage? If you like him, go out with him. There's no rule that says you have to marry every guy you date."

"But we're getting older," Marisa said.

I imagined she had given up on Zack by now.

"Does that mean we're supposed to stop having fun?" Tiffany said. She stretched back in her chair and folded her hands behind her head.

"Hey, speaking of having fun, what happened to that guy you met at El Sol last weekend," I asked Tiffany, while discovering some loose change under a stack of paper on my desk.

"To put it bluntly, he fucked me and ran." Her voice sounded raspier than usual. "After his last number at the club, we ended up back at my apartment. We had a wild night of sex, and when I woke up he was gone. I guess he assumed I was just another groupie after his body, which I guess was partly true."

"You mean he hasn't called since you slept with him?" I gave up trying to find the top of my desk.

"Not even an email, the bastard." But despite her language, she didn't seem overly upset or surprised about it.

"My phone hasn't exactly been ringing off the hook either," Marisa complained.

Meany peeked her head into Tiffany's office, "Ten minutes till the big fungus meeting, ladies." She flashed her patented frozen smile. Meany disappeared as quickly as she appeared.

"Please, don't tell me she's the account executive on the Sterling Campaign," Tiffany said. "I thought Pat had that account."

"She did, but John thought Meany could handle it better," I answered.

"Maybe she has foot fungus," Marisa offered.

"Let's hope she doesn't take off her shoes during the meeting to show us," Tiffany said.

The thought of seeing Meany's toenails made me ill. Then again, the thought of being late to one of Meany's meetings also made me ill, and apparently Marisa and Tiffany felt the same way because we simultaneously popped up from our seats and headed toward the conference room.

We walked in unison, armed with our file folders, marketing proposal, and three cans of ginger ale. "How's the job search going?" I whispered to Tiffany as we walked past the traffic department's cubicles.

"It sucks! Everyone looking for a creative director wants someone with website design experience. After twelve years of experience working as an artist, I might have to go back to school to learn how to design a fuckin' website before I can get another job. It's totally frustrating."

What was even more frustrating was entering the conference room where Meany wrote the disadvantages of foot fungus on her large easel, as if there were any advantages of having crumbling, discolored nails with foul odors. We placed our sodas on coasters at the conference table and silently sat down, listening to Meany's marker squeak along the paper.

When she was done, she asked Tiffany, Marisa, and me to come to the easel to write three benefits of Sterling's cream. When it was my turn to take the large marker, I was transformed from an advertising professional to a scared third-grader who was asked to write the multiplication tables on the blackboard.

As I carefully formed each letter, my heart raced as I pictured all the advertising awards hanging on Meany's office walls. My palms became sweaty as I thought about the international accounts she had handled over the years. And my hands shook as I remembered the list of famous clients Meany had represented.

Damn it! I hated feeling so nervous around this woman who was even shorter and wider than me, especially after working with her for so many years. Her appearance certainly wasn't intimidating. She dressed like she put on the first outfit that fell out of her closet, and despite her need for makeup, she never wore any cosmetics other than lipstick and concealer. Her high-pitched, chirpy voice sounded like it should be coming from a teenager's mouth instead of from a middle-aged woman.

Even knowing all this, I still waited for Meany's reaction like an eight-year-old waiting for her teacher's approval. Meany took her pointer to read my answers, and I was rewarded by her instant smile activator. It was as gratifying as receiving a happy face sticker from my elementary school teacher.

When the Sterling Pharmaceutical product managers arrived, Meany put on her usual glowing performance, never missing a beat when she was asked a question. Somehow she made their foot fungus cream sound like the most extraordinary product ever produced. I was almost ready to buy some before leaving the meeting.

After talking about fungi for two hours, my feet felt itchy as I returned to my office. Maybe now would be a good time to try a pedicure. I considered stopping by Thomas's salon to have one done while I checked my emails.

What a surprise. A message from my mom. *Hi, sweetheart, I found the most beautiful silk flower arrangement that will look perfect in your living room. I'll stop by around seven to show it to you. Love, Mom.*

Oh, great, now I was stuck entertaining my mother all evening. And wouldn't it have been nice if she had called to ask if I had plans? As I glanced at my watch, I realized I better leave now if I wanted to get there in time.

Remembering how I'd overslept that morning and didn't have time to make the bed, I raced out of my office and toward the parking garage, hoping I'd have a chance to tidy up. My mom's spur-the-moment visits were as bad as being inspected by the army's drill sergeant. I always expected her to run her finger down my end tables to test for dust, or to bounce a ball on my bed to see if it had been made it properly. I was sure I would have failed both tests miserably.

Fortunately, my new place was only fifteen minutes from work, and even in traffic I made great time getting home. I walked briskly toward my apartment, where I saw Chris sitting on the front steps, holding a daisy. Since our first date, Chris had been picking a daisy for me everyday. On the days we didn't see each other, he slipped one into my mailbox.

While walking toward Chris, I felt lots of sensations throughout my body, especially when he stood up to kiss me. I was even starting to find the nicotine on his breath to be kind of erotic.

"For you," he said, handing me the flower.

I tried not to stare at the big silver cross he wore around his neck. It must be a good conversation piece when people saw it next to my big Star of David charm.

"Thanks for the flower. You're very sweet." He seemed so rough around the edges, and yet underneath that rough exterior was a kind, sensitive person, which was probably why I found him so irresistible.

"If I'm so sweet, how come we haven't had sex yet?" He pulled me close to his chest, making it difficult to remember why I kept resisting. I couldn't explain to him that it was the only ounce of control I still had left over this relationship, which I wasn't sure was headed in the right direction.

"Let's go away somewhere so I can show you how I feel about you. I guarantee it will be worth your while." He wrapped his arms around me and moved close enough so I could feel his hardness against my legs, causing my heart to practically leap into my mouth. There was no way I was going to be able to hold out much longer. As we kissed like teenagers, my body became so hot I thought I would overheat... until I heard a car door slam and the familiar sound of stilettos on the pavement.

Coming up for air, I pulled my cell phone from my purse to see what time it was. Damn! Damn! Damn! My mother was due to arrive in ten minutes, and she was always early.

"Is something wrong? I swear I used deodorant this morning." Chris reached over to pull me toward him again, but this time I didn't let him.

"Doesn't the night shift start soon?" I inadvertently pulled a white petal off of the daisy.

"Yeah, but if I'm a little late, it's okay. I'll tell my boss that I stopped by my beautiful girlfriend's house to give her her daily daisy."

His girlfriend? We had never officially had that relationship talk, so hearing Chris call me his girlfriend caught me off guard. I liked hearing those words come out of his mouth.

My thoughts were interrupted as the footsteps got closer. "Maybe you should go," I said, looking toward the parking lot for a middle-aged woman with a teenager's body. "I wouldn't want you to be late for work."

"You're not expecting another guy, are you?" Chris smiled confidently. "I suppose we could have a threesome, but I would much rather have you to myself." As he said the words, he moved closer and kissed me so deeply I didn't think I'd be able to catch my breath. I groaned with excitement until those footsteps sounded like they were nearly on top of us.

Fortunately, there were lots of trees and high shrubs leading from the parking lot to the front steps of my apartment complex. Enough greenery, I hoped, to block any X-rated behavior taking place behind them. Through a large bush, I saw my mother's hot pink tank top and denim short shorts.

Without thinking, I pushed Chris away and straightened my silk shirt.

"What's wrong?" Chris looked surprised.

"I'm sorry. I didn't mean to push you away, but those loud footsteps are coming from my mother's shoes, and I haven't told her about us yet."

"Well, no time like the present." His hair was all disheveled, probably since I had spent the past few minutes running my fingers through it. And his face looked flushed, like he had just had sex. I was still feeling extremely hot. What we both needed was a cold bucket filled with ice to dump over our heads, but most likely my mom would offer to do that for us once she found out about Chris's background.

"I'm glad I'll have a chance to meet your mom. I promise to use my charm to win her over."

I realized, of course, that he'd need a lot more than charm to impress her, starting with a good career and a nice home in the suburbs. "Listen, Chris, my mom can be a little difficult at times. Just promise you'll go along with anything I say. I'll explain later," I whispered as she stomped down the path toward us, holding the silk flowers. Dainty, she wasn't.

"Wow, is that your mom?" Chris's eyes practically popped out of his head. "She's hot!"

Great, just how I wanted my boyfriend to react to my mother.

"Hi, sweetie," my mom said to me, while looking at Chris. "Aren't you going to introduce me to your friend?"

"Oh, right. Mom, this is Chris."

"Hi, Chris. You have some of my daughter's lipstick on your shirt."

"Hey, Jen, how do you suppose that got here?" Chris shrugged and gave his best innocent grin, but my mom didn't crack a smile.

"Mom, why don't we go inside? Chris was just leaving."

"I can't believe Jen hasn't mentioned you before." My mom ignored my suggestion, and me, for that matter. "How long have the two of you known each other?"

"We've been dating almost two months." He flashed that irresistible smile that my mom seemed quite capable of resisting.

"So, Mom, how about a glass of wine—"

"Two months!" My mother looked like Chris had just thrown a glass of water over her perfectly highlighted blond hair. "Jen, why didn't you tell me about Chris?"

Because I knew what you'd say when you found out what he didn't do for a living and where he didn't go to school. "I was waiting for the right moment." That was an honest answer. Although I wasn't sure there would ever be one.

"Do you live here, too?"

Uh-oh! The façade was up. "No, actually..." Chris began.

"We met when he was visiting his friend who lives upstairs from me," I interrupted. Chris raised his eyebrow at me. "Mom, Chris is going to be late to work if he doesn't leave."

"You work on Saturdays? What do you do?"

This was it! The moment of truth. I watched Chris open his mouth, as if watching him move in slow motion. As he tilted his head sideways to look at my mom, I couldn't listen. "Chris is in management," I blurted out.

We were back to real time now. My mom looked impressed, probably envisioning him to be some kind of corporate executive who worked seventy hour weeks to make mega bucks.

"Mom, Chris is too polite to interrupt, but he really has to go."

"Unfortunately, Jen's right. I really should get going, but it was nice meeting you."

"Don't worry about it. Besides, I imagine we'll get a chance to talk next week at Stacy's engagement party?"

Oops! Busted! Was it too late to pretend I was deathly ill? Judging by Chris's and my mother's expressions, it was.

"What engagement party?" Chris asked. It was the first time I ever saw his wide smile reduced to a grimace.

"You did invite Chris to the party, didn't you, dear? I know Stacy said you could bring a date." I considered stuffing the daisy from Chris into my mother's big mouth.

"Um, well…I thought I'd introduce Chris to everyone separately. I didn't want you to feel overwhelmed meeting all of my friends and family at one time." I looked into Chris's eyes, hoping he'd understand, but he stared at me, expressionless, which was out of character for him.

"That's ridiculous," my mom continued. "Stacy's party will be a great chance to introduce Chris around. There's no reason to be shy, Chris. I promise you that we don't bite."

"And I promise you, I'm far from shy." The sparkle in Chris's eyes disappeared as he looked at me without saying anything.

"Great, then it's settled. I'll see you at the party."

"I'll talk to you later, Jen. I'm late for Big Al's Mini Mart." Chris clearly pronounced every syllable of the convenience store's name.

"What does he mean about Big Al's Mini Mart," my mother asked as I unlocked the front door.

"Um, I think he wanted some coffee before he went to work."

"He seems nice. Too bad his name's not Noah instead of Chris. You know how much I'm hoping you end up with someone Jewish."

And she didn't know the half of it, I thought as we walked up the two flights of steps to my apartment, where we were greeted by the sound of a baby crying next door. At least I hadn't woken up the little rug rat this time.

It didn't take Chris long to call me. Fortunately, my mother had already left. "Why didn't you invite me to the party, and why did you lie about my job?"

How could I explain to him that my family and friends were on a mission to find me a guy who met certain criteria, and on a scale from one to ten, Chris came in at about a minus thirty-eight?

"I'm sorry if I made you feel bad, but my mom and some of my friends can be very critical sometimes. They think I should be with a certain type of guy, and I didn't want to put you in an uncomfortable situation."

"And what do you think?"

"I think my family and friends can be too opinionated at times… and…I think you're terrific." The second part of my answer came directly from my heart.

"Well, then in that case you're forgiven." An unbearable silence followed.

I glared at the silk flower arrangement that my mom had brought over and vowed to throw it in the trash the next morning. "Are you sure you're not mad anymore?"

"No, but to be honest, now that your mom knows about me, I thought you'd feel comfortable asking me to your friend's party. Are you ashamed to introduce me to your friends?"

"Of course not." Well, it wasn't exactly a lie. I knew what everyone would say and think and I just didn't feel like dealing with it. But I knew now that hiding Chris from my world wasn't fair to him either. "I'd really like you to come with me."

"I hope you mean that." There was a slight edge to his voice that I hadn't heard before.

"I do, Chris. I really want you to come with me." And at that moment I sincerely meant it, despite that gnawing feeling in the pit of my stomach that by the end of the party, Chris would be wishing he'd never asked to be invited.

Chapter 9

How the Marriage Epidemic Affects Your Social Life:

1. Hanging out with the girls now means forming a huddle around them and checking out their diamonds.

2. You spend lots of time "oohing" and "aahing," but unfortunately, it's not during sex; instead it's during engagement parties while watching the bride-to-be open her presents.

After parking my car, I walked briskly toward Chris's apartment, nervously checking behind me every few steps. I stepped over two homeless people and gave a quarter to a woman waving a big cup that read, "Feed me" before I rang the buzzer. I clutched my Mace until Chris buzzed me in.

An old man standing inside the door whistled at me as I walked past him to Chris's apartment. "Hey, babe, you're going the wrong way," he yelled. "My apartment's this way."

I ran through the hallway without looking back. Thank goodness Chris lived on the first floor so I didn't have to travel any farther. As Chris opened the door, the old man screamed, "Yo, Chris, looks like you're getting some tonight."

"Hey, you dirty old man, that's my girlfriend you're talking about. Find yourself your own woman." Chris chuckled as if this type of conversation was routine around here.

"He's a pig," I said, relieved once again to make it inside without being attacked.

"He's not so bad when you get to know him. He's just jealous that you're with me, and how can you blame him? You look incredible."

I was glad I had splurged on the Liz Claiborne royal blue chiffon dress, especially since its tiers hid my wide hips. If it weren't for that blemish on my chin and my unmanageable hair, I would have felt almost attractive.

Chris leaned over to kiss me, and as his tongue felt its way inside my mouth and his hands casually touched my breasts, I forgot all about the homeless people outside and the old man downstairs. Hell, I forgot about everything, including Stacy's party. My only thoughts were about tearing Chris's clothes off and feeling him inside of me.

"Let's not forget where we left off," Chris said, slowly moving away.

"I guess we better go." It was more of a question than a statement, but I couldn't very well miss the party.

"Yeah, we should leave soon. I'll wait here while you get dressed." Chris wore a light denim shirt and dark blue jeans.

"What do you mean? I am dressed."

"Chris, you can't wear that to the party. We're going to a country club. All the guys will be in suits and ties."

"Then I guess I'm going to stand out as the best-looking casual dresser in the room."

"I'm serious," I shrieked louder than I meant to. "They might not even let you in without a tie."

"Why didn't you tell me it was such a fancy shmancy place? I would have bought new laces for my sneaks."

"Chris!"

"Ok, ok. I'll see what I can find." Pushing a pile of clothes off his couch, he handed me his remote. "Have a seat. Oh, by the way, if the TV acts up, hit it on the side a few times. It works like a charm." He winked at me as he walked to his bedroom.

I was afraid to see what Chris would come out wearing. Maybe I should have bought him something for the party. Not wanting to think about it, I turned on the TV. Since Chris didn't have cable, I didn't have much of a selection. I was just about to change the channel when a commercial caught my attention.

"You don't have to be embarrassed anymore about dropping out of high school because the Goodman Technical Institute is here to give you a second chance. In just three short weeks, we'll teach you everything you need to earn your GED so you can start living the successful life you deserve."

I jotted down the number with a pen that I found on the coffee table, and slipped the number into my purse.

"Tada!" Chris shouted. Now he wore a bathrobe and slippers.

"Chris!"

"Gotcha!" He laughed, taking off his robe to display a nice pair of khaki pants and a matching cream tie that complimented his bluish green shirt.

"You look great," I said. The shirt accentuated his green eyes, and the pants and tie gave him a semi-professional look that I wasn't used to seeing.

"I wish I had a camera to capture your expression when I first walked out." Chris continued laughing. "Oh, by the way, I found these loafers in the back of my closet so I won't need these sneaks after all. Sorry about not owning a suit, but this is the best I can do. So do I pass the test?"

"With an A plus," I said.

"I hope I get an extra credit assignment when we get back, preferably in the bedroom," he said.

I simply smiled, still not sure how to respond.

Chris took my hand and led me through the hallway and out the front door. Amazingly, nobody had broken into my car.

"Hey, this is some place," Chris said as we passed various sized love doves carved into the bushes outside of the Enchanted Country Club. We walked through a path of heart-shaped roses as we approached the stone entranceway. Once inside, we stopped to admire the fountain of water flowing from a statue of Cupid's mouth.

"Isn't it beautiful?" I said. Would I ever be coming here as the hostess, or would I always be one of the many guests? And more importantly, could I see Chris co-hosting a bridal event here?

Chris held my hand as we walked into the reception area. "Hey, Jen!"

I had to look twice before I recognized Lori waddling over. Her usual slender figure now resembled the shape of a pear. Her breasts, which had grown proportionately to her stomach, looked like two mountains peeking through a valley. Her face looked larger, too, but despite her significant weight gain, she looked surprisingly good, like she was finally at peace with the world.

"How are you feeling?" I asked.

"Other than barfing my brains out every few hours, great. So are you going to introduce me to this gorgeous hunk, or should I ditch Tony and get the lowdown on him myself?"

"Lori, this is Chris." I was proud to introduce him. Even though he was the only guy who wasn't wearing a suit, he somehow made his wardrobe look elegant, if that was possible.

"Hi, Lori," Chris said. "I take it that's not a basketball in there."

"It better not be." Lori laughed as she gave me a thumbs up when Chris wasn't looking.

"Where's Tony?" I looked around, wondering which guy he was.

"He's getting me a virgin daiquiri. Wouldn't you know the one craving I'm having is beer. I'm going through major withdrawal."

"I used to work with a girl who drank a glass of wine once a week when she was pregnant," Chris said. "Her doctor told her it wouldn't hurt the baby."

"Well, find out the name of that doctor and get me the number," Lori said.

"What number?" a male voice asked as a handsome man wrapped his arms possessively around Lori's large waist.

"Tony, this is Jen and her boyfriend, Chris."

"Nice to meet you," Tony said, shaking hands with Chris.

If a man could be beautiful, Tony was. He had short black hair, long, thick eyelashes and the darkest brown eyes I had ever seen. He was about five foot eleven, but had very small features. His feet couldn't have been bigger than Lori's. I wondered about that saying that you could judge a guy's penis size by his shoe size, but then I remembered this was Lori's fiancé, and imagined whoever made up that saying had gotten it wrong. Tony wore a tweed suit with a narrow gray tie.

"Congratulations, Tony," I said, admiring his appearance.

Lori's face lit up as Tony kissed her and gingerly placed his hand on her belly. Apparently, Lori had gotten over her aversion to public displays of affection because she looked up at him as if he had just given her a winning lottery ticket, and I guessed in a way, he had.

"When I went to Italy, I never thought I'd be meeting my wife and the mother of my child," Tony said. "It's amazing how one moment in time can change your life."

While Tony got philosophical about life, Chris decided it was time for a beer. He excused himself as I listened to Tony express his unconditional love for Lori without once looking at either of her breasts. Tony was so romantic and sweet that I was ready to bear his child.

"Lori, Jen, hi." I looked up to see Amy, another former roommate from college, walking toward us. Even though I had lost touch with Amy a while ago, she and Stacy had remained good friends, which is why Stacy had asked her to be in the bridal party. Amy, whose arms were quite muscular from lifting weights, gave me such a powerful hug that I had trouble breathing. I was afraid if she did that to Lori, her baby would fly out. Fortunately for Lori, she placed her arm around Lori's shoulder and stroked her belly instead.

"It's so great to see you both," Amy said. Although just as blond and buxom as Stacy, Amy was shorter, like me, and more athletic looking, unlike me. She wore her hair up in a French twist that looked like it had been done professionally. Considering Amy came from lots of money, it most likely was. "Lori, when are you due and when's the wedding?"

"The baby's due in January, and Tony and I are getting married at City Hall next weekend. What's new with you?"

"Howard and I are planning our wedding, too. We're getting married two months after Stacy."

I looked around for Chris, but couldn't see him through the crowd. There had to be over one hundred people there, at least.

"You're kidding," Lori said, no longer looking at me. "That's great. Is this the same guy you brought to Stacy's New Year's Eve party last year?"

"That's the guy. Can you believe the three of us are all getting married the same year?"

"What about you, Jen?" Amy asked. "Do you have any big announcements, too?"

Judging from the way she looked at me, the fact that I had just gotten my first pedicure didn't count. "I just moved to an apartment near the Art Museum," I answered.

Amy stared at me, as if waiting for the real news.

"Um, I'm a senior writer at Premier Advertising."

"That sounds exciting," Amy finally said. "Stacy told me that you've been climbing that corporate ladder." Amy, who had also majored in journalism, couldn't be bothered paying her dues to make it in the field, so she got a job at Bloomingdale's squirting perfume on women's wrists.

I was ready to elaborate on my job until Amy asked me the question she was obviously most interested in getting an answer to. "So, any guys in your life?" Amy's persistent questions were getting on my nerves. Now I remembered why I had stopped talking to her after college.

"I've been dating someone for a couple of months." At least I was able to honestly say yes, for once.

"And?" Amy said. None of my answers seemed to satisfy her.

"And, uh, that's about it." I tried desperately to think about some other accomplishment, but I kept drawing blanks.

I was about to search for Chris when Stacy walked over. She looked like a runway model in her black, strapless cocktail dress. "Hi, it's so great to have the old gang together again. Amy, did you tell them your news?"

"I sure did," she answered. "Stace, I don't think I saw your ring."

"And Lori, I never saw yours either," Stacy said. "Jen, did I tell you what a beautiful diamond Tony gave Lori last week?"

Tony smiled proudly as he rubbed Lori's back. Meanwhile, my three college friends formed a football huddle as they admired each other's rings. I stood behind them, feeling like the player who had been placed on the bench. I wanted to play the game, too, but the team had decided I was disqualified for not being engaged.

I wasn't about to stay around for kick-off, so I wandered over to the bar in search of Chris. Unfortunately by the time I found him, my mother had already cornered him. My father stood several inches behind them, sipping a soda.

"How do you expect to get anywhere in life without a high school degree?" my mother asked. "Don't you want more for yourself than a job at a convenience store?"

I was too late. The interrogation had already begun. Fortunately, Chris didn't seem weathered by the storm of questions. He stood up straight with his head high. "I appreciate your concern, Mrs. Greenberg," he said in a sickeningly sweet voice, "especially since we hardly know each other, but please don't lose any sleep over me. I'm doing all right with my life."

"It's not you that I'm worried about." She scowled at him. "I'm concerned about my daughter."

"Don't worry about her." He flashed her a phony smile with lots of teeth. "She's got a great head on her shoulders. She's doing just fine."

I could hear my mom's heavy breathing as I stood next to Chris. "Jen, your mom's such a loving person that she's getting all worked up about our happiness. Isn't she just a sweetheart?" He continued speaking in that sugary sweet tone.

"Chris, you really need to think about your future." My mom was back for one last shot, but she was no match for Chris. As hard as she tried, she couldn't knock down his self-esteem.

"I'll do that, Mrs. Greenberg. And again, thanks so much for all your motherly concern. Can I call you mom?"

Ding! Ding! Ding! Ding! Ding! My mother stormed off, and Chris won the round without a scar.

"Chris, I'm so sorry about that." I took his hand, wanting to make him feel better, but when I looked at him he was wearing his real smile again.

"I'm sorry, too. I hate when I get sarcastic like that, but it's the only way I know how to deal with people who are that rude."

"Well, I apologize for her behavior."

"Don't worry about it. I'm at a point in my life where I truly don't care what other people think of me. If they can't like me for who I am, then they're not the kind of people I want to be around."

"Does that mean you want to leave?"

"Of course not. Hey, Jen, don't look so concerned. I'm here to be with you, not them. As long as you're by my side, there's nothing anyone can say to upset me."

I felt my heart melt as he made that special eye contact with me. We were once again in our own little bubble that nobody could pop.

"You handle these situations better then me." I squeezed his hand. "If that had been your mom saying those things to me, I think I would have run to the bathroom, crying."

"Well, you don't have to worry about meeting my mom." And before I could ask him what he meant by that, he excused himself to get another beer.

Meanwhile, Kathy approached me. "Is he an alcoholic?" she whispered after taking a sip of her mineral water.

"No! I wouldn't date an alcoholic. Why would you ask me that?"

Kathy wore a Chanel vertical striped, black and white dress that was snug enough to show off her slender figure without looking gaudy. Her lively eyes were a bright, almost sky blue color, and her dark brown bobbed hair moved as freely as the wind. There was no denying that Kathy was quite pretty, but it was her energy and spunk that captivated everyone who met her. People gravitated to her like a magnet, except perhaps Chris.

"That's the third beer he ordered since he got here." Kathy looked appalled.

"He's not that big a drinker, and besides I drove so it doesn't matter if he has a little fun tonight." Oops! I hadn't meant to give that last part away.

"You drove?" Kathy's high voice was enough to make me want to put my hands over my ears. "Does he even have a driver's license?"

"Of course I do," Chris said, suddenly reappearing with his beer. "Would you like to see it? If I do say so myself, it's a damn nice photo. I was thinking of having it copied and made into greeting cards this year." Chris handed the license to Kathy.

"You live on Franklin Street? Is that safe?" Kathy opened her mouth so wide I could practically see her tonsils.

"My first choice was Harlem, but all the good apartments were rented so I had to settle for the Philly slums instead."

Chris wasn't kidding when he said he got sarcastic, but I supposed it could have been worse. He could have told my mom and sister to go fuck themselves, and I couldn't say I would have blamed him.

"I'm going to find Jeff." As Kathy walked away, she whispered to me, "I liked that gay guy you dated better."

"Your family needs to lighten up," Chris said after Kathy left. "Are they always so serious?"

119

It was an interesting question. Were we? Maybe that was part of my problem, too. I didn't know how to let go and have fun. And maybe that was why Chris was so good for me because he showed me how to let down my guard and live life like it was meant to be lived, instead of the way people thought you should live it.

"While you're deep in thought, I'm going to hit the head," Chris said.

I turned around to take an hors d'oeuvre and noticed my dad sitting on a stool by the bar directly behind me. I had forgotten he was there. "I guess you heard everything, huh?" I asked him.

"I did." My dad was never one for many words, probably because my mother never let him say much.

"So what do you think of Chris?" I imagined my dad would go along with my mother so he wouldn't have to listen to her scream at him the entire ride home. If they even came to the party together.

My dad got off the stool, took my hands in his, and looked into my eyes with such a serious expression that I was afraid to hear what he said.

Touching me as if I were a frail porcelain doll that might break any moment, he simply said, "I like him if he makes you happy, princess." And with those words, he walked away.

For some reason, I felt like he was trying to tell me something more than his impression of Chris, but I wasn't sure what. I was still trying to interpret my dad's statement when Chris returned, placing his arm around my waist. "Shall we find our table, or would you like to stand here solving the world's problems for another ten minutes?"

"You know us Greenbergs, always so serious."

"Trust me, Jen. You're nothing like your family."

I smiled at Chris, wondering how true that was. I did want a guy with a stable background, but I also wanted to be happy and in love. Was it possible to find both, or was I looking for someone who didn't exist?

We found our seat assignments and made our way to table four, where Stacy, Lori, and Amy were already seated with their fiancés. Lance Horowitz wore a new Armani suit that Stacy had said cost a fortune. He was as charming and dashing as ever as he kissed me hello and introduced himself to Chris. Lance's black hair, dark brown eyes, and olive skin tone complimented Stacy's light coloring and complexion. Stacy and Lance were the golden couple that caught your eye when they walked into a room.

Sitting opposite Lance and next to Amy was Howard Epstein. Even though Howard was tall and toothpick-thin with a nose that took over his face, he carried himself so confidently that you forgot about his looks as soon as he uttered a word.

Tony Riccio sat between Amy and Lori. I had been shocked to find out that Tony was Jewish with such an Italian-sounding name. But Stacy had explained that although Tony's father was Italian, his mother practiced Judaism. According to the Jewish faith, a child inherits his mother's religion. Lori's mother had to be ecstatic considering Lori had only ever dated one Jewish guy, and that was when she was in sixth grade.

And here I sat with Chris O'Reilly. Me, the girl who had gone to Hebrew school three days a week from the time I was seven till I was bat mitzvahed. Me, the only one of my friends who still fasted for Yom Kippur, and endured the bland, tasteless matzo all eight days of Passover.

My Irish boyfriend smiled at me as Stacy's parents welcomed everyone to the party, and ended their opening speech with "l'chaim," meaning "to life" in Hebrew. Everyone toasted with Manischewitz wine, while Chris finished another beer.

"Any new award-winning ad campaigns, Jenny?" Lance, who sat on my right side, asked. "Stace told me you have a cool foot fungus ad coming out."

"I hope that's not my claim to fame." I laughed and told him about some of the other ads I'd been writing.

"So what about you, Tony?" Lance asked. "I heard you own your own business. I'd love to work for myself someday, too."

"Have you ever considered opening your own law practice?" Tony asked.

"I have, but I'm doing so well at my firm right now that I'd be crazy to leave."

"Well, it's something to think about down the road," Howard said.

"Do you work for yourself, too?" Lance asked Howard.

"Not yet, but hopefully someday."

"What do you do?" Lance asked Howard.

"I'm an accountant. I work at Young, Spitzer, and Grant downtown, but I do taxes for so many friends and family on the side that I might as well open up my own business. I've been thinking about it, but with the wedding coming up, I'm going to wait awhile. I don't want to make too many changes at one time."

"What about you, Chris? Where do you work?" Lance asked.

I could no longer swallow the lettuce. I felt like my throat had closed. Desperate for a sip of water, I grabbed my glass, which collided with my soup. I must have hit it really hard because the fine bone china bowl cracked, causing the broth to leak through the broken china, down the tablecloth, and nearly onto Lance's lap. Lance stood up so quickly he knocked over his wine.

"I'm so sorry, Lance." So much for appearing poised at this elegant affair. Instead I felt like an uncoordinated elephant as I grabbed all the embroidered napkins from the table to clean up the mess I had created.

Amy, Stacy, and Lori, who had been comparing marriage proposals, shot up like rockets from their seats. Their first reaction was to check out their clothes to make sure the soup and wine hadn't drifted over to their outfits. "I think Jen wanted to test your reflexes," Chris said to Lance, while chuckling.

"Next time you want to see how fast I move, challenge me to a relay race instead, okay, Jenny," Lance said. Everyone laughed at my expense, of course.

After two waiters meticulously cleaned and dried the table, Lance once again turned his attention to Chris. "So what did you say you did?"

This time, I forced myself to swallow my salad and move slowly without making any abrupt movements.

"I'm an assistant manager at Big Al's Mini Mart," Chris said. "Hey, Howard, could you pass the bread."

"That's not your full-time job, is it?" Stacy gave Lance a nudge with her elbow, but he didn't notice.

"It is when I'm not cleaning pools. Hey, Tony, could you pass the butter?"

"Cleaning pools." Lance laughed. "Jen, your boyfriend has quite a sense of humor. So come on, what's the punch line?"

This time I wanted to knock the soup on Lance's lap. I felt bad for Chris, as everyone, including the women, stopped talking to hear his answer. Chris's profession was now even more interesting than wedding cakes and bridal bouquets.

"There's no punch line, pal. You asked where I worked and I told you. But from your expressions, you must have thought I said I robbed old ladies for a living because I can't imagine anyone would be that shocked to hear someone worked at a convenience store." Chris continued eating his salad, unphased by the seven sets of eyes upon him.

"Sorry, Chris. I thought you were kidding for a minute. So, uh…"

For once, Lance seemed speechless. He probably had never met anyone who hadn't graduated from an Ivy League school or wasn't destined to become a corporate executive or business entrepreneur. "I'm sure working at a mini mart is an interesting job." Lance seemed uncertain how to continue.

"As a matter of fact, it is." Chris said it with such forcefulness and certainty that nobody dared question him again. Chris continued eating while everyone else at the table looked uncomfortable.

When people finally resumed making idle conversation, I looked over at Chris, who winked at me. "You should try the Beef Wellington, Jen," he said. "It's great."

"Are you okay?" I asked, unsure how to read his thoughts.

"Of course, I am. I'm sitting next to you, aren't I." He placed one hand on my leg and his other hand around my shoulders, and for that moment, nothing else mattered.

After eating a full-course lunch, putting me way over my calorie allotment for the day, and watching Stacy and Lance open their presents for over an hour, I looked for Stacy to say good-bye. When I found her in the lobby, she was surrounded with guests, but as soon as she saw me, she excused herself and led me to a private room that was empty.

"I'm sorry about Lance's comments." Stacy said. "I forgot to tell him about Chris." She stood poised in her pointy, high heel, black silk pumps.

"You make it sound like he has a disease." I leaned against the wall, feeling tired from all the commotion about Chris today.

"That's not what I mean. Listen, Jen, I know you think I'm being a bitch about this whole thing, but I'm worried about you."

"You and my mother, it seems."

"I heard she gave Chris a tough time." Stacy sighed. "Look, there's no denying that Chris is a good-looking, charismatic guy who obviously adores you." Instead of smiling at these attributes, she looked concerned.

"So why isn't that enough?" So far, her description was enough to make anyone fall in love with Chris.

"Because it's not, and you know it. You're too smart not to see past all the other stuff. You come from totally different backgrounds and want totally different things out of life. Besides, he's too much of a free spirit for you. Jen, you get upset when they run out of your brand of orange juice!" She crossed her arms in front of her, continuing to stand up perfectly straight.

"People do change, you know. Maybe he needs to become a little more serious and I need to become a little more laid back. Just because he's had an unusual background doesn't mean he'll never settle down. What about all those actors who end up becoming insurance salesmen?" I grabbed a chair and sat down.

"Yeah, but most of them at least graduated from high school. Do you really want to spend your life supporting his carefree lifestyle?"

"Who said anything about spending my life with him?" I rubbed my temples, trying to stop my head from throbbing.

"I'm sure it's crossed your mind. When you get to be our age, you have to look at any boyfriend as a potential husband. Why would you waste your time with him if you didn't think he might be the one?"

"Because I love him." I was just as surprised as Stacy when I said it, but after the words left my mouth, I knew it was true. I loved him for who he was, not what he did or didn't do. But most importantly, I loved the person I was when I was with him.

"Wow. I didn't realize it had gone that far. I hope you know what you're doing. You don't want to waste your time with Mr. Wrong when you could be out meeting Mr. Right."

I thought about the day's events as we drove back to Chris's apartment. I had always believed that getting married was based entirely on falling in love, but now that I was in love, I still wasn't completely happy. All of the things that had always been so important to me like education, professional success, and stability were meaningless to Chris. Had I become so desperate to get married that I had talked myself into loving the first guy who showed any interest in me in over a year? Or had I been wrong about love being enough to seal the glue in a lifelong relationship?

How could someone so wrong be so right?

Chapter 10

Advanced Symptoms of
The Marriage Epidemic:

1. Mr. Wrong makes you feel happier than any guy you've dated.

2. Mr. Wrong makes you feel better about yourself than any guy you've dated.

3. You can no longer tell the difference between Mr. Wrong and Mr. Right.

I walked into Premier's front door carrying dental floss, toothpaste, and enough toothbrushes to distribute to the entire office. At any other type of business, this would be a strange way to come to work, but since I worked in advertising, these items could only mean one thing, namely a major dental account.

We had been awarded The Happy Tooth account the week after Stacy's engagement party, which had been a relief. I was so busy with this new campaign, I didn't have time to listen to my family and friends tell me all the reasons why I should forget about Chris. It also gave me some time to distance myself from Chris, who I barely got to see once a week for the past month.

I needed time to think about what I wanted and needed from a long-term relationship without listening to everyone else's advise. Unfortunately, I wasn't doing a very good job at coming to any conclusions.

As much as I loved being with Chris, was he really right for me? What if I eventually married him and realized that all of our differences made it impossible to have a happy life together? But what if I broke up with him and realized that I had let the only guy who ever made me happy slip away? I was terrified of making the wrong decision, but would I ever really know what that was until it was too late?

As I dropped a box filled with dental floss on my toe, I forced myself to focus on the account, which was difficult since I had only slept a total of four hours last night. I worked till almost three in the morning, which barely gave me enough time to go home before returning this morning for the big photo shoot that was taking place at a nearby studio.

The only reason I stopped in the office was that I needed Rhonda to photocopy a stack of marketing proposals for all of the clients attending the shoot. As usual, Rhonda was on a personal call when I stopped by her desk. I gave a loud cough, pretended to sneeze, and tapped my pen on her desk, trying to get her attention, but she was too busy giggling to notice.

Unlike me, Rhonda appeared well rested and quite animated. "You are so funny," she laughed into the receiver.

"Rhonda, I need you to make these copies right away," I finally said, feeling especially irritable from all the sleep deprivation during the past four weeks. "Rhonda?"

"Just a minute, Jen. Now what were you saying," she asked the caller, totally ignoring my request. I knew I wasn't a VP, but it would be nice if she respected me at least a little.

"Rhonda, now!" I screamed.

Not only did Rhonda's conversation come to a screeching halt, but Meany, who naturally had to be walking by at that precise second, looked at me with a surprised expression. Was it my imagination or was she smiling at me?

"Rhonda, why don't you end your conversation and help Jen out," Meaney said. "She's been working like crazy trying to wrap up this shoot."

"Well, then maybe she should tell her boyfriend to stop calling so much," Rhonda said, giving me her sweetest smile.

"My boyfriend?"

"That's right. Chris has been telling me the most hilarious story about two customers who came into his store this morning. Should I tell him you're too busy to talk?" Rhonda looked particularly pleased with herself.

Of all the people who could have been on the phone, why did it have to be Chris? And why did it have to be the first time I ever exploded at Rhonda? And why, oh why did it have to happen in front of Meany, who for the past two weeks had been preaching all the reasons why we couldn't waste a second of time during today's shoot?

Apparently, the studio was costing Premier a load of money.

Meany nodded at me while staring at her watch, as I told Rhonda that I'd have to call Chris back. After giving Rhonda the original proposals to copy, I snuck into an empty office and returned his call.

"Hi, stranger," he said when he heard my voice. "For a minute there, I thought you were falling for the Happy Tooth."

"I'm sorry, but Meany was standing right there so I couldn't talk." Just hearing Chris's voice made my heart skip a beat. So much for placing distance between us.

"Don't worry about it. I know you're busy. Rhonda's been giving me updates."

"Oh, please don't listen to her." I sat back in the chair that belonged to an account executive who was on sick leave.

"Why? She's very informative. Did you know your creative director is having a fling with your conference planner?"

"Joe? No way! He's married with five kids."

"That's why he's having the affair!"

Something had to be done about Rhonda if Chris was giving me gossip about my office. "Well, don't believe everything you hear, especially when you hear it from Rhonda."

"Then I guess I shouldn't believe all the great stuff she's been saying about you?"

"About me? Really? Rhonda?"

"Yeah. She really likes you. Last week she went on and on about how much time you spent booking the Happy Tooth for the campaign. She said nobody's ever gotten him to endorse a product before. Getting him for your ad must have been like extracting a tooth, if you'll pardon the pun."

We both laughed at his bad joke. "I guess it was, when you put it like that. Rhonda said that, huh?"

"Yeah, I think she looks at you as her mentor."

128

"No way." I placed my feet on the desk in front of me, thankful to have a few minutes away from work.

"Really. Maybe you should give her a chance. Have you ever sat down and talked to her? She's very nice."

I couldn't remember ever having a long conversation with her in all the years I worked at Premier. She was always so annoying that I tried to keep my distance, fearing that our talk would be rebroadcast over the intercom system.

And since when had Chris become so chummy with Rhonda? Chris, having never met her, probably had no idea what she was really like. Knowing Rhonda, she was probably trying to charm him away from me. I'd better keep my eye on her. "If you're getting a crush on her, I may have to stick The Happy Tooth on you," I said, enjoying the solitude of this empty office.

"Oh no. Not that! That guy looks pretty scary on TV with his fangs hanging out. I'm amazed he doesn't scare the kids."

"Believe me, if you met him, you wouldn't lose any sleep over him." I laughed, thinking about the small, scrawny man with acne who had become a national icon dressing up in a tooth costume every morning on PBS to sing songs about dental hygiene. Roger's Dental, Inc., had paid a bundle to lure the little runt into promoting its dental floss and toothpaste to kids in its national ad campaign, and I had spent a good part of two weeks convincing the arrogant little fang to appear in our print ads.

"So once this shoot's over, will we have more time together?"

"Yeah, things will calm down after today. Thanks for understanding about these crazy hours. I'm glad you still want to see me after all this."

"Hey, we've managed to squeeze in some quality time in between molars. Sorry, I couldn't resist. Last bad joke, I promise."

"I'm holding you to that," I said, laughing at his corny joke. "And seriously, I do appreciate you understanding about my crazy hours."

"Jen, I'm proud of you. You have an important job with lots of people counting on you. I would never make you feel bad about your hours, even though it would be nice to see you more. You're lucky you found a job you love so much. I care about you too much to ever ask you to give that up. Besides, I think what you do is really cool. I love hearing all your stories about the world of advertising."

I loved his support and interest in my job. Whenever we spoke, he wanted to hear every detail about my day.

I could easily spend hours discussing my job, but I knew people got bored listening to me after fifteen minutes or so. My few former boyfriends would listen politely and nod sporadically as I spoke, but I could tell that their minds wandered elsewhere.

And they never asked me the probing questions that Chris did. In fact, when I was trying to come up with an idea for the Happy Tooth campaign, Chris had wanted to brainstorm with me to really understand the creative process. Ironically, he helped me come up with the tag line that the client approved.

"So, how can I make it up to you for being so unavailable this past month?" I was really looking forward to spending some quality time with him.

"Let's see, last week I convinced you to go bowling even after you swore you'd make a fool out of yourself by throwing the ball down the wrong lane, and the week before I got you on ice skates for the first time. Now that you've become such a risk taker, how about trying something totally different this weekend?"

Every time we came back from another one of Chris's adventures I felt so great about myself that I was sure I could accomplish anything. Maybe that's what gave me the confidence to lure the Happy Tooth to sign a contract with us, a task that everyone told me was impossible. Chris had proven to me that anything was possible if you put your mind to it. "I admit, trying new things can be kind of exciting."

"That's the spirit. And with that thought in mind, I thought we'd take a hot air balloon ride this Saturday." I could hear the enthusiasm in his voice.

"Yeah, right." My heart raced just thinking about it. "And then we can go parachuting out of planes."

"That can be arranged, but I thought we'd start with something less challenging first."

I knew he was smiling while he spoke. "Please tell me you're joking," I said, feeling my hands begin to sweat. "You know I'm terrified of heights."

"I got you hiking up that hill last month, didn't I?"

"Yeah, but at least my feet were still on the ground." I removed my feet from the desk and planted them firmly on the floor.

"Well, how do you expect to ever get over your fear without facing it?"

By taking trains and buses everywhere I can? I knew Chris wouldn't understand that type of logic so I didn't try explaining it to him. "I thought renting a hot air balloon was expensive," I said. And I knew who would end up paying for it, based on our previous outings.

"That's the best part. We're going to ride for free. The cashier at work just told me his family owns a hot air balloon business in Allentown. He already arranged for our free balloon ride this weekend."

"Chris, there's no way you're getting me up in a balloon. It doesn't seem safe." My calm moment of solitude was becoming stressful. I got up from the chair and paced through the small office.

"If it weren't safe, it would be illegal. It's not like I'm asking you to go bungee jumping, unless, of course, you'd like to. Anyway, the cashier told me that his parents only hire FAA certified commercial hot air balloon pilots, and they all have lots of experience."

"How long would we be up in that thing?" I was beginning to feel nauseous.

"No more than an hour. Here's an idea. Why don't we take a drive to Allentown to check out the balloons. If you don't like what you see, we can go to the mall."

I couldn't help laughing at the image of Chris strolling through department stores on a Saturday afternoon. It was as crazy a concept as...as...well, I guess, as me taking a hot air balloon ride. Somehow I was the one who always ended up giving in, but not this time. I was not going up in a—"

Chris's singing interrupted my determined inner chatter. "Don't you want to fly in my beautiful, my beautiful balloon." Chris's voice was so loud I had to move my cell phone from my ear.

Unfortunately, this was when Rhonda opened the office door with my copies. "I was wondering where you were hiding." She handed me the copies without smiling. "Tell Chris he has a beautiful singing voice."

Oh sure, she liked me. Like a vulture liked her prey. "Listen, Chris, I've got to go or I'll miss the photo shoot."

"I'm not going to stop singing until you say yes."

I wondered what Chris's customers thought of his terrible rendition of the old Fifth Dimension song. "Ok, ok. I'll go for the drive, but I'm not going up in one of those things." It might be fun watching hot air balloons from the ground.

"That's all I ask. I'll take the R32 bus to your house so I can be there by four o'clock."

"Well, at least that will give me time to sleep in tomorrow." I stretched, feeling exhausted from the past few weeks.

"Sorry, Sleeping Beauty. I meant four o'clock in the morning. I have to work at night."

"Four o'clock in the morning? Why so early?"

"They only fly balloons at sunrise and sunset because the winds are lowest then. That means we need to be there by six o'clock. Come on, Jen. Where's your sense of adventure? Imagine how romantic it will be watching the sun rise together from one thousand feet in the sky. What better way to end the summer."

"I wish you hadn't mentioned how high they go. Besides, I told you I'm not going up." My heart raced faster.

"I'm going to start singing again."

I was about to argue my case again until I saw Rhonda lurking outside the office door. "All right," I whispered, "as long as you realize you might be taking that ride alone."

"We'll see," Chris said. I heard him humming the song as he put down the receiver.

After hanging up with Chris, I ran six blocks to the studio where Miles Oskerburger, aka the Happy Tooth, was about as happy as if he had just had root canal work done. The studio was too warm. His costume was too hot. Our gourmet breakfast was too bland, and the copy, which I had spent no less than two hundred hours writing and rewriting, was too dull.

Were all grown men dressed in children's costumes so difficult to get along with? I hated to think of Barney as a miserable old geezer when he took off his purple dinosaur head.

We put up with his complaints and demands for two hours until Meany stepped in when Miles refused to continue working unless he got a break every fifteen minutes. She pulled him aside so none of us heard what they said, but after a mere five minutes, the Happy Tooth miraculously looked happy. Apparently, Meany gave him the fluoride treatment that he so desperately needed.

She told Miles to take a ten-minute break, and while he was gone she called a brief meeting with all of us. "Here's what we're going to do to get through this shoot," she said with an air of authority that nobody dared question. "I want the air-conditioning cranked up as high as it goes.

"Beth," she said to our intern. "I want you to go to the grocery store and buy every flavor of Snapple you can find. Miles tells me it's his favorite drink. Every thirty minutes, I want you to deliver a different bottle to our happy tooth."

Directing her attention to Melissa, the production coordinator, Meaney said, "I want you to order Miles's lunch from Le Bec Fin. Get him whatever he wants." Of course, we all knew Le Bec Fin, one of Philly's finest French restaurants, was also one of the most expensive places to eat.

Next Meany looked at Jason, the production assistant. "Find a group of kids who love the Happy Tooth and invite them to the shoot. Have them make a big fuss over him in between takes."

"And Jen, Miles wants to approve all the collateral materials before he leaves since his photo will be all over them, so I need you to finalize the copy with all the product managers at Rogers Dental before the end of the day."

A half hour later when the shoot continued, I hoped the shiny white tooth costume would decay all over the little dweeb's body. For a mere ten thousand dollars, all he had to do was pose in front of three kids who cheerfully held up our client's toothbrush and toothpaste. Hell, for that kind of money, I was willing to jump into the hot costume and take his place.

While the Happy Tooth complained about the bright lights, I revised the ad copy *again*, reviewed a rough draft of the brochure with our clients, and made some last-minute changes to our direct response mailing, scheduled to go out the following week.

The day dragged on as Meany did everything but cartwheels to get the Happy Tooth to smile. The photographers looked like they wanted to break all of his teeth, along with some other body parts. It took twelve hours to finally get the shots we needed, and by the end of the day nobody looked very happy.

As I sat surrounded by toothpaste at eight o'clock at night, I realized that I had forgotten to brush my own teeth that morning. I doubted anybody had noticed, though. We were all too busy jumping every time Miles Oskerburger raised his gum.

I was ready to collapse as I watched the Happy Tooth whisked away by a stretch limo. While our photo shoot star had dined on Asparagus Risotto for lunch, I had grabbed a cheeseburger and fries from McDonald's that I never had time to eat. Even Meany looked drained as we prepared to leave.

While I packed up the toothbrushes and toothpaste, Meaney approached me, giving me a warm, spontaneous smile, unlike the frozen ones I was used to seeing. "You do good work, Jen," she said.

"Thanks." Meany giving out compliments was as unusual as the Happy Tooth doing stand-up.

"We never could have pulled off this shoot without you," Meany said, while helping me load hundreds of dental floss containers in a box. "Miles told me that the only reason he agreed to this endorsement in the first place was because he liked your writing style. I know it's hard to believe, but he really was happy with the way the shoot went, and he especially liked all of your copy. He approved everything with only a few minor changes."

"Really?" The Happy Tooth had been so miserable all day, I didn't think he liked anything about the campaign.

"Don't sound so surprised. You're a wonderful writer. I always know when someone's going to make a difference in this industry, and I can tell you're one of those few people who will. Mark my words, you'll go far in your career." Meany placed her arm around my shoulder and squeezed it before leaving the studio.

First a genuine smile and then a form of affection from Meany? This was a first. I hated to admit how much her words of encouragement meant to me, but knowing how respected she was in the industry, I realized that her compliments meant the world to me. I had to be doing something right for Meany to offer me so much praise.

For once, I felt really good about myself. The Happy Tooth wasn't the only one leaving happy tonight.

Chapter 11

How to Reduce Symptoms Associated with The Marriage Epidemic:

1. Avoid thinking too much about marriage by taking a hot air balloon ride.

2. If number one doesn't work, try sex and lots of it!

My afterglow from the Happy Tooth shoot faded the next morning when my alarm went off at three o'clock. I jumped into the shower to wake myself up, grabbed a low-fat, high fiber cereal bar, and waited for Chris, who showed up thirty minutes late.

It would have been nice if he arrived on time at least occasionally. The only way of guaranteeing that we got anywhere on time was for me to pick him up. "You could have called if you were going to be late," I said, opening my front door.

"That's a fine greeting after not seeing me for a week. Someone got up on the wrong side of the bed this morning." Chris held his hands behind his back.

"I thought we had to get our balloon by six." Maybe now we would be too late, I hoped.

"Don't worry. We'll make it. I know a shortcut, and besides, we won't hit any traffic at this time."

So much for that thought.

"I have something for you that will make up for it." He disclosed his right hand, which held an entire bouquet of daisies. "I got up extra early this morning to pick them for you."

"They're beautiful. Thank you." I smelled that familiar scent that I now associated with Chris.

"I have something else for you, too." His face lit up waiting for my reaction as his left hand reached out from behind him with a powdered jelly donut. Chris looked at me proudly, apparently pleased with his selection. "I ran into work as soon as I got up to get it for you," he said. "Good thing we're open twenty-four-seven. I know it's your favorite."

"Thanks," I said, taking a bite out of my gift. Okay, so it wasn't long-stemmed roses or emeralds, but then again this wouldn't be Chris if it were.

"Shall we go?" he said.

"Just give me a minute to put these in a vase." I left him by the door as I walked to my kitchen and grabbed a vase where I put the handful of daisies next to three other vases filled with the same flowers. I pulled a few weeds from the stems and returned to where Chris now stood in my living room.

"They're beautiful. Thank you," I said as I sneezed. I didn't have the heart to tell him I was allergic to them, and besides, I found myself looking forward to my daily dose of daisies. I reached up and kissed him lightly on the lips.

"Well, that's more the reaction I was hoping for." Chris immediately reciprocated until we were both out of breath. Breaking away, we looked longingly at each other, and I wasn't sure if we would make it out of my apartment. But Chris broke the spell by taking my hand in his and leading me to the door. "As much as I'd like to continue this, preferably in a horizontal position, we have a balloon to catch."

I groaned, partly because I wasn't ready to stop kissing him, and partly because I was petrified of where he was taking me.

"Jen." Chris's voice became deeper than usual and his eyes grew wide as he gazed directly into mine. "We'll continue this when we get back."

And as he escorted me out the door, I felt like I no longer had any control over my body. Somehow, I managed to lock my door, while listening to Randy and Lisa screaming from inside their apartment. I figured they were yelling at their bratty kids to go back to sleep.

I still felt like I was in a trance as we silently walked to my jeep. Once there, the fresh air seemed to break the spell as I watched Chris jump into the passenger side while I walked around to the driver's seat.

"Should I program the directions into my GPS?" I asked, still feeling hot from our kiss. "I've only been to Allentown once."

"No, I know the way. My stepfather lives there. Just take the Schuylkill Expressway to the Pennsylvania Turnpike. I'll give you the rest of the directions when we get closer. At this time of day, we should make it there in less than an hour."

I put on the air-conditioning and let it blow on my face before turning on my headlights and backing up. I breathed deeply, finally regaining my mental facilities to drive. "You never mentioned your stepfather before. Are your parents divorced?"

"Now there's the understatement of the year. Some people collect sports memorabilia. Others collect comic books. My mother collects husbands." There was an undertone of anger in Chris's voice.

"I'm sorry. How many times has your mother been married?" I squinted as the driver behind me turned on his high beams for some reason.

"Let's see. Father number one left us when I was six months old. I don't remember him at all. Father number two was an alcoholic who thought it was cool to beat up on my mom for kicks. We don't see him anymore either. Father number three, the one who lives near Allentown, decided he preferred the single life to marriage. I still get a greeting card from him once a year. And father number four went to jail for stealing. He should be out before the holidays."

"That's terrible." I wasn't used to hearing Chris sound so serious, and his smile was gone. He never talked about his personal life. Somehow finding out about his childhood made him seem more vulnerable and real. He had a past like everyone else, and apparently had been hurt many times. "That must have been rough on you growing up."

Chris shrugged. "I got used to it after a while. My brother and I made a game out of it. We would guess how long our mother's new marriage would last, and whoever came closest bought the other one a case of beer. Losing was hell, considering we were both under age. I used to wait outside of liquor stores until I spotted a guy who looked like he had already had a few too many. Then I'd give him a ridiculous excuse about leaving my driver's license at home while I slipped him an extra ten bucks. It worked like a charm."

"So are you and your brother close?" I asked, as I followed the signs for the expressway.

"Nah. As soon as he turned eighteen, he got as far away from my mother as possible. Last time I heard from him, he was living in New Mexico."

Next to Chris, my dysfunctional family seemed normal. "So when was the last time you saw him?"

"I don't know. Four, maybe five years ago. We still talk occasionally, but the only thing we have in common these days is our family, and neither one of us wants to reminisce about that topic."

I slowed down as I passed a cop, realizing I was driving too fast, but with so few cars on the rode, it was easy to get carried away. "Do either of you talk to your mother?"

"For a while, every time I moved she tracked me down, but I think she's finally given up. Hopefully, I've heard the last of her."

He was having trouble disguising his anger now, and I couldn't say I blamed him. As difficult as my mother and sister were at times, I always knew that they would be there for me if I needed them.

"I probably never would have become the adventure junkie I am today if it hadn't been for my lousy childhood." Chris looked out the window and stared at the darkness as I drove.

"Huh? What does that have to do with it?"

"Well, when you're growing up watching your stepfather beat up on your mother, and sometimes on you, you need to find someway to escape. I guess I could have tried drugs, but I didn't want to end up like one of my mother's ex-husbands, so I found my own thing." He continued staring out his window as if we were passing some spectacular sights. "I needed a way to forget about my problems, and what better way than diving to the bottom of the sea or jumping out of an airplane. When I'm climbing a mountain or flying down the huge slope of a roller coaster, there's no time to think about my miserable past."

"That makes sense." It made me look at Chris in a totally different way. He didn't thrive on adventure just for kicks; he did it to try to stop hurting, even if it only helped for a little while. I felt sad thinking about all that Chris had endured.

As if reading my thoughts, Chris said, "Don't worry about me. I turned out all right. Maybe I'll become a famous novelist someday when I write my memoir. I bet there are lots of people who would love to read about a poor kid who grew up with four fathers within ten years. I wouldn't be surprised if it made it to Oprah's Book Club."

Chris finally took his eyes off of the dark road, and I could tell that he wanted to transform himself back to his happy-go-lucky self. I wasn't about to push the subject. He had already disclosed plenty, and I felt closer to him having heard about his past.

Chris took a CD out of his denim coat pocket and handed it to me.

"What's this?" I asked.

"It's the greatest collection of campfire songs. I thought it would get your mind off of the balloon ride."

And your family, I thought.

Before long, I forgot about both as we sang "Ninety-Nine Bottles of Beer on the Wall" until we were hoarse. Forty-five minutes later, we pulled into the balloon rental site, singing "A Hunting We Will Go."

"Look at those beautiful balloons, Jen." Chris opened up his window and stuck his head out to see better.

I agreed they were spectacular, but I preferred admiring them from the low altitude of my car. Just watching people take off made me feel ill.

"You can't come all this way without riding in one of those babies."

"Chris, you promised!"

"And you promised you'd really think about it. Let's get out and look around."

I slowly followed Chris toward the balloons. By the time I caught up with him, he was talking to an older man with long gray hair and a matching long beard who looked like a member of the Grateful Dead. I would have preferred a younger, clean cut guy in charge of the object that might lift me off the ground.

I heard Chris explaining that he worked with Bill Walters, who had arranged a balloon ride for him and his girlfriend.

"Chris, I really don't want to do this," I whispered into his ear.

"My girlfriend's a little nervous about the balloon ride," he explained to the man who nodded without any emotion.

That was putting it mildly.

"Lots of people who are afraid of heights come here to conquer their fear," said the Jerry Garcia look-alike, who held a clipboard with nothing on it.

"Does it work?" I asked.

"Sometimes yes, and sometimes no."

His vague response didn't offer me the comfort I needed to get up in that balloon. I was hoping for more of a guarantee than that!

"If you'll wait here, I'll let your pilot know you've arrived," he said.

I paced for ten minutes until he returned with a much younger guy who he introduced as Larry Willard, our pilot. In contrast to the older hippie, this guy looked like a member of The Jonas Brothers. Was he actually old enough to fly a balloon? How many years of experience could he possibly have piloting balloons when it looked like he was barely old enough to drive a car?

"Larry here is one of our most experienced pilots," said the hippie owner.

I was afraid to see how old his inexperienced pilots were.

"Let's go," Chris said, assuming I would jump into the balloon after him.

A part of me really wanted to go up in that balloon. I had always wanted to ride in one. But even as I thought about it, I felt a sharp pain in my chest. What if I had a heart attack while we were up in the sky? Who would save me then?

"Chris, I'm still not sure about this. We don't even know where we'll land."

"None of us do until we're ready to take the balloon down," the young pilot said. "When your time's up, we'll choose a field free of crops or animals. The minivan behind you will be your chase vehicle. It will follow your balloon until you land."

How was this minivan on land going to chase our balloon in the air? Was I missing something here?

"What if we don't land, or we land in a busy highway?" I watched as people gathered in groups to wait for their balloon. Why didn't any of them look as nervous as me?

"Will you stop worrying, Jen," Chris said, staring at the sky with a look of excitement.

"Your boyfriend's right," Larry said. "You have nothing to worry about. Even though the wind dictates the direction and speed of your flight, I can alter the direction of the balloon simply by changing the altitude and finding a favorable wind."

I had to admit this young guy, who resembled Nick Jonas, seemed to know what he was talking about.

"See that, Jen," Chris said. "There's nothing to worry about. When can we go for our ride?" He rubbed his hands together, looking impatient to get our balloon.

"There's no time like the present," Larry answered. "Your balloon is in that canvas bag lying on that trailer, behind the basket."

"Do you mean the balloon that is going to keep me from falling to my death is rolled into that tiny bag?" I was beginning to hyperventilate.

"It has to be inflated first." Larry seemed amused by my reaction, but I had lost my sense of humor, and was afraid that any minute I was going to lose that jelly donut I had eaten.

Larry opened the balloon's basket for us to step inside. "Give me a few minutes to prepare your balloon and I'll come back for your flight," he said.

I wondered if I had time to scribble a will while we waited. Who would take care of Frisky if I died? I hadn't left enough food for him for more than a few hours.

"Chris, I don't think I can do this. Why don't you go and I'll wait for you here."

Chris stopped staring at the balloons to drink me in with his eyes. Once again, I got that feeling that we had left the real world and gone into our own. "I don't want to go without you," he said. "I admit, I thrive on the adventure part of these experiences, but since you've been coming with me, I don't want to do it alone anymore. Jen, I…"

I stared at him, sure he was going to say he loved me. I could see it on the tip of his lips, but he hesitated too long for it to reach his vocal chords.

"I…I want us to experience this together, and I know you'll be absolutely fine once we get up there," he said. "I promise, I'd never let anything happen to you."

Once again, I couldn't look Chris in the eyes and say no. It was like he put me in some kind of hypnotic state with his eyes and that damn sexy voice.

"Okay, I'll go." My voice was a little more than a whisper, but loud enough for Chris to hear. He rewarded me with a kiss that made my knees buckle.

A few minutes later Larry stepped into our basket, where we now both stood. He took his place behind the burner and like the operator of a machine gun, he gave a blast of flame. Within seconds, the flat lifeless mass of fabric began to breathe, rise up and expand until it finally took on the appearance of a hot air balloon. For a split second, I looked up inside the balloon. It resembled the inside of a giant cathedral. That was the last thing I saw because as soon as I felt my body rise, I shut my eyes.

"Open your eyes, Jen," Chris said. "You can see the most amazing view of farms below us." I felt Chris kiss my cheek. At least I assumed it was Chris and not Larry. "I promise I won't let anything happen to you while we're up here." Something about the way Chris spoke made me believe I would be okay. "Just open one eye and take a look."

I felt Chris take my hand as I very slowly opened one eye, and when I did, I felt completely sick to my stomach. I was going to die. I just knew it. Chris placed his arm around my waist to steady me. Good thing, because if he hadn't I probably would have fallen out. "It's you and me against the world, Jen, free of everyone and everything below us."

Now that we were floating through the sky, I could see how taking these adventures made Chris forget about his problems. I, too, liked the idea of being free and leaving all my problems back on the ground. Up here I didn't have to worry about Mr. Wong's vomit cookies or Sterling's foot fungus cream. There were no wedding invitations to respond to, and no Pampered Bride saleswoman giving away all her gourmet pastries.

I opened my other eye and peeked at the view. It was incredible! I could see fields for miles ahead. I couldn't believe I was up here.

"I think we just passed your apartment," Chris teased. "Being up here makes me feel great to be alive. Shall we dance?" He began leading me in a waltz.

"Are you crazy," I said, coming back to reality. "Don't shake the basket. We'll fall out."

"We're not going anywhere. Come on. You've gotten this far. Dance with me." Before I knew what was happening, Chris took me in his arms, while humming "Up, Up and Away, In My Beautiful Balloon." Chris slowly spun me around in the basket, thousands of miles above the ground.

"Don't you feel free?" Chris asked.

"I feel great!"

"Then say it, Jen. Say that you feel great."

"I feel great," I repeated.

"No, not like that. Really feel it and let the whole world know how you feel. Scream it to everyone in their comfortable little homes with their stuffy little picket fences below us. Tell them how you feel."

"I feel great!" I screamed the words, but who cared. Nobody could hear us, except Larry, who waved his hat to us.

"We're free, Jen. We're free."

While holding onto to each other, we screamed in unison, "I'm free!" After repeating the words dozens of times, I looked into the nearby clouds and held both my arms up toward the sky. I wanted to cherish these moments of freedom before our beautiful balloon took us back to the realities of life.

I'm not sure whether it was the fresh air, the high altitude, or the feeling of being totally uninhibited on the balloon ride, but as soon as Chris and I got back to my apartment we practically tore off each other's clothes. To hell with a high school diploma! To hell with responsibility! I wanted him, and I wanted him now.

It was hard to start off slow when we were both so charged from the day. Not to mention, we had waited so long for this moment. Instead of light kisses, our tongues probed deeply inside of each other's mouths. Instead of slowly exploring each other's bodies, Chris sucked on my breasts. I felt out of control as I searched for his penis, wanting to feel its hardness. Before long, I stroked it with my hands and licked it with my tongue, wanting more, always wanting more.

While usually shy in bed, especially the first time with a new boyfriend, I would have hung from a chandelier if Chris asked me to. In between sucking on my breasts, he nibbled on my shoulders, my arms, ultimately traveling downward until he reached the place that longed for him the most. My entire body sizzled as Chris came down between my legs with his mouth. I was ready to explode, but Chris continued teasing me with his tongue until I couldn't take it anymore.

"Now!" I cried.

He placed a condom on with ease, and within seconds I felt that wonderful sensation of pure joy flow through my entire body. We both moaned as our bodies quivered and the final climax raced through our bodies.

Was it possible that I had two orgasms? And so quickly? I was usually lucky if I had one. Two hours later, just to make sure, we tried it again, this time in the living room. Yeah, it was definitely two. We were like rabbits in heat as we went for a third time later in the afternoon, this time in the kitchen.

Chris never uttered the "L" word, but if he had, I would have told him that I loved him, too. Without planning to, or even wanting to, I had given my heart to Chris.

Late that night when Chris returned to my apartment after work, I snuggled into his warm body, glad to have another male in my life besides Frisky. I felt so happy and fulfilled, I was sure I would sleep soundly throughout the night.

—But I was wrong. Every time I fell asleep I was disturbed by a recurring nightmare. I dreamed that I was floating in a hot air balloon with Chris, feeling light and free when suddenly my mother and Stacy appeared from behind a cloud with a huge pair of scissors. Shaking their head at me in disapproval, they slashed the balloon, causing me to fall from the sky toward the ground. Just as I was about to hit the ground, the earth magically opened to expose a large bottomless hole. I kept falling into the eternal abyss until I woke up the next morning to Chris's soft lips on my face.

Chapter 12

False Negative Scores: You Mistakenly Think You're Cured When:

1. You confuse good sex with love.
2. You assume every happy couple ends up like Mike and Carol Brady.

A weekend of sex was just what the doctor ordered to make my recurring nightmare go away. After trying out the kitchen table and the walk-in closet, I finally lived out my fantasy of making love in my brand-new Jacuzzi.

Whether it was all the orgasms, the high altitude from the balloon ride or simply Meany's recognition for my work, by Monday morning I was on a high. For once, everything was going my way, and I felt pretty good.

When I saw Randy and his tribe opening their door the same time I opened mine to leave for work, I decided to be neighborly. After all, they did live next door, and they had come by several months ago to introduce themselves. So what if their son had ruined my new sandals. It's not like he did it on purpose.

"Hi," I said. Randy sure looked good in his navy suit, unlike Lisa, whose blouse wasn't even tucked into her pants. Randy held a brown leather briefcase, while Lisa had a duffle bag so full of junk that she had to bend over three times to pick up fallen items. I wondered where they worked. I waved as I locked my door, but my friendly neighbors didn't seem very neighborly this morning.

"Hey," Randy said so quietly I barely heard him. He glanced at me as if he wanted to say more, but his darling wife nudged him with her elbow while giving him a dirty look. After that, Randy avoided eye contact with me as he picked up the infant carrier.

What was their problem? He and Lisa yawned, while Josh cried and Jessica threatened to scream during the entire car ride to preschool if Lisa didn't buy her a chocolate chip cookie for breakfast. Maybe they were tired again? I was tired just listening to their children. Being in the jovial mood I was in, I decided to try again.

"Did Josh keep you up again last night?" I noticed the dark circles under Randy's eyes.

"Not exactly," Randy said, still avoiding eye contact with me as the unhappy foursome walked past me. The only one who looked at me was Josh, possibly trying to assess the damage he had done to my shoes.

This was hardly the Mr. Rogers greeting I was hoping to receive. Talk about waking up on the wrong side of the bed! Was this family always in such a bad mood first thing in the morning? If so, I was glad I'd never run into them on my way to work.

"Where's your boyfriend?" Lisa asked, with the same look that Frisky got when he was ready to let out his claws and pounce on a field mouse.

Why was she asking about Chris? It's not like I'd ever introduced them, and I couldn't remember running into them while I was with him.

But judging by the look on Lisa's face, Chris was not one of her favorite people. Had she met him at the pool? Maybe the baby pool hadn't been clean enough for her precious baby's bottom.

"He went home," I answered, not sure why I felt a need to respond.

"Too bad. From the sounds coming from your apartment the past two days, I'd say you had a great weekend."

Those damn thin walls! This was worse than being caught singing sitcom openings.

As the elevator opened, Lisa said, loud enough for the entire second floor to hear, "I wish people in this building were more considerate and remembered that there are children living here. It's not like there aren't hotels nearby." Lisa dragged Jessica onto the elevator, followed by Randy lugging Josh inside.

I wanted to tell Miss Prim and Proper Lisa that there were also apartment complexes that catered to families with small children. I wanted to tell her that maybe her little monsters would learn to sleep if she didn't make the whole world tiptoe around them all the time. I wanted to tell her to shove her duffle bag up her ass, but just my luck, the elevator door closed before I had a chance to say anything.

I was sure my face was as red as the apple I carried inside my thermal lunch bag as I walked down the hall to the elevator. Of course, I had nothing to be embarrassed about. It wasn't like I was doing it with a total stranger outside in broad daylight. Surely, Randy and Lisa remembered what it was like to be young and single.

Come to think of it, they were still young. They couldn't have been more than a few years older than me. What happened when they had sex in their apartment? Didn't that wake up their tiny insomniacs? For the first time since I moved, I missed my old apartment filled with senior citizens who turned off their hearing aids by eight o'clock at night.

⁓

I was still feeling bad about my run-in with my neighbors when I got to work. How was I ever going to face them again? Of course, they were way out of line if they expected me to moan quietly during the heat of the moment in my own home, but unfortunately, I still had to live next door to them. Every time I saw them from now on, I'd imagine them imagining me rolling around my apartment naked, performing all kinds of lewd, sexual acts. Judging from the way they looked at me, or didn't look at me, they must have thought I was some sort of slut. If only they knew.

I was glad to put Randy, Lisa, and their obnoxious kids behind me when Rhonda pranced up to me as I walked into Premier's lobby. "Did you hear the news yet?" she said, obviously glad to have an audience.

I imagined someone else had either gotten engaged or pregnant. After all, it had been at least two weeks since our last bridal shower. "What news?" I looked around to see who had a shiny new diamond or the beginning of a big belly.

"Meany gave notice."

"She what?" A few people from the accounting department gathered around us to listen to Rhonda's news.

"You'll never guess where she's going to work." A small crowd of production assistants and coordinators also stopped to listen, and from the glee on Rhonda's face, it was obvious she was loving every minute. Other than the occasional beep from the elevator, the reception area remained silent.

"Where she's going?" I asked, hating having to grovel for details.

"Richardson and Whitaker hired her as their new VP of account services."

"You're kidding." Richardson and Whitaker happened to be the number one advertising agency in the country. It was also the oldest, most prestigious agency on Madison Avenue.

"So she's moving back to New York?"

"She already found a place in Manhattan." The silence was broken as everyone started talking at once about Meany's departure. By the smiles and excitement that filled the room, it was obvious Meany wouldn't be missed. I was surprised people didn't start handing out cigars to celebrate.

"What did John say?" I asked, ignoring the elation in the room.

"The usual thing he says whenever someone quits to go to the competition. He told her to empty her desk and leave by noon." Rhonda glanced around, looking disappointed that I was the only one still listening to her.

"You mean she's leaving today?" I couldn't believe my reaction, but I didn't want her to go. And it wasn't just because she had finally complimented my work for the first time, though I admitted, that had been very gratifying. It was more because Meany had become the heart of Premier since she arrived from a small Madison Avenue agency five years ago.

Of course, I still hated making revisions twenty times until Meany finally approved my copy, and naturally, I resented her for insisting that I be nothing less than perfect for her clients, but when it came down to it, Meany's high expectations of all of us forced us to work up to our true potential. Meany wouldn't let any of us slide, even for a second, to produce anything less than the best that we could create. Without Meany's guidance, I bet I never would have reached the level of writing that I was now capable of achieving.

"I knew you, of all people, would be thrilled to see her go," Rhonda continued, oblivious to my emotions. "She's worked you like a dog since the day she came. Maybe now you'll finally be able to let your guard down a little."

"Yeah, I guess." How could I explain to Rhonda that I wasn't sure I wanted to let down my guard? And what would happen to Premier if we all let down our guard?

I slowly walked to Meany's office, not sure what to say. Her office was across the hall from mine, right past the cubicles, so I didn't have much time to sort out my thoughts.

It was strange that after spending so many hours together in her office and even traveling together to visit clients, I knew very little about Meany's personal life. All of our conversations had always revolved around work issues. All I knew about Meany was that when she was about my age she had been married for a short time. As far as I knew, she never had children.

When I got to her office, her door was wide open. "Hi, Ilene," I said, still standing in the hallway. It felt unnatural calling her by her first name. I had gotten so used to referring to her as Meany, that I rarely addressed her by name, afraid that my nickname for her would come out by accident.

"Hi, Jen. Come on in."

I walked past her boxes of reference books and dictionaries, and felt a tugging feeling at my heart as I saw her easel and pointer stacked up on top of her boxes. "I came to say 'bye. I'm sorry you're leaving."

Meany put down a box of coffee mugs and scribbled something on a post-it note. "I was planning on coming by before I left. It's been a real pleasure working with you, Jen."

"It's been great working with you, too, but it sounds like you've got a great job waiting for you in New York." Her desk was already empty and her bookshelves were just half full.

"I wasn't planning to leave, but sometimes 'life is what happens to you while you are busy making other plans,' as John Lennon once said."

How come I was still waiting for life to happen to me? I made plenty of plans!

"The woman I used to work for at my last job just got hired as the CEO at Richardson and Whitaker," Meany continued. "She called me last week to offer me the VP position. I wasn't sure I wanted to go back

149

to New York, but it was too good an opportunity to let go. I know I would have regretted it if I turned it down."

She handed me the pink post-it note, which consisted of a phone number with a New York area code. "This is my new office phone number," Meany explained. "Make sure you keep in touch. You never know when a writer's position will come up at Richardson and Whitaker."

Was she insinuating that she would recommend me for a job at her new agency? Had she heard that one of the writers was leaving? I couldn't even imagine working at such an impressive ad agency, but maybe Meany would open the door for me, if that was what she was saying.

If things actually worked out between Chris and me, I bet he would move with me so I could be closer to work. He didn't seem to have any problems packing up and moving on.

I was dying to ask Meany what she meant, but I never got the chance. As usual, Meany had to be the one to begin and end every conversation, and as she turned her back to continue packing, I knew that she had just finished ours.

Before leaving Meany's office for the last time, I watched her tape up a box filled with markers and chalk. As she sealed the box, I felt like a part of Premier Advertising had just died.

I didn't feel very motivated to work after Meany left. Even the great photos from the Happy Tooth shoot didn't cheer me up so I told John I wasn't feeling well and left early.

Fortunately, Chris had the day off, so I called him from my cell phone to let him know I'd be by earlier than planned. We had already decided to go to the Pennsylvania State Fair that evening, but all I really cared about was seeing Chris.

I didn't even let the blind person playing the drums outside Chris's apartment upset me, and as I stepped over a roach to knock on his door, I just wanted to fall into his arms and tell him all about my day. I knew he'd listen carefully to everything I said, and understand exactly how I felt. For a guy, he had great empathy for my feelings.

I also wanted his interpretation of Meany's pre-job offer. I still wasn't sure if I should get my hopes up for a job that might never materialize.

As soon as Chris opened the door, I relayed my entire day's events, beginning with my neighbors' complaints about our lovemaking and ending with Meany's departure. I took off my shoes and put my feet on Chris's ripped ottoman. It was amazing how comfortable I had become with Chris after less than four months.

Chris sat across from me without saying anything. I loved how he let me talk, making sure he heard everything I said before offering me his opinion or advice. But when I finished, he was still silent. Had I said something to offend him? Did my feet smell? Or maybe he was upset about me moving to New York?

"Is something wrong?" I became worried when Chris continued to sit there without speaking.

"Chris, what's going on?" Had he decided that I wasn't experienced enough for him in bed? I did have a little trouble maneuvering myself in the Jacuzzi.

"Look, Jen. You obviously had a stressful day, so maybe we should talk about this later."

Oh sure. I was going to spend the rest of the day riding roller coasters with him, unsure whether he was going to break up with me. But why after this weekend, of all times? Maybe I was really bad in bed. "I want to know now. Did I do something to upset you?"

Without saying anything, he handed me a crumpled piece of paper. "I found this under my sofa cushion today."

I opened the paper to see my own handwriting. It was the phone number from the Goodman Technical School that I had copied from that GED commercial. "Is this why you're upset?"

"Uh, *yeah*," he said, dragging out his last word. "I thought you understood that I didn't want any part of school."

"I do, but this place helps you get your GED in a few weeks. You'd only be in school for a really short time, and then you could get a better job, if you wanted to."

Chris got up and paced back and forth between his stack of empty beer cans and his pile of dirty laundry. "I feel like you're trying to change me, and I don't want to change. I like me the way I am, and I thought you did, too."

"I do." Okay, that wasn't exactly true, but I was suddenly scared of losing Chris, and I wasn't ready to let go, not yet anyway.

"I'm not so sure about that." Chris's jaw tightened. "I spent all day thinking about us. I remembered how you lied about my job to your mother and how you didn't want to take me to Stacy's engagement party. Can you honestly look me in the eyes and tell me you like me the way that I am, or are you planning to change me into one of those professional geeks who your friends are marrying?"

This time I sat silently. I didn't have a black or white answer. Of course, I didn't care if he worked on Wall Street so I could live in a single home with maids. But I'd be lying if I told him that his lack of education and motivation didn't bother me. Would he understand that my answer fell into some large gray area?

"Don't you believe in compromise?" I finally answered.

"Sure, I'm glad to find a happy medium for lots of issues, like if you preferred a red carpet to a blue one, I'd be the first one to suggest an orange one. And if you absolutely hated the smell of peanut butter, I just wouldn't eat it when I was with you.

"I think I'm pretty easy to get along with, but I'm not talking about small compromises, and I don't think you are either." He continued walking back and forth through his small apartment like a caged animal. "I'm afraid that you want me to compromise my values and beliefs, and I just can't do that."

I knew he was right. When it came down to it, our core set of beliefs were so different that it seemed impossible to find any way to bridge the gap, but I still didn't want to lose him. One of the reasons I loved Chris so much was because he was so different.

"Chris, just because we're different doesn't mean we can't be happy together." I got up and tried to take his hand, but he pulled it away before I could reach it and continued walking.

"I totally agree with that, but I hope you understand that I won't let you change me. I am what I am."

"I understand." And for the first time, I really did. There was no compromising with Chris. Either I accepted him exactly the way he was, or I left. Any fantasies I had about him eventually becoming more settled or more career-oriented were just delusions.

Then I became angry because Chris didn't care what I wanted or needed. If he really loved me, wouldn't he be willing to work toward a compromise that we could both live with?

Maybe that was the problem. Maybe he didn't love me. Even though it felt like he did by the way he looked at me, he still hadn't told me how he felt about me.

For some crazy reason, I always believed anyone I had sex with loved me.

It must have been my way of rationalizing becoming so intimate with someone. Or maybe it was because I wanted a guy to fall so desperately in love with me that he would do whatever he could to make me happy?

"So what's it going to be?" Chris asked without any emotion in his voice. He seemed so matter-of-fact about the whole thing, as if he were asking whether I wanted two or three sugars in my coffee.

"I promise that I won't try to change you. I like you the way you are." And I did, in many ways.

"You're sure the next time I check under my sofa cushion I won't find a phone number for a headhunter." He finally stopped pacing.

"I promise." I sat back down on his sofa, feeling drained from the conversation.

"Or a classified ad for a new job?"

"You have my word."

"Or a winning lottery ticket?"

"What?"

"Just checking to see if you were paying attention." At last, Chris's voice sounded somewhat animated, and as usual, I couldn't help laughing.

"Okay then." Chris's face seemed to relax and he had the beginning of a smile on his face. "Why don't we go to the fair and forget about all this for a while."

Before I could speak, Chris kissed me deeply on the lips, hugging me so close that I could feel his heartbeat. I wrapped my arms around his back as if I were holding on to a life preserver.

"Come on," he said, grabbing my shoes. "We have a Ferris wheel waiting for us."

As we walked hand in hand through the fair grounds, Chris asked me lots of questions about Meany. I was glad to be talking about something besides our relationship.

"It sounds like she's really interested," he finally said. "If I were you, I'd keep calling her. Make sure to send her holiday and birthday cards. Don't let her forget about you, even for a minute."

"I don't want to make a pest of myself, especially if she was just being nice by mentioning a possible job."

"Are you kidding? High-powered, controlling women never say anything just to be nice. Believe me, I've worked for enough of them to know. If she mentioned a job, she wants you."

That had been my initial reaction, too, but hearing Chris say it made it seem more believable. It was hard to conceive that someone like Meany would think that highly of me.

"How about some cotton candy, my treat," Chris said. Chris was always good about paying for the inexpensive stuff like a can of soda or a game of air hockey at the arcade. I seemed to be in charge of the larger ticket items, like dinners and nightclubs. Lately, Chris always seemed to be short of cash, and without realizing it, I had begun paying for most of our outings.

Is this really what I wanted for myself? Was it too much to ask for my boyfriend to spring for a movie from time to time?

I am what I am! I am what I am! Over and over throughout the evening, I heard Chris's declaration of independence. It was like a loud echo between my ears that wouldn't stop.

"There's a petting zoo over in that barn," Chris said, returning with a small cotton candy. "Want to check it out?"

"Sure." We walked silently to the barn. Even after Chris's intense kiss back at his apartment, things still felt tense between us.

As we entered the barn, a woman dressed in a long white bridal gown walked past us. She continued walking toward a vacant tent with her gown trailing behind her in the dirt. "That's weird," Chris said. "It's not everyday you see a bride walking past pig shit, although it would certainly be appropriate."

I wasn't thrilled with his analogy, but I hoped he was making one of his corny jokes. "I read something about a wedding taking place here," I said. "The article said that the couple decided to get married at the fair because the groom proposed here two years ago on the Ferris wheel. It is kind of romantic, if you think about it."

"I'll try not to," Chris said, as we entered the barn. "Hey, take a look at that! Have you ever seen such a large cow before. It almost looks like a bull."

But I wasn't looking at the cow. "What exactly is it you try not to think about?"

"Huh?" He was busy feeding that damn cow pellets from a food dispenser.

"You said you try not to think about it. What don't you like to think about?"

"Oh, that." He patted the cow on his head. "Marriage. After living with my mother, I've seen enough marriages to last me a lifetime."

"So you're saying that you never want to get married?" I couldn't believe it. I knew Chris was unsettled, but I assumed he would eventually want to get married. But then I remembered that I couldn't assume anything about what Chris would do. He was what he was. Again, his words echoed in my head like a mantra.

"I wouldn't say never, but if I do, it's not going to happen for a long time."

"And what exactly is a long time?" I didn't want to sound like a nagging girlfriend, but didn't I have a right to know if my boyfriend had a hang-up about marriage?

"I don't know, Jen. Ten, maybe twenty years, who can say?"

You can, I wanted to scream in his ears, but I knew it wouldn't do any good.

Chris finally turned away from the cow. "I suppose you want to get married like all your friends."

Was that so terrible? I mean, it didn't have to happen right away. But it would be nice to know if I'd still be young enough to have children before Chris got around to popping the question. The way he was talking, I'd be living in an assisted living home before he handed me a ring. "Yes, Chris. I do. I'm not trying to rush you down the aisle today, or even this year. But I would like to know that if things work out between us that eventually we would get married."

"I don't understand why so many women want to get married. Believe me, from what I've seen it's way overrated. What's wrong with just living together?"

"Nothing, if that's what you want. But I do believe in marriage and commitment and everything else that goes along with it."

"But I am committed to you. Why do I need to give you a ring to prove that to you?"

"Because you just do." I couldn't think of anything profound to add. I guess I was who I was, too. And the person I was wanted marriage and stability.

"I see." Chris gave the cow the rest of the pellets. "Then I guess there's nothing else to say."

"I guess not." There were lots of things about Chris that I might have overlooked, but marriage wasn't one of them. I wanted it too badly to accept Chris's unacceptance of it.

And so we stood at the barn for what seemed like hours, but was probably only minutes, staring at that mammoth cow who seemed pleased to have Chris by his side.

"I really did love you, Jen," Chris said, petting the cow instead of taking my hand.

Oh sure, now he said it. Too bad it was in the past tense.

"I loved you, too," I said, feeling the first of many tears fall down my cheek.

When Chris turned toward me, I thought I detected a tear in his eye, but I wasn't sure. "I'm obviously not the guy you're looking for, Jen. I wish I was, but I know that I'll never make you happy. You want a lot more than I can give you."

I knew this wasn't entirely true. He was capable of giving me a lot of what I wanted, but he chose not to. He could have changed, compromised, met me halfway. But then, I guess, he wouldn't have been Chris.

"I guess you better drive me home," Chris said. For a moment, I felt like someone had super-glued my feet to the ground because I couldn't move.

And then I felt a familiar liquid warming my feet. It was the same feeling I had experienced when Josh barfed all over my shoes. When I looked down, I discovered that this time my feet were covered in cow pee. I couldn't believe that one cow held so much fluid, but its bladder was apparently as massive as the rest of him because clear fluid flowed from him like a hose.

At any other time, Chris would have found this incident to be hilarious. His new-found friend's lack of bladder control would have provided him with enough comic material to make jokes the rest of the night.

But as Chris looked down to see my feet submerged in urine, he said nothing. That's when I knew that our relationship was really over.

Chapter 13

Overcoming Setbacks:

1. When the love of your life no longer loves you, find a designated driver and head for the closest bar.

2. Seek out support people, preferably other single females, who have had more relationship failures than you.

3. Beware of married couples who use you as a pawn to play matchmaking games.

"Typical male asshole," Tiffany said, taking a drink from her third beer at Tina's Bar in Chestnut Hill.

"At least you found out now that he was against marriage," Marisa said, sipping a Sea Breeze. "You could have dated him a lot longer before he told you."

"I guess," I said, taking my second shot of tequila. I needed something to numb the pain I still felt after dropping Chris off at his dilapidated apartment for the last time.

It was even harder returning to my apartment where everything reminded me of him. Just walking through my parking lot made me remember how he had rescued my mop the first day we met. When I turned the key to my apartment I wanted to scream so Lisa and Randy would hear that there wouldn't be anymore moaning coming from this apartment for a long time. That ought to give that pesky Jessica a few questions to ask.

Walking inside my place was the worst because it still smelled like Chris. I hadn't even put the chairs back up from where they fell when we pulled each other's clothes off under the kitchen table. Next to my nightstand, I found a package of Chris's Marlboro Lights, and in my bathroom I found one of his razors. These small tokens were simply memories of yet another broken relationship.

For some reason, this breakup seemed harder to accept. At first, I thought it was because I was older this time. But then I realized that this relationship had been a lot more intense than the others. I had lost control of my feelings too fast this time, and I was paying the price.

The second shot didn't dull my pain so I ordered another one and then another. "Easy, Jen. Remember, you have to be at work tomorrow," Tiffany said. We usually didn't go out on Sunday nights, but it had taken me a day to get out of bed, and another few hours to find the energy to call Tiffany and Marisa.

"Who cares," I said. I knew I was slurring my words, but it didn't matter. Nothing did. "Maybe I shouldn't have pushed the topic of marriage. We had only been dating a short time. I should have just waited until he was so in love with me that he would do anything to avoid losing me." I put my head against the corner booth where we sat.

"But what if he didn't?" Marisa asked. "Imagine finding out when you were thirty-five that he still didn't want to get married." She looked horrified at the thought.

"It doesn't sound like marriage was the only issue that did you in." Tiffany took a drag of her cigarette and blew it out away from where we sat. "Any guy who can't afford to pay for a movie shouldn't be dating."

"Tif's right, Jen. There were too many problems."

Of course, they were both right, but that didn't stop my heart from throbbing. For the first time, I truly understood the definition of heartache.

"You know what you have to do now," Tiffany said. "You need to look around this room, find a guy, and get laid. Breakup sex always helps." She gazed around the smoky bar, as if trying to find the perfect guy for me to have sex with tonight.

"I don't think so." I couldn't be that close to anyone right now. It was too soon.

"Even if you're not up for sex, why not look around anyway." Marisa certainly hadn't stopped looking around since we walked in. "You know what they say about getting back on that horse again after you fall off."

"Whoever said that must not have fallen as hard as me."

"Trust me, Jen. We've all taken that fall," Tiffany said, while puffing smoke into the air. "I think Marisa's right. Brush yourself off and get out there again. But this time, you take control of the saddle. Make this guy your transitional boyfriend. Everyone needs a transitional boyfriend between breakups. That way, you call the shots and you break it off when you're ready."

But I didn't want breakup sex or a transitional boyfriend. I wanted the real thing.

"Oh my God!" Marisa screamed, practically flying out of her seat.

"What's wrong?" We both jumped up, reminding me of all the times I had run out of bars being raided when I was underage.

"It's him." Marisa's eyes were larger than I'd ever seen them.

"Who? Chris?" If he was already with another girl, I swore I would spill every last shot of tequila over his head. Had he already found his transitional girlfriend?

"No, not Chris, Zack!" Marisa shrieked.

"Well, go tell him to screw himself," Tiffany said as she banged her beer bottle on the table.

"Which one is he?" I was so relieved that it wasn't Chris that I took a few minutes off between shots. I was also curious to see the mysterious Zack.

"That's him, in the red polo shirt."

He looked like he could have been Marisa's twin brother with the same big brown eyes, full round face, even the same rimless glasses. His eyes lit up when he saw Marisa.

"He's coming over," she beamed. "Do I look okay?" She whipped out a cosmetic mirror to take a quick look.

"Marisa, get real," Tiffany said. "The guy blew you off months ago. If he did it once, he'll do it again. Don't waste your time with him."

But as Zack approached our booth, Marisa smiled widely at him, ignoring Tiffany's advice. "You're a hard person to find," he said, smiling equally as wide as Marisa.

"What do you mean?" Marisa sounded out of breath as she spoke.

I wished Marisa would play it a little cooler instead of practically drooling over his every word. But I had to admit, Zack was looking at Marisa as if he had just found a lost treasure.

"The night after we met, the consulting firm I work for sent me to an emergency meeting in Detroit." Zack wasn't nearly as quiet as Marisa, but he was soft spoken. "I got stuck there for over a week and when I got back I couldn't find your phone number. I could have sworn I put it in my pocket, but it wasn't there."

"Oh, great, the old I couldn't find your phone number line," Tiffany whispered to me.

"I remembered your last name," he continued, "but when I called information they said your number was marked private. Then I tried to remember where you worked, but I couldn't think of the name. I even went back to the Flamingo Club where we met, hoping to see you again."

"Really? You did all that to find me?"

Okay, I admitted, the guy sounded sincere, but there was no need for Marisa to bat her eyelashes every time he spoke. It was entirely possible that he had met another girl, broken up with her, and now wanted to try his luck with option two.

"I hope you didn't meet anyone since we met." He looked concerned. "I would hate to have lost my chance."

"No, I haven't met anyone," Marisa gushed.

"Great, then can I buy you a drink to make up for losing your number?"

Marisa resembled a jack-in-the-box as she bolted out of her seat to walk toward the bar with Zack.

"So much for playing hard to get," Tiffany said.

"No kidding. You'd think she would have learned by now." But then again, who was I to offer advice about men? My tactics hadn't gotten me anywhere either. And with that thought, I finished another shot.

A few minutes later a tall guy wearing multiple earrings asked Tiffany to dance. I encouraged her to go, even though she seemed hesitant to leave me and my shots of tequila alone.

I sat at my booth watching girls staring at guys, making it quite obvious that they wanted their attention. Some of the guys eventually caught on and asked them to dance. Later on, some of them took out pens, most likely to write down their phone numbers.

And where would it get everyone? Would the guys actually call? And then what? Would they all go off and live happily ever after, or would the girls end up alone at the back of some bar surrounded with tequila?

I woke up the next day depressed and hung over, a lethal combination, especially when I heard someone knocking on my door before I had my first cup of coffee. Could it be Chris? Maybe he realized how much I meant to him and was willing to meet me halfway on some of our differences, particularly his viewpoint on marriage.

"Who is it?" I shouted toward the door, not having the energy to walk all the way through my living room to look in the peephole.

"It's me," Stacy shouted from the other side of the door.

I dragged my body across my floor and opened the door to see Stacy's smiling face. "I have a client meeting around the corner so I thought I'd surprise you."

"Great." This wasn't the surprise I was hoping for. Without returning her smile, I left her standing in my living room, while I headed to the kitchen for an aspirin and a chocolate éclair. I had bought both at an all-night convenience store on my way home last night. The fact that I had lost five pounds since I met Chris obviously hadn't motivated him enough to want me, regardless of some sacrifices he might have to make for our relationship to work. So why bother dieting? I bit into the cream-filled pastry while Stacy caught up with me.

"What's wrong, Jen? Uh-oh. You're eating again. That's never a good sign."

"Chris and I broke up on Friday." I didn't bother blotting the cream off of my lips.

"I'm sorry." She sat down at the table, giving me a knowing look without actually saying I told you so. "I know how much you cared about him, but I'm not surprised."

"Why do you say that?" I noticed Stacy's black duffle bag bulging with this month's bridal magazines. Just what I felt like looking at.

"I knew that as much as you liked him you'd realize eventually that he wasn't right for you. How did he take it?"

Funny, how she automatically assumed that I dumped him. "It was more like a mutual break up." I sighed. "Want some coffee?"

"Yeah, thanks. It feels like old times, coming by before work again," Stacy said, making herself at home by pouring a glass of orange juice and grabbing a bagel from the bread basket in front of us.

I didn't think so. Those were pre-Chris days and pre-Stacy engagement days. A lot had changed since then.

"So what made the two of you break up?"

As I munched on my éclair, I told her all the gory details beginning with that damn GED phone number and ending with the cow pee on my shoe.

"You deserve someone much better than him, Jen. You have so much more to offer him than he could ever give you. I know you probably feel like shit right now, but I bet in a few months, you'll look back at Chris and wonder how you ever got involved with him."

I knew she was trying to make me feel better, but it wasn't working. As my best friend, I wanted her to understand why I had loved him so she'd realize how much I was hurting right now. But she just didn't get it.

"What's up with you?" I asked. There was no point talking about Chris to Stacy anymore. As far as she was concerned he was history, and there was no reason to look back. I got up, scrounging around for something else chocolate to eat.

"Things have been really hectic this week, between ordering invitations, hiring a calligrapher, and choosing the wedding cake, but everything's finally booked."

My life should only be as hectic as Stacy's. Choosing a wedding cake didn't sound nearly as exhausting as watching a cow pee on your foot while your boyfriend and you broke up.

"So are you happy with everything?" I asked, waiting to see if Stacy would put her empty orange juice glass in my sink. I was determined not to bus her table this morning.

"Yeah, it's been tiring, but exciting and wonderful at the same time, if you know what I mean."

Unfortunately, I didn't, and Stacy's glass remained on my table. "How's Lori feeling?"

"Oh, I'm glad you mentioned her. That's the other reason I stopped over. She and Tony are having a small dinner party Friday night, nothing fancy, to celebrate their marriage. She tried reaching you at work on Friday, but you'd already left. When I told her I'd be popping by today, she asked me to invite you. So can you make it?"

I was happy for Lori, and at any other time I would have loved to celebrate, but I wasn't in a partying mood at the moment. "Who will be there?" I found a stale Jewish apple cake in the back of my refrigerator and returned to the table to cut a large slice.

"It's going to be really small, just Lori's two sisters and their husbands, Lance and me, Amy and Howard, and you."

Great, I loved going to a couple's party when I was only half of a couple. Unlike most single women, I didn't have a gay male friend willing to escort me to any occasion that required a date. "I might have to work late on Friday."

"Oh, come on, Jen. Lori will be really disappointed if you miss it." She pouted as she spoke. "Besides, it will be good for you to get out with people."

Not with these happily married and engaged people. It was hard to believe that Stacy didn't realize that I might be uncomfortable being the only single one at a couple's dinner. At another time, she would have figured it out right away. I could remember the two of us searching for excuses to miss couple's events when neither of us had boyfriends. It was like Stacy had totally forgotten what it was like to be single.

"I'm usually tired after a full week of work. I hardly ever go out on Fridays anymore."

"You went out this Friday." Her voice perked up.

Damn, I was never good at coming up with excuses. That was always Stacy's department, but since I obviously couldn't count on her this time, I reluctantly accepted. "Tell Lori that I'll drop by for a little while, but I'll probably have to leave early."

Real early, I thought, while finishing my apple cake.

As I stood outside of Lori's apartment Friday night, I was ready to drop her present at the door and run, but just my luck, Lori happened to be opening it to let her neighbor out at that precise second.

"Are you feeling okay, Jen?" Lori asked as I handed her a gift. "You look tired."

"Yeah, you look like you haven't slept in weeks," Amy agreed.

And you look like the fat lady at the circus, I wanted to tell Lori, who had put on quite a bit of weight. Her boobs had grown so large, they practically sagged down to her knees.

"You do look a little flushed," Stacy said. My confidence level plunged right into the ground as my college friends lavished me with compliments.

"Other than being tired, I'm doing fine," I lied. And looking at all the couples who greeted me at the door didn't make me feel any better either. Howard stood with his arm around Amy, Lance held Stacy's hand, and Tony stroked Lori's belly. Lori's sisters sat on a couch in the living room, each next to her respective husband.

I walked past the three pairs of love birds and sat down next to Lori's Labrador retriever in the living room. While everyone else expressed their affection toward their significant others, I petted the dog. Other than me, he was the only single person in the room. Too bad he was furry with a cold nose.

"Come on, Jen," Lori said. "I'll show you the nursery."

I left my date eating scraps from the carpet as I followed Lori down the hallway of her small two-bedroom apartment. The first room, which had been Lori's guest room, now contained a crib, changing table, and matching dresser. I liked the Disney border slightly below the ceiling.

"My mom had a fit when she saw we already set up the nursery," Lori said. "She still believes that old Jewish superstition that it's bad luck to bring anything into the house before the baby's born, but I think that's a load of shit."

I hoped Lori's baby wasn't listening from inside. "It looks great." A lot different from her bedroom with the mirrored ceiling at her last apartment. "Do you know whether you're having a boy or a girl?"

"I could have found out last month when I had the ultrasound, but I decided to wait and be surprised. Oh, Jen, the baby just moved. Do you want to feel it?"

I really didn't. I never understood why pregnant women assumed everyone wanted to touch their bellies. I would have been happy waiting until the baby was born to feel its movements for the first time.

"Sure," I said, feeling obligated. All of a sudden, I felt a jolt. It reminded me of the time I'd bought a goldfish and they'd handed it to me in a plastic bag filled with water. The fish squirmed around, poking its head against the bag. I couldn't imagine how it felt to have your own baby squirming around inside of you. Then again, according to that magazine article, chances were I'd never find out.

"Tony, come here!" Lori screamed. "The baby's moving."

Within seconds Tony was by Lori's side, beaming with pride as he placed his hand on her stomach. He gave her a long kiss and stroked her hair as I stared up at Mickey Mouse and Pluto. Tony and Lori continued to kiss, apparently forgetting I was there.

I was relieved when Stacy and Amy walked in. "We heard you say that the baby's moving," Stacy said. "Can we feel?"

Oh, good grief, now everybody had their hands on Lori's belly. Was this the next logical step after inspecting each other's ring fingers? Did it ever end?

Finally, the baby stopped moving, probably sick of so many hands trying to stroke it through Lori's big belly. When the main attraction ended, we all headed to the living room, where my date sat wagging his tail. Apparently, nobody had hit on him yet.

As we sat making small talk, Lance came over and sat opposite me. "Sorry to hear about you and Chris," he said. "So, are you doing all right?"

I had been until Lance brought up his name. "Yeah, I'm fine. Plenty of other guys in this world, right?" I used my self-assured, business voice, hoping I sounded more convincing than I felt.

"That's a good attitude," he said, looking pleased.

Whew, he bought it.

"I know, let's help Jen find a new boyfriend." Amy came over and sat next to Lance.

Was this some kind of new party game? Whatever happened to charades? Without realizing it, everyone had sat down around me, as if I were the game pawn.

"My neighbor's looking for a girlfriend," Lori's older sister said.

"Your neighbor's always looking for a girlfriend, even when he has one," her younger sister said.

"Have you tried that new eighties club in Cherry Hill?" Lori asked.

"Clubs are just meat markets," Stacy chimed in, wanting to play, too. "What about somewhere different like the produce section of the supermarket?"

"I read that some supermarkets actually have singles nights," Tony said, looking thoughtful.

"I know," Howard said, raising his hand. "How about a bookstore like Barnes & Noble on a Saturday night."

"That's a great idea," Lori said. "You could find out what the guy was interested in by whatever section you met him at."

And so the game continued. Instead of Trivial Pursuit, tonight's entertainment featured Husband Pursuit, and I was the game piece. Object of game: Find poor single Jen Greenberg a potential husband. Rules: Move Jen from one imaginary meeting place to another until she finds acceptable mate. Do not pass ex-boyfriends along the way.

To determine winner: Add up the number of horrible dates Jen has before she finally gets lucky. Whoever has the least amount of points by the wedding wins. In order to play: must be married or engaged.

Everyone seemed disappointed to end the game when Lori announced that dinner was ready. I, on the other hand, practically knocked Lance over to race toward the dining room.

"Now, let's see," Lori said, standing by a table set for eleven. There was no question who the odd person was. "Where shall we put Jen?" she asked, as if I weren't in the room.

"Put her next to me," Stacy offered.

"You always see each other," Amy said. "Jen, sit next to me so we can catch up."

"Actually, I was thinking you could sit next to me" Lori said. "That way, you and Tony can get to know each other."

"Hey, I want a chance to sit next to her, too," Lance teased.

Oh great, another party game involving me. This time we were playing musical chairs, and I seemed to be the only one who would be moving from place setting to place setting. What was next? Pin the tail on the single girl?

"Why don't we let Jen decide where she wants to sit," Tony said.

How about next to Lori's dog in the next room? Guess not. I chose Stacy as my table buddy. She filled me in on her final wedding plans and I told her about work. Other than that, we had very little left to say so we ended up reminiscing about high school and college.

The night dragged on until I finally made my exit at nine o'clock. How could it possibly be so early? It felt like midnight.

I drove home to my empty apartment. At least Frisky seemed happy to see me. Was it my imagination or was I hitting it off better with animals than people these days?

I put on my fuzzy pajamas and my old faithful Pound Puppy slippers. Not exactly the sexy lingerie I had worn for Chris, but since it didn't matter anymore how I looked in bed, I might as well be comfortable.

Before going to sleep, I pulled out the only box I hadn't unpacked from my closet. Inhaling deeply, I inflated Mr. Wow until he was staring me in the eyes. I didn't feel like using him sexually yet, but I needed to put my arms around something that didn't have fur, claws, or tails.

As I held him tightly against my chest, the tears I had held back for the past week fell quickly down his plastic body. Before long, I was sobbing, wishing Mr. Wow could console me.

Unfortunately, nobody could. Chris was gone and I had to let go, but for a few last minutes I held on to his memory, twirling Mr. Wow around as I hummed, "Wouldn't you like to fly in my beautiful balloon."

Chapter 14

Your Marriage Epidemic Survival Kit Should Include the Following Vital Statistics About Each Potential Date:

1. Full name (make sure his last name sounds good with your first name).

2. Work history (if he gets a blank expression when you ask him where he works, get a blank expression when he asks you out).

3. Family history (beware if his mother had more than three husbands).

4. Medical history (find out if he ever had a head injury that caused his brain to shut down at the mention of marriage).

5. If all vital statistics are favorable, proceed slowly to first date.

I waited to cross the street with fifteen other people until the police officer finally waved us on. I thought I had left early enough to avoid this mob scene, but if the police were already directing traffic, I knew I was in for a long wait.

Sure enough, as I approached Moish's Deli, I saw a crowd lined up outside. Damn, too late again!

With this much excitement, you would think we all came to see a famous actor or singer, but our mission was completely based on hunger.

Today was Yom Kippur, the Day of Atonement in the Jewish religion when you asked God for forgiveness for your past year's sins.

It was also the day you fasted for twenty-four hours as a form of self-denial.

I couldn't imagine that I had committed enough sins to justify starving for an entire day. I should only be so lucky! But being the good Jewish girl I was raised to be, I had only broken my fast once my whole life, and that was when I was sick during my freshman year of college.

Every year, Moish's opened between one and three on this sacred day for the sole purpose of selling its traditional holiday fish trays. And every year, the Jews from Pleasantown flocked to the deli like seagulls flock to the ocean. It didn't seem fair that after starving ourselves since the evening before, we had to once again suffer by waiting in this incredibly long line.

My mom, Kathy, and I took turns every Yom Kippur waiting for our tray, and this year was my turn. In the past, Moish's had made us stand in line while we waited for our food, but this year, they placed a few benches outside.

Nobody ever looked happy on these occasions. And who could blame us? We had just spent the day sitting in synagogue listening to our stomachs growl for food. As I sat down, waiting for the line to move, I was glad I brought a copy of *Advertising Age* to read.

"Do you work in advertising?" someone asked as I skimmed through the magazine.

A guy who looked a little older than me sat down beside me.

"Uh, yeah. I do." Well, this was different. Not too many guys showed up for the infamous deli tray line. It was mostly women around my mom's age and older, with a few females around my age mixed in.

"I always thought advertising seemed like an interesting job," he said.

"It is." The mysterious Jewish stranger had almond-shaped brown eyes, bushy brown eyebrows, and light brown, wavy hair. Even if he hadn't been sitting at a deli tray line, I would have guessed that he was Jewish. He had that ethnic look about him. He was cute, not gorgeous, but still, attractive. "Where do you work?" I asked.

"I teach history at Penn."

"That sounds interesting, too." More than interesting. A Jewish history teacher at an Ivy League college! Okay, so what was wrong with this one? Maybe he was married? No, nothing on his ring finger. Of course, I had already learned that that no longer meant anything. And if he wasn't married, he still could have a girlfriend. But wouldn't she be here with him if he did? There was always the chance that he was gay. Once again, I knew firsthand that was also impossible to detect right away.

He was probably just being friendly, trying to pass the time until he could eat, but that was all right with me. It was better than three years ago when I'd come here and ended up listening to an eighty-something-year-old woman tell me all the gory details about her recent gall bladder surgery.

"So do you live around here," I asked.

"Not too far." He stretched his long legs out in front of him. "My bubby lives around the corner and she's not feeling well so I offered to pick up the tray."

I wasn't used to hearing a grown man refer to his grandmother as bubby, but I thought it was nice of him to help her out. My mom would say he sounded like a nice Jewish boy. "What street does she live on?"

"Newtown Avenue." He had a pleasant, soothing voice, the kind you'd expect a radio announcer to have.

"You're kidding. I grew up a block away from her on Yardley Road. My parents still live there, which is why I'm picking up the tray for them."

"That's funny. I wonder if they know each other. What's your name?"

"Jen, Jen Greenberg."

"I'm Mike Robinowitz."

Robinowitz! That was a lot closer to what I was looking for than O'Reilly, but I wasn't going to ruin this moment thinking about Chris.

"Does your family belong to a synagogue around here?" Mike said. Ironically, he wore a Star of David charm, very similar to mine.

"We go to Beth El."

"That's where my bubby goes." He moved over to make room for a woman on crutches. "We were there for services today."

"So were we," I said. "Last seat in the back."

"Small world." Mike picked up some change that a little boy had dropped and handed it to him. "So where do you live now?"

"I live at the Royalty Apartments by the Art Museum." The smell of food was making my stomach growl and I put my hand on my stomach as if I could silence it.

"Nice place. Do you live alone?"

"Yeah, I do. What about you. Where do you live?" Growl. Grumble. Growl. Grumble.

"I live with my mom in Huntingdon Valley. I was going to move out a while ago, but then my dad got sick. I wanted to be close by to help out. After he died, I felt bad leaving my mom alone so I stuck around." He got a faraway look in his eyes, like he had just stepped away for a moment.

Nobody could accuse this guy of not being family-oriented. What a difference from Chris. But as soon as I thought about him again, I was mad at myself. Considering he hadn't called once in the two months since we broke up, he had obviously gotten over me pretty quickly. Little by little, I was getting over him, but it was still hard.

Our line began to move, and as we stood up I was surprised at how tall Mike was. He had to be well over six feet, which made me look tiny in comparison. He wore black dress pants with a vertical striped IZOD shirt that made him look really thin.

"Are you having a lot of people at your bubby's house?" I asked, stretching my neck up to look at him. Maybe he'd recite the guest list so I'd know if his girlfriend was waiting with his sick, elderly grandmother.

"No, not really. I have a pretty small family." He smiled at a small baby being strolled past us. "What about you?"

Well, if he wasn't spilling the beans, neither was I. "The same, not too many people."

"So did you go to Jefferson High School?" he asked. "Here, let me get that for you." He raced in front of me to open the door.

I wasn't used to this type of treatment. Chris never even opened my car door for me when I drove. Uh-oh, there I went again, making comparisons. I had to stop that. "Yeah, I graduated in nineteen ninety-eight." We slowly inched our way to the deli.

"You must know my cousin, Larry Gorenstein. He graduated the same year."

"Sure, I remember him." How couldn't I? Everyone in the school used to tease him for wearing suits and carrying a briefcase to school. "So, how's he doing?"

"Great, he got a job working for Microsoft when he graduated from college and now he's a VP."

"Are you and he close?"

"Yeah, he and I have always been like brothers. He's a great guy."

I wondered if Mike used to carry a briefcase to school, too.

Finally, at the deli, I gave my name to the man behind the counter, who handed me my tray. Even before I held it, I smelled the lox, herring, and white fish salad. Too bad after waiting all this time I didn't even like fish. I usually ended up eating bagels with cream cheese and, of course, dessert.

"That looks heavy. Why don't you let me carry it to your car," Mike offered.

This was a good sign. Did this guy make a habit of picking up girls at the deli, or was he genuinely interested in me?

As Mike picked up his tray, I went through my potential husband checklist that I had developed after Chris and I broke up: Jewish, check; educated, check; professional, check; family-oriented, check. I imagined it would be inappropriate to ask him about his feelings toward marriage. Too bad. I hated to waste my time on another guy, only to find out that he wanted to remain single until he received his first social security check.

Chris had taught me that love wasn't enough to maintain a long-term relationship so I decided to do things differently this time. I developed a list of criteria that I planned to use before getting involved with someone else. I wanted to be sure from the start that whoever I dated now shared the same beliefs and philosophy that I did on subjects that mattered to me.

I didn't feel like I was selling out, becoming a clone of Stacy or Kathy, because I still wasn't interested in materialistic things like how much the guy earned. I wasn't looking for a doctor or lawyer to provide me with a status symbol. I was mostly concerned with the guy's values and interests.

No more diving in head first. This time I was going to float around for a while. And I was determined to think with my head, not my heart, until I felt sure I met the right guy.

Okay, I was definitely getting ahead of myself. Mike hadn't said anything about going out on a date. But as he looked through my order with me to make sure everything was there, I had a feeling he would ask for my number. Nobody had ever cared enough to check my fish tray before.

We talked for the next fifteen minutes as we paid for our trays, and then walked across the street to my car. Mike gently placed my fish tray in the back of my jeep before asking me out.

Who would have thought I could meet a guy waiting for a fish tray at a Jewish deli? Why hadn't anyone come up with that suggestion at Lori's dinner party?

"Good Yuntiv," Kathy said, smiles dripping off her face as she wished me a happy holiday. She blew me a kiss, as if I'd catch it.

"You, too," I said, ready to sink my teeth into a bagel. Even the smoked salmon was starting to smell good.

I was ready to lunge toward the food when Kathy shoved the blueprints of her home in my hand. "Take a look at the vaulted ceiling we're adding in the study upstairs. We thought it would make the house look bigger."

I couldn't imagine why she needed her 4,000-square-foot home to look any bigger, but I agreed, not having any idea how to read blueprints.

"It's been so much fun watching our home being built. There's nothing like buying new construction." You'd think I'd be used to her high voice by now, but it still sent shivers up my spine.

"I'm glad everything's going so well." I supposed telling her that I was still thrilled with my walk-in closet would sound strange to her.

"I heard you've been busy at *work*," Kathy said. "Sounds like you're doing really *well*." The last word of every sentence Kathy said always went up an octave, making her sound like she was celebrating some kind of special occasion.

"Yeah, work's going well."

"Hey, how's my favorite sister-in-law doing?" Jeff leaned over to kiss me.

"Good. I wasn't sure if you'd make it here tonight."

"Neither was I, but I just finished a week of twelve-hour shifts so they let me out for good behavior." Jeff wore his dirty blond hair short, which made his bluish-green eyes stand out. Unlike Kathy's outgoing, bubbly personality, he was a lot quieter and more subdued, but they seemed to compliment each other.

"Don't worry, Jeff. All that work will pay off when you're a doctor," my mom said from behind us.

"Mom, a resident is a doctor." Kathy giggled, while placing her arm around my mom's waist.

"I mean when he's done his residency and becomes a real doctor."

"Oh, Mom, you're impossible." Kathy laughed, hugging my mom closer to her.

That was the difference between Kathy and me. I would have argued with my mom until she admitted that a resident and a doctor were the same thing, but Kathy just let it go.

"All the food looks wonderful." Kathy continued gushing at my mom. "As always, you're the perfect hostess."

Oh, barf! Give me a break! My mom couldn't make toast without burning it. And by the way, did Kathy remember that my mom's only contribution to dinner was supplying the paper goods?

"You're sweet." My mom kissed Kathy on the cheek.

"Hi, princess." My dad came over and kissed me. "Thanks for picking up the tray."

"Glad I could help." He had no idea how glad I was.

"Everything's set up so grab a plate and help yourself," my mom announced.

Without looking back, I grabbed a cinnamon raisin bagel and smothered it with strawberry cream cheese. Apparently, Mike didn't mind chunky girls because in the past eight weeks I had gained back the five pounds I lost while dating Chris.

The doorbell rang and my mom ran to the door to let Barb in. Surprise, surprise. I was hoping she'd be with her daughter and new grandson tonight. It's not that I didn't like Barb. She was always very nice to me, but lately whenever she was around, my mom acted kind of weird. It was almost like they went into their own world. If I didn't know better, I'd think they were having a fling, but of course, that was ridiculous. Barb had been happily married for over forty years before her husband died, and my mom...well, my mom did marry my dad.

I watched my mom lead Barb to the food trays. "I have an especially great assortment of fish this year," my mom told Barb, as if she had skinned the fish herself.

After putting some lox and cream cheese on a sesame seed bagel, Barb followed my mom to two chairs by the steps, where they sat huddled in the corner, giggling like teenagers. What was with them anyway? They sure were chummy. What could they possibly have left to say to each other? They had just spent nearly the entire weekend together, shopping, going out for drinks, and playing mahjong. They both wore short, tight sweaters that made their boobs bulge out. Funny, I couldn't remember Barb dressing like that before her husband died.

My dad startled me. "Sorry, didn't mean to sneak up on you, princess. I just wanted to make sure that you're doing all right."

"Sure, why wouldn't I be?"

"With, uh, you know, with Chris. Are you okay?"

I wanted to jump into his arms and cry on his shoulders. He was the only one who seemed to care how I was coping without Chris.

"Yeah, Dad, I'm okay. Thanks for asking."

He smiled at me like I had just lit up his world again. If only a guy would look at me like that someday. Meaning the right guy, of course.

"So what about you and Mom? Have the two of you been out together lately?"

"No, your mom keeps telling me how busy she is." My dad looked tired again. "I don't want to spoil her fun." He sighed.

Wasn't he supposed to be her fun? "Dad, you're her husband. You should be doing things together."

"Oh, princess, there's a lot of things about life that you're too young to understand."

"Like what?"

Before he could answer, my mom stepped between us. "Take a look at these." She handed me three brochures of the Mirage in Las Vegas.

"It looks beautiful, but who's going?"

"Didn't I tell you," she said. "The Springtown Theater gave Barb and me two round-trip plane tickets to Vegas to thank us for all the time we spent volunteering there."

"They gave you plane tickets to Vegas for selling theater tickets?" Had I known, I would have volunteered, too.

"We did a lot more than sell tickets, Jen." My mom sounded hurt. "We recruited new customers, got donations, helped set up shows…"

"Okay, okay, I get the idea. So when are you leaving?"

"Next week. We'll be gone for ten days. I hope the weather's nice. I hear October's a great time to go."

She bolted off with her brochures to show Kathy. "Did you know about this?" I asked my dad.

"No," he said sadly. "I didn't." He let out another sigh and excused himself.

This must have been another one of those things in life that I was still too young to understand.

Chapter 15

Setting Goals –
Your Next Boyfriend/Potential Husband Will:

1. Believe the sun rises when you enter the room (or at least be mildly pleased to see you).

2. Worship the ground you walk on (okay, if he appreciates a few of your positive attributes, you'll be satisfied).

3. Put you up on a pedestal (a short ladder will do).

"Ilene Meeney?" I said to the receptionist at Richardson and Whitaker as I looked down the street to make sure nobody from work was walking by. Even after walking over a mile from Premier on my lunch break, I still worried that someone would overhear my conversation. I leaned against the wall of a high-rise hotel, hoping I would get a good signal on my cell phone here.

"Just one moment, please," the receptionist said.

It had taken me over two months to get up the courage to call her, and I was still nervous about talking to her.

The truth was that I had avoided making this call because I was afraid of more rejection. My career was still the one thing I could count on in my life, and I didn't want Meany to pull the rug out from under me by telling me I had misinterpreted her future job offer. Other than my internship, I had never applied for a job I wanted, and I really wanted this job. That was the problem. I wanted it too much, and I felt like Meany held my entire future in her hands.

I was beginning to hyperventilate. Remembering the one meditation class that Stacy had dragged me to, I slowly inhaled from my diaphragm and then exhaled. There, that was better.

What was taking so long for her to come to the phone? I hoped they didn't put me through to her voice mail. I always ended up stuttering on those machines when I really wanted to sound impressive. I knew! I could write a message, and then recite it on her voice mail to make sure I didn't sound like an idiot. That way, I would have time to formulate my thoughts. That would work out even better than talking to her and then...

"Hello, this is Ilene."

So much for that idea. Maybe I should hang up and call back later, hoping to get her voice mail. But then she might know I was the one who hung up on her.

"Hello," she said again. I recognized her impatient voice.

"Uh, hi. It's Jen Greenberg." Damn, my voice cracked as soon as I said my name.

"Jen, hi. How are you?"

"Um, good. I, uh..." Okay, I had to get a hold of myself. She obviously liked my work, and she was the one who suggested I call. Besides, what was the worst thing that could happen? If she didn't help me get a job at Richardson and Whitaker, I'd just stay at Premier until something better came along. It wasn't like I was unhappy there. Inhale, exhale, inhale, exhale. "I called to see how your new job was going." Hey, that didn't sound too bad. My voice didn't even quiver that time. Maybe I should try another one of those meditation classes.

"It's going really well. I'm glad you caught me because I just got back from France on business."

"That sounds exciting. What were you doing there?"

"A lot of our accounts are international so I travel a lot now. I went to France to meet with Jacques Montan."

"The designer?" Could she tell I was drooling all over my cell phone? Jacques Montan was the most sought after designer in Hollywood. Whenever I watched the Emmy Awards, almost every actress interviewed proudly announced that her gown was a Jacques Montan.

"The one and only. He's really quite charming."

Meany had come a long way since appeasing the Happy Tooth. "I read somewhere that he's starting a more affordable line of clothing," I said, continuing to search for any familiar faces from work.

"That's exactly why we met. He wants to reposition himself as the designer of choice for women of all incomes. Julia Roberts has agreed to be the spokesperson targeted to celebrities and high income women. We're still looking for someone who appeals to middle class women. We're launching a big international print and television campaign to create Jacques's new image."

"It sounds exciting." I always wanted to write for television. I always wanted to work on international accounts. I always wanted to travel to Europe. Inhale, exhale. Or was it exhale, inhale? I suddenly couldn't remember, and I felt dizzy again.

"So have you ever thought about moving to New York?" she asked.

Why couldn't she just ask if I wanted to work there? It was like she was dangling a carrot under my nose, and every time I went for it, she pulled it higher. "If the right job came along, I would." Okay, the ball was back in her court.

"That's good to know because we'll probably be expanding soon. We're pitching three multi-million dollar accounts. If we get them, we'll need to increase our staff. Of course, I can't make any promises right now, but if we were to get those accounts, would you be interested in coming to work here?"

There, at last, she said it! Should I tell her I'd pack my bags and wait by the phone for her call? Probably not. "I'd love to work there," I said, trying to tone down my enthusiasm. "Keep me posted on those pitches."

"I will. By the way, don't say anything until it's a sure thing. You know how John gets when former employees try to recruit his staff. That's why I didn't say too much before I left. I thought it was better that a little time went by before we discussed it."

"I understand. Thanks for thinking of me."

"Don't thank me. I'm being selfish. Good writers like you are hard to find. And the fact that we have a history working together is an added bonus. Try calling me in a about a month. By then I should know more about the expansion."

I didn't realize I could skip until I headed back to work. Meany wanted me to work at her agency! This was the big leagues. I threw my sandwich to the pigeons at the park, and handed a five-dollar bill to a homeless person lying near a gutter.

Tiffany and Marisa cornered me as soon as I got back to my office. "Judging by your expression, I'd say it went well," Tiffany said.

I motioned them to close the door, and swore them to secrecy before filling them in on the details.

"Pretty impressive," Tiffany said after I repeated my conversation with Meany to them.

"There's still a good chance that it won't even happen." I was trying not to get my hopes up too high, even though I was afraid it was probably too late. "If those new accounts don't pan out, there won't even be a new job."

"I doubt Meany would bring it up if she didn't think it was a good possibility," Marisa said, and I was glad she didn't look distressed at the prospect of me leaving. In fact, her eyes looked particularly bright even through her glasses.

"I hope so. And if there are lots of openings, maybe you guys can come work there, too."

"Come on, Jen," Tiffany said. "Do you really think Meany would want me working there? Let's face it, I was never one of her favorite people." Tiffany coughed so hard, I was afraid she was going to break a rib. "Meany thought I was some kind of a smart-ass."

"Then she was right," I laughed.

Tiffany made a paper airplane and threw it at my head.

"Anything new with your job search?" I asked her as I ducked from the plane.

"Not a thing. I finally gave in and enrolled in a website design course at the Philadelphia Art Institute. I start next week."

"That should help," Marisa said, looking more beautiful than I had ever seen her. Since she started dating Zack, she seemed to stand up straighter and her nails had never looked better. As an added perk, she had raised the volume of her voice a few octaves so I could hear her better.

"So I assume that instead of job searching, you'll be ring searching," Tiffany said.

Marisa got a pensive look on her face. "I certainly hope so."

"Are things really that serious?" I was surprised. Even though this was Marisa's longest relationship, they had only been going out a little over two months.

"When the right guy comes along, you just know it." She spoke so confidently, I had to look twice to make sure it was really her. "That's why I was so upset when Zack didn't call. I knew as soon as I met him that he was the one for me."

Interesting. Is that how I felt while Mike scrutinized my deli tray to make sure they didn't gyp me out of a pound of lox? I had been excited when he called to ask me out for this weekend. I guess time would tell whether my Prince Charming finally found my glass slipper.

Naturally, my face was broken out on Saturday night. Couldn't I ever go on a first date without a blemish? I was also bloated like a stuffed cabbage because I was due for my period any second. My hair had a frizz attack from the rain outside and my eyes had dark circles under them from working overtime all week. Hopefully, Mike wouldn't run back to the deli to find another date when he saw me.

My heart beat fast when my doorbell rang. *Please let this go well this time. Please let him be the right one.*

When I opened the door, I was greeted by two dozen roses. There were so many flowers I could hardly see Mike through the petals. "Wow, this is a nice surprise!"

"It's really good to see you again." As opposed to Chris's constant wide grins, Mike didn't smile as much. His eyes seemed more expressive than his lips, and at the moment they beamed at me. "I wanted to start the evening off right."

"Well, you certainly did. Come on in. I'll go find a vase." I wasn't used to receiving flowers that hadn't been hand-picked from a park or someone's garden. But as I placed the flowers in water, my eyes got watery and my nose became stuffy. I had to pop an allergy pill to make sure I didn't sneeze all over Mike.

"This is really nice," he said, looking around my apartment. He looked good in his light blue cardigan IZOD sweater and off-white pleated pants. I liked his brown suede jacket.

"Thanks. I'm still trying to fix it up, but little by little it's getting there."

"I'd say it's already there. I love that TV. Is that a fifty inch?"

"Yeah, my parents gave it to me as a housewarming gift."

"That's some gift. You must be really close to them."

Probably not a good time to mention that my mom was on vacation without my dad. "Yeah, they're great." Well, they were, in an unusual kind of way.

"I always feel bad for people who have little to do with their parents," Mike said. "A lot of my friends moved away after graduating from school, and they barely see their family once a year. I would hate that."

"Sounds like you're a real homebody."

"After my dad died, I realized how important your family really is." He got that same distant look in his eyes that he'd gotten at the deli. "Sorry, I don't want to start the evening talking about something upsetting. Why don't we figure out where we're going for dinner. Is there any place you've been wanting to go to?"

Too bad I no longer ate Mexican food, or this would be a good chance to try the new Mexican café on Hobb Street. "I wouldn't mind Chinese."

"Chinese it is, then. I know a great place in Chinatown. Would that be all right with you?"

"That would be great." As I locked my front door, I was ready to keep my keys out until I remembered I wasn't driving.

Once outside, Mike led me to the passenger side of his shiny gray BMW, where he closed my door before walking to the driver's seat. I could get used to this!

"I forgot to tell you that my bubby knows your mom," Mike said, sounding excited.

I wasn't so sure this was a good thing. "Really, how do they know each other?"

"She sees her every Sunday night during bingo at Beth El." Mike turned on the ignition and backed out of my parking lot. "I'm surprised your mom didn't mention it."

How could she when she didn't even know about him yet. I knew as soon as I recited Mike's resume, she'd start planning our wedding. I didn't want her excitement about Mike to influence how I felt about him, but now I'd have to tell her. She'd be back from Vegas next weekend, and I didn't want Mike's bubby spilling the beans. "My mom's away on a business trip so I haven't had a chance to mention your name." I rubbed my hand against the car's gray leather interior.

"Oh." Mike seemed disappointed. "Where does she work?"

"She doesn't actually work. She and her friend volunteered so much of their time at the Springtown Theater that its managers gave them a free trip to Vegas."

"That's a pretty generous gift. I guess your dad's there, too?"

This was way too early to explain my parent's relationship, especially since I still didn't understand it. Telling him that Kathy suspected my dad had cheated on my mom since our birth probably wasn't the best way to impress this family-loving guy. "No, my dad had to work. He's an accountant and it's coming up to his busy season. He likes to prepare before he's overloaded with paperwork."

"Your dad's an accountant? That's what my dad did." His eyes grew larger as he spoke. "Where does he work?"

"He has his own business in center city."

"You're not going to believe this, but so did my dad. Next time you talk to him, mention Robinowitz and Family Accountants. They're pretty well known."

"I will. Who took over the business after your father died?"

"My two uncles still run it." His eyes returned to their normal size.

We spent the entire car ride talking about all the connections that our families had to each other. It turned out that his aunt was best friends with my parent's next-door neighbor, and his grandfather used to sell antique jewelry to my great-uncle.

"Talk about coincidences," Mike said as he pulled into a parking place outside of the restaurant. Before I had a chance to open my door, Mike leaped out of his seat to open it for me.

"So when do think you'll see your father again?" Mike asked. "I'd love to find out whether he knew my dad."

"I'll probably see him next week. I promised my mom I'd stop by to see the gift she bought for my best friend's bridal shower."

Mike nodded and took my hand, leading me down the street. "This is the place," Mike said, pointing to the restaurant in front of us. As we walked inside, I admired the Imperial Chinese décor.

"So when's your friend's wedding?" Mike asked, while a waiter led us to our table.

"She's getting married in June." After opening my menu, I told Mike all about Stacy and how we'd known each other since we could walk.

"That's great that you've stayed in touch so long. So I imagine you're her maid of honor?"

"I am," I said, enjoying the smell of barbecued spare ribs being served at the table next to us. "Have you been in any wedding parties?"

"That's an understatement," he said, closing his menu. "When I was about twenty-eight, I was in so many weddings that I finally bought a tux. I would have liked to have gotten married then, too, but I was too busy writing my thesis and working on my Ph.D. Unfortunately, now that I'm ready to settle down six years later, most of the girls I meet are already married."

Did he say settle down, or was I hallucinating?

"Can I take your order?" the waiter asked.

"Jen? Jen?"

Oops. Too much daydreaming. "Yeah, I'll have a small bowl of wonton soup, an egg roll, and a small portion of chicken chow mein."

"Same for me," Mike said, giving me one of his crooked grins.

Okay, if six years ago Mike was twenty-eight, that meant he was thirty-four. That made him four years older than me, which seemed like a perfect age difference. If he really wanted to settle down, he must be searching for a potential wife. Maybe we should just skip the wonton soup and elope now. "So how do you like working at Penn?" I bit into a Chinese noodle and took a sip of tea.

"It's great. I love teaching college students. It's so rewarding when I can tell that they suddenly grasp a new concept. It's like watching a light bulb go on above their heads."

"What made you decide to teach history?" I leaned back, enjoying Mike's look of enthusiasm as he talked about his job.

"I was always fascinated with past events. Besides, it's pretty cool taking an entire classroom of students anywhere in the world, without ever leaving the room."

"I bet you love traveling."

"No, not really. Believe it or not, the farthest I've ever traveled was to Florida. I'd rather relax at a beach down the shore."

"Oh…I figured you'd want to see all the places you taught about." The waiter brought us our egg rolls and soup.

"But that's the beauty about textbooks. You can visit so many great places every time you turn the page."

Just like Chris, I thought, and then got mad at myself again for making the comparison. "Have you ever worked anywhere else besides Penn?" I bit into my egg roll, hoping I didn't have cabbage hanging out of my teeth.

"No, I was really lucky to get this job." Mike blew on his spoon before trying the soup. "I went all through school at Penn, and when I was working on my Ph.D., I also worked there as a graduate student. I made a lot of contacts while I was there, and the day after I graduated, they offered me a job."

"Do you think you'll stay there, or would you eventually like to work somewhere else?" Was it my imagination, or was I asking all the questions? I was beginning to feel like Barbara Walters.

"I'd love to spend my life teaching at Penn. In a couple of months, I'll be eligible for tenure. That means I'll have job security until I retire. I'm hoping to be promoted to a full professor in the next two years."

He might not ask many questions, but I liked his answers. "You must have a long commute to work." I continued my interview as we made room on our table for the waiter to serve our dinner. I loved the smell of Chinese food, even though everything on the menu pretty much smelled the same to me.

"It takes me almost an hour to get to Penn, but I avoid morning rush hour because my first class doesn't begin till ten o'clock. I usually leave my house a little before nine."

"Do you get home late since your day begins later?"

"I teach two nights a week, so on those days I get home around nine o'clock, but I make sure to give myself a two-hour break before my last class so I have time to unwind. The rest of the week, I'm home by six o'clock, at the latest. What's your schedule like?"

"My schedule makes yours sound like banker's hours. I normally get to work around nine o'clock, but I rarely get home before seven o'clock. Lately, I've been staying till ten o'clock. Sometimes, when we're pitching a client, I'll pull a few all-nighters."

"That's awful. You must hate that." He looked horrified.

"It probably sounds ridiculous to somebody who doesn't work in the industry, but the hours go by fast because I like what I do."

"Even so, expecting someone to work those hours is insanity."

"Well, I guess you shouldn't go into advertising." I was trying to lighten the mood because Mike's soft-spoken voice suddenly sounded rather harsh. I didn't want my schedule to turn Mike off, but I couldn't hide it from him either. If we were going to continue dating, he'd find out about my long hours soon enough.

"How will you have time for a family when you have to work so much?"

Now I felt like I was being interviewed, and I suspected that a lot was riding on my answer so I took a few seconds before answering. "Lots of women I work with are married, and they manage. I think if you want to do something badly enough, you find a way." I looked into Mike's eyes to see how my answer had registered on his Richter scale. I was relieved to see him grinning at me.

"So I take it you're one of those women who think you can have a family and work?"

"I am." It was weird talking about starting a family on a first date. It was almost as if Mike had his own list of guidelines for potential wives that I had to meet. "I know I could juggle a career and a family because they are both things I want more than anything."

"That's good to know. Too many women today are so focused on their careers that they don't care about getting married or having kids. It's nice to know you want a family, too." Mike took my hand and squeezed it gently.

I squeezed it back as if sealing some kind of a pact. Apparently, we had each met each other's marriage criteria.

After seeing the new Woody Allen movie, which Mike let me pick, he walked me to the front door of my apartment. "When can I see you again?" he asked, leaning close to me.

"I'm free next weekend."

"You're going to make me wait that long?" He looked disappointed.

He liked me! He really liked me! "I might be able to leave work early on Wednesday night."

"Great, I'll call you tomorrow to make plans." As he bent down to kiss me, I had to stand on my toes and stretch my neck up high to find his lips. My heart skipped a beat anticipating his taste. but when the moment of truth came, I was overwhelmed with saliva dripping all over my mouth and around my chin. And why was his mouth open so wide if he wasn't planning on using his tongue?

"Thanks for a great evening," Mike said. "I'll wait here to make sure you get in safely."

That meant I couldn't wipe off my face until I was inside. Once the door closed, I took a tissue to clean off my face. Okay, so he wasn't the best kisser in the world. We could easily work on that. What mattered was that he and I appreciated each other's values and beliefs, and we had an understanding about what we wanted for our future, namely marriage and a family.

If I played my cards right, I might be the next one arriving at Premier with a shiny new diamond ring!

Chapter 16

Prognosis: Good

If you're hoping to make a quick recovery, seek treatment immediately with a serious boyfriend ready to make a commitment.

"I can't believe you've been dating Mike for a month and a half and I still haven't met him," Stacy said as we waited for the rest of her bridal party to arrive at the Pampered Bride.

I glanced at my watch, hoping they'd be there soon. I had to get back to work in less than an hour. I usually didn't take lunch breaks, but made an exception today.

"When do you think we can all get together?" Stacy asked while browsing through the bridal salon as if she had all the time in the world.

"How about next weekend," I suggested, taking off my black down jacket and placing it on the back of a chair. I poured a glass of champagne for myself before anyone could object.

"Oh, I wish we could, but Lance and I are spending the weekend looking for wedding bands on Jeweler's Row. If we have time afterward, we're going to talk to travel agents about honeymoons."

"That sounds like fun." It was hard to top a weekend like that. "Well, maybe the following weekend?"

"Jen, I'm sorry, but that's when Lance's aunt is coming in from New Mexico. She can't make it to the wedding so she wants to spend that weekend celebrating with us."

Well, maybe after you're married and your kids are in college. "I'm sure we'll figure out a time to get together."

"We better. I really want to meet him. He sounds absolutely perfect."

"Are you talking about me," Lori chimed in. We had to move a rack so she could fit through the clothes.

"You're perfect, too," Stacy laughed. "But I was talking about Jen's boyfriend, Mike."

"Is this someone new?" asked Amy, who arrived at the same time as Carla and Becca, Stacy's friends from work.

"You didn't hear about Mike, did you?" Stacy said to Amy. "He's been wining and dining Jen since they met."

"Really?" Amy's mouth dropped open. "What does he do, Jen?"

Couldn't she be a little tactful and ask what was he like instead. "He's an associate professor at Penn. He teaches history."

Amy's eyes grew so wide, I thought they might bulge right out of her head. "He must be really smart to teach at an Ivy League college."

"He is. He went all through school at Penn, and even got his Ph.D. there." All right, I admitted I enjoyed flaunting my new boyfriend's portfolio, especially to this crowd.

"Do you have a picture of him?" Lori asked, trying to hold herself up with a rack.

"No, but he looks a little like Adam Sandler."

"He sounds adorable," Amy said.

Now how could someone sound adorable from that description? The only adorable things Amy heard were Penn, professor, and Ph.D.

"Not only is he smart and cute, but he treats Jen like a royal princess," Stacy said, placing her arm around my shoulder. "Since they met, he's taken her to two Broadway plays, the Pennsylvania Ballet, and the Philadelphia Orchestra."

"You better hold on tight to him," Carla said. "A guy like that could easily slip away."

"She's right," Becca agreed. "A nice guy who's smart and cute doesn't come around too often."

"You're so lucky you found him," Amy said.

They all nodded in agreement. Wasn't anyone going to mention how lucky he was to find me? Guess not. But I didn't care. I was too busy enjoying all the attention. It was nice having a boyfriend everyone accepted for a change, even if they hadn't met him yet.

And after listening to the bridal party rave over Mike, I felt especially pleased to be dating him. So far, he was the nicest guy I ever met. All I had to do was mention that I wanted something and, like magic, Mike made it happen.

Just last week, I told Mike that I always wanted to see Bruce Springsteen in concert. My sister had been a big fan, and I grew up hearing his music blaring from her room. The next day, Mike arrived holding two tickets to Springsteen's sold-out show in New Jersey.

Three days ago, I mentioned that I loved KitKats. I forgot all about it until yesterday morning when I received a package at work filled with enough KitKats to last me an entire year.

I was daydreaming about Mike until I looked up to see that same snooty saleswoman who had given me the Twinkie last time we were here. Didn't anyone else work at this place besides her? "How can I help you ladies, today?" she asked in that familiar husky voice.

"Now that my maid of honor picked out her gown, I want the rest of the bridal party to try on gowns that match hers," Stacy said, while trying on a tiara.

"Make sure you add at least fifteen pounds when you fit me for mine," Lori said.

More like thirty, I thought.

"Why don't we start by having your maid of honor try on her gown so everyone gets an idea what style they should look for." The saleswoman gave one of her smiles that showed off her gums. "I assume that's you," she said, looking directly at me.

"You have a great memory. With all the bridal parties, it must be hard remembering every maid of honor." Maybe complimenting the old bag would at least earn me one gourmet pastry this time.

"Oh, I couldn't remember all those details." Ms. Snooty Face rolled her eyes.

"Then how did you know I was the maid of honor?"

"That was easy, dear. When Amy bought her wedding gown last night, she told me she would be in today for a *bridesmaid* gown for Stacy's wedding. And all three of them are wearing wedding bands," the obnoxious saleswoman said, turning her head toward Carla, Becca, and Lori. "Since you're not wearing a wedding band, you're *obviously* not the matron of honor, so that leaves you as the only potential maid of honor."

I was surprised she didn't add, *and the only potential old maid.* Feeling like a total reject, I followed Ms. Snooty Face into the dressing room at the back of the store, once again feeling alienated for my empty ring finger. I looked at my watch, relieved that my lunch break would soon be over.

Roses are red,
Violets are blue,
It's been almost twenty-four hours,
And I miss you.

When I gratefully returned to my office, I was greeted by one of Mike's corny but sweet poems, which he had emailed me. Obviously, he was no Shakespeare, but his poems made me smile, which was all I cared about.

When Mike wasn't emailing poems or notes to me, he was sending them via snail mail to my apartment or my job. It was so nice finally meeting someone who appreciated me for who I was.

"You have a call from that new guy," Rhonda announced through my intercom.

"Okay, I'll take it."

"I liked the other one better." Click.

Well, who the hell asked for her opinion anyway?

"Hi, beautiful, how are you?" Unlike my other boyfriends, I never worried whether Mike would call again. Before I even had time to think about him, he was on the phone, checking in.

"Good, how's your day?" I asked while opening a diet Pepsi.

"Okay. I just taught a class in one of those large lecture halls that holds two hundred people."

"I'd love to see you lecturing a room full of students." I found the idea of Mike completely in control of a lecture hall to be very exciting.

"Stop by anytime. I'll make you my assistant for the day."

"I just may do that." I unwrapped my lunch, a package of six peanut butter crackers. "So what did you do after class?"

"I went to the library to read. I hate going through a day without knowing what's going on in the world, so I always read the *Philadelphia Inquirer* and the *Wall Street Journal* from cover to cover."

"Everyday?" I had trouble talking because the peanut butter was sticking to the roof of my mouth.

"Since I was in high school."

Mental note: Never get into a lengthy conversation about current events with Mike. Most of the time, the only way I got my news was from the headlines that popped up on AOL.

"After the library, I stopped by Barnes & Noble on campus and bought that new book that analyzes each president of the United States. I've been dying to read it."

I guess he wouldn't be too impressed with the newest Janet Evanovich novel that lay on my nightstand.

"Then I grabbed a copy of *Newsweek* and headed back to my office," Mike continued. "I have fifteen papers to mark before my next class, but I couldn't get through the rest of the day without hearing your voice. So how's my favorite writer doing today?"

"Busy as usual." I smiled at his description of me. "I have back to back meetings for the next four hours, which means I probably won't even start writing until at least five o'clock. And I have a nervous account executive waiting for my copy, which we're pitching to a new client tomorrow."

"Sounds like I won't be seeing you tonight," Mike said. Was it my imagination or did his voice sound slightly abrupt?

"I doubt it. The account executive wants to see a rough draft by the end of the day." Which was likely to be around eight or nine o'clock.

"What about tomorrow night then?"

"Tomorrow I have a client meeting in North Jersey that doesn't start till four o'clock. The meeting could easily run three to four hours."

"Don't they ever give you a break?" Now I was certain he sounded upset.

"People in advertising don't work traditional hours like you do."

"So I see."

I could tell he wasn't happy, but what could I do? He couldn't expect me to jeopardize my job to go out with him. Or did he?

"So when are you free this week?"

"Wednesday and Thursday nights I'll be at photo shoots, but I should be caught up on Friday, so if you want, we can go out then." I took a large sip of soda to wash down the peanut butter crackers.

"You mean I have to wait another five days to see you."

"It looks that way." I had never heard a man with such a deep voice whine before. I felt like I was talking to a child. Okay, time to be less critical. I should be glad he wanted to see me so much.

"I wish I hadn't made plans to go to that Foreign Film Festival on Friday," Mike said. "Remember, I told you I was going with a bunch of guys from work."

"Oh, that's right. Well, we'll see each other on Saturday at that outdoor jazz concert so don't worry about it."

"No, that's okay. I'll cancel with the guys. I don't want to wait another day to see you."

"You don't have to do that. I know how much you wanted to go. One more day won't make a difference." Had I really said that? Being the jealous type, I didn't make a habit of persuading my boyfriends to go places without me, but with Mike, I didn't feel threatened by other women.

"I know I don't have to cancel, but I want to. I miss you, Jen." I was glad the warmth returned to his voice.

"I miss you, too." But I could have waited one more day to see him.

"Okay, then it's settled. So what do you want to do on Friday?"

"Why don't you choose this time," I suggested.

"I like it when you decide. Besides, you always come up with great ideas."

Last week, I had suggested pizza. I didn't realize that was such a brainstorm. "How about going out dancing? We've never done that before and I heard the Paradise Club is great."

He hesitated so long before answering I thought we'd been disconnected. "Would you be upset if you picked something else? I really don't like going to smoky places, and to be honest, I can't even dance."

"Oh, okay." So much for my brilliant suggestions. "There's always dinner and a movie."

"Now that sounds more my speed. I hope you're not upset about the club."

"No, not at all." Just because I'd gotten used to hiking and roller coasters didn't mean I couldn't return to my old routine.

"You're the best." Mike hung up, telling me how excited he was about seeing me Friday night.

I hung up, remembering how excited Stacy, Amy, and Lori were about Mike. As they said, guys like Mike didn't come around too often.

I got home from work at nine o'clock. Meany's replacement was far less demanding than Meany. The new account executive had accepted my copy with a few minor revisions, while Meany would have handed it back to me covered with red comments.

I gave Frisky his dinner and then popped a Weight Watcher's Smart Ones in the microwave. Now that it was only a matter of time before Mike saw me in the flesh, I had to lose all that excess weight I had gained after breaking up with Chris.

While sitting in front of the computer eating my chicken marsala and mixed vegetables, which looked like they were portion controlled for a small child, I checked my emails.

"You've got mail," the familiar male voice said. It should have just said, "You've got more poems from Mike." All three of them were about how hard it would be getting through the week without seeing me. I really was lucky to have such a caring, devoted boyfriend.

Strange, how difficult it was to find the right words to reply to his messages. I was supposed to be a writer, for goodness sake. Of course, writing about liquid detergent was a lot less personal than expressing your emotions. I'd wait till tomorrow when I was more rested to concentrate.

The next email was from Marisa. *Jen, call me as soon as you get home. I need to talk to you before eight o'clock. It's really important.*

But it was way past eight o'clock. Marisa had left two similar messages on my answering machine. What could have happened that was making her so frantic?

Marisa wasn't home when I called her apartment so I tried Tiffany.

"I got the same messages," Tiffany said, "but I got them too late, too." I could hear the clanging of a glass in the background and imagined she must be having a nightcap. "I wish Marissa would pay for unlimited texting."

"I know. I keep telling her emailing won't work if she needs to reach me right away," I said, tapping my nails on my desk. "I don't remember seeing her at work today, do you?"

"I'm already ahead of you. I called Rhonda who said she called out sick."

"That's not a good sign. I wonder what's going on." I watched another email pop up from Mike, without reading it.

"I hope Zack didn't do another one of his disappearing acts on her, like when they first met." Tiffany must have been smoking a lot today because her voice sounded like Lucille Ball during the late years of her life.

"But Marisa seems so sure that he's Mr. Right." I turned off my computer, wanting to focus on where Marisa might be.

"And how many Mr. Rights have you met who turned out to be Mr. Wrong?" Oh, so true. "Call me if you hear from her before work tomorrow, and I'll do the same."

I was still worried about Marisa when I lay down next to Frisky in bed. I hoped that Zack hadn't become Mr. Wrong. At what point did you realize that Mr. Right was Mr. Wrong? Was it ever possible that Mr. Wrong was Mr. Right? And what made Mr. Right so right?

With so many questions racing through my head, Frisky was snoring long before I fell asleep.

Marisa wasn't at work on Tuesday and this time, nobody heard from her. "What exactly did she say when you talked to her yesterday?" I asked Rhonda.

"All she said was that she wasn't feeling well." Rhonda, who wore four long, beaded necklaces and three earrings in each ear, all different colors, seemed disappointed that she didn't know more.

"That's it? Nothing else?" I didn't know why I bothered asking that. Naturally, if there was more, Rhonda would tell me.

"That's it." When Rhonda turned to answer the phone, I walked to Tiffany's office, starting to panic. It was so unlike Marisa to disappear without calling anyone.

Tiffany, who was drawing a beautiful illustration of a fly for the Bug Off Spray account, put down her pencil when I told her Marisa was still missing.

"Should we call her father?" I asked Tiffany.

"You know she's barely talked to him since her mother died. I don't even think she listed his name and number on her emergency contacts."

"Maybe we should find out who she did list," I suggested.

We called the HR director who said she'd call her three contacts. Three hours later the director called me to say she had struck out. Nobody knew where she was.

The police weren't very helpful either. They didn't seem too concerned that our adult friend who hadn't been heard from since yesterday morning was missing. They told us to call back the end of the week if she still hadn't turned up.

The week dragged on without any calls from Marisa. On Friday, Tiffany and I were about to call the police again when Rhonda announced that I had a caller on line one.

"Hey, Jen, it's me," that familiar quiet voice that wasn't so quiet anymore spoke into the phone.

Oh my God! It was Marisa. "Are you okay?" I shouted. Tiffany closed my office door so we could put her on speaker phone.

"I'm fine. In fact I'm great."

"Where the hell are you?" Tiffany screamed, which made her start to cough. "You've had us worried sick."

"I'm sorry. I really wanted to talk to you before I left, but there was no time."

"No time for what?" Tiffany continued shouting.

"Zack and I eloped on Tuesday."

I looked at Tiffany, who looked as shocked as I was.

"Are you pregnant?" Tiffany asked, still looking stunned.

"No," she giggled.

"Then what's the rush?" Tiffany continued probing.

I couldn't understand it either. It was so out of character for Marisa to do something so spontaneous, especially something like this.

"Zack found out last weekend that he was getting transferred to Detroit. His consulting job in New Jersey was coming to an end, and they needed someone right away at this other pharmaceutical company. At first, I was just planning to go with him for a week, and eventually move there. But then we realized that we couldn't be away from each other that long." She sounded elated.

"Zack proposed an hour before he was supposed to leave on Monday. I didn't have to think about it for a second. I was never so sure about anything in my life. It's not like I have a big, close family to invite to a wedding, so eloping seemed like a good idea. Of course, it would have been perfect if you both could have been there.

"Anyway, I called you both around dinnertime, but neither of you were home. I didn't want to tell you over your answering machines that I was getting married so I figured I'd wait until Tuesday, but that's when we got married, and we wanted to have some kind of a honeymoon so we've been locked in our hotel room for the past few days. I hope you're not mad."

I was too stunned to feel anything. Marisa was married! Marisa, who had never dated the same guy more than three times, had found true love with her first real boyfriend!

"I still don't understand what the rush was," Tiffany said. "Couldn't you just live together for a while until you knew each other longer?"

"I guess we could have, but neither of us wanted to. I wanted to marry him and be his wife. I've never been more sure of anything in my life."

We were both silent for a moment.

Tiffany finally backed down. "In that case, I'm really happy for you. It sounds like you know what you're doing."

"I absolutely do. I've never been happier before." And she truly sounded it.

"Congratulations," I said, feeling a lump in my throat. "You certainly deserve to be happy."

"Thanks, guys. I'll be back in a month to get all my stuff so we'll get together then, okay?"

"Hey, by the way, how did you get past Rhonda without her recognizing your voice?" Tiffany asked.

"I had Zack call and say he was calling on behalf of Miles Oskerburger."

"Pretty clever," Tiffany laughed.

Marisa asked us to transfer her to John so she could give him the news. He would flip when he found out she was gone. It had taken him months to finally replace Meany.

"I hope Zack treats her well," I said after putting the receiver down.

"If he doesn't, we'll just have to go out to Detroit and take care of him." Even though Tiffany talked tough, I saw some redness developing in the corner of her eyes, and her voice cracked a few times. Looking at her was like looking at the proud mother of the bride. "I'm sure going to miss her," Tiffany said, looking away from me. When I saw her blot her eyes with a tissue, I realized how much Marisa meant to both of us.

"Can I have one of those, too," I asked.

Tiffany smiled through a few tears and handed me a tissue.

I left work early so I would be ready when Mike picked me up. Feeling hopeful, I realized that Marisa's Mr. Right had really turned out to be Mr. Right. If it happened to her, it could happen to me, too. For the first time all week, I desperately missed Mike. Now I could finally reply to all his saved emails.

"We found Marisa," I told Mike as soon as he walked through my front door.

"That's great. Where was she?" Mike knew how worried I had been about her.

"You're not going to believe it, but she eloped with that guy she just met a few months ago."

"Why wouldn't I believe it? Relationships move faster when you get older. Besides, when it's right, it's right."

I couldn't have said it better myself.

Chapter 17

Possible Cures:

1. Find a guy who your family immediately embraces as part of the family (regardless of whether he fits in better with them than you do).
2. When you find the right guy, reel him in like a fish.

After postponing the inevitable for another four weeks, I couldn't put it off any longer…it was time to introduce Mike to my parents. I was afraid if I didn't, my mom and Mike's bubby would set it up without me.

I hoped that for one night my mom didn't act like my mom. I was sure Mike didn't expect my mother to dress like Britney Spears and act like Samantha from *Sex and the City.*

When Mike came to pick me up for the big meeting, I was surprised to see him wearing a suit and tie. "You look really nice, but you didn't need to get so dressed up."

"I want to make a good impression," Mike said, fixing his collar. "This is an important occasion."

Maybe I should have worn a dress instead of my black bootleg jeans and a sweater. Now I felt completely underdressed.

"How are you, beautiful?" Mike gave me a kiss before coming in. I had finally asked him to close his mouth when he kissed me. I think I hurt his feelings, but all his slobbering was making my chin break out. He was getting better, but he still needed reminders from time to time.

"Are you nervous?" I asked, while looking for my black wool coat in my closet.

"Of course I am." Mike straightened his tie and checked to make sure his top shirt button was buttoned. "It means a lot to me that they want to meet me."

He had no idea how much they wanted to meet him, especially my mom. After returning from Vegas, my mom immediately sought out Mike's bubby at bingo night. Since then, my mom, Barb, and Mike's bubby played at the same table every week.

Mike thought it was great that they were getting to know each other. I thought it was just plain scary. I certainly didn't want Mike's bubby finding out things about me that I hadn't told Mike yet.

"Are you ready?" Mike said. "I don't want to be late." He was starting to fidget.

"Ready," I said, finally locating my coat in the back of the closet.

As I locked my door, I heard Josh crying and Jessica screaming something about a lost baby doll. Weren't those kids ever happy?

"Why don't I drive tonight?" I offered as we walked toward the parking lot. "After all, you are coming to meet my family."

"No way. I'd be embarrassed if they saw you driving me around. I guess I'm old-fashioned, but I think a guy should always drive on dates."

As independent as I liked to think I was, I didn't mind being chauffeured around. "Well, if you insist."

When Mike opened my car door, I saw a Jewish apple cake already in my seat. "My mom baked this for your parents for dessert tonight. Would you mind holding it while I drive? I don't want it to fall."

Taking the cake, I kissed Mike on the cheek. "You're very thoughtful."

"I hope they like it," he said. Looking at his watch, he seemed concerned. "If we don't leave now, we're going to be late." I never saw Mike move so fast as he ran to the driver's seat.

I didn't tell Mike that he could arrive late with a stale rye bread and my mom would still like him. After all, he was the nice Jewish professional she had been praying I'd meet since college.

"You just sit back and relax." Mike put on the seat warmers as he pulled out of his parking spot.

There was nothing like having your butt toasted like a bagel on a cold December evening.

As soon as we pulled into my parent's driveway, my mom raced down the steps to greet us. Before we got out of the car, my mom stood outside the driver's door. I thought Mike would have to knock her over in order to get out.

"Mike, I am so very glad to meet you. I'm not used to Jen bringing home a male friend for dinner."

Go ahead. Just tell him I haven't brought home a boyfriend for two years.

"It's nice to meet you, too. Jen, please, let me get that door for you." I was already halfway out of the car, but Mike insisted that he race around and help me out.

"I just love your car," my mom gushed. "A BMW is such a nice car for a man your age."

"Thanks. And I love your house. The stone front makes it look very cozy. By the way, my mom baked this cake for after dinner." Mike placed the cake I was holding into my mother's hands.

"Jen, look, a Jewish apple cake!" From my mom's reaction, you'd think Mike had just handed her the winning lottery ticket.

"Why don't you come in out of this cold," my mom said, while holding on to Mike's coat sleeve as she coaxed him into the house. It was as if she thought he might escape if she didn't physically pull him inside.

"I hope you're hungry because I've been cooking all day."

My mom? Cooking? Had I just stepped into *The Twilight Zone?*

After walking into my parent's living room, Mike handed my mom his gray London Fog coat. "Everything smells wonderful," he said, looking toward the kitchen.

I was relieved that all of the buttons on my mom's silk shirt were fastened. Her skirt almost reached her knees. For once, it didn't look like you could peel off her makeup. And was that an oven mitt on her hand? Had an alien taken over my mother's body?

"Everyone, Mike's here," my mom announced.

Everyone? Who was everyone? But I found out seconds later as my father, Kathy, Jeff, and even Barb appeared, looking Mike over like I had just brought home a movie star.

Since when had this become a dinner party? I was supposed to be introducing Mike to my parents. Meeting my entire family seemed a lot more serious. My mother better not scare Mike off with all these people. And why was Barb here again?

After introducing Mike to my entire entourage, my mom invited him to sit down in my father's favorite recliner. Everyone else gathered near him on the couch.

"Sorry for staring," my dad said, standing next to his chair, "but you look exactly like your father."

"A lot of people tell me that." Mike seemed pleased by the comparison.

"Would you like a drink?" my mom asked. "An appetizer? How about a piece of bread? It just came out of the oven."

Why didn't she just offer him a massage and spa treatment while she was at it?

"No, thanks," he said. "I want to save room for dinner."

I wondered if he'd still feel that way after tasting it. The last time my mom cooked, which was probably sometime in the 1990's, everything she took out of the oven was completely black. There was so much smoke in the kitchen that the smoke detectors went off. We ended up ordering pizza that night.

"So, Mike, have you been keeping track of the football game?" my dad asked, pointing toward the TV. "The Eagles just scored a touchdown."

"Harris, Mike doesn't want to talk about football," my mother snapped. "He's here to get to know us."

"Sorry, Mike. I just thought you'd be interested in the game."

"Well, he's not! Mike, please sit down, and Harris, will you turn off that TV. We have a guest."

"Sylvia, it's the last quarter, and the score is tied." My dad stared longingly at the television screen. "This might be the last game that the Eagles win this season."

"I'm sure you've seen them win many games before during other seasons. You can see all the highlights from the game tonight on the news." My mom placed her hands on her hips. "Now turn that thing off. You're embarrassing me."

He was embarrassing her? Did she have any idea how much she was embarrassing me?

"Oh, it's okay, I don't mind having the TV on," Mike said, seeming oblivious to my mom's flip tone toward my dad. "When I was younger, my dad used to buy season tickets every year to the Eagles game. No matter how cold it was, we'd be out there cheering them on."

"No kidding?" my dad said. "I've been getting season tickets for the past twenty years." He turned his attention to Mike as a deodorant commercial came on the TV. "I remember seeing your father there with a young boy. I guess that must have been you. That's quite a coincidence."

"It really is. Jen told me that you and my dad knew each other. Did you see each other a lot?"

"Every month. He and I were both on the board of the local chapter of the American Association of Accountants. Your dad never missed a meeting. He was a really good man, Mike." My dad's voice became somber. "I was very sorry when Jen told me he had passed away."

"Well, it's always nice talking to someone who knew him so well. It makes me feel closer to him."

"He is such a warm, sweet guy," Kathy whispered, her voice getting progressively higher as she finished her sentence.

When Mike got up to pour himself a soda, Kathy leaped up from her seat. "I'll get it for you, Mike. What would you like?"

"A Pepsi would be great. Thanks. So what's the age difference between you and Jen?" he asked Kathy.

"We're four years apart." Kathy poured Mike's drink, not surprisingly, into a large Waterford glass.

"I guess you've always been close since you're so close in age." He carefully took the glass from Kathy.

"Oh yeah." Kathy beamed at him. "Jen and I have always had a great relationship."

We did? Had she forgotten that we had absolutely nothing in common other than our dysfunctional parents?

"That's nice." Mike smiled.

"Jen and Kathy are as close as Mary Kate and Ashley," my mother shouted. Even though we couldn't see her from inside the kitchen, her voice came through loud and clear.

Was she for real? I bit my tongue to refrain myself from setting the record straight.

"Where do you live?" Kathy asked, returning to the couch, coincidentally with a Pepsi also.

"In Huntingdon Valley." Mike sat on the couch next to Kathy and me this time.

"Oh, that's a nice neighborhood." Kathy's grin got larger with every answer Mike gave.

"We like it," Mike answered.

"We?" Kathy looked concerned for the first time.

"Yeah, me and my mom." He took a sip of his drink and placed the crystal on a coaster on the glass table in front of us.

"You live with your mom? That's so nice." Once again, my mom's voice came through the kitchen walls. Wasn't she supposed to be cooking?

"So I hear you're a nurse," Mike said, addressing Kathy. "Where do you work?"

"At Jefferson Hospital. Jeff works there, too. He's a cardiologist."

"That's a great hospital," Mike said. "I have a few friends who are doctors there, too."

"Really, what are their names?" Jeff asked, sitting down on the opposite side of Mike. The guys seemed to hit it off right away. They had similar personalities, being that they were both quiet and soft-spoken, and slightly on the introverted side.

"My friend, Matt Steinberg, is an internist and my other friend, Rich Zeitz, is an oncologist," Mike said.

"I know Matt," Jeff said. "He and I meet for lunch almost everyday."

Still another coincidence. It seemed like Mike had more connections to my family than I did.

For the next twenty minutes, Mike and Jeff talked about their mutual acquaintances. Finally, Mike excused himself and walked over to the kitchen.

"Can I help you with dinner, Mrs. Greenberg?" Mike opened the kitchen door where Barb was keeping my mom company while she prepared dinner.

"No!" my mom shrieked, causing Mike to back up. Apparently realizing that she had just screamed into my new boyfriend's ear, my mom peeked her head through the door. "Sorry, I didn't mean to shout, but I want to surprise you with everything I'm making. You just relax and let me do the work. And please call me Sylvia."

Mike returned to the couch, looking slightly startled from my mom's sudden outburst.

What was she up to? I decided to see what good old Sylvia was doing in the kitchen. I quietly opened the kitchen door as Barb pulled a roasted chicken out of the oven, while my mom filed her nails. "Just as I thought. Mom, you could have ordered deli."

"No, I couldn't. Mike's bubby told me that his mother cooks him a full-course dinner every night when he gets home from work. How could I throw some corn beef on his plate when he's used to home cooking?"

"I don't cook," I reminded her.

"Well, maybe you should start," my mother said. "You can't exactly serve your husband and children Lean Cuisines every night."

"You did!"

"I did a lot of things I shouldn't have," she said, putting the nail file in her purse. "Now don't give me away."

I promised, wondering what things she had done that she regretted.

"Dinner," my mom announced.

We all piled into the dining room while Barb offered to help my mom serve. Of course this made sense, considering she had cooked the entire dinner.

"Have some potato knishes," my mom said, shoveling three on Mike's plate.

"Thanks." He smiled graciously.

"And try this fruit noodle kugel. My grandmother gave me her secret recipe before she died."

Where did my mom come up with this stuff? Her grandmother had such bad arthritis, she could barely hold a spoon. Her grandfather had cooked all their meals.

"How about a piece of challah?" I watched my mom pile gefilte fish, chopped liver, and brisket on Mike's plate before going back in the kitchen to get kreplah for the soup. Mike now had enough food to last till breakfast and we had enough Jewish food at our table to feed an entire synagogue.

"I'll try one of those apple blintzes," my dad said, holding up his plate.

"Harris, I'm serving our guest. You'll have to wait."

"That's okay, Sylvia," Mike said. "I have plenty. Go ahead, Harris, help yourself."

I still couldn't figure out whether Mike detected the tension between my parents, but how couldn't he see it? Maybe he was so busy trying to impress them that he didn't notice. Or maybe he just didn't want to notice.

"I think it's nice that you still live at home," my mom said, sitting down at the table. "I wish Jen still lived here, but she was determined to move out as soon as she graduated from college. So what do you think about a young girl living alone?"

"Mom!" I felt my face grow warm.

"I think a girl as pretty as Jen has to be careful." Mike dug into his fish. "There are a lot of crazy people in this world."

"Exactly." My mom looked pleased. "Kathy didn't move out until she got married."

Nobody mentioned that Kathy was only twenty-two when she got married. I didn't like where this conversation was headed.

My mom and Mike spent the next fifteen minutes talking about the dangers of living alone, while I silently ate Barb's dinner. Mike seemed to be getting along better with my family than me. Perhaps they would adopt him if we broke up.

"How do you like working at Penn?" Kathy asked. I couldn't imagine that her lips were long enough to smile any wider than she already was.

"It's great. We have some of the best professors in the world. It's really an honor to work with such intelligent people."

"They're lucky to work with you," Kathy said.

"I'm sure your hours are much better than Jen's work schedule," my mom said, rolling her eyes in my direction.

"I think anybody's hours would be better than Jen's," Mike said, and I didn't like the tone of his voice.

"She would probably work less hours in a sweatshop in Chile," my mom said, obviously enjoying having an ally.

Why did I feel like the outsider at my own home, while Mike appeared to have become part of the family?

"I've been telling Jen for years that they expect too much of her time," my mother continued.

"I agree, but they obviously think very highly of her if they keep giving her promotions," Mike said, this time gazing at me with a look of adoration.

What was that? A compliment? About me? I was so surprised, I almost choked on my knish.

"I hope they appreciate how devoted you are to them, Jen." Mike said, while placing his hand on mine under the table.

It was the first nice thing anyone had said to me since we arrived. Come to think of it, it was the only thing anyone had said to me since we arrived.

"They're really lucky to have such a great employee," he said. "Almost as lucky as I am to have met you."

"He's so sweet," Kathy said, swooning over his words.

Now I felt bad for getting mad at Mike. He was probably just going along with my mom so she would like him.

"Jen told me that you've been taking her to see all the new Broadway shows in New York." Kathy sounded giddy. "I just love the theater. Have you always been a fan?"

My mom served Mike another portion of chicken. Amazingly, nothing had landed on his lap yet.

"Oh yeah, I've always loved seeing shows," Mike said, diving into a chicken breast. "When *Phantom of the Opera* first came to New York, my sister and I got tickets to the first performance. It was awesome."

"How old is your sister?" Kathy asked, leaning forward on her elbows as if watching a one-person play.

"Allison's twenty-seven, and she's the greatest," he said with total conviction in his eyes.

"What does she do?" Heaven forbid, Kathy didn't ask that question.

"She's a pharmacist," he said proudly, as if talking about his child. "She works at a hospital in Boston."

"You must miss her," Kathy said.

"I do." But the pride had disappeared from his face. "I was really upset when she moved to another state, but her boyfriend found a better job there."

"Oh, they live together?" My mom raised her eyebrow. Strike one against Mike's family.

"Unfortunately." He squirmed in his seat, looking distressed.

"It sounds like you don't like him," my mother probed. Perhaps it wasn't a strike after all.

"I admit that I'm overprotective of Allison, and I guess in my eyes nobody will ever be good enough for her, but her boyfriend's not exactly the type of guy I wanted her to end up with." He sighed in between finishing the chicken breast and picking up a chicken wing.

"Why's that?" My mom seemed very interested in Mike's opinion.

"Well, first of all, her boyfriend isn't Jewish. I think it really helps when you marry someone in your own religion. Marriage is hard enough without marrying out of your faith."

"I agree with you one hundred percent," my mom beamed. "Marriages last longer when you marry someone who has your same religion and nationality."

If that was the case, why was she vacationing in Vegas without my dad?

"Exactly," Mike said, now eating some kasha.

My mom continued the interrogation. "Is Allison's boyfriend a pharmacist, too?"

"Well, that's the other problem. I don't want to sound like a snob, but her boyfriend is a mechanic. I always hoped my little sister would marry a white-collar professional like my dad. I hope you don't think I'm terrible for saying that." Mike's eyes shifted from side to side waiting for their reaction, but he didn't have to worry too long.

My mom and Kathy smiled at Mike with love in their eyes.

"I think you're perfect for saying that," my mom said, as she served Mike a third portion of Barb's chicken.

~

Kathy and I helped my mom clear the dining room table. "Jen, I'm so glad you finally met the right guy," my mom said. "I know the two of you will be very happy together." The way she talked, you'd think we had just announced our engagement.

My mom returned to the kitchen with a few dirty plates. Maybe she was going to ask Barb to put them in the dishwasher for her.

"He really is great," Kathy said. "And he seems really serious about you." Her voice hit its highest note on the word serious.

"What makes you say that?" I carefully removed some leftover chicken from a Wedgwood plate and threw it in a big trash bag.

"He said that fate must have brought you together in that deli, that he'd been looking for the right girl for so long and there you were sitting right in front of him at Moish's."

"Really? He told you that?" I stopped clearing plates to look up at her in surprise.

"Yep, he sure did. He also told me how much he enjoys being with you, but that's obvious by the way he looks at you. Jen, the guy's crazy about you, and he's such a perfect catch. All you have to do now is reel him in."

"You're talking about him like he's a trout." I threw a wishbone in the trash bag.

"The same principles of fishing apply to husbands." She spoke as if she were reciting the theory of relativity as opposed to her own theory on marriage. "You throw in your line and bring in the fish. You return all the fish with imperfections back to sea, but when you finally catch that delicacy, you cast out your line and pull it in until it can't remember what the ocean behind it looked like."

Nothing like taking the romance out of a relationship. "Kathy, do you realize that you just compared the entire institution of marriage to a fishing expedition?" I placed a tie around the closed trash bag, wishing I could place one around her smiley, giggly mouth.

"Okay, even if you don't like my analogy, I still think Mike's the right guy for you. Not only is he a Jewish college professor, but he treats you like a royal princess. What else could you possibly want in a husband?"

And for the rest of the evening, I pondered that question. After saying good-bye to *everyone*, and returning to Mike's BMW, I thought about it some more. What else could I possibly want my future husband to have? Unable to think of anything specific, I sat back and turned on my seat warmer.

Chapter 18

Sexual-Related Complications of The Marriage Epidemic:

1. If your boyfriend is old-fashioned about having sex too soon, you recite all the virtues of celibacy (even if you don't believe them).

2. If he looks like a gorilla without clothes, you close your eyes and pretend you're making love to John Stamos on a bear-skin rug.

3. If he's bad in bed, you convince yourself that a few issues of *Cosmo* and a relationship book written by Dr. Phil will cure him.

"Hello, you have reached Ilene Meeney. I'm sorry, but I'm not available to take your call…"

Well, why not! She was never available to take my call. I slammed down the cordless phone in my bedroom, tired of hearing Meany's voice mail message. I had been listening to it for the past three weeks.

Last week, after hanging up on her answering machine for the fiftieth time, I spent two days writing a message that I could leave on her voice mail. I wanted it to sound professional, intelligent, and witty.

Unfortunately, I never bothered reading it out loud before the moment of truth because I ended up sounding like one of those annoying robotic messages you get from your doctor's office to remind you about your upcoming appointment. The message looked great on paper, but sounded way too formal for a telephone message. No wonder I wrote for print and not broadcasting.

Naturally, when Meany didn't call me back, I assumed it was because my message had sounded so strange. How could I possibly call her multibillion-dollar clients who barely spoke English when I couldn't even leave one intelligent-sounding message for her?

Still, it would have been nice for her to get back to me. She had sort of, kind of offered me a job. Hadn't she?

Now, on New Year's Eve day, I couldn't take it anymore. I knew most ad agencies closed by noon today, so I decided to give it one last try at ten o'clock. This time, instead of dialing Meany's extension, I dialed zero for the operator.

"Hi, uh, I was, uh...What I mean is, I'm, uh, looking for, uh..." What was wrong with me? I was talking to a receptionist who probably didn't make much more than I did when I worked at that linen store during college.

"Yes? May I help you?" asked a very professional sounding receptionist. Well, she certainly didn't have any trouble speaking. What was my problem?

Deep cleansing breath. Inhale, exhale, inhale, exhale. "I'm trying to reach Ilene Meeney. Do you know when she'll be back in her office?"

"I'm sorry, but she's in Venice on business until the first of the year." Within five seconds, I was back in that bottomless voice mailbox.

I banged the receiver down with such force I half expected to hear Randy knocking on my door with advice on handling the phone in a quieter fashion.

I shouldn't even have been calling her now anyway. I should have been packing for my special New Year's Eve getaway with Mike, so why couldn't I get motivated? It was the first time Mike had asked me to go away with him. This was a big deal.

So far Mike had been the perfect gentleman, barely getting past second base, or was it third? I could never remember. Whichever it was, his hands and mouth had still never made it down south, but I had a feeling that would change after this weekend.

Starting the new year at a historic Victorian bed and breakfast in Cape May certainly sounded romantic. Mike said he wanted to start the new year holding me in his arms. Since I had agreed to go away with him, his poems had taken on a new twist. Now they all included lines about how much he wanted to get to know me better and get closer to me. He never actually mentioned the word sex, but the message was definitely implied.

I inventoried my overnight bag to make sure I had everything. New lace lingerie, three pairs of matching black panties, thong, just in case, and condoms, also just in case. And finally, the new velvet Liz Claiborne cocktail dress I had spent an entire week's salary on. Looked like all the essentials were there.

The phone rang as I surveyed my makeup. "Ready for the big weekend?" My mom asked. Why didn't she just ask me if I was looking forward to a sex-filled weekend with Mike? And didn't most mothers feel uncomfortable thinking about their daughters having sex? I bet she'd be thrilled if I told her I'd been practicing my sucking skills on a banana.

"I'm almost done packing."

"Do you think tonight's the night?"

"Mom!" Was she for real?

"Sorry, I'm not trying to rush you, but I thought maybe Mike would pop the question, being that you'll be together on New Year's Eve."

"Oh." Okay, she wasn't as perverted as I thought. "Mom, we've only been dating for a short time."

"Your father and I didn't date much longer than you when we got engaged."

I really wished she'd stop comparing us to them. It wasn't very reassuring.

"I wouldn't go chilling those champagne glasses yet," I said. I closed my suitcase, hoping I had everything I needed.

"Well, make sure you let me know when I can."

"You'll be the first one I call. So what are you doing tonight?" I sat down at my vanity to refresh my makeup.

"Barb and I are going to her friend's party downtown. We made reservations at the Four Seasons in case one of us has too much to drink."

"I assume Dad's on his own again this year." I tweezed out three new gray hairs, feeling old just seeing them.

"You know your father. He'll be snoring by nine o'clock. I spent too many years sitting by the TV, watching that ball drop from Times

Square while your father slept." The resentment in her voice was obvious. "This year, I'm having fun."

I wasn't sure I wanted my mom to have too much fun, especially with Barb.

After wishing each other a happy new year, I finished packing and waited for Mike. I always got nostalgic thinking about the end of another year. Had I kept any of my New Year's resolutions this past year? I couldn't even remember what they were.

And what would I be doing next year at this time? Perhaps looking down at a shiny diamond on my finger? Maybe planning a wedding with Mike? Would this be the year I got engaged, and maybe even married? Or would I be spending next New Year's Eve alone? If only I had a crystal ball to look into the future.

"So what do you think?" Mike asked. We had just checked into the Duke of Wellington Bed and Breakfast, and were sitting on the front porch.

"It's beautiful. I feel like I just stepped back in time to the Victorian days. Do you know this place dates back to 1896? It says it right here in this brochure." I had picked one up while Mike carried both of our suitcases up the spiral staircase, all three flights.

"I always feel like I'm walking through history when I stay at one of these bed and breakfasts," he said. "This one is my favorite. I like its Queen Anne detailing and its dramatic sixty-five-foot tower. And these pillars on this porch are indicative of the Colonial Revival period."

I couldn't add anything to that description. I imagined calling this bed and breakfast awesome would sound rather shallow compared to Mike's eloquent choice of words. "That's pretty impressive." Did that sound stupid? Hey, what was I worried about? This was Mike. He practically worshipped the ground I walked on. I didn't have to worry about how I sounded with him.

"I'm glad you like it because I want this to be a special weekend," Mike said. "And can you believe how lucky we got with the weather? The woman at the check-in counter said it's supposed to go up to sixty degrees today."

214

"I knew it was supposed to be warm, but that's amazing for December." I leaned against the step, enjoying the warmth of the sun. "Maybe we can go for a walk on the beach."

And as always, Mike eagerly agreed.

We crossed the street, holding hands. I loved seeing all the Victorian homes lined up on every street. As we got near the beach, a trolley filled with tourists passed by. Feeling very relaxed, I took off my New Balance sneaks and tied them together.

"Aren't you going to take off your shoes?" Mike wore a pair of brown loafers.

"No, I hate getting sand between my toes." He scrunched his nose. "I never walk on the beach barefoot."

"Oh." Guess that ruled out having sex under the boardwalk. I had always fantasized about doing it there. Of course, there were lots of places to have sex that didn't involve sand.

The ocean roared as we walked down four steps to reach the beach. "I'm really glad you wanted to go away with me this weekend." Mike trudged through the sand with his leather shoes. "I hope you know that I'm not trying to rush you into something if you're not ready, but I wanted some quality time together. So even if nothing happens, I'll still be happy."

Well, I wouldn't! Rushing me into something? Was he kidding? I was getting worried that he hadn't tried something yet. Maybe he wasn't sexually attracted to me. If he had driven me all the way out here to tell me he just wanted to be friends, I swore I would convert and become a nun.

"I don't feel like you're rushing me into anything." *I'm ready to have sex with you, you moron!* Okay, time to get a grip. He was just being nice.

"Glad to hear it." Mike took my hand. "As much as I love living with my mother, it definitely has its drawbacks. It's a good thing you have your own place, or we'd never have any time together."

"I'm sure your mom appreciates having you around." I wiggled my toes, feeling the cool powdery grains beneath my feet.

"She does, and she's a great roommate. She even makes my bed and does my laundry."

Was it a good thing for a grown man to let his mother do these things for him? And hadn't his bubby told my mom that she cooked him dinner everyday? Didn't she have anything better to do with her life than wait on Mike? "She sounds…uh…very caring."

"She's great. I can't wait for you to meet her. She'd like you to come over for dinner next month. Would that be okay with you?"

"Yeah, I'd like to meet her." His mother! To most people meeting a guy's parents probably wasn't a big deal, but considering none of my ex-boyfriends had ever introduced me to their families, this was huge.

"I'd like to meet Stacy one of these days, too." Mike stopped to shake some sand out of his shoes.

"She wants to meet you, too." I tried to pull Mike closer to the ocean, but he resisted. "The problem is finding a time when she can make it. Lately, she spends every second that she's not working, planning her wedding."

"That sounds like a fun way to spend your time." His eyes lit up as he spoke.

Another encouraging statement.

We continued strolling along the beach, passing many other people along the way. The shore was so crowded, it would have looked like a typical beach day had everyone not been wearing long pants and jackets. We passed lots of couples who were holding hands, walking arm-in-arm, or kissing. I loved being part of a couple. I never wanted to spend another New Year's Eve alone again.

I hadn't told Mike, but this was only the second time I ever had a date for New Year's Eve, and the first time was when I was fifteen and Joel Saltzberg invited me to go roller skating with him. I always seemed boyfriendless whenever major events took place, like Valentine's Day, birthdays, and graduations. But not this time.

"I'm surprised you've never been to Cape May before," Mike said. "I think it's the nicest shore point in Jersey."

"It is really nice, but my family always went to Atlantic City or Wildwood for vacation."

As we got older, I had stopped thinking of them as vacations. By the second day, my mom usually stormed out of our hotel room, leaving my dad sitting on the balcony, staring aimlessly at the ocean. If it weren't for Kathy, I would have spent my summer vacations parked in front of the TV. She and I usually escaped to the amusement piers.

"My parents owned a home in Cape May while I was growing up," Mike said, while staring at the ocean. "I used to go for long walks along the beach with my dad. He and I had some of our best conversations during those times. It was during one of those walks that my dad helped me figure out that I wanted to teach."

"How'd he do that?"

"I had originally planned to become an accountant and work at my dad's office. My dad and uncles had always talked about it, and I never considered doing anything else, even though I never really enjoyed working with numbers. I figured I'd get used to it eventually."

"Was your dad disappointed that you didn't want to become an accountant?" I enjoyed the cool breeze that blew my hair away from my face.

"Just the opposite. The summer I graduated from high school, my dad and I were walking along this shore, when he surprised me by telling me that he realized I didn't like accounting work." Mike pushed his windblown hair off of his forehead.

"Apparently, he had watched me struggle through paperwork in his office. He asked me what I enjoyed doing, and I ended up telling him how much I loved tutoring kids, how I got a great sense of satisfaction when someone I tutored finally understood a new concept. He said that if I enjoyed tutoring so much I should think about becoming a teacher where I could teach new ideas to students all day long. He said I had the patience and the knack of explaining things to others that would make me a great teacher."

It must be great having parents who were so supportive. The only thing my mom ever encouraged me to do was get married and have babies. So far, I had been nothing but a big disappointment to her. "So did you always want to teach at a college?"

"No, at first I thought I'd teach grade school. I've always loved being around little kids, and the idea of opening the world up to them at such a young age seemed really exciting. But the more I attended college, the more I wanted to learn. I think I'd still be a full-time student today if I could afford it." Mike steered me farther away from the ocean to avoid a flock of seagulls attacking two kids who were eating French fries.

"So when did you decide to get your Ph.D.?"

"Ironically, it was during another walk on this beach with my dad. This time, I was in my junior year of college and I was trying to decide exactly what I wanted to teach after I graduated. My dad said that if I loved college so much, I should think about going to graduate school. He even offered to pay some of my tuition."

"That was nice," I said, remembering how thrilled I was two years ago when I paid off my last student loan.

"It's funny how some decisions seem so clear after someone makes the simplest suggestion," Mike said. "As soon as he said the words, I knew I wanted to get my Ph.D. in history. I felt so relieved that I had figured out what I wanted to do with my life. If it weren't for my walks right here with my dad, I might never have become a teacher."

"No wonder you like coming here so much. You obviously have a lot of nice memories of your father on this beach."

"Yeah, I miss being here with him, but now I have another incredible memory on this beach because now I've been here with you."

His words were so beautiful that I wanted to cry. Was it possible for someone to be too good to be true?

We celebrated the new year at the restaurant attached to our bed and breakfast. We started out with brie baked in some kind of puffy pastry and baked shellfish. This was followed by lobster bisque and a tossed salad with lemon poppy-seed vinaigrette. For the main entrée, I selected the twin lobster tails, which of course meant that Mike chose the same thing. The dessert tray had some of the most incredible cakes and pastries I had ever tasted.

Throughout the night, a great band played festive music. The dining room was decorated with wreaths and garlands. Each table had a poinsettia plant as a centerpiece, and in the middle of the room stood an enormous Christmas tree decorated with Victorian ornaments.

I was convinced that my fairy godmother had transformed me into Cinderella for the evening because it was truly a magical evening. All the women wore cocktail dresses or gowns. Some of the men even wore tuxes.

"Ten, nine, eight..." We all counted down to the new year.

As we screamed the number one together, Mike bent over to kiss me while the band played "Auld Land Syne."

"I have a feeling it's going to be a wonderful year," Mike said, smiling at me.

Oh, I sure hoped so.

As soon as we toasted the new year, we returned to our warm, cozy room with two antique dressers and a handcrafted four-poster iron bed with a large woven bedspread draped on top.

Why did that bed make me so nervous, especially after the incredible evening I'd just had with Mike?

I had barely taken off my jacket before he began kissing me, unlike any kisses he had given me before. These were deeper and more urgent. "Maybe we should get comfortable," I suggested. "I think I'll use the bathroom."

He nodded as I walked into the bathroom and closed the door behind me. I changed into my black negligee and panties, and brushed my teeth. Next to the toilet was a magazine rack filled with all kinds of pamphlets and brochures about New Jersey shore points. Before long I was reading about the history of Cape May. I never realized it was the oldest seashore resort in the United States. Interesting.

"Are you okay in there?" Mike called from the other side of the door.

Oops. What was I doing? The nicest, kindest, most wonderful man I ever met was waiting to make love to me and I was reading. I was really losing it. I put on my red satin bathrobe and closed the bathroom door behind me.

"Is everything all right?" Mike looked concerned.

"Yeah, fine." No need to mention the history of Cape May right now.

"You're more than fine. You're beautiful."

He was so sweet. And he looked really cute in those blue IZOD pajamas. I didn't know IZOD made pajamas. Did all of Mike's clothes have alligators on them?

Mike turned off the light while I climbed into bed. Then he moved over to me and kissed me lightly at first, and then with more force. I tasted his lips with my tongue and he moved his hands up and down my back. We continued kissing and hugging each other for a while. Finally, Mike began exploring my breasts with his hands.

Now I was getting charged up. I decided to take matters into my own hands. I slipped out of my lingerie, leaving only my panties on. Mike moved his head down to my breasts until they grew hard.

After going four months without sex, it wouldn't take long for me to explode with passion. I unzipped Mike's pants and let my fingers wander between his legs until I found what I was looking for. As Mike grew hard in my hands, he groaned and held me tightly against him.

Just when was he going to take off his clothes? And had he noticed that my legs were wide open waiting for his touch? I tried to nibble on his breasts, but I couldn't get to them through his shirt.

I wanted to feel him naked next to my body so I once again took the lead. I slowly unbuttoned each button, making a show out of it as I licked him and teased him with my tongue after each one was unfastened. After I opened the last one, he slipped it off.

Yikes! Where did all that hair come from? It looked like he was wearing an angora sweater. He was a lot thinner than I realized. In between all that hair, I could see his bones sticking out of his rib cage. I bent down to kiss his stomach and came up with a wad of hair in my mouth. Maybe I should work on the more important areas.

I helped Mike take off his pants so I could wander down yonder with my tongue. Okay, how about a little action for me? He continued nibbling on my breasts, but I needed his mouth much lower right now.

I was getting very hot and didn't want to lose the momentum so I took his hand and placed it between my legs. Mmm. Finally! But what was he doing? I needed him to move faster, faster, but he was moving so, so slow. I was going to lose it.

As if sensing my anxiety, he rolled over and slipped on a condom. "Ready?" he asked.

"Yeah, ready, ready." *Let's go already.*

Ahh, now that was better. He was inside me and I was completely wet. I wanted to hold on a little longer, had to hold on…but, what the hell? Mike let out a mammoth groan and grew limp inside me.

What about me? Hadn't he forgotten something inside, like my orgasm? Where was Mr. Wow when I needed him?

"I knew being with you would be great, but I never imagined it would be this incredible," Mike said.

Probably not the time to critique his performance, but he obviously needed a few lessons on foreplay and climax. With all the subjects he studied at school, couldn't he have at least taken one sex ed course?

Okay, so we had a little problem here, but I had already improved the kissing issue. I was sure Dr. Phil would agree that we could work on this, too. We simply had to communicate our needs to each other. I couldn't exactly hold his lovemaking style against him, could I?

Chapter 19

Psychological-Related Complications of The Marriage Epidemic:

1. You believe a *nice* boyfriend will automatically make a good husband.

2. You believe ending up alone is synonymous with living in hell.

3. You believe that telling your partner how to improve his sexual techniques will make it happen immediately and consistently, forever.

After oohing and aahing through pretend orgasms for the next six weeks, I realized I could and did hold Mike's performance in bed against him. I was beginning to feel like Meg Ryan in *When Harry Met Sally*. As nice as Mike was, there was no way I could live the rest of my life having fake orgasms.

Since our first night together in Cape May, he had become like a dog in heat. He was like an adolescent who suddenly discovered that he had erections. Unfortunately, his techniques in bed weren't much better than a teenager's, and rarely lasted much longer than a boy who had just reached puberty.

We had gotten into a routine where as soon as we returned to my apartment after a date, Mike would immediately lead me to my bedroom, but not tonight. I could no longer pretend that he was the next best thing to Tarzan in bed.

After returning from dinner this evening, Mike was already halfway down my hallway when he realized I wasn't following him. "What's wrong?" Mike asked, looking confused.

"Mike, we need to talk."

"What's up?" He looked worried as he returned to the living room.

"Nothing major." Okay, it was major, but I thought I'd play it down. "Mike, when was the last relationship you had before me?"

"Why?"

"Just curious. I mean now that we're sleeping together, it's sometimes good to talk about these things."

"Oh. You don't have to worry about that." He looked relieved. "I've always been sure to wear a condom, and besides, I haven't been with that many girls anyway."

No kidding. "So about how many girls do you think you've been with?"

He hesitated a little too long. "To be honest, there really haven't been too many?"

"How many?" I wanted numbers here.

This time he paused for a good few minutes. "Just one," he answered.

That's it? A thirty-four-year-old man who only had sex with one other woman? Well, that explained a lot. "Who was she?" Without realizing it I had folded my arms across my chest.

Mike sighed as he sat down next to me on the loveseat. "I met her my freshman year of college at a Hillel party. We dated for three years, but never had sex because she was an Orthodox Jew, and as you can imagine, pretty religious."

"You didn't mind going without sex all that time?"

"It's not like I didn't want to, but I respected her beliefs. Besides, I was in love with her and I was afraid I'd lose her if I pressured her. Anyway, around senior year, things really started heating up between us. Are you sure you want to hear this?"

"Yeah, go on."

"Sarah decided she didn't want to wait anymore and we began sleeping together." He got that same sad look on his face that he got when he talked about his father. "I was going to ask her to marry me after we graduated, but a week before graduation, she broke up with me. She said she was ashamed of her behavior, and looking at me was a reminder of what she had done."

"That's terrible." I reached over to put my arm around him. "You must have been crushed."

"I was. I was so upset that I wouldn't accept it. For the next six months I tried everything I could to get her back. I even hired a small orchestra to play in front of her apartment to serenade her with love songs, but nothing worked. She wouldn't even look at me."

"And that was it?"

"Yeah, that was it." After ten years, Mike still looked upset. And after ten years, he still hadn't had sex with anyone else?

"That must have been hard for you. So there was nobody else since then?"

"I dated here and there, but never found anyone who seemed right for me again...until you."

This was going to be harder than I thought. "So you never had any one-night stands in college?"

"Nah, I don't believe in casual sex." He put his hand on my lap. "I think you should really care about someone before you become intimate."

Well, there was one for the Oprah show. A guy who didn't believe in one-night stands. "Wasn't there anyone before college who you slept with?"

"I was so shy in high school, I barely spoke to anyone, let alone girls," he said, staring at his shoes. "It wasn't until I started college that I came out of my shell a little. So you see, you have nothing to worry about. I'm totally clean."

I almost laughed out loud when I realized Mike had absolutely no idea why I was asking all these questions.

"So, ready for bed now?" Looking hopeful, Mike stood up and held out his hand.

"Uh, no."

Mike sat down, looking worried again. "Why all the questions, then?"

"Well, uh, this is hard to say, but, um, Mike, I really do care about you, and I'd like things between us to work out, but, um..."

"What is it?" Mike looked terrified.

"I think we need to change the way we do things in bed." All the women's magazines made these conversations sound so easy. Simply tell your partner what you need in bed, they instructed. Yeah, right. There was nothing simple about this.

"Like what?" His voice was a mere whisper.

My mouth became dry as I searched for the right words. It was one thing to tell your boyfriend that he needed a haircut, but telling him he needed to spend more time sucking on your breasts was completely different.

"Jen, just tell me," he pleaded.

I took a deep breath. "Well, first of all, it would help if you took off your clothes."

"Okay, I can do that." He looked slightly encouraged.

"And then there's the foreplay. I mean, I know you get excited really quickly, but you need to give me a chance to catch up. Do you know what I mean?"

"Am I that bad in bed?"

Yes. "No, not at all. Lots of couples have this problem. We just need to talk about our needs so we both feel fulfilled." I was quoting from a recent article in *Women's Circle*.

"Anything else?" Was it my imagination or was he holding his breath?

"Well, it would be nice if you let me come first sometimes. Maybe we could take turns, like sometimes, I could work on you, and then you could work on me. And maybe we could change positions. You don't always have to be on top. And it might be nice to do it in another room besides the bedroom and…"

"I get the idea." Mike looked down at his shoes again.

Oops. Had I gotten carried away? Maybe I shouldn't have offered so much feedback at once.

Silence. I watched Mike stare at the floor for the next five minutes. Now I felt awful. I was a jerk. How could I be so mean when Mike had always been so sweet to me? Maybe I should have given him some more time to figure these things out for himself.

Finally, Mike kneeled before me and took my hands. "Jen, I promise that I will do anything to make you happy. I don't want to lose you. You tell me what to do in bed, and I'll do it."

And he did. The night before Valentine's Day, for the first time since Cape May, I finally fell asleep with a smile on my face.

"So what did Mike give you for Valentine's Day?" Rhonda asked, as I walked in late Monday morning.

An orgasm for the first time. No, probably not the appropriate answer. "This," I said instead, proudly showing off my new diamond heart necklace.

"Ooh, that's pretty," she said, checking out my hand. "Nothing for your ring finger, then?"

What a bitch. "No, no ring." I tried to walk past her, but she walked around her desk and blocked my path.

"Did you hear that Julie and Lynn got engaged last night?"

I put my hands in my pockets so Rhonda wouldn't see my clenched fists. "Both of them?"

"Yeah, and I think Julie met her fiancé right around the time you met Mike."

"How about that." *Asshole.*

"That reminds me," Rhonda continued. "After you and Tiffany are done lunch with Marisa, John wants to have a surprise wedding shower for her. Nothing fancy, but he ordered a cake, so make sure you make up some excuse to bring her back here."

"Will do." Rhonda got out of my face so I could walk past her. I was glad that Marisa would finally get her shot at a wedding shower at work. For the longest time, we had been so sure that we would be the last ones at Premier to get married. Apparently, only one of us had been right.

"How's married life?" Tiffany asked. She sat opposite Marisa and me at the diner around the corner from work.

"It's the best," Marisa said, glowing from ear to ear. She spoke confidently and more surprisingly, quite audibly. And her fingernails were manicured. Go figure!

"So, I take it Zack was worth moving six hundred miles away from home," Tiffany said, taking a bite out of her BLT.

"I would have moved to Alaska if he had asked me to."

"Do you think it was love at first sight?" I asked. I was really curious because I never believed you could fall in love after talking to someone for a few brief hours. Maybe in lust, but not in love.

"I don't know if I loved him the second we met, but there was some kind of chemistry that drew me to him. It's really hard to explain."

It was really hard to understand, but shouldn't I? Hadn't Mike and I immediately clicked when we first met?

"I miss you guys," Marisa said, taking a sip of her coffee. "Jen, what's up with Mike?"

"Things are going really well." Did my voice sound flat or was it the potato chip I was eating that made my voice sound funny?

"So what's he like?" Marisa asked, while reaching for her pickle.

"He's a really nice guy."

"Yeah, and what else?" Tiffany said, looking at me as if I had given the wrong answer.

"What do you mean? I thought nice was a good thing."

"Do you realize whenever I ask about Mike, you always tell me how nice he is, but you never say much more."

"Oh, well...he treats me really nicely." For some reason I was having trouble swallowing my chip.

"Oh brother, I give up," Tiffany said. "I'll have to find out myself when I meet him."

"I wish I could meet him, too, but we have to get back tomorrow," Marisa said. "So do you think he might be Mr. Right, Jen?"

"Could be." Better be! I was ready for Rhonda to plan my surprise wedding shower.

"That's so great." Marisa no longer cracked her knuckles or tugged on her hair. "You must be thrilled. No more blind dates and singles dances, huh?"

"Yeah, that would be great." Wouldn't it? I pushed my chips aside, unable to eat anything else.

"Well, if you do marry him, promise me you won't aim your bouquet at me," Tiffany said, wiping her chin with a napkin.

"I thought you met someone, too," Marisa said.

"Oh, that's over." Tiffany took her cigarettes out of her purse. "After dating that guy for only a few weeks, I felt like he was smothering me. I couldn't take a piss without him asking me when I'd be back. He was like a noose around my neck."

"Don't worry, Tif," Marisa said. "I know you'll find the right guy, too."

"Who's worried?" She didn't look the least bit concerned. "You know how I feel about that. If I find Mr. Wonderful out there, that would be great, but if not, I'll survive."

"I always wished I could be as independent as you," Marisa said. "Before I met Zack, I was so scared of ending up alone."

"Sometimes being alone is better than being with the wrong person," Tiffany said, crumpling her napkin into a ball.

And sometimes being alone can be the most terrifying feeling in the world, I thought.

"So whatever happened with Meany?" Marisa asked me.

"Absolutely nothing, and I'm not leaving one more message on her voice mail." I pounded my fist on the table to make my point.

By the middle of January I had left Meany a second message, convinced she had never received my first one. I thought it was possible that I hadn't spoken loud enough on her machine for my voice to register. Now one month after the second unanswered message, I had given up.

"She's probably really busy," Marisa said. "Don't rule that job out yet."

"Too late, I already did."

"What does Mike think?" Marisa said.

"Uh, well.."

"Go ahead, tell her." Tiffany covered her mouth to cough.

"Tell me what?" Marisa asked, looking from Tiffany to me.

"Well, uh…I haven't actually told him about it yet."

"What? How can you keep something like that from him? Moving to New York is a big deal."

Okay, now I felt even more guilty than I had for the past few months. "I know I should have told him, but when Meany first mentioned it, I wasn't sure she was serious. Besides, it isn't exactly the kind of thing you mention on a first date in between discussing your favorite restaurants and what you like to do on weekends for fun. I still don't really believe it's going to happen so maybe I should just wait to tell him at this point." I came up for air since I didn't think I breathed during my entire explanation to Marisa.

"But what if it does happen?" Marisa asked, starting to get on my nerves.

"Did you know from the beginning that Zack could be transferred anytime?" I asked.

"Yeah, I always knew there was that chance." I wasn't sure, but I thought Marisa looked disappointed in me.

"And that didn't bother you?"

"Well, of course I would have been happier if we could have stayed here, but I knew eventually he'd have to move. Neither of us was expecting it to happen so quickly."

"You're changing the subject, Jen." Tiffany never let me get away with anything.

"Yeah, what happens if the job comes through and you haven't even mentioned it to Mike?" Marisa asked again.

"I guess I'm a little worried about what he'll say," I finally admitted. "He's such a homebody that I can't imagine him moving to New York. Besides, he's got a great job where he'll have tenure soon. He's not going to give that up for me. I don't want to lose him over this job, but I don't want to give it up either."

"You shouldn't have to give either up," Tiffany said with her usual air of authority. "If things are meant to be between the two of you, you'll figure out a way."

"Maybe he'll surprise you and offer to move with you," Marisa said, pushing her empty plate away. "Don't forget, I gave up my job for Zack."

"But you didn't like your job, Mike does." Our waitress came by to clear our plates.

"If he wants you badly enough, he can always find a job teaching in New York," Tiffany said. "There are plenty of colleges out that way."

"And if he doesn't want to move, you could always compromise and move somewhere in between," Marisa offered. "I know lots of people who live in Bucks County who commute to New York."

"Well, that might work." Why hadn't I thought of that? What a great solution!

"I'd tell him soon before you get an offer," Marisa said.

"I guess you're right." Besides, it wasn't going to happen anyway, so there was no reason to make too big a deal out of it.

"New York?" Mike said, after finishing dinner at the Poppy Stream Inn. I had left work early so I could talk to Mike in person about Meany's offer. Now that I had decided to tell him, I wanted to get it over with. "Why would you want to work in New York?" He looked stunned.

"Mike, that's where all the big agencies are. I'd be working on Madison Avenue."

"When would I see you if you moved?" He looked concerned.

"Well, if I did get the job, I thought I'd move somewhere in between New York and Philly, like Bucks County." I didn't think Marisa would mind if I took the credit for her idea. "That way, I'd only be forty minutes from your home and a little over an hour from New York by train."

"Would you be working fewer hours if you got the job?"

"Uh, well, no, probably not. Anyway, there's probably no reason to even be having this conversation because I haven't heard from Meany in months. Chances are the expansion will never happen or she's decided to hire someone else for the job."

"But if she does offer it to you, would you take it?"

I was a little worried when he inhaled without exhaling. I knew I'd better answer quickly before he turned purple. "I'd be crazy not to. It's the biggest agency in the country. I'd never get a chance to work at a place like that again."

I was relieved when Mike slowly let out his breath. I knew he was deep in thought as I watched him move his tongue from side to side. I had recently discovered that when Mike was contemplating a serious topic, he chewed on his tongue, making a swishing sound through his teeth. At first I thought he was chewing gum, but I soon realized he preferred his own flesh to Trident. I wondered if he had any idea that he had this gross habit.

The slurping sound faded, which meant Mike was getting ready to say something.

"If she offers you the job, when would you start?"

"Probably not for a few months. Expansions take time, and I'd still have to interview for the job. Even with Meany's recommendation, I might not get it."

"In the meantime, if you get another once-in-a-lifetime offer in Philly, would you take that?"

"Well, sure." I couldn't imagine any offer being better than Meany's, but there was no reason to debate the issue when this entire conversation was hypothetical. "So are you okay with me taking the job if Meany ever gets back to me?"

"As long as you promise to keep your options open. A lot can happen in a few months."

"I promise. And thanks for being so great about the whole thing." Whew. I didn't realize how worried I'd been about Mike's reaction until he gave me his blessing. What a relief! If I had known how easy it would be, I would have told him sooner.

"So now that we're done dinner, how about going back to your place," Mike suggested.

In the past I would have stalled over coffee for an hour or so, but after this past weekend, I agreed and waited for Mike to pay the check.

Once back at my place, Mike started to walk me back to my bedroom, but stopped abruptly before reaching the hallway. "How about trying another room," he said, smiling at me.

"That would be great. What did you have in mind?"

"Why don't you choose."

"Okay, how about the couch?" I was getting excited at the prospect of a new location.

We made our way to the couch, and Mike immediately took off all his clothes, which of course was a step in the right direction, but I was hoping we could ease into it slower instead him disrobing completely before he even kissed me. I probably needed to be a little more specific about that.

"So tell me what I can do to make you feel good," he said.

I felt uncomfortable giving him play-by-play instructions, but I knew he was just accommodating my request. I should be grateful that he was that willing to make me happy.

"How do you feel about oral sex," I asked. "Maybe you can do me and then I can do you?" So far, Mike had only used his hands between my legs.

"Let's do it." Mike looked like a child who was about to explore a candy store.

Unfortunately, once he arrived at the goodies, he had no idea how to get to the sweets.

"Just use your tongue. No, slower, higher. No, lower, a little faster now, keep going, that's it, don't stop!" I soon felt that delicious wetness between my legs. I was getting hotter and hotter until I felt like I was burning up.

"Keep going?" Mike asked, moving his mouth away to ask.

"Don't talk, just keep doing what you're doing. A little faster now, that's it, don't stop till I tell you." I hated narrating the entire experience, but at least he was getting me where I needed to be. "That's it." Before I could say anything else, my body exploded.

I took a deep breath. "That was perfect," I said, enjoying the tremendous release. "Now tell me what I can do to make you feel good."

"You just did," Mike said, coming up to kiss my mouth.

What could I say? He really was a nice guy.

Chapter 20

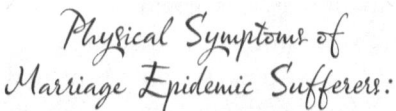

Physical Symptoms of Marriage Epidemic Sufferers:

1. You develop migraines when hearing about your blissfully happily married friends (especially when they seemed miserable when they were still single).

2. You develop marriage cravings (similar to food cravings that pregnant women get, but revolve around planning your wedding instead of planning your next meal).

3. Your heart skips ten beats when your sweetheart tells you he "loves" you (even if it skips another ten beats before you're able to say the "L word," too).

"Lori had her baby and it's a girl!" Stacy yelled into the phone.

"That's great! What's her name?" I carried my cell phone outside on the balcony, and despite the cold air, sat on my lounge chair.

"Samantha. She's really cute. I just got back from seeing her at the hospital."

"How's Lori doing?" I asked, watching the sun set above a young couple kissing by the Schuylkill River.

"Better now that the labor's over. She swears she'll never go through that much pain again, but after watching her with Samantha, I think she might change her mind. You should see her with the baby. She wouldn't put her down the entire time I was there. She just kept rocking her back and forth and kissing her."

"Wow, that doesn't sound like the Lori we once knew. Apparently, married life has been good for her." I wondered if that couple by the river was married.

"I'll say. Did you ever think Lori would become a mother and a homemaker?"

"Not in a million years. Remember that time we got stuck babysitting your neighbor's bratty kids and Lori refused to come by unless she could use the master bedroom with her new boyfriend?" The couple outside stopped kissing to smile at a mother strolling her baby. Perhaps they were expecting one, too.

"I'd forgotten about that," Stacy said.

"I didn't. Don't you remember when she and her boyfriend got there, she took one look at the screaming baby and whining toddler, and decided right then and there that the only little creatures who would ever live in her home would be dogs or cats. Then she left us with the dirty diapers and bottle sterilizer, and spent the next three hours rolling around in bed with her boyfriend." I smiled as I watched the guy by the river make silly faces at the baby in the stroller.

"That part I remember," Stacy said, "because she never bothered making the bed when she was done. You and I had a tough time explaining who had been sleeping in my neighbor's bed after Goldilocks left the scene of the crime."

"Yeah, she was always such a free spirit." I watched the couple wave good-bye to the mother and her child until I couldn't see them anymore. Then I walked back inside to my kitchen where I popped two extra-strength Tylenols for my pounding headache. "What happened to that carefree, reckless girl from college?"

"She grew up. I guess we all have."

Stacy answered with such decisiveness, but I wasn't so sure that was it. Hadn't Lori gotten her breasts stuffed with silicone just months before meeting Tony? Was that growing up? And hadn't Marisa complained like a child about wanting a boyfriend until she met Zack less than one year ago?

Was it really their age and maturity that had changed them or the contentment they got from finding true love that they knew would last them a lifetime? I didn't buy the fact that celebrating so many birthdays had profoundly changed their thinking and actions. Getting older hadn't done it; marriage had.

And after seeing Marisa on Monday, and hearing about Lori today, I was craving marriage. I needed it, wanted it, and had to have it as soon as possible. Was this how junkies felt when they needed their next hit? If so, I was ready for mine.

I was glad that tonight happened to be the evening Mike had invited me to meet his mother. At least, it was a step in the right direction toward satisfying my craving.

"This is it," Mike announced as we pulled up to a big, single colonial home. It was one of those older homes that was built entirely with bricks and stone, unlike the newer ones that were constructed with vinyl siding. His home looked solid and stable, much like Mike.

"Have you always lived here?" I asked, as we pulled up into his long driveway.

"All my life. I've had the same bedroom since I was born. It's that one up there with the plant in the window." Mike pointed to the middle window on the second floor.

I couldn't imagine still living in the same room where my mom once diapered me.

"Well, hello," a cheerful voice sang out. I could tell by the food stains on her apron that Mike's mother didn't have a friend cooking for her. "I'm so glad to finally meet you," she said.

This matronly, plump woman hugged me as if we had always known each other. Her sudden outburst of affection startled me, probably because my own mother hadn't hugged me for years.

"It's nice to meet you," I said, still locked in her embrace. Her genuine warmth and friendliness reminded me of Mrs. Cunningham on *Happy Days*. She even wore her hair in a bun like the mother on that TV show, except Mike's mom was completely gray.

"You're even prettier than the pictures of you that Mike carries in his wallet," she said. "And I love your outfit. Please come in and sit down. Mike, why don't you get Jen something to drink."

I followed his mother into their family room, which resembled an antique shop. No wonder Mike was so fascinated by history. Everything in this house must have been at least one hundred years old. "You have a beautiful home." I sat down on a chair by the fireplace.

"As you can see, I adore antiques. The older, the better."

I looked around, feeling like Mike had taken me to an earlier period of time. "Do you know the history of some of these items?"

"I wish I knew more, but I do know that the chair you're sitting on dates back to the early eighteen hundreds. The antique dealer I bought it from told me that President Andrew Jackson once owned it."

"That's pretty impressive. I didn't know I was sitting on such an important chair."

"Well, you're a very important guest. Here, would you like a piece of candy?"

As she held up the candy dish, I noticed her huge emerald-cut diamond set in a thick gold band. "That's a beautiful ring, Mrs. Robinowitz. Was that your engagement ring?"

"Thank you, sweetie. Yes, it was. It's a family heirloom, on Mike's father's side. It belonged to Mike's grandmother before me, and to his great-grandmother before her."

"That's nice. It must mean a lot to you."

"It does." She stroked the ring, as if touching a precious treasure. "I never take it off."

"I can see why."

"I'm going to check on dinner, and then I want to sit down with you so we can get to know each other."

I listened to her humming as she left the room. "She's really nice," I said to Mike, who was obediently pouring my diet Pepsi.

"I knew you'd like her. Come to think about it, you two have a lot in common. She once worked in advertising a long time ago."

"You're kidding! Mike, why didn't you tell me that before?"

"To tell you the truth, it was such a long time ago, I almost forgot," he said nonchalantly. "She gave it up after she married my dad. He didn't want her to work."

"Why not?" I sat up straight in my seat.

"I guess he didn't see the point. He was making enough money to support her and a family."

"Oh…well, how did she feel about quitting her job?"

"I don't know." He shrugged. "She never talks about it."

"Do you know which agency she worked for?"

"I have no idea. You should ask her. Now that we're talking about it, I wouldn't mind hearing about her past life in the world of advertising. I'm not sure why, but I've never asked her about it."

I couldn't imagine why either.

"Dinner's ready," Mike's mother announced.

We followed the smells of spices and sauces into the dining room where Mike's mother had already served Mike and me.

"Mike, I made sure to take out all the tomatoes from your salad. I know how they make you break out," she said, pouring his salad dressing for him. "Jen, what kind of dressing would you like?"

"This one's fine." I picked up the low-fat Italian dressing.

"No, you're the guest. Let me pour that for you."

Now I knew where Mike got his nurturing personality. While Mike's mom returned to the kitchen to get the soup, I looked up to see a portrait of an older version of Mike, who I imagined was his dad. If I put a gray wig on Mike and painted wrinkles around his eyes and mouth, the two men would look identical.

I was surprised that Mike's dad hadn't smiled in the picture. His mouth and eyebrows both formed a straight line.

The only difference in features between Mike and his dad were their eyes. Unlike Mike's warm, gentle, brown puppy dog eyes, his father's dark brown eyes almost looked black as they stared intently at us, making me shiver. It was almost like someone had cut slits through the photo so his father's ghost could stand at the other side of the wall to check out new visitors. "When was that picture taken?" I tried to avoid his father's gaze.

"My father and uncles hired a photographer about ten years ago to take photos of each of them. All three portraits hung in their office until my dad died. My uncles thought we should keep it."

If I saw that picture hanging at someone's office, I would leave. It didn't exactly paint a warm, fuzzy picture of their business. "My dad was right," I said. "You really do look like him."

Mike seemed pleased, but I wasn't sure it was a compliment.

"So, Jen, would you like soup before or with dinner?" Mike's mom returned with a huge bowl of chicken noodle soup.

"Either way is fine with me."

"I know how serious Mike is about you so I want to make sure everything's right."

How serious? What had he told her? Would someone please fill me in? But instead of elaborating on her comment, his mother excused herself to get a soup ladle.

"Is something wrong, Jen?" Mike asked, taking a bite of his tomato-free salad.

"No, it's just I was kind of surprised that you told your mom about how serious we were."

"Why? I thought it was obvious by now how I felt about you."

This was it! He really was the one. And if he already told his mother how much he cared about me, it was probably just a matter of time before he proposed. And then I would be telling Stacy about my wonderful wedding plans, and beaming like Marisa and Lori. My marriage craving was about to be satisfied! And with that thought, I swung my arm over the side of my chair, knocking over the bread basket, which caused all of Mike's mother's homemade bread to roll on the floor.

"I'm so sorry, Mike." I bent down to clean up my mess, but Mike beat me to it.

In his typical Mike fashion, he refused to let me pick up one piece of bread. While picking up crumbs, he looked at me with concern in his eyes. "Are you okay, Jen? You look a little pale."

"I'm fine, really." Why wouldn't I be fine? I had finally found the guy who would help me live happily ever after, and he had once again come to my rescue. Mike returned to the table after throwing away the bread.

"How is everything?" Mike's mom carried a roasted chicken that smelled incredible.

"Everything's great," I said, grateful that Mike didn't mention the bread incident. I sure hoped she liked me. After all, this was going to be my mother-in-law. "By the way, thanks for all those cakes and pies Mike's been bringing over to my place. I've never eaten such unusual desserts. Are they your own recipes?"

"They are," she said proudly. "I couldn't even tell you the precise ingredients I use, but after baking and cooking for so long, I know that if I take a bit of this and a handful of that, I'll have a chocolate éclair or a strawberry shortcake."

"I wish I could cook like that." Oops. Maybe I shouldn't have said that. Now she'd know I wouldn't be preparing homemade meals for her son. Would she hold that against me?

"I'm sure you don't have all the time on your hands that I do to putter around the kitchen all day. Cooking and baking have become my life. The only bad part is that I spend all day cooking and then I have nobody to eat my meals. Mike is gone all day and he works some nights, as you know, and Allison obviously lives too far away to stop by for some home cooking. I end up giving away my food to strangers. Just yesterday, I gave the mailman two trays of chocolate covered marshmallows to bring to his family, and this morning I gave the gardener three dozen chocolate chip cookies."

"If you love cooking so much, maybe you should teach a cooking class. I bet the JYC would be interested in hiring you."

"You're sweet, but I don't have any teaching experience. Besides, I don't want to teach. I want to cook." It was obvious by the way she took a large second helping of everything that she also liked to eat.

"Well, you could always write a cookbook if you could figure out exactly which ingredients you're using."

Mike's mom let out a loud, hearty laugh. "Mike, your girlfriend wants to find a career for me. No, sweet girl. I'm too old to begin exploring the world of publishing. I had a great job at one time, but that was a long time ago. I think I'll just continue cooking. It makes me happy when the people I love enjoy my meals."

"Mike just told me that you worked in advertising before you got married. Is that the great job you're talking about?"

"It is, but I don't want to bore you with my past life. Mike's father always told me that it was better to leave the past in the past. Can I get you some more peas?"

"No, thanks. So where did you work?"

"I'm sure you're not interested in hearing me ramble on about that..."

"But I am. So which agency did you work for?"

"I worked for JBM&P. You probably never heard of it because it's pretty small now, but at the time it was the biggest one on Madison Avenue."

Why did that name sound so familiar to me? "You worked in New York?"

"We lived there, too. Mike's father and I were born in Brooklyn. We didn't move to this area until we were married for a few years. That's when Mike's father decided to go into business with his brothers. They already had an established accounting firm in center city."

"So what did you do at JBM&P?" I stopped eating, too interested in hearing about Mike's mother's former career.

"I was an account executive. Jen, I used to get so excited whenever we pitched a new account." For the first time since we arrived, she spoke with enthusiasm and animation. "I loved watching the artists draw their sketches. In those days, artists didn't have all this fancy graphic design software so they drew everything on paper. My favorite part was brainstorming with the creative team until we came up with a new idea. I always knew when we had hit on something big because you could almost hear a hush in the room as we all got ready to put our thoughts down on paper."

Finally, someone who knew exactly how I felt. It was like finding a long-lost friend.

"Were the work weeks as long as they are today?" Mike asked, with a mouth full of food. "Jen works some insane hours. Would you believe that last week she worked three thirteen-hour days in a row?"

I looked up at Mike's father, and wondered if he had asked that same question thirty years ago.

"I remember those days well." As Mike's mother reminisced, her tired eyes looked refreshed. "In fact, I remember sleeping overnight at the office for an entire week, while preparing for a big pitch."

"No wonder Dad made you give it up," Mike said. "Can I pour you some more soda, Jen?"

Before he could pick up the bottle, I poured it myself. "So do you ever regret leaving the field?" I asked Mike's mother.

"Sure I do, but my husband insisted that I quit. It was really important to him that I stay home and raise our family. I think he was afraid that his friends would look down on him if I worked, as if he couldn't earn enough money to support a family."

Was this the same man who had inspired Mike to teach? The man who my own dad spoke so highly of? All the warmth I felt toward him suddenly froze. How could he have forced his wife to give up her job that she loved so she could stay home and cook for him? And now all she had left was cooking for contractors.

"Don't feel sorry for me," Mike's mom said, as if reading my mind. "I miss the excitement of advertising, but getting married and having children were the most rewarding jobs in the world. I guess my husband was probably right. It would have been hard doing both."

"Of course he was right, Mom," Mike chimed in. "It would have been too much for you to do both. Besides, everything worked out okay, right?"

Maybe for Mike and his sister and father, but what about his poor mother? She had accepted her life sentence without questioning her husband's demands. I shot his photo a dirty look as I finished eating.

After Mike's commentary, his mother changed the subject. "Mike, I forgot to tell you, I picked up three new IZOD sweaters for you and left them on your bed."

"Thanks, Mom," he said, kissing her on the cheek.

"Oh, and I found a new Rolodex for your office at work. I remember you mentioned that you needed one."

"You're the best, thanks."

I was beginning to feel nauseous. This woman who had once been a corporate executive at a Madison Avenue agency was now spending her days shopping for her thirty-four-year-old son. And why the hell wasn't he doing his own shopping?

"You're been awfully quiet since we got back from visiting my mom," Mike said, settling down next to me on the couch.

"Have I?" I put my head against the cushion.

"Did my mom say something to upset you?"

"No, your mom's terrific. She couldn't have been nicer."

"Then what's wrong?" He had that let's go to bed look in his eyes, but I was definitely not in the mood.

"Do you really believe that your father was right about making your mom give up her job?" I blurted it out before I realized it had left my lips.

"You're still thinking about that?" He let out a big sigh.

Every second since you said it. "It's been on my mind."

"Our parents grew up in a different time, Jen." Mike inched closer to me. "Women didn't have careers like they do today."

"But your mom sounded so happy when she talked about her job." I inched myself away from Mike.

"Don't worry about my mom. She's had a good life." He looked at the sudden distance between us with dismay. "She's okay with her decision, really."

Considering he never even knew what she did in advertising, I doubted he had ever taken the time to ask her if she was happy with her life, which seemed to revolve around catering to his every need. "So you're saying that if your parents grew up today, he would have been wrong to ask her to give up the job she loved?"

Uh-oh. More swishing with his tongue. This obviously required some thought. I was ready to rip his tongue out of his throat when he finally stopped chomping on it.

"If it happened today, I think my father would have been more willing to let her continue working as long as it didn't interfere with their marriage and their family."

"What do you mean he would *let* her continue working? Since when is the guy in charge of the woman?"

More swishing. Couldn't he find a normal annoying habit like biting his nails? Finally, he moved over to me and took my hands in his. "Jen, I promise you that I will never ask you to give up your career. Okay?"

I squeezed his hands. "That's good to know." This time I let him move closer to me.

"There's something else you should know," Mike said, squeezing my hands even tighter. "Jen, ever since I first met you, I knew you were special, but the more I know you, the more I want to know you. You're the first thing I think about every morning and the last thing I think about every night. It's hard to get through a class without picturing your face and remembering how you feel when you're close to me. I hope I won't scare you away by telling you this, but I want you to know that I love you, Jen."

He loved me! He'd said the "L" word, and now it was my turn. All I had to do was say it, and we would be taking our relationship to a whole other level.

I opened my mouth to say it, but nothing came out. I felt like swishing my spit for a while. How did I really feel about Mike? Of course, I really liked him. I might even love him as a friend. I'm sure I could learn to love him in time. Maybe I was already in love with him, and just didn't realize it. Could I tell him that I was on the periphery of loving him?

"You don't have to say it if you're not ready," Mike said, looking sad. "I don't want you to feel pressured to say it just because I did."

Then I remembered the pact I had made with myself after I broke up with Chris. I had sworn that I would think with my head, not my heart. That was the problem! Up until now, I hadn't let myself fall in love with him because I didn't want to get hurt. Not to mention, I didn't want to find out again that we had a different viewpoint about a major issue that could prevent us from getting married.

But now I knew that Mike would be the ideal husband for me. He still met all of my marriage criteria, and best of all, he loved me.

It was time to stop treading water and dive right into this relationship. Relieved that I now understood my feelings, or lack of them, I looked Mike directly in the eyes and said, "I love you, too."

Even though it wasn't entirely true yet, now I could let myself start feeling it.

Chapter 21

People to Avoid When Suffering From The Marriage Epidemic:

1. Engaged couples who can't keep their hands off of each other.

2. Engaged couples determined to convince your boyfriend that you're the next best thing to Mother Theresa.

3. Engaged friends who can no longer relate to women who aren't married or planning a wedding.

Damn! I had only stepped out of my office for three minutes the entire morning, but in those one hundred and eighty seconds, Meany had called. Figured! "Hi, Jen. Sorry I haven't gotten back to you the past few months, but I've been out of the country a lot. I'm leaving for Australia for a month, but when I get back I was hoping we could get together. I'll call you then."

Did that mean the expansion was taking place, or that she wanted to tell me in person that Richardson and Whitaker wouldn't need a new writer after all? No way was I waiting another month to find out what she meant.

I called her back, assuming she'd still be in her office. After all, she had just called, but as soon as I asked to talk to her, I heard that familiar voice mail message. "Hello, you have reached Ilene Meany. I'm sorry, but I'm not available…"

No! No more messages. If she really wanted me, she would have to make the next move. I was tired of spending so much time tracking down somebody who waited months before calling me back. The ball was in her court now. I had had it!

Mike picked me up from work to meet Stacy and Lance at La Stromboli Restaurant in center city. I didn't tell him that Meany had left me a message. What was the point? I didn't have anymore information to tell him than I had last month.

When we arrived at the small, quaint Italian bistro, Stacy and Lance were already seated at a table by the door.

"Glad we could finally get together," Lance said, shaking Mike's hand. "Hey, Jen, you look terrific. Did you do something new with your hair?"

"Uh, no, not really."

"And I love that outfit, Jen," Stacy said. "I don't think I've ever seen you wear it before."

What was she talking about? Stacy had been with me when I bought it.

"So, Mike, sorry we've been so difficult to get together with, but with the wedding only a few weeks away, things have been pretty crazy," Lance said, putting down his menu.

"I understand," Mike said, sitting opposite Lance. "It's not everyday you plan your wedding."

"So what's the final head count?" I asked, looking at the wallpaper of gondoliers rowing gondolas through the canals of Venice.

"Probably somewhere around two hundred," Stacy glanced at her menu before closing it. "We're not sure exactly. Can you believe we're still waiting for people to RSVP?" Stacy looked indignant. "Their responses were due over a week ago so now my mom has to call them to see whether they're coming. People can be really rude."

"I guess if that's your worst problem, that's not so bad," I said. I sure wished it was mine.

"Yeah, we've been pretty lucky with all of our other arrangements." Lance placed his arm around Stacy's shoulders. "We're especially happy with the videographer. He uses all kinds of special effects throughout the video, like all of a sudden you might be looking at a table of guests and Demi Moore might appear."

"Or Ashton Kutcher," Stacy teased. "And our photographer does a wonderful panoramic shot during the service and reception."

"What song did you pick for your first dance?" Mike asked, while looking at his menu.

"We're dancing to 'A Whole New World,' you know, the song from *Aladdin*," Stacy answered, while resting her hand on Lance's. "It was the song playing on the radio the first time Lance told me he loved me."

Had the radio been on when Mike told me he loved me? I hadn't noticed.

"So how long have you known each other?" Mike asked.

"The day of our wedding will be five years." Stacy leaned her head on Lance's shoulder.

"That's a long time," Mike said. "You must really know each other well."

"Yeah, we're already like an old married couple," Stacy said.

"Hey, are you saying we're boring?" Lance stuck out his lower lip and pretended to pout.

"I still wuv you even if we are," Stacy said, kissing his wounded lip. Lance eagerly responded by returning the kiss until I felt like I was watching a make-out scene from some R-rated movie. I really could have done without seeing their tongues in each other's mouths. This was one of the reasons I never liked double dating with them.

Not sure where to look, I stared at those gondolas on the wall while Mike looked out the window, fidgeting in his seat. It would be nice if they waited till they got home to do their business. From the way they kissed, I was afraid they were going to pull off the tablecloth and do each other on the middle of the table. When the waiter came to pour our water, they finally came up for air.

Lance cleared his voice and straightened his shirt before returning his attention to us. "So what about you guys?" Lance said, trying to catch his breath. "I hear you've gotten pretty chummy awfully quickly."

"That's easy to do when you're dating someone as incredible as Jen," Mike said, still looking slightly uncomfortable. "But considering Stacy and she have been best friends for so long, I'm sure you both already know how terrific she is."

"That I do." Stacy squeezed my arm. "Jen has a heart of gold and will go out of her way for anyone she cares about. I remember when a bunch of us from college were supposed to go to Florida for spring break. The day before we were planning to leave, I fractured my leg and my doctor put me on bed rest for a week. Instead of going on vacation with the rest of the gang, Jen insisted on staying home to keep me company."

Stacy turned to face Mike. "Jen exchanged a round-trip ticket to a sunny week on the beach for a quiet seven days watching videos in bed with me. That's just the type of person she is."

"Yeah, and remember that time our car broke down in the middle of the night in Jersey," Lance said, looking directly at Mike. "Both of our parents were out of town, so we called Jen, and thirty minutes later she came to our rescue."

"And what about that time I forgot my wallet at home," Stacy continued. "You'll never believe how Jen …"

I quietly sat behind my menu, listening to Stacy and Lance describe all the good deeds I had done for them over the years. I felt like a Jewish Mother Theresa. After fifteen minutes of listening to "Jen the Heroine" stories, I was becoming uncomfortable. It was almost as if they were trying to sell me to him, as if I couldn't do it myself. Perhaps that was because in the past I never could.

I was waiting for one of them to say, "And now for just one diamond ring you too can reap the rewards of spending your life with Jen Greenberg!" Enough already! I was glad when the waiter finally came to take our order.

But when he left, Stacy continued where she left off. "Jen's not only sweet and kind, but she's funny and smart. She even…"

Oh great. Now she was reciting all my positive attributes. She was using her marketing skills to market me. What if Mike thought I told her to say all these nice things about me so he'd be impressed?"

I dropped my napkin on the floor and as I bent down to pick it up, I whispered, "Enough" into Stacy's ear. While under the table, I saw Stacy kick Lance's leg.

"So, Jen, uh…hey, did I mention that we ran into your mom at the liquor store right before we came here?" Stacy mouthed "Sorry" to me when Mike wasn't looking.

"No, you didn't." The waiter came by to deliver a bread basket that I vowed not to knock over. "What was she doing around here?"

"She said Barb invited her to her friend's party." Stacy placed a piece of garlic bread on her plate.

"Really? She didn't mention that to me." I wondered why she hadn't stopped by on her way to the party, not that I wanted to see her.

"Your mom's really looking hot these days," Lance said.

"Lance!" Stacy gave him a warning look.

"Sorry, but she does look incredible. Of course not as incredible as you." He kissed Stacy's neck, obviously trying to redeem himself, which seemed to work because Stacy giggled.

"What was she wearing?" I asked, not wanting to know.

"Some kind of red, sequined, very low-cut dress." This time, Lance sounded more matter-of-fact as he described her.

Sequins? That sounded unusually dressed up for a house party. What was she up to now? "Was Barb in sequins, too?"

"We didn't see her," Stacy said, as Lance stroked a strand of her hair. "Your mom was meeting her at the party."

Huh. It was more unusual for my mom to go out without Barb than to go out without my dad.

"So, did you tell Jen about the house?" Lance asked Stacy without taking his hands off of her.

"Nope, I was waiting till tonight." Stacy sat up straighter, if that was possible and leaned toward me. "Jen, you'll never believe it, but we put a bid on that house in Delaware County and we got it."

"That's great," I said. "Congratulations."

"Here's a picture," Lance said, proudly displaying it on the table as if showing off his first born.

"Hey, that's really nice," Mike said. "Mazel tov."

"Thanks," Lance said, admiring the photo.

It looked more like a mansion than a home. Stacy and Lance could probably go days without ever running into each other there. "It's magnificent, Stace. It looks practically new."

"It is. It's only two years old, but the couple who lived there are getting divorced. We got really lucky with the price because the woman wanted to sell quickly so she'd get the money as soon as possible. We make settlement the day we get back from our honeymoon. Is that unbelievable or what?"

For anyone else it would be, but for Stacy, it was not only believable, it was expected. Stacy got what Stacy wanted.

"What part of Delaware County is this?" Mike asked, looking at the picture.

"It's in Media. Do you know the area?" Lance asked, after taking a piece of bread and dipping it in olive oil.

"Yeah, my dad had a small office not far from there that he worked out of once a week."

"Really, that's great because I'm still not that familiar with the area. I was going to call our realtor tomorrow, but maybe you already know the answers to some of my questions."

"Why don't we let the boys talk real estate while we powder our noses," Stacy said to me.

I nodded and followed her past a small bar until I glanced up to see Randy sitting on a stool, sipping a beer. Unable to avoid his eyes, I stopped at his stool, not knowing what to say. I had gone out of my way to steer clear of him and his annoying family for months at my apartment. Just my luck, I had to run into him away from home.

"Hi, Jen," he said, smiling at me for the first time in months.

He looked good in his gray business suit. Being that it was six-o'clock, I imagined he must have come from work. "Um, hi," I said. This was awkward. Since the moaning incident with Chris, none of us had spoken. They must be happy that I'd met Mike because I now had a much quieter, subdued sex life. There was no chance of furniture being knocked over when we were in the heat of the moment.

"Jen, I'll meet you in the bathroom," Stacy said, walking passed us.

Great, now I was forced to make conversation.

"I've been wanting to talk to you," Randy said. He seemed more relaxed than he typically appeared at our apartment complex.

"It's okay, Randy. You don't have to say anything." I really didn't feel like talking about my sex life, especially my former sex life with Chris.

"But I do. Sometimes Lisa can be very judgmental and outspoken, especially when the kids are involved. I think she feels guilty about working full-time, and she overcompensates by becoming excessively nurturing and overprotective when she gets home. I would never have complained about your singing that first day you moved in, but she kept nagging me to say something."

And you had to obey her orders? "Don't worry about it."

"And when you and your boyfriend kept waking Josh and Jessica all weekend…"

"Really, let's just forget about it." I closed my eyes, trying to forget about that weekend.

"Plus, Jessica was worried when she heard screaming coming from your place." Randy got a mischievous look in his eyes that I wasn't sure how to interpret. "She thought you were hurt."

I guess trying to explain that I wasn't hurt until *after* we had sex would only confuse her more. "Oh…um…well, I'm sorry I upset her."

"Don't get me wrong," he continued, slurring his words slightly. "I don't mind the sound of good sex. I wish I heard more of it coming from my apartment. I keep telling Lisa we need to get out more, but she refuses to leave the kids with a babysitter, even for a few hours. Needless to say, this takes a toll on our sex life."

Okay, I had heard more than enough. Randy apparently had a few too many drinks because he was beginning to sway back and forth. "Listen, why don't we just start over," I said. "I promise to keep the volume down if you promise to let me live my life in my own apartment."

"That sounds fair. So are you here with anyone besides your girlfriend?" Randy stood up and moved so close to me that I had to take a step backward.

"Yeah, my boyfriend is waiting for me back at the table."

"Oh…well, I better let you go, then." He returned to his bar stool and took another sip from his drink. "I'll see you around."

Had my married next door neighbor just hit on me? It had to be my imagination. Randy seemed like a committed family man. This was the first time I ever saw him without Lisa. What was I thinking? He was just being friendly…and drunk. All of those positive, uplifting stories that Stacy and Lance had just told Mike about me must have gone to my head.

⌒

I found Stacy putting on lipstick by the sink. "Who was that guy?" she asked.

I took out my cosmetic bag and grabbed some concealer to cover a blemish I somehow missed at home. "He lives next door to me."

"He's the one always complaining that you make too much noise?"

"He's the one."

"He doesn't look the type. The way you described him, I pictured a much older, pot-bellied, balding guy who had nothing better to do with his life than make other people miserable, but he's actually kind of cute."

"I agree he's not bad looking." I dotted on the concealer to cover my zit. "He even apologized for complaining so much. He claims his wife put him up to it."

"He sounds like a wimp. Otherwise, he would make his wife do her own dirty work." Stacy took a mint Altoid out of her purse and placed it in her mouth. "Fortunately, you don't have to deal with any other guys anymore. Jen, Mike's wonderful! I really hope you end up with him."

"Yeah, I could tell from your cheerleading routine out there. I'm surprised you didn't stand up on the table with pom poms and make everyone at the restaurant give you a J-E-N."

"I'm sorry if we got carried away, but I really like him for you. He's so nice."

There was that adjective again. Nobody could argue that Mike was genuinely a nice guy. "I'm glad you like him so much."

"I really do. Oh, Jen, wouldn't it be incredible if he proposed soon. Then we could each start out our married lives together, like we always talked about."

"That would be nice." I turned my back to the mirror, not wanting to face anymore surprises on my face.

"Lance and Mike seem to be hitting it off, too, so now the four of us can go out together all the time." She used a tissue to blot her lips. "It will be just like old times."

"I would like that because, to be honest, since you got engaged, I've felt like we've been drifting apart." My words got choked up in my throat. I hadn't realized how much I missed Stacy the past ten months until now. I wanted my best friend back.

"I'm sorry, Jen. I didn't mean to make you feel left out. I guess I got so wrapped up in my wedding plans that I didn't make enough time for us."

"It's okay, and I understand. This is a very exciting time for you, and you should be wrapped up in your plans. It's just lately, our lives have been moving in different directions, and there's not a lot we can do about it." *Especially when you refuse to talk about anything besides weddings and marriage.* "As you said a few weeks ago, we're all grown up now."

"But that doesn't mean we have to give up our childhood friendships. I promise that once Lance and I get settled in our new home, things will go back to the way they were. Besides, now that you met Mike, I bet we'll have a lot more in common again. I have a feeling you'll be engaged before long. From what you say, Mike's ready to settle down, and once you get engaged, our lives will be right back on track again."

I liked the idea of reconnecting with Stacy again. It seemed like Mike would be the glue to secure our friendship. But what if I didn't marry Mike? Would Stacy and I continue to drift apart? And why did our lives have to be on track for us to maintain our close friendship?

Chapter 22

Why Attending a Wedding Can Worsen Your Condition:

1. You're repeatedly forced to explain why you're still not engaged, as if you've been put on the witness stand.

2. You're surrounded by people who seem to have forgotten how to talk about any topic unrelated to marriage.

I couldn't believe that after talking about weddings since we were kids, Stacy was actually getting married today. It didn't hit me until I walked through the entrance of the Starlight Country Club and saw the marquee that read: "Stacy and Lance's Wedding."

I stood in my teal maid of honor gown for a while staring at the sign, while hearing Stacy's childhood voice singing "Someday My Prince Will Come." My eyes filled with tears, realizing her prince had finally arrived with her glass slipper. Even if he had come walking into a bar instead of riding through a forest, his shoe had obviously fit her foot.

Stacy no longer had to fantasize about what her husband would look like, or play dress-up games to get an idea of how she'd look in a wedding gown. Her dream had become a reality, and I felt a rush of emotion as I pictured that little girl in my house who would soon be a married woman.

I finally peeled my eyes off the marquee when a man approached me from behind, startling me. "Are you here for the Horowitz wedding?" asked the man, who had more hair on his face than on his head.

"Uh, no. I'm here for Stacy Siegel's wedding."

The man looked confused as he checked his clipboard. "But Stacy Siegel is marrying Lance Horowitz."

He gave me a strange look, and I didn't blame him. Of course I knew she'd be taking Lance's last name. Apparently, I was in denial. I'd miss the Stacy Siegel I once shared every intimate secret with.

Then again, I already missed her and she hadn't changed her name yet, just her personality. Since she got engaged she hadn't been the same person I once knew. And if an engagement ring had such a profound change on her, what would a wedding band do to her?

"Sorry, I, um, got confused." I heard a weird giggle come out of my mouth. "I'm still used to people using Stacy's maiden name, but I am here for the Horowitz wedding."

The man stared at me as if I were some kind of an idiot. "In that case, you can follow me. The photographer is about to start taking pictures of the bridal party."

I followed the man who walked with a limp past the marquee, and this time I didn't bother to glance at it.

"Okay, ladies, smile," the photographer said for what seemed like the fiftieth time. He had set up all his equipment in a small room in the basement, apparently not wanting to take any chance of the bride running into the groom, who was getting ready on the second floor. On cue, all six of us shouted "cheese" and were once again blinded by the flash.

"How about a few pictures with the bride and maid of honor?" he asked. The other girls moved aside as I stood beside my oldest friend. That four-year-old little girl playing Cinderella in my bedroom would have been thrilled if she had known how beautiful she would look on her wedding day. She wore a strapless white silk sheath that showed off the contours of her body. Her three-foot train was trimmed with lace. *Snap.* "Okay, I think we have enough shots for now."

"So, are you nervous?" I asked Stacy as we moved aside to let the photographer through. He was going to take some photos of Lance and his ushers.

"Not at all," she answered without hesitation. "I was expecting to feel some last-minute jitters, but I feel great. I can't wait to become Lance's wife and start our life together."

It must be great to be so sure. Lance Horowitz truly was her Prince Charming. Would Mike Robinowitz turn out to be mine?

Stacy excused herself to go touch up her face, as if she needed to, when I heard Amy's irritating voice. "Jen, where's your boyfriend?" Amy caressed her diamond ring, as if stroking a sick family pet.

"He's sitting with my parents." I tried to remain poised standing in my three-inch heals.

Amy, along with the rest of the bridal party, had chosen a gown similar to mine, except the front of their gowns were low-cut as opposed to my sweetheart neckline. God forbid they should hide their buxom cleavage. "So when do you think you'll be getting engaged," she asked.

So much for small talk. Tact was never one of Amy's strongest traits. And how the hell did I know when I'd get engaged? It wasn't as if I was the one doing the proposing. "I'm really not sure." I held on to a chair in front of me as I wobbled slightly.

"But Stacy said things were getting serious between you two," she whined like I was letting her down. "I assumed you'd already talked about marriage."

Bitch. "Well, we haven't."

"Well, maybe you should bring it up. Sometimes guys need a little nudge."

I wanted to give her a big nudge. "I'll keep it in mind."

"Before Howard proposed, I kept showing him pictures of the engagement ring I wanted." She smiled smugly. "He finally got the message."

He probably just wanted to shut her up. And why did I feel like I was suddenly on trial, defending my single status?

Carla, who I had only met during fittings and bridal parties, joined us and chimed right in. "Why do you think he's taking so long to propose?" she asked, looking perplexed.

"It hasn't even been six months," I said, wanting to take off my shoe and stuff its heel down her throat.

"Yeah, but relationships move faster when you get older. Once you turn thirty, people spend a lot less time dating before they get married. It's like a dog's life," Amy reasoned.

"Huh?" Why was she comparing my relationship with Mike to a dog?

"You know how one year of a dog's life is equal to seven years of a person's life?" Amy said, not having a clue how stupid she sounded.

"Uh-huh?"

"Well, after you turn thirty, six months of a person's dating life is equal to one year of the dating life of someone in their twenties. So according to that theory, you've been going out with Mike for almost a year." She titled her head to the side and gave me a puzzled look as if she couldn't believe I'd never heard this information before.

"And whose brilliant theory is that?" I asked.

"It's in that new bestseller for singles. What's the name of that book again, Carla?"

"*Thirty-Something Singles*?" The title rolled right off her tongue.

"Yeah, that's it," she nodded.

If that book compared single people to dogs, I was glad I had never unwrapped my mom's birthday gift.

"I'd start dropping some hints if I were you," Carla said.

Great, now she was my relationship counselor, too. Did every married or engaged woman think she had a right to give unsolicited advice to single women? I couldn't wait to spend the rest of the night listening to all their *helpful* suggestions. After they had a few drinks, I could only imagine what kinds of animals they'd be comparing me to.

"Do you Stacy Siegel take Lance..." I stood next to Stacy under the chupah, wondering how Stacy felt knowing that in a few minutes she would be married.

"And do you Lance Horowitz..." Lance looked so handsome in his black tux and white cummerbund.

We all listened as the cantor sang some prayers. Right before my eyes, Stacy was leaving the world of singlehood behind. At last, she had a clear view of that faceless groom we had talked about for so long. Come to think of it, he did look a little like Tom Cruise from the side.

"...I now pronounce you husband and wife," announced the rabbi. And as Lance kissed Stacy passionately on the lips, I looked over at Mike who sat between my parents. I tried to fill in my faceless groom with Mike's face, but every time I tried all I could see was John Stamos.

Stacy's reception took place at the grand ballroom, next door to the room where the ceremony had taken place.

"You look beautiful," Mike said as he selected a shrimp cocktail from a waiter holding a generous selection of hors d'oeuvres.

"Thanks. You don't look so bad yourself." He had bought a Pierre Cardin suit just for the wedding, and he looked quite handsome. Thank goodness I had a date for the wedding. It was bad enough being single at this wedding, but coming alone would have been slow torture.

"Come on, Mike. They're doing the hora." I held out my hand.

"Jen, you know I don't dance." He took a step back as everyone else began moving forward toward the center of the room.

"You don't have to dance to do a hora. Just hold my hand and follow the circle."

"Why don't I meet you at our table." His hands fidgeted as the lead singer of the six-piece band sang the first few notes of "Hava Nagila."

"It's just a hora, Mike. You don't need any coordination to dance in a circle."

"I know, but I get nervous dancing in front of people. I guess it's always been one of my fears."

"Well, sometimes you have to face your fears." I suddenly remembered Chris telling me the same thing when he wanted me to take that balloon ride.

"I've managed thirty-four years without dancing, so why start now?" And before I could say anything else, he headed back to the table where my dad sat alone.

I lost track of Mike when Amy grabbed my arm to spin me around inside the circle. I didn't see him again until the bandleader asked everyone to find our seats so dinner could be served.

I was glad that Stacy had seated spouses, fiancés, and, in my case, boyfriends, with the bridal party because I couldn't have endured an entire dinner listening to all the reasons I had to tackle Mike until he proposed.

"Hey, Jen, aren't you going to introduce me to your boyfriend?"

Oh great. Amy again, and now I was stuck sitting next to her. "Mike this is Amy. We know each other from college."

"I've heard a lot of good things about you." Amy winked at him.

"I hope I can live up to the review," Mike said, sitting down next to me.

"I would say you already do. You're a good-looking college professor at an Ivy League college. You've already exceeded all expectations."

Could this woman possibly be anymore obnoxious? Didn't that bestselling singles book say anything about using tact when meeting your friends' boyfriends?

Mike was still looking at Amy with a strange expression when Lori and Tony approached us and introduced themselves. "So you're Jen's fiancé," Tony said, sitting next to Mike. "Congratulations, have you set a date yet?"

"No, Tony, they're not engaged," Lori whispered loudly enough for everyone at the table to hear her.

"I'm sorry," he said. "I thought Lori told me you were getting married."

"I didn't mean right away," Lori told him, as if we weren't sitting there.

"Mike, why don't we get a drink," I said, grabbing his hand.

As we approached the bar, I felt better just seeing all those alcoholic beverages. If I ever needed a drink, now was the time. "Mike, I'm really sorry about Tony's comment. I never told anyone we were engaged, and as far as Amy goes, she's just plain rude, which is why I never kept in touch with her after school."

"Hey, you don't have to apologize for them. I know you wouldn't be friends with someone like Amy, and don't worry about Tony either. My friends and family have been asking me when I'm going to propose since our third date."

And your answer to them is...?

"Mike, have you met all of Jen's friends yet?" Even for my mother, her dress was revealing. It had a slit that practically opened down to her belly button. Was that her nipple hanging out on the side? I hoped she had mistakenly put the dress on backward, but feared she hadn't.

"We're still making the rounds, Sylvia," Mike answered.

I could tell he was trying not to stare at her cleavage, but how could you avoid it?

"Don't Stacy and Lance look terrific?" my mom gushed. "I bet you'll look great in a tux, too, Mike."

"Mom, please, not now, okay?"

"What's wrong with telling Mike that he would make a handsome groom?" she asked, trying to look innocent. "I didn't say he'd be marrying you, did I?"

"I think you said more than enough, Mom. Can we please change the subject?"

"Well, we are at a wedding so the subject of marriage is going to come up."

And it did. For the next hour during dinner that topic came up over and over again. It was like nobody had ever spoken about anything else before. When the lovely ladies in Stacy's bridal party weren't talking about their own weddings, they were preaching about the joy of marriage or wedding planning to Mike and me.

As the waiter cleared our plates, I was ready to get another drink, preferably a strong one, when I heard the announcement I was dreading all night. "Will all the single women please come to the dance floor," the bandleader announced.

"Go ahead," my mom said, appearing out of nowhere.

"I think I'll skip it this time." I hated this tradition. I felt so pathetic standing with the other single women as if we needed to catch those flowers in order to find a husband. Besides, I had already caught the bouquet at two other weddings and where had that gotten me?

"Jen, please, you have to go out." Stacy was now at our table, begging me to go out to the dance floor that appeared empty. "I promise to aim my bouquet at you."

"How could you miss, Stace? There's nobody out there. Am I the only single woman at your wedding?"

"Of course not. My cousin Sherrie is single and so is Lance's niece."

"So why aren't they out there?"

"Probably for the same reason that you're not. Nobody wants to go first, so can you please do me a favor and go out there so that they'll follow your lead?"

"I better not be the only one out there, Stace." I hesitated before getting up.

"Don't worry, I promise you won't be."

As I walked toward that ominous, empty dance floor, I saw two other females leave their seats to join me. Stacy had been right. I wasn't alone up there. What she hadn't bothered to mention was that neither of them looked older than fifteen. Lance's niece couldn't have been older than twelve. I was going to kill Stacy!

I heard a drum roll and watched the flowers fly through the room. As promised, Stacy threw them directly to me. I reached for the leaves and felt the tip of a petal until Lance's niece jumped up in front of me and grabbed the bouquet right out of my hand. "Better luck next time," she said, holding up her trophy.

The only thing more embarrassing than standing with two young girls trying to catch the bouquet, was losing it to one of them who was probably still wearing a training bra.

"Too bad you missed," Kathy said as I headed back to the table. "Maybe if you had jumped up on your tippy toes, you would have caught it." She giggled.

"Thanks, I'll remember that next time." But there wasn't going to be a next time. I was hereby boycotting weddings until I had a diamond on my finger. Weddings were definitely meant for married people.

Chapter 23

How to Avoid Obsessing Over Your Condition:

Work till you drop or are too exhausted to think.

The Presto Cosmetics pitch was driving me crazy! John, who normally didn't get involved with the daily operations at Premier, insisted on taking an active role in every step of the creative process. He even assigned himself as Presto's account manager.

For the past two weeks, John had been calling meetings with the entire creative team every night around five o'clock, and as a result of these daily gatherings, we normally ended up making revisions at least until the sun rose the next morning.

When John walked into the conference room tonight, nobody looked up. Without bothering to sit down, John spoke in that deep, baritone voice that was sometimes a little intimidating, especially coming from a man close to seven feet tall whose face and stomach were twice the size that they should have been. But tonight, nobody seemed unnerved by his voice or size, just tired. "Listen, I know everyone's exhausted," he said, "but here's the good news. Only two days till the pitch and we're done."

"What's the bad news?" Tiffany asked, resting her head on the glass conference table.

"I was waiting for you to ask that, Tif." He smiled, always amused by Tiffany's quick comebacks. "Okay, here's the deal. We need some more revisions."

I joined in a group "ugh."

"Now we all know that Presto Cosmetics is targeted to teenage girls, right?" John ignored all of our grunts and sighs. "So what do teenage girls want more than anything else?"

"Teenage boys," Tiffany said. Lots of laughter followed.

"Well, Tiffany's actually got the right idea. Girls want to look attractive and sexy to attract guys. I've just spent the last eight hours going over this campaign, and I think we're really close to giving Presto what they want, but I think we'd be right on target if we made the campaign even sexier."

Another group ugh.

"Would you like me to design the models without clothes?" Tiffany asked.

"Let's put it this way, if you can get away with it, do it." And he looked completely serious.

"You've got to be kidding," Tiffany said. She lifted her head up long enough to give him a dirty look.

"Of course, you can't make them naked, but you can shorten their dresses and skirts."

"If I shorten them anymore, readers will be looking at their asses," Tiffany said.

"Hmm, there's an interesting thought," he responded.

"And Jen, your copy needs to be sexier." He placed two fingers on his mouth as if pondering his idea. "I don't want you to rewrite it because your message is strong, but maybe you can make it sound sexier by using a different voice. Imagine how one of Howard Stern's strippers would read the copy, and then write it as if it's coming out of her mouth."

Gee, I never thought I'd be using my writing skills to promote sex to teenagers. Too bad they didn't teach Sexual Advertising 101 in college.

"All I'm saying is that this campaign has to be as close to crossing that line without actually stepping over it," John continued. "Presto is notorious for pushing their ads to the limit, and I don't want to disappoint them."

"What if they're looking for something different this time?" I asked. I didn't even listen to Howard Stern.

"Yeah, maybe this time they want something with a little class?" Ashley, our new graphic design coordinator, agreed, looking hopeful.

"That's what I thought at first, too, but after looking at their website for the hundredth time and rereading their mission statement, I realized that their entire foundation is based on getting a sexual response from their audience." He began passing out former Presto ads. "I just received tear sheets from all their ads dating back to 1950, and even back then they used sex to sell their product. Of course, back then they couldn't get away with as much as they can now."

"So basically you're looking for an X-rated ad that will somehow be approved for submission," Tiffany said, looking bleary-eyed. This time, she didn't bother to lift her head.

"Exactly." He smiled, looking relieved that she got it, but nobody else seemed to have the energy or enthusiasm to return his grin. "And I don't think you have far to go. Everything you've done has been great, but I need you to get rid of any conservative photos and wording and increase the sex."

Tiffany's eyes seemed to wake up as she looked at a tear sheet of a woman who was practically nude. "Maybe if we get this account we can take on *Playboy* next," she said, still staring at the semi-naked lady.

"And on that note, I'll make my exit," John said. "Why don't we meet back here at nine o'clock and see what we have then." And before anyone could protest, John's heavy footsteps thumped through the conference room and out the door.

Had John said nine o'clock? Mike was going to have a fit. This would be the third time this week I'd canceled dinner plans with him.

Maybe I could tell him I had food poisoning. That would lay me up for at least a couple days, No, knowing Mike, he would insist on sitting by my bedside holding a bed pan until I was better. Would he believe I had some kind of family emergency? No, my mom would give me away when she saw his bubby at bingo this weekend. Of course, I shouldn't lie to him anyway. He had to get used to this kind of thing happening.

I dragged my feet back to my office, hoping Mike would be understanding.

But when I called him to explain why I couldn't see him again, I could actually hear him swishing his spit.

"I'm really sorry, Mike. I was looking forward to tonight, too." I searched through my files till I found the Presto copy that I thought was done.

"Couldn't you make some kind of excuse?"

"Not really. When you have a big pitch like this, it takes priority." I was having trouble keeping my eyes open long enough to skim the ad.

"What if it was your son's birthday? Would it take priority over that, too?"

Ouch! I wasn't expecting that curveball thrown right at my heart. "Obviously, that would be different," I said. At least, I thought so... "Anyway, for now I don't have a son, but I have a restless boss who's waiting for my copy." My head throbbed, trying to reason with Mike. "Can you please be patient for a few more days? I promise that once this pitch is over, I'll have a lot more time on my hands. Why don't we make plans for Friday?"

Why was he swishing now? I understood why he was upset, but it wasn't like we had major plans tonight. We probably would have gone out for Chinese food or pizza.

"I was hoping we could have dinner at my bubby's tonight, but I guess it would be okay if we went over there Friday instead." His statement was filled with a nice heavy dose of guilt.

"Your bubby's? Mike, why didn't you tell me she invited us for dinner?" This was a much bigger deal than take-out at Mia Shu Lu.

"Um...she just invited us today."

"Oh, well, I hope she didn't go to any trouble." Some first impression I was going to make. She'd probably hate me now. I wondered if she was as fanatical with her cooking as Mike's mom. I pictured a really old gray-haired, robust woman, shaking her head as she froze uneaten kreplah. I bet my mom would hear all about it at bingo on Sunday.

"This isn't just about my bubby, Jen. It's about us. I miss you."

"I miss you, too, but my job is a big part of who I am."

"I thought I was a big part of who you are, too." He had this Jewish guilt thing down pat.

"Of course you are. You're a big part of my life, but you have to understand how important my job is to me, too."

More swishing and then finally, "Believe me, I do," but he didn't sound happy about it. "I'll reschedule with my bubby for Friday."

"Make sure you tell her how sorry I am that I can't make it."

"I will." His voice sounded so sad that I felt terrible. "I know she'll love you as soon as she meets you. So can I count on you for Friday night then?"

"I promise."

"Okay then." Mike's voice rose slightly. "Can you be ready by seven o'clock? My bubby hates eating later than eight."

"That won't be a problem. The pitch is in the morning so that will give me plenty of time to go home, take a nap, and be ready on time."

"I love you," he said so easily I could tell it came from the heart.

"I love you too." I did, didn't I?

"I can't believe I'm sitting here at midnight making this girl's boobs stick out of her bathing suit." Tiffany was furious with John when I stopped by her office on my way back from getting some coffee.

"I know. Who's going to even see her makeup when she's wearing a shirt that looks more like a bra." It looked like something my mom would wear.

"I never thought I'd say this, but things have really gone downhill since Meany left." Tiffany stared at stock photos of sexy models. "She never would have taken an account like this. Remember when that company wanted us to promote their wine coolers by showing girls in string bikinis drinking on the beach?"

"Yeah, Meany refused to handle it." I sat down next to Tiffany's desk, too tired to stand. "She told John our agency would get a bad image if we took on accounts that degraded women like that."

"Not to mention, she didn't want to be responsible for using sex to sell alcohol." Tiffany pounded at her keyboard, looking for sexy colors.

"Well, I'm with Meany." I knew I could confide in Tiffany. "I'm not really thrilled with John's new approach to advertising. It seems so sleazy. It's not like John, either. Why do you think he's taking on these accounts? He used to be a lot more conservative."

"I was wondering the same thing," Tiffany said, while transforming a pair of tight jeans into short shorts. "I wonder if it has something to do with all the accounts we've lost in the past few months."

"Of course it does," said a familiar voice in the dark hallway. A moment later Rhonda's image appeared outside of Tiffany's office. So much for our private conversation.

"Rhonda, what are you doing here this late?" I wasn't used to seeing her later than one minute past five.

"John asked me to stay." Rhonda slowly inched her way inside Tiffany's office. "I've been working in the accounting office helping Fran with the billing."

"That can't wait till tomorrow?" I asked.

"Not when so many of our vendors are threatening to stop working for us unless they get a check first thing tomorrow." She looked like she might explode if we didn't ask her for more information.

"So what's going on?" Tiffany stood up to get a chair for Rhonda, who seemed thrilled to join our midnight chat session.

"Well, *supposedly* the reason nobody's gotten paid lately is because Ali used to help Fran with all the bookkeeping and since she left, Fran's gotten really behind."

"And what do you think?" I could tell she was dying to say more.

"Promise not to say anything?"

"Promise," we said as sweetly as possible.

"Well, when I was sitting outside Fran's office, I happened to hear her talking to John. Apparently, Mr. Wong doesn't want to do anymore advertising with us."

"Weren't we his agent of record?" Tiffany asked, sounding surprised.

"No, he only hired us to do the initial campaign and collateral materials, and they're all done," I answered.

"That's right," Rhonda said, looking quite chipper considering it was the middle of the night. "John was hoping Wong would advertise another one of his product lines with us, but it sounds like he's going to Meany's agency. John sounded pretty frantic because he was expecting to get that account. He had even figured it into our budget."

"So what does that mean?" I asked. For the first time since I started working here, I was worried about my job.

"Well, between losing Wong and those other clients you were just talking about, we really need to get Presto's business. Haven't you noticed our project status reports get thinner and thinner every week?" Rhonda looked thrilled to be spilling the beans.

"No wonder John's been micromanaging the Presto account like a baby," I said, suddenly feeling wide awake. "I had no idea things were so bad."

"Did all the other clients go to Meany's agency?" Tiffany asked.

"I heard most of them left because their own companies were losing money and they had to cut back on their advertising," I said.

"That's true, but not having Meany here doesn't help either," Rhonda said. "A lot of those clients came here in the first place because they liked working with Meany, or because they had heard about her reputation from her New York agency days. A few of them complained that Marisa had left, too. They said they felt like our creative teams were falling apart."

Tiffany, who rarely let things bother her, looked alarmed. She really couldn't afford to lose her job considering all of her credit cards were completely maxed out. "Did John tell you all this?" she asked.

"Uh, well, he didn't exactly tell me directly. Let's just say that Fran's office door is pretty thin."

"Shit, I better shorten these dresses some more." Tiffany returned to her computer to add more flesh tone to the girls' photos.

"And I better go make my copy sound sexier." I ran out toward my office, wishing I had satellite radio so I was familiar with how Howard Stern's sexy models spoke.

By Friday afternoon, I was functioning only from caffeine and sugar. Three cups of coffee and two jelly donuts had gotten me through our presentation, but I was gradually losing momentum.

John had called a meeting after the presentation and I was hoping it would be short so I could go home and collapse. We barely moved as John entered the conference room.

"I'll make this brief so you can all go home, but I want to thank you for all your hard work these past few weeks. I know it's been hard on you, but I really think it's going to pay off. The product managers at Presto told me they liked our pitch, especially the graphics." He smiled at Tiffany. "The VP told me if it were up to him, he'd give us the account today, but he has to meet with one other agency as a courtesy."

"That sounds like a good sign," Tiffany said, looking unusually anxious.

"I know it's too early to celebrate yet, but I want to do something for all of you to show my appreciation so I've made reservations at the

Palace Inn Restaurant for dinner tonight. After dinner, we can go to their nightclub. Dinner and drinks are on me."

I joined in the cheering as we talked about which shots we would do.

"You all deserve an evening of fun, so go home, get some rest, and let's meet back here around seven o'clock. Oh, and feel free to bring a date if you want."

Uh-oh.

"What's wrong?" Tiffany asked as we left the conference room. "You have a strange look on your face."

"Tif, I can't go tonight. Mike will kill me." I stopped walking and leaned against an empty cubicle. "I've been canceling dates with him for weeks and I'm supposed to meet his bubby tonight. What am I going to do?"

"That is a problem." Tiffany joined me in slumping against the cube until we were practically holding each other up. "Any chance of postponing dinner with his bubby till tomorrow night, and bringing Mike to the Palace Inn tonight? You heard John. He said that would be okay."

"Not with Mike. He's been pretty upset about my schedule lately. Besides, how can I cancel on his bubby twice in one week? The woman's eighty-something years old. I don't think she understands the concept of career women."

"You never know. Sometimes older people are hipper than you think."

"You don't know Mike and his family. Tif, I don't want to lose him over a work party. I gave him my word that I'd be there tonight, and I know it's important to him." My sudden anxiety gave me an adrenaline rush to stand up straight.

"Well, you might be spending a lot of time with him because if we don't get this account, John's probably going to have to lay some of us off." Now Tiffany looked like she had received a shot of energy as she stood up to look directly at me. "Listen, Jen, I've been through a couple layoffs before, and believe me, you want to stay on John's good side at a time like this."

Just great. Now I had to decide between my job and Mike's bubby. I couldn't lose my job. Since college, it was the only thing I could count on, but I couldn't lose Mike either. He held the key to my future.

"Just talk to him," Tiffany insisted. "Tell him what's going on here. I bet he'll understand."

"All right. I'll give him a call."

"Good, I'll see you tonight, then."

But as soon as I invited Mike to the party, he swished so loudly, it sounded like he was gargling.

"You just spent every moment of the past week with these people. Why would you want to spend the rest of the evening with them?"

"I just told you why. If we don't get this account, I could lose my job!" I didn't mean to yell at Mike, but I was caught in a bad situation and he wasn't helping matters any.

"I thought your agency was doing well," he whined.

"So did I, but since Meany left it's been going downhill."

"Who?"

"Meany, you know that account executive who left Premier for that job in New York."

"Uh-huh?"

Still no recognition. How could that name mean nothing to him? "The woman who sort of offered me a job in New York."

"Oh, her." Silence followed.

"Listen, Mike, I don't want to offend John by not going tonight. What if he uses it against me when he decides who to fire?"

More silence and swishing. I wish he'd get angry and yell at me instead. At least I could respond to that.

"Tonight's really important to me, Jen. Please come with me instead of going to that party."

He sounded so sad, and I was so tired I didn't have the energy to talk him into going with me. Besides, I understood why he didn't want me to go. It wasn't fair to him to keep canceling dates. I just hoped I didn't pay the price of choosing his bubby over John. "Okay, forget about the dinner, I'll see you at seven."

"Oh, sweetie, I promise you won't regret it."

I certainly hoped not.

Chapter 24

It's Possible to Go into Remission When:

1. You receive your ticket to marriage (in a small square box).
2. You no longer have to worry about checking your mail for singles events.
3. You can tell all your *loved ones* that you're done wrestling single women for bridal bouquets at weddings.
4. You utter the words, "I do," even when you don't.

"You look particularly pretty tonight," Mike said as he drove toward the expressway.

"Thanks." Apparently, Mike needed of a good pair of glasses. I had been so upset about missing the party that I hadn't been able to sleep when I got home. My eyes were bloodshot and the creases around my eyes looked especially deep tonight. I really needed to look into botox treatments.

"You're so quiet," he said, driving agonizingly slowly behind a tractor trailer.

I watched at least twenty cars speed up and pass the trailer, while we crawled behind. "Mike, why don't you pass that driver. At this rate, we won't get to your bubby's until breakfast tomorrow."

"Don't worry, we'll be there soon." He looked over to where I sat. "Are you thinking about work? Is that why you're not saying much?"

I knew he'd be upset if I told him the truth, but what did he expect? It wasn't everyday you found out you might soon be signing up for unemployment. "I guess I'm a little worried about losing my job."

"Jen, they'd be crazy to let you go. You're as dedicated to that place as anyone could be."

I hoped John still felt that way when he read my email, explaining that I had come down with a migraine and couldn't make the party. Of course, if I had gone to the party, I'd probably be sitting there now, worrying that Mike was going to break up with me. It was a no-win situation. Now that I'd made my decision, I had to put Premier out of my mind and focus on Mike. I really liked his new striped IZOD sweater. I wondered if it was one of the sweaters that his mom had bought him.

"Why are we turning here?" I asked. Mike pulled into the parking lot across the street from Moish's Deli.

"I told my bubby we'd pick up a rye bread for her. Is that all right?"

"Of course. Oh, Mike, I forgot to bring her something for dessert. Maybe I can pick up some Danish while we're here."

"Um…okay," he said, taking my hand. "It's hard to believe it's been over six months since I carried your fish tray to this parking lot."

It did seem like a long time ago. "I wasn't even sure you'd call me."

"I knew as soon as I met you that I would."

We crossed the street, and this time, nobody was directing traffic. I continued walking toward the front door when I realized that Mike was no longer beside me. When I turned around, I saw Mike standing by the bench where we first met. "This is a very special spot," Mike said.

I walked over to Mike. "I have to admit, I never thought I'd meet someone at a Jewish deli."

"Did you ever think you'd get engaged at one?"

"Huh?" It took a minute, a long minute, for Mike's words to register. It wasn't until I saw him take out a small square box from his pocket that I realized what was happening. Oh my God!

"Sweetie, I've been waiting a long time to meet the right woman. I'd stopped believing it would ever happen until I met you. And now that I have, all I want to do is be with you. Jen, I want to spend the rest of my life loving you. I want to wake up every morning next to you, knowing that we belong to each other."

Mike waited for a bunch of older women speaking Yiddish to pass us before he knelt down on his knee in front of me by the bench. "I know it's only been a short time, but I feel like I've known you forever, and I want to know you forever. Will you please do me the great honor of becoming my wife?"

This was it, the moment I'd been waiting for all my life, the moment I had fantasized about since I was four. Of course, my fantasy didn't include the smell of corned beef or the sound of clanking dishes, but nevertheless, this was it. It was finally my turn to plan my wedding, my turn to announce my engagement. Look out world, Jennifer Greenberg was getting married!

"Of course, I'll marry you."

"Oh, Jen, you've made me the happiest guy in the world," Mike said, reaching over to kiss me. A moment later, he opened the box, which contained a diamond ring. Gently, he placed it on my finger.

Hah! I finally had one, too. Wait till Stacy saw the size of this. I couldn't wait to see the look on Rhonda's face. And my mom would absolutely flip! "Mike, it's so beautiful." I stared at the shiny emerald-cut stone, wanting to hold it up in the air for everyone in the deli to see. It didn't have the fancy baguettes around the sides, like Marisa's and Stacy's, but I didn't mind because its plain gold band made the huge diamond stand out even more.

"I'm glad you like it." He stood up to admire it on my finger. "It's three carats, and practically flawless."

As if I would know what a flaw looked like. "You have great taste. Did you pick it out yourself?"

"No, don't you recognize it? It's my mom's engagement ring. This week is exactly forty years since my dad gave it to her." He stroked the ring with affection. "I thought it would be nice to get engaged on their anniversary, but since you couldn't make it on Tuesday, I figured tonight was close enough."

"You mean you were going to propose on Tuesday?" I felt my mouth drop open.

"Guilty," he said.

And here I had gotten mad at him for wanting me to leave work early. How selfish could I be?

"My dad always told me that when I met the right girl, he wanted me to give her this ring…and now I have."

While admiring my new treasure, I recalled the grim expression of Mike's father from the photo in his dining room, and for a moment I felt a chill run through me.

"Is something wrong?" Mike looked concerned. "I hope you like it because it means a lot to me seeing it on your finger."

I was being ridiculous. Mike wasn't his father, and besides, other than making Mike's mom give up her career, he sounded like a nice guy. Even my dad had said so. "I love it." And I would love walking into work on Monday with my newest piece of jewelry.

"Was your mom okay about giving me the ring? I mean, after all, it really was hers."

"Yeah, she was happy to give it to me. She always knew that my father wanted my wife to wear it someday."

But what did his mother want? I hoped she had some say in the decision...Had Mike said wife? Oh my gosh. I was going to be a wife, and I didn't even need breast implants to get that title.

"You really scared me when I thought you were going to cancel on me tonight," Mike said. "I was afraid I'd have to call your mom again and tell her to put the champagne back in the fridge."

"My mom? My mom knows?"

"Yeah, I went to your parent's house last week to tell them I was going to propose," he said sheepishly. "I really wanted their approval before I asked you to marry me."

I touched my bright shiny diamond, still stunned to be wearing one on my finger. "I hope my mom didn't pass out when you told her."

"Not quite," he laughed, "but she was pretty ecstatic."

I pictured my mom jumping on the furniture and screaming, and I imagined that her reaction wasn't too far off.

"I promised your parents we'd stop by tonight." Mike glanced at his watch.

"But what about dinner at your bubby's?"

"Hope you don't mind, but that was a little white lie so you wouldn't suspect why I was bringing you here. Knowing my bubby, she's probably shutting the lights off to go to sleep right about now."

"Of course I don't mind." Mind, how could I possibly mind? I had my ring, I had my fiancé, and I had a wedding to plan. It would take a lot more than a cancelled dinner with Mike's bubby to upset me.

"Your mom's dying to see the ring," Mike said, staring at it on my finger.

I bet she was. She'd only been talking about it for the past six years. Huh, this meant no more email links to singles websites, no more singles dance notices, no more articles on finding your soul mate. I was free. And if we got married soon, I might even beat *Today's Modern Woman's* deadline of having children before I turned thirty-five. All the pieces of the puzzle were coming together in my life, and I had Mike to thank.

"Before we go, I want you to know that I will always do everything I can to make you happy." Mike placed his hands on my shoulders and looked into my eyes as if he had never seen them before. Where had I seen that expression before? Was it from Chris? No, his was more lustful and passionate. Then I realized it was my dad's look of adoration in Mike's eyes. At last, someone other than my dad was looking at me like that.

"Jen, I want us to always to be as in love with each other as we are now, even when we're too old to walk." Mike smiled at me with that tender look in his eyes, but that "L" word still made me uncomfortable.

What was wrong with me? Here, I had everything I always wanted bottled up in one person, and I felt nervous when he told me how he felt about me. Of course I loved him. How could I not?

When we pulled up at my parent's house, we were greeted by "Congratulations" balloons waving on the railings of the front steps. I was surprised one of the balloons didn't read, "Jennifer Greenberg finally found someone to marry her."

Before I even walked into the living room, my mom and Kathy grabbed my hand, as if it was an object I carried around in my pocket. I forgave them as they swooned over the ring. "It's beautiful," they said in unison.

"Your father had great taste in jewelry," my mom said to Mike.

"Well, I have great taste in fiancées," he responded.

My mom and Kathy uttered a simultaneous, "Ooh," extending the *o* for about ten seconds.

"I love the setting," Kathy said, while moving my finger around in different positions to inspect it.

Hey, did she forget there was a person attached to this ring? My finger wasn't meant to bend that way.

"Well, Dad, what do you think?" I walked over to my dad, who sat on his recliner, looking at us but saying nothing.

"As long as you're happy, I'm happy." But for some reason, he didn't look too happy. My mom must have insulted him again.

"Of course, she's happy, Harris," my mother interrupted. "Look who she's marrying."

"Make sure you save me a dance at the wedding, princess." My dad winked at me before getting up and walking upstairs.

"And speaking of weddings, have you set a date yet?" my mom asked.

"Mom, we just got engaged thirty minutes ago. Give us a chance."

"I think the spring is a beautiful time for a wedding, don't you, Mike?" She focused all her attention on Mike while I silently gazed lovingly at my ring.

"It's funny you mentioned the spring because I always imagined getting married in May," Mike agreed. "How does that sound to you, Jen? We could plan our wedding after finals next year so I have plenty of time for our honeymoon."

"May sounds like a perfect month," my mom answered for me.

Hello? Remember me? The bride-to-be. Maybe I should have left the room and let Mike plan the wedding with my mom.

"I hope you're planning to have a band instead of a DJ," my mom said. "I think live music is much more elegant."

"I agree," Mike said. "Maybe you could get the name of Stacy's band, Jen. I really liked them."

I listened as Mike and my mom talked about our wedding plans. My wedding! I'd never have to attend a couple's party alone again. And no more wrestling with single women over bridal bouquets at weddings. I now had a steady date to every major function for the rest of my life.

~

"Aren't you going to come to bed," Mike called from my bedroom.

"In a minute. I still have one more phone call to make." I had already called Stacy, Tiffany, and Marisa, but I still wanted to call Lori.

Hell, maybe I'd even call Amy. Not that we socialized anymore, but after all her comments at the wedding, I'd love to let her know that Mike had proposed without me having to drop one hint. So much for that *Thirty-Something Singles* book that Amy had quoted from.

I loved listening to everyone's reaction when I told them I was engaged. Naturally, they all wanted to hear every detail, and I was thrilled to share all the information with them. Okay, I would have preferred telling them that he had proposed at a French restaurant or by Penn's Landing. Getting engaged in front of a deli took some of the romance away from the story, but I recovered quickly by describing the ring, and how Mike wanted to get engaged the same time his father had proposed. They all ate that up, telling me how sweet Mike was.

"Jen, we'll still be engaged tomorrow. Come to bed."

Darn. Lori had her answering machine on. Maybe the baby was sleeping. I'd have to wait to tell her tomorrow. I didn't want to leave that kind of message on her machine. I preferred hearing her initial reaction.

When I climbed into bed, I saw Mike was wearing his usual pair of blue IZOD pajamas. "Your neighbors really should keep the volume down on their TV," he said, sounding annoyed.

"What are you talking about?" But then I heard the loud voices, too, and I knew right away that they weren't coming from the television. Lisa was screaming at someone. Had she finally flipped out at Josh for keeping her up? Or maybe she had had it with Jessica's constant demands for fast food. But wait, that wasn't a child's voice shouting back. That was Randy. If Mike hadn't been there, I would have put a glass up to the wall so I could hear better. But just as I started listening, I heard the door slam.

"What were they arguing about?" I whispered in case there was more to hear.

"I don't know. I was reading the paper."

That was the difference between males and females. A female would have heard every word.

"So are you done filling everyone in?" Mike smiled. "I'm glad you want the whole world to know, but I was hoping I'd have you all to myself tonight."

Mike stroked my face and kissed my hands. "So what would you like tonight," Mike asked, as if taking my order at a restaurant. But all

I had to do was hear his heavy breathing to realize he wasn't talking about French fries versus onion rings.

"Why don't you surprise me this time?" After all these months, he must have caught on to what I needed by now. And I was getting tired of playing teacher in bed. I was ready to have him graduate so we could get on with our sex life.

Mike kissed my lips deeply until I started getting really hot. Okay, now we were getting somewhere. Next, he lowered his mouth to my neck and nibbled for a while. I loved when guys nibbled on my neck. So far, he got an A plus. He continued lowering his mouth until he found my breasts under my sweater. Bingo. That's just what I would have asked him to do. My nipples grew hard as he sucked on them for a while. Oh, yeah, this was good. I felt his cock harden beneath my hands as he continued moving downward. He unzipped my pants and probed between my legs until he found the spot I had showed him.

Perfect! He must have been the world's greatest student at school. He was using his tongue between my legs. Now I was on fire. I moaned as he increased his speed, faster and faster and...Hey, what the hell? Why was he slowing down? I hadn't taught him that. I needed him to increase the pace. Now! He had totally lost the rhythm. No wonder he couldn't dance.

Mike's score was going down now, and so was my sex drive. "Mike, can you move your tongue faster the way I showed you?"

"Oh, yeah, sure, sure." But it was too late. He just couldn't get that same motion back and within seconds my orgasm was history. Unfortunately, he was now hard as a rock. He lowered his pants enough for me to see his cock and then lowered mine. We lay in bed with our shirts still on and our pants down to our ankles. Apparently, he'd forgotten the part about taking our clothes off first.

"Go slowly," I instructed. Okay, now his cock was pressing on the right spot. All he had to do was continue...Too late. Mike grew limp inside me and I grew frustrated.

I couldn't very well give him step-by-step instructions every time, but as I looked at my diamond shining in the darkness and thought about our wedding, preparing sexual lesson plans didn't sound like such a terrible idea anymore. At least they gave me the results I needed.

When I drifted to sleep, I dreamt about our honeymoon. I could see Mike and me sitting on lounge chairs by a swimming pool on a cruise ship. But when I woke up, I realized that Mike had been sitting at the pool with an IZOD sweater and pants, while everyone else wore bathing suits.

Chapter 25

Even While in Remission, You're Still Contagious When:

1. You first become engaged (remember, an engagement ring is toxic to single women).
2. You spread your happiness to females without boyfriends.
3. You become the person you once avoided like the plaque.

"I can't believe you missed the party on Friday," Rhonda said first thing Monday morning. "John seemed really disappointed that you weren't there. You were the only one who didn't show up."

Good old Rhonda. I could always count on her to make me feel like shit, even when I was in a great mood.

"You must have had a really bad migraine."

Oops. Good thing Rhonda reminded me about my excuse. I had almost forgotten about the email I sent John.

"Yeah, it was really bad, but fortunately, I felt much better on Saturday. Otherwise, Mike might not have been able to give me this." I held my ring finger up the way I had seen so many other women proudly displaying their diamonds.

"Wow, Jen. Congratulations." Rhonda kept one eye on my ring and the other one on the elevator until it opened. "Hey, Sandee," she yelled before Sandee had taken one step into the office. "You've got to come see Jen's engagement ring." The production assistant walked over and made the appropriate oohs and aahs.

When our new account coordinator came by for some office supplies, Rhonda once again spread the news. "Renee, Jen's engaged.

Forget about the paper clips for a minute and come see her ring." Renee was quickly by my side, breathing down my arm.

Within five minutes, Rhonda had called over just about everyone at Premier, and I found myself in the center of a large circle, surrounded by well wishers and admirers. This was my moment, and I was enjoying every second.

Apparently, Tina, our traffic manager, didn't feel the same way. When she saw what all the fuss was about, she turned around to leave the reception area. I caught her look of dismay as she tried to slither out, but Rhonda was too fast for her. "Hey, Tina, where are you going?" Rhonda yelled after her. "You haven't even looked at Jen's ring yet."

Tina slowly returned to stand in line so she could take a peek. And just when Rhonda got her where she wanted her, she blurted out, "So Tina, when do think your boyfriend's going to propose? Didn't you meet him around the same time Jen met Mike?"

"Yeah, I guess I did," she said, barely glancing at my diamond before making a quick escape.

Whew. Thank goodness nobody would ever ask me that question again. I felt like I belonged to an elite club that only accepted members with diamond rings. Looking down at my emerald-cut stone, I felt relieved, knowing Mike had just bought me my membership.

I let everyone take a look at my ring before walking to my office. As always, I immediately checked my email, but for once I was hoping for personal messages. I was rewarded with a message from Stacy who had written "Congratulations" in the subject line. *Jen, just wanted to tell you again how happy I am that you and Mike are engaged. You're going to have such a wonderful time planning your wedding, and you'll love being married. It's the most wonderful experience in the world. Love ya, Stace.*

I wasn't even annoyed with Stacy's overuse of the word wonderful.

Next message: *Jen, Barb and I volunteered to sell tickets for the Springtown Theater's big benefit concert. We thought it was a good cause since all proceeds go to help homeless people. I'll probably be staying over her place occasionally since she lives so much closer to the theater. The box office opens everyday at eight o'clock and you know how much I hate to miss my beauty sleep. If you need me, call me on my cell phone. I can't wait to go shopping for gowns with you. Love, Mom. PS: Make sure you tell my Mike I said hi.*

My mom now referred to Mike as "my Mike," almost as if she had officially adopted him. Hmm, when had my mom become such a big philanthropist?

I skimmed through a message from Mike, another poem expressing his unconditional love for me. I would get back to that one later.

Then I flipped through my Rolodex. Let's see. Who else could I call to tell about my engagement? I hadn't talked to my cousin in Florida for a while. Maybe I'd give her a buzz. And then there was my old college friend who moved to Arizona after graduation. I could call her, too… But before I could dial, my phone rang. Probably another well-wisher.

"Hello, this is Jen."

"Hi, Jen, it's Ilene Meeney, how are you?"

I will not get my hopes up. I will not get my hopes up. "I'm good. How have you been?"

"Busy as usual. Since we last spoke, I've been to Australia, Japan and China."

I wondered if she saw Mr. Wong while she was out there. "Sounds like business is good."

"It really is. So what's been going on with you?"

"Well, actually I have some big news." Telling Meany wasn't as exciting as telling Rhonda, but still, it gave me another audience. "I'm engaged." I looked at my ring for the hundredth time to reassure myself that it was still true.

"Congratulations. So, who's the lucky guy?"

"His name is Mike. I think I met him right after you left. We've been dating for almost seven months."

"That's great. I'm really happy for you." And I could tell from her voice that she was. "So what will your married name be?"

"Robinowitz."

"Michael Robinowitz. Hmm, that name sounds familiar. What does his father do?"

"He was an accountant, but he passed away a few years ago. His mother once worked in advertising. Maybe you know her."

"Not Doris Robinowitz?" She sounded incredulous.

"Yeah, that's her." I scratched my head, wondering how they knew each other.

"I don't believe it. Do you have any idea who she is?"

I guessed the correct answer wouldn't be Mike's mother and servant. "Not really," I said, feeling rather stupid.

"Jen, Doris Robinowitz was one of the most successful account executives on Madison Avenue in the 1970's."

"You're kidding." Now I really felt like a big dimwit. "Did you ever meet her?"

"Meet her! If it weren't for Doris, I probably would never have broken into advertising. I interned for her at JBM&P."

That's where I had heard that agency's name before. Meany had worked there before coming to Premier.

"It's probably hard for you to believe, but at the time, JBM&P was as big as Richardson and Whitaker is now," Meany explained. "Doris took me under her wing and taught me all about advertising. I guess you could say she was my mentor, but we also became friends. When I realized I didn't want to teach anymore, she was the only one in New York willing to take a chance with an inexperienced kid like me. Doris offered me my first job in the field."

"You mean you worked for Doris?" I couldn't imagine such a strong, powerful woman like Meany working for such a meek, sweet woman like Doris.

"She hired me as her assistant. Most of the Madison Avenue shops made you pay your dues at the smaller markets before considering you for a job, but not Doris. She insisted that the CEO at her agency give me a break."

To think, I'd now learned more about Meany during this one telephone conversation than I knew about her during the five years that we worked together.

"I owe my entire career to Doris," Meany continued. "Whenever I got discouraged or questioned whether I would make it in the industry, Doris always gave me the encouragement and support I needed to keep going. We really missed her when she left. Did you know that Mike's father made her quit her job?" For the first time since talking about Doris, Meany was uncomfortably silent.

"Uh, yeah. She mentioned it."

Meany let out a big sigh. "It was such a shame because she was so good at her job. She brought in some of the largest accounts the agency ever landed."

"Have you kept up with her at all over the years?"

The Marriage Epidemic

"I tried, but after a while she stopped returning my messages. It was like she wanted to forget all about the world of advertising."

Maybe because she was too busy waiting on Mike's father.

"The last time I saw her was at an advertising convention in New York, about five years after she left JBM&P. Even though I remember her eyes lighting up when she showed me pictures of her children, I could tell she wasn't the same woman who I remembered. It was like someone had extinguished the light inside her soul."

Pretty deep.

"So how's Doris doing now that her children are all grown up? Did she ever go back to advertising?"

"No, she spends most of her time at home, cooking." *For people who don't eat her food.*

"What a waste of talent. If you think about it, give her my phone number. I'd love to see her again. If she's interested in getting back into the field, I might be able to help her out. I happen to know of a Philly agency looking for a part-time consultant. She'd be perfect for the job. She really is a remarkable woman. You're getting a great mother-in-law. By the way." Long pause. "Does Mike know about my job offer?"

Is that officially what it was? "Uh, yeah, he knows about it."

"Great." She exhaled loud enough for me to hear it through the phone. "I'm glad he's supportive of your career. That's really important. And speaking of your career, I was hoping we could get together tomorrow. I'm sorry it's such short notice, but I just arranged a client meeting in center city tomorrow morning."

"That's okay. I can make it." *With bells on.*

"My client's staying at the Ritz Carlton, so why don't we meet at the hotel's restaurant for breakfast."

"I'll be there." I wouldn't miss it.

Even though meeting with Meany wasn't an interview, I wore my new dark blue Calvin Klein business suit. Meany was already waiting for me when I arrived ten minutes early.

"Jen, it's good to see you." Meany wore a short burgundy blazer with a long gray skirt.

We both ordered coffee. "I heard Premier's having some problems lately," Meany said, while looking at her menu.

283

"Yeah, we've lost a few accounts since you left."

"According to *Advertising Age*, it's more than a few," she responded rather abruptly.

Had she invited me here to get information from me? Well, I wasn't giving anything away until I got some information about Richardson and Whitaker from her.

"It's a hard time for most agencies." I tried to be as vague as possible.

"That depends on which accounts you go after. Richardson and Whitaker just had its best year ever." She put down her menu and looked directly at me. "Are you still interested in working there?"

Yes! Yes! And yes! "I would certainly consider it." *Yahoo!*

"Good, because we got all three accounts that I mentioned to you, and we're looking for some new talented people. I already told David Jeffreys, our copy director, about you, and he's interested in hiring you. You'd still have to meet him, of course, but that would be more of a formality. As far as he's concerned, you have the job if you want it."

"I want it!" Had that sounded too pathetically desperate? According to *Career Women Magazine*, you were supposed to take a few days to consider a job before accepting it, but I had been considering this job for months now.

"Great." She smiled naturally without triggering her smile activator. "I'll schedule a meeting with David for sometime next week."

I couldn't believe I was going to work at Richardson and Whitaker! This was my big break! All my hard work had actually paid off!

For the next hour, Meany filled me in about my new job description. I tried hard to listen, but found myself daydreaming about working on Madison Avenue, handling huge international advertising campaigns.

From what I did hear from Meany, I'd still be a senior copywriter, but I'd actually have my own staff, two assistants and a coordinator, who'd all report to me. David was planning on assigning me the Jacques Montan account. I'd even get to travel a little, although most of the time I'd be in the office, which worked out well. I wasn't sure how Mike would feel about me traveling abroad when I was supposed to be planning our wedding.

Thank goodness I had listened to Marisa and told Mike about Meany's possible job offer. Now I didn't have to worry about breaking the news to him.

I left the restaurant feeling elated. I couldn't believe how lucky I was. I got the job and the guy! It was like living out the happy ending of a movie. I didn't even care that I had to walk through the entire hotel past the main lobby to grab a taxi back to work.

But before I got to the front door, I couldn't stand it anymore. I was about to burst with excitement if I didn't tell someone about Meany's offer. I started to call Tiffany back at the office, but stopped before hitting the last digit. I really should tell Mike first. Weren't you supposed to share this type of big news with the person you planned to spend your life with?

So I dialed his office number instead. Assuming I'd probably get his voice mail, I was surprised when he picked up on the first ring.

"Hey, sweetheart. How's my beautiful bride-to-be?"

"Oh, Mike, I've had the greatest day. For the second day in a row, I spent the morning showing off the ring that my very generous fiancé gave me."

"That sounds like a great way to spend the day."

"It was. And then I met Meany for breakfast. You'll never believe it, but she offered me the job in New York."

Swish. Swish Swish.

"Mike? Mike?" If it weren't for the sound of saliva, I would have thought we'd been disconnected.

"You're not going to take it, are you?" He spoke in a whisper.

"I was planning to. Mike, we already talked about this." I was beginning to panic and felt myself at the verge of hyperventilating. "You said you wouldn't mind."

"And you said if a better offer came up in Philly, you'd take it."

"But it didn't," I said emphatically.

Swish. Swish. "Yeah, it did." Long pause. "I made you that offer when I proposed."

That was the offer he had talked about? He tricked me! "So the only reason you said you wouldn't mind if I took the job is because you always expected me to change my mind once you proposed!" I didn't realize I was shouting until two women in business suits who were walking through the lobby shot me a dirty look as if I had interrupted their very important conversation.

"Look, sweetheart, I would never tell you to turn down that job. I was just hoping that after we got engaged, you would want to. It's going to be hard having a marriage when you're commuting to New York everyday."

"But now that we're engaged, it's the perfect time." My heart raced as I tried to reason with Mike. "We can buy a house that's right between both of our jobs so neither of us have to commute more than an hour and a half."

"That's a long commute," he complained. "You know how I hate traffic." Maybe because he refused to pass anyone going more than ten miles an hour.

"You already commute almost an hour each way. What's an extra thirty minutes?"

"What about all those late nights you work? By the time you get home from New York, I'll be sleeping."

"You're sleeping half the time when I get home now. I'm telling you, it won't make that much of a difference."

I was so involved in my conversation that I didn't notice an old lady listening to my phone conversation until I backed into her. Before she decided to give me advice, although I probably could have used it, I moved away from her and closer to the check-in desk.

While I was walking across the lobby, Mike continued his tirade. "I'm not sure I like the idea of you traveling home from New York late at night. What if you get mugged?"

"So I'll carry Mace with me. Besides, lots of women commute late at night from New York. I'm sure I won't be the only one on that train."

I watched a large crowd of people get out of the elevator and approach the check-out line. It must be nice to calmly go about your day without suddenly having to work out all the details of your entire future.

Sigh. Swish. Sigh. Swish.

"Mike, will you please stop with the sound effects and say something?"

"What sound effects?" He sounded totally perplexed.

"Never mind." Ugh. I wasn't about to get into that now.

"Why can't you just stay at Premier?"

The old woman who'd been eavesdropping appeared next to me again. I turned my back to her, not wanting to have another argument with someone else.

"Mike, I told you how bad the agency's doing. I couldn't even buy binders yesterday because we haven't paid our office supplier for three months. Not to mention John's taking every sleazy account just to stay afloat."

"I understand, but there's lots of other agencies in the area. You could always work at one of those." His voice pleaded with me over the phone.

The old woman moved closer to me until I finally shot her a dirty look and gave her the finger. She walked away with her head down as if I'd truly upset her. Too bad!

"So you're telling me that you don't want me to take the job." I nearly choked on the words.

"No, I'm just saying that I hope you don't accept it until you've really thought about it. I also hope that when you're considering it, you put our marriage before your job. Just follow your heart, Jen. Okay?"

"It sounds like you want me to choose one or the other."

"I never said that." But he didn't have to.

We barely said good-bye to each other, and as I cleared my cell phone, I wondered if this was how Mike's mother had felt thirty years ago. Of course, Mike hadn't actually demanded that I turn down the job, but in his passive way, he had made his point.

So much for getting the job and the guy. Why couldn't my life resemble a fairy tale for more than a few minutes? Was I being difficult? Maybe starting a new job and getting married at the same time was too much. Maybe I should find another job nearby? Hadn't Marisa said she would travel to Alaska if Zack asked her to? Then why wasn't I willing to stay in Philly for Mike?

My head pounded as I glanced up at the check-out counter. Huh. That woman in line could have passed as my mom's double. Even her halter top and tiny short skirt looked exactly like something my mom would wear. Amazing. How could two people look and dress so much alike. I tried to see the woman's face, but she wore dark sunglasses and a large rimmed hat that made it impossible to get a good look.

Wait a second. That woman next to her? It couldn't be. Barb? It was. That meant that mysterious woman who looked like my mom was my mom. Why on earth were my mom and Barb checking out of the Ritz Carlton on a Monday morning? Weren't they supposed to be selling tickets for some benefit show? Oh my God, they must be gay. No wonder my mom lost interest in my dad.

Hey, who were those two men in front of my mom and Barb, and why were they talking to them now? And why was one putting his arm around my mom's waist? And why was he kissing her? And more importantly, why was she kissing him back?

I felt physically ill as I heard my mom's familiar laugh, the laugh that had once responded to my dad's jokes, the laugh that had once made my dad smile whenever he heard it.

As my mom raised her head to touch her male friend's face, her dark sunglasses met my eyes. Unable to speak, unable to breathe, I ran out of the hotel as fast as I could.

Chapter 26

You Might Experience a Relapse When:

1. You discover that nice guys sometimes do finish last.
2. Your prince turns back into a frog.

My mom and another guy! Why? Why? Well, this was certainly enough to forget about Mike's semi-ultimatum for a while. As I walked around Independence Mall for the tenth time, I still couldn't figure it out. My dad was the sweetest, kindest man in the world. How could my mom do this to him?

Kathy had been right about someone cheating in our family. She had just guessed the wrong person. I knew my dad would never do anything to hurt my mom. So why was my mom hurting him? What had he done that was so horrible that he deserved this kind of treatment?

My cell phone rang, but as soon as I saw my mother's cell phone number, I let it ring. She continued to call every few minutes, but I didn't care. She began texting me, but I ignored it. What could I possibly say to her? So, mom, nice hotel beds? Or, how's your sex life now that you decided to do it with other men?

How could I have been so blind that I hadn't even suspected this before? Here I thought she might be having an affair with Barb when she was just using her as her decoy. In some ways it would be easier to accept another woman than another man. Then at least I could rationalize it by saying that my mom didn't like men. It was much less personal than believing she truly didn't like my dad.

That trip to Vegas must have been a getaway for my mom and Barb with their boyfriends. Or maybe Barb hadn't even been there at all.

And all those late nights out weren't really with Barb. That must have been why Stacy saw her all dressed up at the liquor store last month. She must have been buying her lover a nightcap.

I bent over to heave, but nothing came out. I was too numb to throw up. All I could do was continue circling around the square. Had there been other guys? And if so, how many? And how long had this been going on?

I pictured my loving dad sitting alone all these years, while my mom paraded around the city with other men. Did he suspect what was going on? Maybe he had cheated on her, and now she was getting him back. No, not my dad. He wouldn't do that, but if my mom did, why wouldn't he?

My head pounded and I no longer knew what to believe. I wanted to talk to someone, but I didn't know who to call. I didn't feel like telling Mike yet, and that bothered me, too.

I was getting tired of walking so I headed back to the only safe place I had known for years; my office.

When I reached my desk, I had five voice mail messages, all from my mom, which I erased without listening to. I wasn't ready to hear what she had to say. I wasn't sure I wanted to know.

"You look like hell," Tiffany said, closing the door behind her. "What's wrong?"

As I relayed the past hour to her, tears poured down my face. "How can I ever look at her again?"

"You have to talk to her. That's the only way you'll know what really happened."

"Like I can believe anything she says."

"Jen, your mom's here to see you," Rhonda announced into my intercom.

"Give her a chance to explain." Tiffany put her arm around me as I dried my eyes.

"How can she possibly explain cheating on my dad?"

"Hey, there's always two sides to every story. Why don't you go find out what her side is."

I silently followed my mom outside to a bench in front of my office building. My mom tried to touch my hand, but I pulled away. "Jen, honey, you're the last person I ever wanted to hurt."

"Too late." I wasn't letting her off the hook. She was totally, one hundred percent wrong and nothing she said would make me change my mind. "Did Dad cheat on you?"

"Never."

"Did he hit you?"

"Of course not!"

"Did he treat you badly?"

"No."

"Then why?" I felt like Perry Mason, except he didn't cry like I did.

"Because I screwed up. I should never have married your father in the first place, but I thought I was doing the right thing."

"Okay, Mom, if this is supposed to make me feel better, it's not working."

A man with a parrot perched on his shoulder sat down on the bench next to us. At any other time, I would have thought that was peculiar. But after my mom's recent behavior, this man who now carried on a conversation with his feathered friend appeared quite normal.

"Jen, you know how poor your grandparents were. They could barely speak English after coming from Russia right before I was born. And working as a butcher didn't exactly make your grandfather Joe Millionaire."

"Yeah, I know all that. What's your point?" I wasn't going to let her sob story about growing up poor change my mind about what she had done. She was still wrong!

"Going to college was never an option for me," my mom continued, apparently oblivious to the parrot. "According to your grandmother, if I ever wanted to live a comfortable life, I needed to find a husband who would take care of me and a family. So my job after high school was to find a suitable spouse, someone who could take me away from the old neighborhood and give me a fresh start."

"I still don't understand…"

"Please, Jen, let me finish. Anyway, I went to every singles event I could find, but nobody wanted me. That was long before I had lost all that weight and stopped wearing those hideous secondhand clothes from thrift shops. I kept watching my friends get married, but I couldn't find anyone, and I felt like a complete failure.

"And then one night I met your father, a nice Jewish boy who was studying to become an accountant. And for whatever reason I still don't understand, he fell in love with me. I knew he would be able to support me and a family."

"Did you love him?" I clutched my hands together, trying to hold on to something tangible.

"I thought so, but I was so young. Looking back, I didn't know anything about love at the time. All that really mattered to me was that he could give me the life I had always dreamed about. Marrying your father meant buying a nice home in a good neighborhood, and never having to worry about money problems again."

"So were you at least happy when you first got married?" I ignored the parrot's squawks as my mother did enough of her own squawking.

"Oh, yeah. Your father was always so good to me. He was such a nice guy; he still is. And for a while that was all that I needed. I was so thrilled to be living the good life, as your grandmother called it, that I never questioned our relationship.

"Of course, you know, within a year of getting married, your sister was born. And for the next ten years, you and Kathy kept me pretty busy. I didn't have time to think about love. But then one day you were both in school all day. You had your own lives, which meant your father and I were alone in the house for the first time. That's when I realized something was wrong, that I needed more than what we had. Our relationship lacked passion. Sexually…"

"Okay, I get the idea." I really didn't want to hear the rest of that sentence. "So you never did love him?"

"Of course I loved him. He was my best friend. But that was the problem." She looked directly at me, never once glancing at the man with his bird. "When it came right down to it, I never felt more than friendship toward him."

"Does Dad know how you feel, or should I say, don't feel about him?"

"That's been the hardest part. He really does love me, even knowing how I feel. He's always believed I would change my mind, that you could grow to love someone."

"I take it you haven't."

"No, not the way I should." Now she was crying. "Jen, I've felt so alone all these years. I couldn't very well tell you that I wasn't in love with your own father. And the one time, many years ago, that I was brave enough to tell your grandmother how I felt, she simply shrugged her shoulders. She just didn't get it. To her, getting married meant stability and security. To this day, I'm still not sure whether she really loved your grandfather."

"If you were that unhappy why didn't you leave him?"

"How could I? I never went to college so I couldn't make enough money to support all three of us, and I was terrified of going back to the life I once lived. I felt completely trapped. Not to mention, your father had been so wonderful to me, I felt ungrateful leaving him."

"So you paid Dad back for his kindness by cheating on him! You sound like you're doing him some kind of a big favor by staying with him. Give me a break!" I turned my back to her, unable to look my mother in the eye.

"Jen, please look at me."

"I don't think I can." I stared at a pigeon devouring a French fry that had fallen on the ground in front of us. "You're just making excuses. Maybe you couldn't go to college when you were younger, but you could have gone back once Kathy and I were older. And if you didn't want to go to college, you still could have gotten a job. That way you'd have the money that you claim you need so desperately from Dad."

"You know I've never worked a day in my life." Her boisterous voice sounded unusually quiet and meek.

"Well, maybe that's the problem! You're a grown woman, Mom. You can't blame Grandmom for your problems anymore, and frankly, I can't stand listening to you sound like the victim." I finally turned to face my mother, feeling my face grow red with rage as I screamed at her. "The only victim here is Dad, and I guess Kathy and me, too, indirectly."

"We all make mistakes." This time my mother's voice cracked.

"Yes, we all do, but most people learn from their mistakes and do something about them. Instead, you're trying everything you can to rationalize what you did and I don't buy it. Personally, I think the real reason you've stayed with Dad is because you're scared to leave him. Even though he might not be the true love of your life, you like

293

knowing he's there to take care of you. I think you're afraid to be alone and take care of yourself. You want the best of both worlds. You want Dad there in case you need him, plus you want other men to fulfill the void that Dad can't fill."

When my mother averted my eyes, I knew I was right.

"You make me sick." I stood up to leave, just in time to see the man walk away with his parrot still on his shoulder.

"Jen, please don't go."

I was going to head back to my office until I looked down at my hip mom with her snug shirt, short denim skirt and tight black leggings, looking old. She had cried off all her makeup, displaying a surprising amount of wrinkles and creases along her face. When I looked down at her, the sun reflected a few lone gray hairs that Thomas must have missed. She sat hunched over like some frail woman in a nursing home, and suddenly my anger turned to pity. She had spent her life camouflaging her bad marriage, much like she had spent her life covering up her age. How sad it must be to spend your whole life pretending to be someone you're not, living a life of lies. I almost wanted to put my arms around her and tell her everything was okay, but then I remembered that everything most definitely was not. Instead, I returned to my spot next to her on the bench.

We sat in silence for a while, each apparently lost in our own thoughts. I was consumed with visions of my poor dad sitting home alone while my mother had sex with someone else to try to mask her pain.

"Does Dad know about your secret rendezvous?"

My mom looked startled when I broke the silence. "I think so. Neither of us talks about it."

"Is it serious?" And did I want to know the answer?

"No. Not at all. But it's romantic and it's passionate, which is something I've never experienced before."

"Well, if you're cheating on Dad and he most likely knows about it, why are you the one always snapping at him? Why are you so mad at him?"

"I've been wondering that for a long time, and I think I've finally figured it out."

"And?"

"I've been so mad at myself for getting into this situation that I've taken it out on him. As much as your grandparents were struggling to make ends meet, I could have waited a little longer to meet the right guy, but I was too damn anxious to get married and move on with my life. The nicer your father gets, the angrier I become. It would have been so much easier to leave him if he had cheated on me or hit me. But he's always treated me like the fairy princess I wanted to be. How can you leave someone who's given you the world?"

I couldn't answer that question because I suddenly had a tugging feeling at my heart. Her words were hitting a little too close to home.

"Do you hate me, Jen?"

Funny, just one hour ago I had. I had planned to hate her for the rest of my life, but for the first time, I understood her better than I ever had. Maybe it's because I finally understood myself. "No. I don't hate you, but I do feel sorry for you." And for myself, considering I now realized that I almost took the same road that my mother had taken a little over thirty years ago.

My mom nodded sadly and reached for my hand again. I reluctantly let her, feeling her bones protruding from her unnaturally soft skin thanks to her dermatologist's anti-aging lotion. "Mom, there is one thing I still don't understand. If you've been so unhappy with your marriage all these years, why have you been pressuring me to get married since I graduated college? Don't you realize that you've been doing exactly the same thing to me that your mother did to you?"

"Oh, Jen, I'm so sorry." My mom was now sobbing. "That's the last thing I ever wanted to do. I guess after growing up poor, I've always wanted to make sure that you and your sister were well taken care of, that your husbands could give you the lives you deserved."

"But Mom, I can take care of myself. I make plenty of money. I don't need a husband to pay my bills."

"Not right now, but what if you have children one day and you decide to become a full-time mom, or maybe you'll just decide to take some time off. If you don't marry the right guy, you won't have that option."

"That's not going to happen. I'd never give up my career."

"What if, God forbid, you get really sick and can't work? Then what? Your father won't always be around to pay the bills."

"Mom, don't you get it? I don't need Dad to pay my bills anymore. I'm a grown woman with a good income and even health insurance. I don't need to depend on anyone to take care of me."

"But I want to make sure that you and my grandchildren never have to live the way I once did. Does that sound unreasonable?"

"Actually yes, especially in this day and age. This is the twenty-first century, not the 1960's. Women can live fulfilling lives without a man by their side." Somehow I felt stronger declaring my independence to her. However, as I looked over at my mother, she suddenly appeared weaker, as if she were sinking lower into her seat every time I disagreed with her.

We once again sat in silence, watching people in business suits walk past us. While my mother squeezed my hand, I felt an overwhelming sadness that she had settled for someone who she had never loved, and I felt equally sad for my dad, who had accepted his fate.

We sat for at least an hour on that same bench without saying a word to each other. After all, what else could we possibly say that hadn't been said? People scurried in and out of office buildings, while we remained idle, glued to our same spot on the bench, as if someone would come by and make everything okay. Needless to say, there were no fairy godmothers in sight.

Finally I peeled myself off the bench. Without another word about my mother's unsettling disclosures, I got up to leave. My mother reached over to hug me, but before she got too close, I backed away. Even though I understood her motives better, I wasn't ready to forgive her. I wasn't sure I'd ever be able to.

Sometime between saying good-bye to my mom and walking toward my office, I promised myself never to lower my expectations for anyone. I would not turn into my mother.

Every time I tried to write, all I could see was my mom kissing that guy at the hotel. That image was followed by Mike's mother throwing homemade blintzes down the garbage disposal. There was no way I was going to write anything that made sense today so I left work early, hoping to clear my head.

When I pulled up at my apartment, I grabbed the four bridal magazines I had bought first thing that morning. Without glancing at their covers, I held them under my left arm so I could carry my briefcase with my right hand.

Damn! Where had that tricycle come from? I fell forward, catching myself with my hands. Naturally all the magazines fell along with me. I made a face at the bride staring up at me with the bluest eyes I'd ever seen. They had to be fake. Nobody had eyes that blue. And what about her smile? Was she really that happy, or was that fake, too?

I stood up to wipe myself off and then bent down to pick up the magazines. "We've got to stop meeting like this." I didn't have to look up to know whose voice it was.

"Hey, Chris. How have you been?" I asked, while standing up with my magazines.

"Apparently not as well as you. That's quite a rock on your finger. Congratulations."

Just looking at him made my heart flutter and my body tremble. "Thanks."

"When you said you wanted to get married, you weren't kidding."

"No, I guess I wasn't."

"I've thought about you a lot since we broke up. I almost called you a few times, but I figured it would be better if we got on with our lives, and judging from those magazines, you have. So who's the lucky guy?"

"Um, nobody you know."

"Well I hope he knows what a great catch he got. If I ever did want to get married, which I'm sure I won't, it would have been with you."

We stared at each other for a long time, without saying a word. While looking into his familiar green eyes, I realized I really had loved him. Funny how sometimes love wasn't enough, and how other times sharing all the same values didn't work either. Maybe the trick was trying to find a happy medium. Or maybe the trick was forgetting the tricks and just letting it happen, like I had once thought.

"So how's your job going?" Chris asked, breaking the silence that felt more like sexual tension. "Did that Meany woman ever make you an offer?"

Here Mike had no idea who she was, and Chris remembered her name after all this time. "As a matter of fact, she did."

"Hey, that's great. Knowing you, you'll be running her agency in a few years. So does this mean you and your fiancé are moving to New York?"

After my conversation with Mike, I wasn't sure what it meant. "I may commute instead."

"That's cool. I love taking the train into the city. Either way, working on Madison Avenue is a pretty big deal." He gave me that wide smile that still made my heart melt. "Not that I'm surprised you got the job. I always knew you'd be successful. You work too damn hard for people to overlook you."

Now this was the kind of reaction I was hoping for. Too bad it was coming from the wrong guy. "Thanks. I appreciate it." More than he knew. "So what have you been up to? Are you going to be our pool cleaner again this year?"

"Nah, I moved on to greener pastures, but I will be working here part-time. I ran into your superintendent last week and he mentioned that his handyman had retired. He remembered how good I've always been with my hands. Of course, you already know how good I am with my hands, right, Jen?"

Boy did I.

"Judging by the color of your face, I'll assume you do. Anyway, I agreed to take the job as long as the hours were flexible enough to work around my other part-time job."

"Aren't you still working at Big Al's Mini Mart?"

"No, I left there a few months ago. As much as I miss the free coffee, the smell of gasoline was starting to get to me. After one of their gas attendants quit, they had me pumping gas for a while."

How ironic that Stacy had been right after all about Chris working at the gas station. "So what are you doing?" I asked.

"Let's just say that my new job lets me travel all through the city, and it's even helped me get my own set of wheels."

"Are you working as a tour guide again?"

"In a way. I do take people for rides, but it's not aboard a tour bus."

I smiled, remembering how Chris could always make me laugh. "Are you going to give me a hint, or are we playing twenty questions?"

"Okay, here's one hint. You passed my car right before you tripped over that bike."

"Now I'm totally confused because the only car I noticed was that gray stretch limousine." I pointed to the vehicle behind us.

"Don't be confused. You just guessed it."

"But that limo has funeral stickers on the back window."

"Right again." He continued smiling, as always.

"You're driving a stretch limo during funerals?" I didn't know why I was so surprised. It was such a Chris thing to do.

"I started working for Danza's Funeral Home two months ago. He has some pretty prestigious clients. Last week I drove the late Senator Pickster's entire family to Washington Memorial Cemetery. The week before I drove Spencer Myers, you know that famous silent film star who lived to be one hundred? I even got to meet some celebrities before the procession."

"That's, um, great. I'm glad you like your new job so much."

"Speaking of which, I better go. I have a funeral starting in thirty minutes, and Danza has some crazy rule about never making the deceased's family late to the funeral. Go figure."

Chris kissed me lightly on the cheek before leaving. For a moment, I felt an electric current pulling me toward him, but I knew I had to resist, for all the reasons we had broken up before. He was all wrong for me. Wasn't he? Besides he still didn't believe in marriage and I did. But was it as important as I once thought? Wasn't spending your life with someone you loved more important than marrying someone you didn't? As I watched Chris put funeral stickers on all the windows of his limo, I wasn't sure about anything anymore.

Chris beeped the horn as he waved goodbye and I smiled at him as if he had just driven by in a Rolls Royce. Even if I never saw him again, at least he reminded me how it felt to be in love. Seeing him again also made me realize that I had never had those same feelings for Mike. You couldn't force yourself to love someone anymore than you could force someone to marry you. Otherwise, you ended up cheating on him thirty years later.

And with that realization, I threw out my new bridal magazines, returned to my car and headed straight to Mike's house.

Chapter 27

Treatment Options:

Option One: Marry the first guy who proposes so you'll finally be able to walk down that aisle, playing the role of a princess.

Option Two: Remain single till that glass slipper fits. Even if it's only a half-inch too small, it will still hurt!

"Jen, where have you been?" Mike opened the door to let me in. "I was getting worried when you didn't return my messages."

"Sorry, I didn't know you called." I looked around, hoping Mike's mother wasn't home. The kitchen light was off, which was a good sign that she was gone.

"Didn't you listen to your voice mail at work before you left?" Mike followed me inside as I walked aimlessly around his living room.

"I did, but I left early today."

"That's not like you. Are you feeling okay?" Mike sat down on the couch, but I was having trouble standing still, let alone sitting. "Can I get you something?" he offered.

Oh, this wasn't going to be easy. "I'm okay now, but we really need to talk. Do we have the place to ourselves?"

"Yeah. What's wrong? Please sit down." He pointed to the spot beside him, and I forced myself to sit next to him.

"Well," I sighed, "a lot has happened today."

"Is this about the job offer?" This time he sighed.

"Partly, I guess. I was really upset when we got off the phone. I feel like you're giving me an ultimatum, that I have to choose between our marriage or this job offer, and I don't like that. You promised you wouldn't do that."

I watched Mike chew his tongue with such vengeance I was sure he would bite right through it. "You're right. I did promise…if you really want to take that job, um, I guess, it's all right with me."

"I'm not so sure about that." I wished I couldn't see his father's photo from where I sat. "I know you. Maybe you're not going to make a big fuss about it now, but you're obviously not happy about it, and eventually that's going to affect our marriage. When I think about it, I've always known how you'd react to this job, but I never wanted to admit it. You don't want a wife who's as career-oriented as me. You want someone who will be there when you get home to serve your dinner and ask you about your day."

"Well…that would be nice, but I know you're not like that, and I love you anyway." He looked at me with that same adoration as my dad. It was a damn shame that wasn't enough to win my heart.

"Do you love me enough to spend the rest of your life married to someone who comes home late at night?" I asked. "Who might have to travel for business trips? Who might have to cancel plans with you at the last minute? Or in the back of your mind, are you secretly hoping I'll change my career plans after we get married?"

There went his tongue again. Too bad it was never that active when we were in bed.

"Um…I guess I've thought about it." He leaned forward to rest his head on his hands.

"Of course you have." I leaned back and placed my head against the cushion, suddenly feeling drained. "You can't change the way you feel about things anymore than I can."

We both looked forward without making any eye contact. It was strange talking to someone right next to me without looking at him, but it felt safer to continue looking straight ahead.

"Jen, I know you're probably thinking about my parent's situation, but I'm not my dad."

"But you think like him, don't you?"

"I guess in some ways." Mike dropped his head lower into his hands.

"In a lot of ways. You said yourself that he was right about making your mom quit. I think someday you're going to regret marrying me when you could have found someone more like…like…like June Cleaver. And if I don't take this job, I'll regret that decision. I don't

301

want either of us to be unhappy." I turned to look at Mike. "So, I've decided to give this back to you." I slowly, painfully took off the ring I had so desperately wanted for so long. "I don't think we're right for each other."

"Jen, don't." Mike's head shot up like a jack-in-the-box and he placed his hand in front of him, refusing to take the ring. "This is crazy. We love each other. Isn't that enough to get through anything?"

I took a deep breath. "That's what I've realized over the past eight or ten hours. Love is enough to get through anything. And it should be enough to help us find a solution. But the problem is…I don't love you, Mike."

Mike flinched as if I punched him in the stomach. Even his tongue stopped moving. I was a horrible person. How could I hurt someone who was so nice? But then I remembered my mom's desperate search for passion and realized it was better to do it now than wait till we were in our fifties.

"I don't understand, Jen," Mike said with tears in his eyes. "You told me you did."

"And that was my fault. I never should have. Mike, I haven't been honest with you. Up until this afternoon I hadn't been honest with myself. I do love you, Mike. And I really care about you. But I'm not in love with you. I wish I were. I really tried. But I just couldn't do it. I'm so sorry. I never meant to hurt you."

"I still don't get it." He looked totally perplexed. "How could you suddenly decide after all these months that you don't love me?"

"I think I've known for a long time. The problem is that I was in love with being in love, with getting married and living happily ever after. Everyone I knew was either getting married or telling me all the reasons why I had to do it too, and without realizing it, I got that marriage bug, too. I wanted to wear a long gown and walk down the aisle with all of my family and friends cheering me on. But my fantasies always ended after the wedding with us walking toward the sunset. I never thought past the happily ever after part. I wanted to get married for all the wrong reasons. The only reason someone should get married is because they're in love. If you have love, everything else can fall into place."

I felt tears falling down my cheek, but they weren't for Mike; they were for Chris, the one guy I had truly loved, who I had let walk out of my life. Even though he was a high school drop-out who drifted from job to job, when I was with him I was whole. Wasn't that what marriage was all about? Two people coming together to become one? Maybe Chris had been right after all. Maybe you didn't need an engagement ring to have that. I had one now and I'd never felt so alone.

"Maybe you just need more time to let your feelings develop. We can still be engaged, but wait to set the date."

I looked at Mike's wide hopeful eyes and wanted to say yes. But then I remembered how my mom was still waiting to fall in love with my dad. "Mike, you told me yesterday to follow my heart, and my heart is telling me you're not the one. If it hasn't happened yet, it's not going to happen."

Mike nodded sadly as if he understood. This time he took the ring.

"You're a good person, Mike. Besides my dad, you're the nicest guy I've ever known. You're going to make someone very happy some day. And you know what?" Now I was crying for Mike. "You deserve to find someone who truly loves you. Don't settle for anything less."

Mike wouldn't look at me. He stared at the floor while swishing enough spit to drown an army of ants. I kissed him on his forehead and got up to leave.

Before closing the door behind me, I took one last look at the man who I almost married. My mom had been right about one thing. He would have looked great in a tux.

Feeling dizzy and dazed, I didn't even notice Mike's mother sitting on a lounge chair knitting on the front porch. "Hi, sweet girl. I saw your Jeep parked outside so I decided to give you lovebirds some privacy."

"That was nice." Now what? Should I tell her? No, Mike should do that. "I better be going."

"So what's going on?"

"Excuse me?"

"You look like you've been crying and you're not wearing your engagement ring." She continued to knit.

"I'll let Mike fill you in."

"You broke up?"

"Yeah, we did." I leaned against the screen door, not sure how much to say.

"Is this because of your job offer in New York?" She didn't look angry, just curious and concerned.

"Um, it has something to do with that." *And the fact that I don't love your son.*

"I'm truly sorry it came down to that." She reached in her knitting bag for some more yellow yarn. "Mike can be as stubborn as his father sometimes."

"I think Mike will be happier with a woman who's more of a homebody." And with someone who really loves him.

"It took a lot of courage for you to stand up for what you believe in. I wish I had had your strength when I was your age."

I sat down next to her, starting to feel weak from this emotional day. "According to Ilene Meeney, you were quite a dynamo back then."

"You know Ilene?" Mike's mother stopped knitting long enough to look up at me.

"She's the one who offered me the job. She's working at Richardson and Whitaker as a VP."

"Huh, Ilene Meeney." She whispered her name as if referring to a ghost. I guessed in a way, she was. Ilene was part of the life Mike's father had killed. I watched Mike's mother search for a new needle and then continue knitting.

"I better go," I said, standing up.

"Take care of yourself," she said, switching to orange yarn.

"Oh, by the way. I have something for you. Meany, I mean Ilene, asked me to give you this." I handed her the piece of paper I had put in my purse. "It's her work number. She said she'd love to hear from you. If you're interested, she might even know of a job in Philly that you'd be great at."

Without looking at the number, she handed me back the piece of paper. "Thanks, Jen. But that part of my life is in the past."

And what was her future? Sitting on a porch alone knitting? Cooking meals that nobody ate? "It doesn't have to be. Go ahead, just take the number."

For the first time since I stepped onto the porch, she put down her knitting needle. "Well…maybe I'll give her a call, for old time's sake."

"That sounds like a good idea." Mike's mother stood up and gave me the biggest bear hug I ever felt. "Jen, you remind me so much of myself when I was your age. You go out and set the world on fire."

I wanted to remain buried in Doris's warm embrace forever, but after a few seconds she returned to her bench, and I was left standing alone. I took her cue and walked to my car. As I pulled out from Mike's childhood home, I waved at Mike's mother, but she never looked up from her knitting.

Chapter 28

In Order to Recover, You Must Endure a Journey of Self Discovery Where You Ultimately Acknowledge That:

1. Being with Mr. Wrong can be a lot lonelier than being alone.

2. Mr. Right is sometimes Mr. Wrong.

3. Creating your own path in life is a lot more fulfilling than following in other people's footsteps.

I sat outside my parent's home for a half-hour. My childhood home was nothing more than a façade. From the outside, it looked like any other single suburban home, but from the inside it was completely empty, void of emotion or love. My parent's entire existence as a married couple was an act.

When Kathy and I were young, our family room had served as their stage where they'd played the roles of a loving married couple, but when their audience left they went back to being the strangers they've always been. My mom was never the best actress, and recently she had given up acting entirely. I was just glad that I would never have to serve as her understudy.

When I walked into the living room, my dad as usual was parked in his favorite recliner watching the Phillies game. "Hi, princess," he said, smiling that warm smile that still lit up my world. It was hard looking him in the eye, knowing what my mom was doing behind his back.

"Hi, Dad. Can we talk?"

"Sure. Is something wrong?"

How ironic. I should really have been asking him that question. "I broke up with Mike last night."

"I'm so sorry. Are you okay?" My dad turned off the TV.

"Yeah. Actually, I'm fine."

"What happened?" When my dad put the remote down, I knew I had his full attention.

"Remember at Stacy's engagement party you told me to find someone who made me happy?"

"Yeah."

"Well Mike didn't. I mean in a lot of ways he did, but not in the important ways."

My father walked over and put his arm around my shoulder, giving me a much needed hug. "You didn't love him, huh?"

I was surprised how quickly he guessed the reason. But then again, when you've lived the problem your whole life you could probably identify it quickly. "No, I didn't."

"You did the right thing, princess. I'm glad you broke up with him before you ended up like…"

"Like who, Dad?" Was he finally going to open up to me? I so wanted to be there for him.

"Uh…like…so many unhappy married couples."

So much for that father daughter heart-to-heart talk. Without planning to delve any further, I lost control of my mouth. "Are you and Mom one of those unhappy married couples?" The words flew out of my throat faster than I could catch them.

My dad looked surprised by my question and hesitated before answering. "I still love your mother," he said, looking sad.

"Come on, Dad. Even though you love her, it's obvious that you and Mom have been having problems for a long time. I mean, how many women book a trip to Vegas without bothering to tell their husband?"

"Your mother and I." His voice trailed off. "Let's just say we have an understanding."

"What kind of understanding? That she gets to go out and have fun while you stay home and watch television?"

He looked hurt, and I felt terrible for being so blunt. "I'm sorry, Dad. I didn't mean to sound so harsh. I'd just like to see you out having fun, too."

"I like staying home. I'm comfortable here. Besides, I'm too old to start going out on the town."

"I'm not saying you should go out and have an affair." Oops! I hadn't meant to say that and my dad looked as startled as I felt when he looked at me.

"Look, princess. Why don't you let your mother and me work out our own problems."

"I just want you to be happy." I felt a tear ready to slide down my cheek.

"I am happy," he said, unable to meet my eyes. "Having you and Kathy in my life is more than I ever wished for. And as far as your mother goes, well, let's just say, we're managing."

"But you should be doing more than just managing. Dad, there's something I need to tell you about Mom." I hadn't come here planning to say anything, but I was tired of my dad being used as a doormat. For all I knew, my mom might have just told me that my dad knew about her fling so I wouldn't say anything.

But before I could tell him what I'd witnessed at the Ritz Carlton, my dad very gently covered my mouth with his hand. "I may be quiet, princess, but I'm not stupid. You don't need to say a thing." He looked so intently into my eyes that I felt like he was reading my thoughts.

"So you know…"

"I know everything I need to know." My father refused to let me finish my sentence. You and Kathy are grown women now with your own lives to live. I don't want you worrying about your mother and me. And Jen, please promise you won't go calling your sister about this and getting her all upset. I may have made a lot of mistakes in my life, but I refuse to let them interfere with my children's lives. I don't want you girls wasting your energy worrying about my marriage. Okay? Promise you won't say anything?"

I knew my dad was serious when he called me by my real name. "I promise." Although it would have been nice to confide in Kathy, I respected my dad's request. He asked for so little. Unfortunately, he received very little in return.

"My marriage might not be the ideal situation, but I can deal with it." My dad spoke as if he were trying to convince himself as much as me. "Besides, I don't feel like starting over again. Not at my age. And who knows? We could surprise everyone by living happily ever after."

He didn't sound very convincing as he returned to his recliner and put on the TV just as the Phillies scored.

I watched him cheer for the Phillies, wanting to scream some sense into him, but what was the use? Apparently, it was easier for my parents to accept their miserable marriage than to risk being alone. The sad thing was that they were probably more alone being together than they would be if they were apart.

I looked around for my mom, wondering if she was home. "Is Mom around, Dad?"

"I think I heard her in the kitchen."

I started walking toward the kitchen door, but just when I was about to open it, my dad called over, "I love you, princess." For the first time since we started talking, his voice sounded strong and self-assured.

"I love you, too." He was such a nice man. It was a damn shame that couldn't be enough for my mom, but I knew firsthand that it didn't always work that way.

When I walked into the kitchen, my mom was making a salad.

"Hi, Jen. Did you see Dad?" She looked nervous as she stopped cutting up radishes.

"Don't worry. I didn't blow your cover." Of course she could thank my dad for that.

"I hate putting you in the middle of this."

"I hate it, too. Listen, Mom, I didn't come here to talk about that again."

"Oh good. I was hoping we could put that behind us."

Was she kidding? Did she really think I was ever going to forget what I saw or heard yesterday? I would probably need some major therapy before that ever happened.

"How about a nice salad," she offered. "I have your favorite low-fat dressing."

"I'm not really hungry."

"That's okay. I'm sure you'll want to lose some weight before your wedding. Speaking of which, is my Mike in the living room talking to your father?"

"No, Mom. That's why I'm here. He's not your Mike anymore."

"Getting jealous, are we?" My mom poured a teaspoon of salad dressing in her salad and sat down at the table.

"Mom, he's not my Mike anymore either."

"I don't understand! What happened? Did he break up with you?"

"No, I did." Leave it to her to assume he ended it.

"What on earth made you do that?"

"You did."

"I don't understand."

"I almost made the same mistake that you did," I said, shaking my head. "Of course, I wasn't marrying Mike for financial stability, like you, but I was marrying him for the security of knowing I'd never be alone. I don't love him anymore than you loved Dad when you got married. And if it wasn't for our conversation yesterday, I'd probably still be moving forward with our wedding plans. I was so scared of being alone, that I didn't realize how scary it might be to marry the wrong person...until I saw you checking out of the Ritz Carlton. Now I know. So I guess I'm grateful to you because if it weren't for your romp around the hotel, I'd probably be following in your footsteps."

"I see." I heard the clock ticking away as she looked at me as if she was trying to find the right words. "Are you absolutely sure you're doing the right thing, Jen? Mike is such a nice guy."

"So is Dad, Mom. So is Dad."

I waited till evening to tell Stacy the news. She'd been asking me to drop by her new castle so I figured this was as good a time as any. I probably should have called first now that she was married, but I wanted to tell her in person.

It took me several minutes to drive from the street down her driveway until I could even see her home. Holy cow! They didn't call these houses estate homes for nothing. It looked more like a hotel than a place where someone lived. And who cleaned all those windows. I counted fifteen, and that was just in the front.

When Stacy had said it was a *wonderful* place to bring up a family, she wasn't kidding. She had also raved about how *wonderful* it was to have so much privacy. There must have been at least three acres between her house and the home next door, if you could even call it next door. If Stacy was upstairs, it would probably take her an hour till she reached the front door.

While turning off my ignition, I saw the door was already opened. Well, that would save some time. And there were Lance and Stacy walking outside. Even better. The whole time I was driving over, I was afraid my spontaneous visit might interrupt some spontaneous action of their own. After all, they were still newlyweds and they certainly acted like it.

I was about to open my car door when I saw Lance making all kinds of gestures with his hands. It almost looked like he was using sign language. And was Stacy crying? Damn! I should have called first. As they walked closer to my car, I could hear their conversation.

"Don't you dare walk out on me again, Lance. For once in your life, can't you stick around long enough to finish an argument?"

"And for once in your life, can't you let me come home from work without starting one?"

"Well, maybe if you weren't always breaking your promises and you did what you said you would, I wouldn't always be upset."

Oh, this wasn't good. And now I was trapped. I couldn't very well back up without them hearing my engine, and I sure as hell wasn't getting out of the car in the middle of an argument. I'd just sit here till they calmed down and went inside. Then I'd call Stacy from my cell phone, like I should have done in the first place, and tell her about Mike.

"I feel like I'm walking on eggshells with you, Stacy," Lance screamed. "If I forget the most minute detail, you have a complete fit. It's ridiculous."

"How is forgetting to pick me up from work a minute detail?"

"I said I was sorry."

"You're always sorry until you make the same mistake a week later."

I slid down in my seat, hoping they wouldn't see me, but their voices were getting closer. Why were they getting so close? And why were they arguing like this when everything was so wonderful? Wasn't this supposed to be the best time in a person's marriage?

"Stacy, I need to get out of here for a few hours. I think we need some time to cool off. I'm going to Moe's Bar to get a drink."

"Oh, great, that's the perfect solution. Go get drunk, like you always do."

He did? Stacy never mentioned that Lance drank. Apparently, Stacy never mentioned a lot of things.

"Damn it! Whose car is parked behind mine? I can't even get out of here!"

So much for my hiding place. Now what?

"Jen, is that you?" I pushed myself up from behind my steering wheel to see Stacy and Lance staring at me through the window. I felt like a caged animal at the zoo.

"Great, Stacy, now we have your friends spying on us."

What was his problem? Why would I waste my time spying on them? Okay, I imagined I looked a little strange rolled up in a ball in the front seat of my car. "I'm really sorry. I came to surprise you, Stace, and when I heard you arguing I figured I'd come back at a better time."

"Most people drive away when they decide to leave," Lance said.

Was this the same charming, charismatic Lance I knew? This guy had to be an imposter. "I thought you'd be uncomfortable if you knew I was here, listening to your, uh, your disagreement, so I was waiting till you went inside till I left."

"How thoughtful," Lance said. "Now can you move your car so I can get the hell out of here?"

"Lance, you don't have to snap at her. She's not the one you're mad at. Jen, I'm sorry. Why don't you let Lance pull out and then you can park in his spot."

"Why don't I just come back some other time?"

"No, don't go. I want to show you around." Stacy's eye shadow and mascara covered her face, and her turquoise eyes looked grayish tonight. Her free-flowing hair looked limp. For the first time since I could remember, her nails weren't polished, and was it possible that was a pimple above her lip?

"Are you sure you don't want to be alone or lie down?" I asked. After hearing Stacy and Lance scream at each other for the past ten minutes, I was ready to lie down.

"No, of course not."

"Okay, then." As soon as I backed up my car, I heard the screeching sound of Lance's tires as he took off.

I followed Stacy into her foyer. "So would you like to see the upstairs or downstairs first?" she asked as if she had just come from a stroll in the park.

Hello? I wasn't an idiot. I really did witness their outburst. Did everyone live in the land of make-believe these days? "Are we going to pretend that I didn't see what I just saw?"

"Every couple has arguments," she said nonchalantly.

"Sure, Stace. It's really none of my business anyway."

"Of course it is. You're my best friend." She put her arm around me, but my muscles tensed up.

"Am I?" I stepped back, needing to place some distance between us.

"Why would you ask that?"

"Best friends confide in each other and they share their thoughts with each other. You know, like we used to do."

"But we still do that."

I wanted to laugh out loud as I looked at the recent photos of Lance and Stacy smiling during their honeymoon. The pictures were prominently displayed on their baby grand piano in the next room.

"Stace, for the last year, you've been telling me how wonderful your life is and for the past month you've been telling me how wonderful married life is. I realize that no relationship is perfect, but come on now. That was no small you-forgot-to-take-the-trash-out disagreement. That was a major you-need-to-change-your-way-of-thinking blow-up."

Sigh. "You're right. I guess I haven't been completely honest with you. Lance and I have some issues to work out, but I wasn't lying when I said I loved being married. I love coming home, knowing my husband will be there to spend the evening with."

Was I missing something here, or did she forget her wonderful husband just took off for the bar, while she spent her evening with me?

"Marriage can be hard work," Stacy continued. "You'll see that when you and Mike get married."

"Actually, I won't. That's what I came over to tell you. Mike and I broke up."

"Broke up! That's terrible." She looked horrified. "Why would he do something like that?"

Was I that pathetic that everyone assumed I was the one who was dumped? "He didn't. I did."

"Why?" She looked at me like I had grown antlers. "He was so perfect."

"On paper, yes. Live and in person, no. After a lot of soul searching, I realized I wouldn't be happy spending the rest of my life with him."

"Jen, we're not four years old anymore, singing 'Someday Our Prince Will Come.' The reality is that he doesn't. But even though you aren't Cinderella and Mike isn't Prince Charming, that doesn't mean you can't still have a good life together."

"Are you happy, Stace?"

"Of course I am. Why wouldn't I be?"

If she didn't know, I wasn't going to be the one to fill in the blank. I rolled my eyes and stared at Stacy's vaulted ceiling.

"Look, Jen, I knew what I was doing when I got married. I was ready. When I met Lance, I was so sick of the dating scene, the clubs, the bars, the pick-up lines. And from what I hear, it gets worse as you get older. I couldn't take a chance of never finding the perfect guy. For all I know, I might never have found anyone better than Lance. Even though he's far from ideal, he does have a lot going for him."

"I understand." And I did, even though I didn't agree with her.

"So what are you going to do now that you and Mike broke up?"

"I'm going to live my life. In fact, I might be moving to New York. I just got a great job offer at an agency on Madison Avenue."

"Wow, that's great. Why didn't you tell me?"

"I'm not sure." In the past, Stacy would have been the first person I told about Meany's offer, but this time, I didn't even think of calling her.

"Well, it sounds like your career is going really well. Now all you need to work on is your personal life. Aren't you worried now that you broke up with Mike that you'll never meet anyone else who wants to get married?"

When was she going to drop the subject already? "Of course, I'm scared, but I was more scared about marrying the wrong guy."

"I still don't understand how marrying Mike could be a mistake. He seemed so right. Do you think you're being a little too critical? Maybe your expectations are just too high."

Now I was mad. I hadn't driven an hour for her to question my decision. She was supposed to be my best friend. Weren't best friends supposed to support each other's decisions? "Did it ever occur to you that your expectations might not be high enough? Maybe the perfect guy for you is out there, but now you'll never find him because you settled for Lance. Or maybe you just want me to marry Mike so I'll be as miserable as you. That way, our lives will be right back on track again."

Uh-oh. For the second time that day, I had spoken my thoughts without meaning to, and we both looked equally surprised by my new assertiveness.

We continued standing in her foyer, frozen in a time warp until Stacy spoke. "What happened to us, Jen? We used to agree about everything. I can't remember ever having an argument like this in all the years we've known each other."

"Our lives have changed a lot in the last year. Let's face it, life's a lot more complicated than deciding what to do on Saturday nights and whose party we should go to."

"I'd like to think our friendship has been more than just parties." She looked hurt.

"It has been, and we've faced a lot of tough decisions together, too. The difference is that we always made the same decisions at the same time. I guess it was easier to fit in than do our own thing. Besides, it always felt right."

"It did feel right," Stacy said.

"But this time it doesn't, Stace. I can't follow your lead, along with Lori and Amy, just because it's easier to fit in. I need to do what's right for me. Can you understand that?"

"I guess so." She sounded unconvinced.

"Listen, Stace, the only way we're going to stay close is if we both realize that we're not always going to make the same decisions anymore."

"I know we can't always do the same things, but I still think you should give Mike another chance. He was so nice!"

"I've got to go." And for the first time in ten minutes I moved, realizing my left foot had fallen asleep. "Hope you and Lance work out your problems. I truly want you to be happy and have the wonderful life that you've been talking about."

"You make it sound like we're never going to talk again."

"I'm sure we'll still talk, but I have a feeling that our conversations will be a lot different."

"I miss things the way they were."

"So do I, Stace."

While driving home, I felt a wave of sadness pour into my heart. After thirty years, Stacy wasn't my best friend anymore. Come to think of it, she hadn't been for a while. A best friend wouldn't make me feel bad for making a decision I knew was right. A best friend wouldn't encourage me to spend my life married to someone I knew was wrong for me. And a best friend wouldn't expect me to conform to her lifestyle.

Maybe someday I would have another best friend. Who knew? Maybe someday, Stacy would be that friend again, but for now I was content knowing I had become my own best friend over the weekend, and I was confident that my new best friend was never going to let me down.

Chapter 29

After You're Fully Recovered, You Will Gain:

1. An appreciation of being single.
2. A feeling of self-confidence.
3. The ability to talk to happily married women without experiencing one marriage craving.

"Maybe you can win the Guinness world record for the shortest engagement in history." It was good hearing Marisa's voice even though it came from six hundred miles away through Tiffany's speaker phone. "So have you heard from him since you broke up?"

"You should see her office." Tiffany let out a few hacking coughs in between answering for me. "It looks like a flower shop. Everyday for the last week, Mike sent her every conceivable type of flower. Today's were so exotic, I swear he must have sent someone to a tropical island to hand-pick them."

"You're kidding." Marisa sounded like her new happy-go-lucky self. "Have you spoken to him, Jen?"

"I called him a few times to thank him for the flowers, but he spent the entire conversation begging me to take him back. It's like he's trying to buy my love. I finally stopped calling."

"But he hasn't stopped sending flowers and candy and fruit baskets and teddy bears," Tiffany said.

"It is getting to be excessive," I admitted. "I sent him an email thanking him for everything, but asking him to stop sending me gifts. He replied with a poem about never giving up on the one you love."

"That's spooky," Marisa said. "It's almost like he's stalking you."

"If it were anyone else maybe I'd worry, but it's just good old Mike being the nice guy he's always been. It's a damn shame I didn't love him."

"Well, thank goodness you figured that out before you planned an expensive wedding," Marisa said. "Tiffany told me you ran into Chris. Any chance of you getting back with him?"

"I doubt it. He certainly didn't seem too upset to hear I was getting married. You'd think he would have at least acted a little jealous if he still loved me. I think for now I'm going to forget about guys and concentrate on my new job. Working sixteen hour days is less stressful than finding a husband."

"How did John take the news?"

"He was relieved. Apparently, I was targeted for the next wave of layoffs. He said he would rather accept my resignation than have to hand me my walking papers."

"You mean he was going to lay *you* off?" The shock in her voice managed to travel all the way from Detroit. "After all the hard work you've done for this agency over the years."

I had been thinking the same thing. And I would have been a lot happier if John hadn't told me I would have lost my job. There was really no reason to let me know. Maybe he was pissed off that I hadn't gone to that party after the Presto pitch.

"I worked on the two largest accounts that Premier lost." I felt a need to explain. "According to John, almost everyone on those creative teams lost their jobs, or are about to. He said that he considered giving me other accounts, but he was afraid if he broke up another creative team, he might lose the few existing accounts he had left."

"It sounds like he's really afraid of going under," Marisa said.

"Since we didn't get the Presto account, John's developed a nervous twitch," Tiffany said. "Whenever we start working on a new pitch, John's double neck goes into overdrive."

"Oh that reminds me, John did offer me a compliment," I said. "He told me I did a great job writing from the voice of a stripper. Maybe I missed my calling."

Marisa laughed. "At least you don't have to worry about finding another job, Jen. Meany's offer came at the perfect time."

"You're not kidding. I would have killed Mike if I had turned down that job and then ended up out of work. And now that Mike's out of the picture, I was able to tell Meany's boss that I can travel anywhere, anytime."

"That's great, Jen. So where does that leave you, Tif?" Marisa asked.

"Tiffany is one of the few people around here who landed on her feet," I said, smiling at my hoarse co-worker.

"Yeah, when John heard I was learning how to design websites, he promoted me to creative director. Now instead of paying an art director, a creative director, and a webmaster, John will only have one salary to worry about. And I'll finally get the experience all the other agencies are looking for. John also promised to give me more creative control over the accounts we bid on. Needless to say, we won't be taking on clients who require more flesh than clothing in their ads."

"So you're staying?" Marisa asked.

"For a while. Until we go under, or I found something better. Either way, I'll at least be more marketable next time I look for a job."

"Congratulations. I'm glad things worked out for you."

"So how are things with you?" I asked Marisa.

"Great." And she truly sounded it. "Zack and I have been taking weekend getaways almost every week. By the time Friday comes, I can't wait to have him all to myself."

After getting a glimpse of Stacy's *wonderful* marriage, it was nice to talk to a happily married person. It gave me hope that fairy tale endings did exist, provided of course, that you really found your prince. "Have you decided whether you're going back to work, or have you permanently given up on corporate America?" I asked.

"Well, as a matter of fact, I just got a job working as a tour guide at a local art museum. The pay's not great, but the job is a step in the right direction. And it sure beats feeling the texture of paper everyday."

I smiled at the phone. "That is so great, Marisa. Congrats! How does Zack feel about you going back to work?"

"He's the one who suggested it. I would have been fine playing the happy homemaker for a while, but Zack was afraid I'd get bored. And when he found the ad in the paper for the tour guide position, he talked me into interviewing for it. It's really important to him that I find a job that makes me happy."

Now that was the kind of supportive husband I wanted... someday.

After chatting for a few more minutes, we signed off. "So when are you packing up the rest of your stuff?" Tiffany asked.

I had been putting off that moment as long as possible. In a lot of ways, it would be harder than packing up my apartment. "I don't have much more to take home. I'll probably finish tomorrow."

"Make sure you stop by before you go," she said.

I could tell she was upset. I recognized her expression from when we found out Marisa eloped. "I'm going to miss you, Tif. Who's going to speak up for me when I'm lost for words?"

"And who's going to come to our office parties with a notebook and pen?"

We both laughed until Tiffany put her arms around me and hugged me almost as securely as Mike's mother had.

"You really are an old softy, aren't you?" I laughed at her through my tears.

"Just don't tell anyone or I'll kick your butt."

Before leaving, I stopped at the ladies room. But when I opened the door, I heard sobbing. "Who's there?" I called. I tried to see through the opening of the stall, but I couldn't make out the figure.

"Go away!"

I'd know that voice anywhere. "Rhonda?"

"I said go away."

Rhonda was crying? Had someone gotten the scoop on an office scandal before her? "Are you all right?"

"No, I'm not all right." Good thing I wasn't standing behind the stall door or I would have been flattened like a bug when Rhonda stormed out. "I got canned."

For some reason, I never expected Rhonda to lose her job. Maybe because no matter how annoying she always was, nobody ever questioned her job performance.

"They're replacing me with an automated switchboard. Isn't that great? After being here fifteen years, my replacement is a goddamn machine." Rhonda's red swollen eyes had eye shadow smeared around them, and her green mascara was running down her face. Her bright red blush had been replaced with red blotches. The only thing about her that resembled the Rhonda I knew was her strong flowery perfume that filled the air.

"I'm really sorry, but if it makes you feel any better, I would have been laid off, too."

"It doesn't," she snapped.

"Rhonda, you're not going to have any trouble getting a job. There's always a need for receptionists out there."

"You just don't get it, do you, Jen?" She grabbed some toilet paper to blow her nose. "You and all your almighty friends who never had the time of day to ask me to go to lunch with you, just once."

Okay, now I felt like shit. "I'm sorry. Why didn't you ask if you could come?"

"I didn't think you'd want me tagging along." Rhonda turned on the faucet and splashed some water on her face. "I'm just a lowly receptionist who will never amount to anything."

"But you always seemed so confident and outgoing. I wouldn't think you'd have trouble inviting yourself."

"Well, I did, and I'm not confident. Far from it. How can I be when I see people like you getting promoted every few years, while I'm still doing the same thing day after day, month after month? All I wanted was for someone to notice me, to give me a break. All these years, every time one of the assistants got promoted, I always thought I'd finally get a crack at that position, but it never happened. No matter how much information I shared with John. No matter how super nice I was to all the account executives, nobody ever considered giving me a chance." She slammed the stall door closed behind her.

So that was it. Rhonda didn't have a thirst for knowledge, she had a thirst for attention, and I was just as guilty as everyone else for never giving it to her.

"Do you know that in all these years, you never even asked me if I had a boyfriend, Jen? Whenever I asked you about Chris or Mike, I thought maybe you'd ask me about my life, about me, but you never did." She stood before me with her arms crossed, looking at me like the enemy.

Huh.

"I always wished I could be more like you. You're a great writer, you're smart, and everyone likes you. I thought maybe someday I'd make a difference at Premier, like you did."

So Chris had been right.

"But after devoting fifteen years of my life to this agency, where the hell did it get me? All I'm getting for my hard work is a small severance check and a long wait on the phone to get unemployment benefits."

"I wish you had told me how you felt before now."

"What good would it have done?" Rhonda tore out of the ladies' room as if someone set her feet on fire.

Who would have thought Rhonda was so insecure and angry? When I walked toward the empty receptionist desk, a group of people from the production department were standing by the door. "Poor Rhonda," Ashley laughed. "For once she was the last one to know something that was going on in this office."

Everyone laughed, except me.

After taking the escalator downstairs, I stood in the lobby that I had walked through hundreds of times over the past eight years. I looked up at the atrium and gazed around at the marble walls. How was I going to survive without my sanctuary? Where would I escape when things were going badly in my life? Would I find the same comfort at Richardson and Whitaker?

As I looked into the mirrored elevator doors, I stared at my reflection with the zit on my right cheek, the wiry, disheveled hair, the small chest and large waistline, and the creases around my eyes. All the hair color, weight loss programs, and botox treatments in the world couldn't change who I was inside.

I couldn't hide from myself anymore. I was getting too old for that. Look at Rhonda. She had been so worried about showing her true self to anyone that she never gave anyone a chance to get to know who she really was.

Raising my head up high, I realized I didn't need a place to hide out anymore. From now on, I would have to find peace within myself.

Chapter 30

Getting Back to Normal:

1. You stop believing that everyone's wonderful life is so wonderful.
2. You start believing that perhaps Mr. Wrong could be Mr. Right.
3. You realize that being single doesn't mean you can't live happily ever after.

Oh, how I hated packing, especially when I was also surrounded by boxes. I wouldn't be moving to New York for another month, but I already had my first real business trip. I was meeting Meany in France to meet Jacques Montan himself. Why hadn't I spent more time studying the fashion section in *Cosmo* instead of always going straight to the relationship articles?

France was supposed to be rainy in the spring so I packed my raincoat, several umbrellas, and a rain slicker. I wasn't sure if I should dress casually or formally so I threw in every outfit that fit. I packed mostly short sleeved clothes, but then worried that it might suddenly get cold. If only I could empty all of my drawers into my suitcase.

I was just about to jump on my suitcase to get it to close when the phone rang. My Caller ID showed it was my mom, but I picked it up anyway.

"I wanted to wish you a nice trip," she said.

"Thanks," I said, wondering if I should bring a sweater for the airplane in case it was cold.

"Please be careful. I'm not crazy about you traveling alone."

Neither was I. I had already packed a pill dispenser filled with tranquilizers. "I'll be okay. Don't worry. And my boss is meeting me at the airport so I won't be alone for long."

"I wish I was going with you. You know how much I'd love to meet Jacques Montan. I just bought one of his purses this weekend."

And I bet it wasn't the economy-priced one. "I'll be sure to send him your regards." *Not.*

"By the way, Mike sent me the most beautiful flower arrangement. The card says he misses me and our family. Wasn't that sweet of him?"

"Well, maybe you should go out with him." What was I saying? At this rate my mom was likely to take me up on that suggestion. "I hope you know that was a joke, Mom."

"I know, dear. By the way, if you need to reach me during the week, call me on my cell phone."

"Why your cell phone?"

Silence.

"Mom? What's going on?"

"Well...Barb and I will be staying at the Borgata in Atlantic City for the next five or six days."

"Barb and you, huh? Yeah, right."

"Jen, I know you think I'm being horrible to your father, but don't you think it's time I did something for me?"

"If you're talking about getting a manicure or spending a day at the spa, I'm all for it. If you're talking about cheating on my dad, I have a slight problem with your choice."

"So you'd rather I live a miserable life with someone who doesn't make me happy."

"I'd rather you tried to turn your miserable life into at least a tolerable one. Have you ever considered seeing a marriage counselor?"

"I think we're way past that, Jen."

"Whatever you say, Mom." I realized even Cupid couldn't save my parent's marriage so why should I exert so much energy into helping them make it work. My dad was right. I had to let them deal with their mistakes by themselves. I needed to take care of myself.

"If it makes you feel any better, I feel terrible that it's come to this," my mom said. "I don't like myself very much anymore."

I didn't like her very much either, but I bit my tongue before I let that news flash slip out. "Listen, Mom, I don't have time to talk about this. I have a plane to catch."

"Have a nice week, Jen."

I hoped she wasn't waiting for me to wish her the same. "Take care, Mom." Click. I tried not to picture what she'd be doing for the next week while I was gone and was glad I wouldn't be around to bump into her and *Barb* anywhere.

I held the phone for a few minutes deciding whether to call Stacy to say good-bye. We had only spoken once since my visit four weeks earlier, and our conversation had been strained and uncomfortable. Stacy spent most of the call telling me about her wonderful new living room furniture that Lance had been wonderful enough to help her pick out. I talked about the weather in France. After five awkward silences, I had given up and ended the phone call. Hmm, maybe I'd just send her a postcard from Europe.

I hung up the phone and jumped on my suitcase until it closed. Next, I pulled the two ends of my duffle bag as close together as possible until it zipped. Oh great. I forgot to pack my straight iron. There was no way I was spending three weeks in France with poofy hair. I jammed the iron into the side pocket, but when I picked it up, the zipper broke. Just wonderful. And I didn't have a spare bag.

I frantically grabbed a piece of duct tape from my kitchen drawer and secured the bag closed. There, that ought to hold it until I got to France. Maybe Jacques would be so impressed with my writing, he would give me one of his designer bags.

At least I fit all my clothes and makeup into my suitcase and garment bag, but what about my pajamas, underwear, and the rest of my hair accessories? I solved this dilemma by stuffing everything left on my bed into a large shopping bag from Macy's. I would try shoving this stuff into my suitcase before I checked in at the airport. For now, I had to go.

I was glad Kathy had offered to take care of Frisky while I was gone. I was afraid if I left him with my mom, my poor feline friend would be forced to eat celery and carrot sticks for the next three weeks.

I walked through my apartment one last time to make sure I hadn't forgotten anything. As much as I would miss living here, it wouldn't be as hard as the last time I moved. I had stopped resisting changes.

I remembered how Meany had recited John Lennon's quote, "Life is what happens to you while you are busy making other plans." While I was busy planning a life with Mike, my mom was busy screwing around with other men. While I was busy working at Premier, our clients were busy losing money or finding other agencies. Maybe I'd pick up a Beatles greatest hits CD when I was in Europe.

I closed the door behind me and took the elevator to the first floor. After lugging all my stuff outside, I was grateful to sit down on the front step to wait for my cab.

As I did, I saw Randy carrying suitcases toward the parking lot. He disappeared behind the trees and bushes for a few minutes until he reemerged empty-handed. When he saw me, he walked over to where I sat. "Going on a vacation?" I asked.

"Not exactly. Lisa and I are getting divorced." He looked more tired than upset.

"I'm sorry," I said. I wasn't sure what else I should say at a time like this. Nobody I knew was divorced. Of course, that didn't mean they shouldn't be.

"I'm sorry too," he sighed. "We tried counseling for a while, but it didn't work."

"It must be rough getting divorced when you have children."

"That's the hardest part. I can't stand the idea of not seeing Josh and Jessica everyday, but I know it's not good for them to see all of our arguments."

If I were him, I'd be relieved to get away from those annoying kids for a while, but then again, what did I know about having children? "How long were you married?"

"Too long," he answered almost too quickly. "It's been ten years, but we've known each other since high school. Getting married seemed like a logical step after we graduated school. We really loved each other back then, too. I'm still not sure exactly what happened." He sighed again.

"Well, you're obviously not the same people you were back in high school."

"Yeah, maybe that's it." He had dark circles under his eyes, but of course that could be due to his two light sleepers upstairs. At least now he'd get some rest.

"Where are you moving?" My neck was starting to hurt from looking up at him.

"I found a condo in North Jersey. A friend and I are starting our own practice."

"What kind of practice?" After living next door to him for over a year, I still knew very little about him.

"I'm a lawyer."

Figured. I wondered if that's why Lisa had married him.

"Are you moving, too?" he asked, eyeing all of my luggage.

"Right now, I'm going on a business trip, but when I get back, I'm moving to New York."

"New York, hey, that's not too far from North Jersey. Here's my card. Give me a call when you get settled."

I took his card without saying anything. There was no way I was going to give him that transitional sex or be his rebound girlfriend. He needed time to heal. We both did. His card read, "Randy Ruttenberg, Esquire." He was even Jewish.

I stuffed his card into my pocket and glanced at my watch. Two o'clock. Where the hell was my cab? If it didn't pull up soon, I'd miss my flight. Maybe the cab driver thought I'd be waiting by the parking lot, even though I told the dispatcher exactly where I'd be. Then again, he didn't speak English very well.

I began dragging my suitcase, garment bag, and Macy's bag, and my purse toward the parking lot. I had only made it a few feet from the step when I heard a loud thud and watched my round brushes, combs, and hairspray tumble out of the Macy's bag, followed by my underwear.

Now I would definitely be late getting to the airport. I crawled around the parking lot, grabbing my runaway hair items, and was about to retrieve my hair clips when I stared face to foot at someone's sneakers. But they weren't just anyone's sneakers. I slowly looked up to see Chris looking down at me.

"Haven't you ever heard of a jumbo suitcase on wheels?" Chris said, handing me my favorite pair of black panties.

Just once it would be nice if he found me walking gracefully through the parking lot.

"Can I help you up?" Chris held out his hand and I let him ease me back up. The problem was that once I felt his skin against me, I didn't want to let go.

"Looks like you're missing something," Chris said.

"What?" I automatically looked around the parking lot. "Did I drop something else?"

"Not from your suitcase, silly. From your hand." He smiled that irresistible smile that still did weird things to my body. "Did that big rock get too heavy?"

"In a way." I was once again unable to remove my eyes from his.

"Perhaps lover boy should have gone for a smaller setting?"

Did I detect some anger in his voice? Good! "I broke my engagement," I blurted out.

"Really? You must be upset. I know how much you wanted to get married."

"I did want to get married, and I still do, but only to the right person." I forced myself to peel my eyes off of Chris. "I got so caught up in getting married that somewhere along the way, I lost sight of what marriage really means."

"So have you figured it out?" He took a step closer to me.

"Yeah, I have, and it's a pretty simple concept," I said, holding my head up like I'd seen Stacy do so many times. "I need to be in love and know that my husband feels the same way about me. That's it."

"What about marrying a rich professional geek who you can flaunt to all your friends?" He took another step closer to me, making me feel tingly inside.

"That's not what I want. I'm sorry for writing down that phone number, Chris. I shouldn't have tried to change you. I like you the way you are, GED or no GED."

"You mean that?"

"I do." I smiled, realizing it was true.

"Well, maybe I was a little rigid in my thinking, too."

"Really? What does that mean?"

"My brother called me two months ago to tell me he was getting married. I told him he was an idiot and he hung up on me. The next day I called him to find out what on earth had ever possessed him to propose. I thought maybe he was on drugs, or was using the girl for her money."

"And?"

"And he said he loved her, that he couldn't imagine spending his life without her and he wanted to be with her forever. You've got to understand that forever in our house meant about a year or two, but when I reminded him of that, he said he didn't care. He said just because our mother couldn't make any of her marriages work, didn't mean he would have the same problem. My brother's even inviting our mom to his wedding. Can you believe it?"

"It sounds like he finally forgave her."

"Yeah, I guess he has," he said, still sounding surprised.

"And what do you think?"

"Well, after talking to my brother, I realized that I can't assume every marriage is going to end in divorce just because of my mother's lousy track record. But I would still never get married unless I was one hundred percent sure that I was marrying the right person. I would never want to put children through the hell my brother and I went through."

Okay, this was definitely progress. He wasn't talking about marriage as if it were something he would do on his death bed. And had he mentioned children, too?

"I think you're absolutely right," I agreed. "The one thing I learned after getting engaged to the wrong guy is that you should never rush into a lifelong commitment. It's too important."

He took a third step closer to me, and this time I could smell the nicotine on his breath. "So you're saying you would be okay waiting a while before you got engaged."

"Yes, I am." I casually popped a stick of peppermint gum in my mouth, having forgotten whether I brushed my teeth. "Are you saying you would consider getting married before you grew too old to walk down the aisle without a cane?"

"What about a wheelchair?"

I threw my black underwear at him.

"Ooh, nice panties," he said. "I'd sure like to see them on you."

He moved forward and kissed me gingerly and slowly on my lips. So that was what a real kiss felt like. It had been so long.

"Where are you off to with all those bags?" Chris asked, without moving away from me.

My cab! My plane! "I almost forgot. I've got to call another cab. I'm going to miss my flight."

"Don't despair, your limo is here. I'll drive you to the airport."

"Thanks, I'd really appreciate it."

He smiled at me and for a few minutes our eyes locked, immobilizing both of us to the same spot in the parking lot where we met. Chris finally broke the lock. "I almost forgot. I have a surprise for you. Wait here for a minute while I get it."

I imagined it was probably another daisy he had picked from the park. I smiled to myself as I realized I'd rather have one daisy growing weeds from Chris than ten exotic flower arrangements from Mike.

But when Chris returned, he handed me a large manila envelope. I couldn't remember ever seeing a fresh flower stuffed in an envelope before. I tore open the seal and took out a certificate with Chris's name on it. "Is this what I think it is?"

"If you think it's my GED, then it is."

"You got it, after everything you said?"

"I realized you were right. If I ever want to find a good job, I'll need it."

"I can't believe you changed your mind. You seemed so sure that you didn't need or want one."

"Well, to be honest, I had a lot of trouble getting a job after I left Big Al's. I couldn't even get this part-time job driving dead people around without a GED, so I took the plunge. Good thing someone tipped me off about the Goodman Technical Institute. Did you know that in just three weeks you could enroll in a program there that helps you get a GED?"

We both laughed. In fact, I laughed so hard that tears ran down my face. When we stopped laughing, we stood for a few moments smiling at each other.

"I'm really proud of you, Chris."

"Thanks, I'm kind of proud of me, too. So shall we go?"

"Just one minute." I took out Randy's phone number from my pocket and threw it into the same trash can where I had thrown away my bridal magazines. Who cared if he was a Jewish lawyer? I had a Catholic funeral car driver waiting to take me to the airport, and for now that seemed a lot better than a horse-drawn carriage waiting to take me to the ball.

Chris led me to his limo, and this time, I managed to walk across the entire parking lot without dropping a thing.

www.ingramcontent.com/pod-product-compliance
Lightning Source LLC
Chambersburg PA
CBHW030925260626
47169CB00002B/381